Road to Hanging Rock

Barbara Gurney

JASPER BOOKS
PERTH
AUSTRALIA

Award-winning writer and published poet Barbara Gurney lives in Perth, Western Australia. Barbara attended Como State School and Applecross Senior High School where she enjoyed netball, bookkeeping and the creative aspect of English lessons.

After retiring from fulltime work, she joined Gosnells Writers Circle in 2008, and the Writefree Women's Writing Group at the Katharine Susannah Prichard Writers' Centre in 2009. Her first published work was a children's story, *Fairies of the Milky Way*, which appeared in *Stories for Children Magazine*, a US online publication, in 2009. She has since won several awards for short stories.

In 2012, Ginninderra Press of Port Adelaide published her poetry collection, *Footprints of a Stranger* and in 2015, *Life's Shadows*. Her poems focus on life experiences and philosophical musings.

Road to Hanging Rock is her debut novel.

The Promise, a novella published by Austin Macauley of London, was released February 2017.

www.barbaragurney.webs.com

ISBN 978-0-9944802-3-1

www.caterocchicom.com/jasper.html

To my husband, Graeme – there aren't enough words

Road to Hanging Rock

Time present and time past
Are both perhaps present in time future,
And time future contained in time past
If all time is eternally present
All time is unredeemable.
What might have been is an abstraction
Remaining a perpetual possibility
Only in a world of speculation
What might have been and what has been
Point to one end, which is always present...
T.S. Eliot
Burnt Norton

PROLOGUE

Michael let his mobile phone slip from his hand. He watched it hit the ground. He sat motionless for a few seconds then pushed at the phone with his foot. He wanted to toss the lifeless device into the bush, but despite his frustration, he wasn't about to discard his only potential lifeline.

As he pulled his keys from his pocket they caught on the stitching. The thread snapped and the keys jolted against his thumb. Holding the keys at arm's length, his eyes narrowed as he glared at the brass front door key, then at the thick black plastic of his car key. Michael hoped that they too wouldn't disappear. They were the only reality in this nightmare. Proof that his car did exist. Proof he wasn't going insane.

ONE

Rebecca was trying to avoid Valentine's Day. Jess had invited her to a "Singles Only" breakfast and Amy was trying to convince her to spend Saturday afternoon at a local football match.

'Come on, Bec,' said Amy. 'I'm going. My brother said most of the guys hang around after the scratch match. It could turn into a party. Come on. You don't have anything better to do.'

'You mean a lot of sweaty blokes after a game? No thanks. I'm not that desperate.' Rebecca curled up her lip and shook her head. 'Take Jess with you. She's single, too.'

'Yeah, but she's going to that breakfast. It's bound to run all day.' Amy grinned, 'Come on, they do shower after they've finished beating the hell out of the footy, you know. Bec, it'll be fun. Valentine's Day and all that.'

Rebecca knew she wouldn't receive anything romantic in her email, or on her unattended Facebook page, but ... a football match! Standing around pretending to be engrossed in discussions on the umpire's poor decisions, the length of the winning kick or someone's miraculous mark ... no, she couldn't think of anything worse.

Fobbing off her friends' invitations, Rebecca decided that some retail therapy in Woodend would be an ideal alternative.

The drive to the country was pleasant enough, but she was glad to reach Woodend. Rebecca parked outside the bakery and wandered in for coffee. The cappuccino was strong and hot, and the smell of fresh pastries was tempting. She watched two giggling teenagers share a vanilla slice; the sticky custard clung to their fingers. She took her empty cup to the counter and checked out possible options for lunch.

Rebecca strolled past the fruit shop and entered the cool interior of a boutique. A yellow dress, displayed with an embroidered black over-skirt, caught her attention. However, an apologetic assistant couldn't find a size twelve.

Further up the street, a window full of teddy bears made Rebecca think of Thomas, her nephew. *Nuh, he has enough stuffed toys.*

She headed across the road to Bits & Bobs Collectables.

A basket of plastic flowers, several wooden chairs and a cane pram that held three vintage dolls, sat under a distinctive red and white striped awning. Numerous woollen handicrafts covered a coat-stand that partially obstructed the doorway. A musty smell of old belongings hung in the air.

Rebecca browsed through cabinets of discarded family possessions and paused for a moment to look at a chair, which, with ornate splayed feet, looked similar to the one in her father's study. Then she squeezed between some larger furniture and discovered delightful pieces of crockery on the shelves at the back.

'Hello, dear,' came a voice from somewhere behind an oak wardrobe.

'Oh, hi. Didn't see you there,' Rebecca answered, as a petite woman with smoky-coloured hair piled on the top of her head appeared.

'Are you after something in particular?'

'No, just looking.'

The shopkeeper's flowery skirt caught on the corner of a dressing table as she approached. She unhooked it before picking up a silver-plated mirror. 'What about this? Isn't it pretty?'

Rebecca shook her head. 'It's lovely, but no thanks. I bought a mirror last time – a couple of months ago. My mum loved it.'

'I thought you looked familiar. I remember your dark eyes and the fair hair – unusual combination. Such gorgeous curls. You bought the little mirror with the white painted frame, didn't you?'

'Yep, that's the one,' Rebecca answered, surprised that she was remembered.

'Well, dear, if you do find something, I'll give you a special price.'

Running her finger around the rim of a cup decorated with pansies, Rebecca said, 'Thanks, I'll keep looking.'

The shopkeeper hovered, watching Rebecca as she picked up indiscriminate objects and put them down again. She kept hold of a decorated trinket box for a while, but decided against it. Then the *ting* of the door-bell announced another customer and the woman hurried off. Rebecca tried to find something unique that would satisfy her need for a purchase. *Maybe the cup and saucer. No.* Checking her watch, she thought, half past twelve, perhaps I should go for some lunch.

On the way to the door, Rebecca spotted a small embroidered bag. She picked it up and unclipped the clasp. Cute. Faded pink lining felt cool as her fingers touched the bottom. *It's lovely, but I don't really need another bag.*

'That's just the ticket, dear. Not a bad price either.'

Rebecca almost dropped the bag. She hadn't real-ised the shopkeeper was so close.

'Well, I'm thinking about it.' Her eyes lingered on the bag as she placed it back on the shelf. 'It would seriously not go with anything I have.'

'What about this brooch then? It's only costume jewellery, but it's sweet.'

Touching the bag again, Rebecca said, 'No, I'm not into brooches, and the pearl ... no thanks.'

'You should treat yourself. It's Valentine's Day. What better way to spoil yourself than with a heart-shaped brooch?'

'I was trying to forget about that.'

'Go on, dear, buy it. Might be just the lucky charm you need to find the man of your dreams.' She held the brooch out and nodded. 'Why not?'

Rebecca came away with the brooch and the bag.

She strolled past the bank – a sign urged cricket players to join the local team. Then she took a photo of the clock tower in the centre of town. After eating a chicken sandwich and slurping the last of a milkshake, she checked her phone. *Nothing.* She was tempted to text Jess. *I wonder if she's home yet.*

She took the brooch out of the paper bag and turned it over. *Good luck? Man of my dreams? Yeah, right.* She rubbed her finger across the pearl. *Pearl for tears – can do without that.* Rebecca lifted out her other purchase. She noticed a couple of broken threads. It is pretty, she thought, as she pushed both items back into the bag.

An elderly couple strolled by enjoying ice cream. Cars and small trucks drove up and down the street.

Rebecca entered another gift shop. The owner convinced Rebecca to purchase a nursery rhyme book illustrated by a local artist.

By the time she walked back to the bakery and finished another hot drink, the clock tower showed a quarter to three. She sent a text to Jess and decided that if she was to stop in at the produce store in Mt Macedon and be home before dusk, it was now time to set out. On the way to her car, Rebecca bought a bottle of water and some mints for the trip home.

As her car settled into the comforting hum of speed, she sang along with the blaring radio. Masses of green rushed by in her peripheral vision. The detail of the scenery went unnoticed.

Twenty-five minutes later, without warning, her car coughed. Rebecca glanced at the gauges. *Enough petrol. Temperature's okay.* Another splutter of the engine. She eased her foot off the accelerator. *Please don't break down here.* A rusty gate led to a dry paddock. There was no sign of people.

The car shuddered violently. Rebecca's pulse increased. Her hands felt clammy. Slowing the car even more, she peered through the windscreen. A green sign on the side road indicated: *Hanging Rock.* Shivery sensations started at the back of her neck and, in an instant, reached her toes. Her ears rang. A sharp pain jabbed her back. Rebecca jumped. Her car swerved and hit the edge of the bitumen. She stabbed at the brakes, then manoeuvred the car along the stony verge. It slid to a halt with a convulsive jolt. Rebecca sucked in several deep breaths. She wiped her damp palms on her jeans and rolled her head around. The ringing in her ears continued and her stomach felt pummelled. She reached for the water bottle that had fallen from the seat.

Then, the sky darkened. A willy-willy came out of nowhere. It charged into the car with ferocity. Rebecca shrieked and dropped the water bottle. The wind leapt around the car. It pounded on the mirrors and snapped at the aerial. She gripped the steering wheel and bit the inside of her cheek. Dust blew in through the vents and made her cough. Small twigs bounced across the bonnet. A leaf, caught in a wiper blade, flapped incessantly. Rigid with fear, she clung onto the steering wheel. The car rocked, buffeted by another burst of wind. An empty can hit the windscreen. Rebecca ducked.

With a final thrust of power, the willy-willy attacked the car again. Rebecca tightened her grip and tried to stop shaking. A twisted branch landed on the bonnet when the wind terminated abruptly. The radio was silent, but the windscreen wipers screeched their way across the dry glass. Hypnotised by the wipers, her eyes followed the blades back and forth. The wipers finally stopped in mid rotation. The claustrophobic smell of dust lingered.

Rebecca released her hands from the steering wheel and watched the blood run back into her finger-tips. All she could hear was the grating of metal on metal as her car keys swung vigourously in the ignition. Just as she reached out to grab them, they fell to the floor. Her stomach contracted and she held her breath as she stared at the keys. *How did that happen?* Taking a gulp of air, Rebecca bent down and picked them up.

She checked the view through each window. The trees were like statues. Not even the leaf in the wiper blade moved. The eerie silence, which seemed to extract the air out of the car, was almost as frightening as the noise the wind had created. It was as if time took a moment to re-start.

It was several minutes before Rebecca felt calm enough to continue her trip home. Thankfully, the car started immediately and gave no hint of its earlier failings. She locked the doors and drove slowly. The Mt Macedon shops were no longer appealing and she was relieved to reach the Calder Highway. Trucks rumbled past. A bloke in a silver four-wheel-drive blasted the horn as he overtook. She continued to travel well below the speed limit until she reached the outer suburbs of Melbourne.

The unsettled feeling lingered as she drove to her flat. Her hand shook as she wriggled the key in the keyhole. Missy, her cat, sprang from a chair and landed on her foot, startling Rebecca. It wasn't until she showered and finished a cup of green tea that she relaxed. However, she was sure there was something in the background. Something that had gone unnoticed. Something important.

The feeling of expectation lasted for weeks. She checked emails constantly, stood looking at the phone for minutes at a time and her mobile hardly left her hand. At work, she imagined every customer would be of particular importance. As she offered suggestions or showed them the latest range of giftware, she searched their faces for recognition. Even when Jess and Amy provided distractions, Rebecca felt detached. Her stomach remained in an unrelenting state of edginess waiting for something significant to happen.

In the middle of May, something else added to her restlessness.

As Rebecca fed Missy a television news item caught her attention. *Man missing from Hanging Rock found after three months.*

Hanging Rock! She stopped with the tuna-laden spoon poised between can and bowl. Missy wound her grey fluffy body around Rebecca's legs, but the spoon stayed in mid-air as she gawked at the screen. A prickly sensation ran down the back of her neck. She sat down on the edge of the couch. An image of the large road sign with the direction to Hanging Rock flashed across her mind. *What's with that?* Rebecca blinked rapidly. *Why does it feel so personal?* She stared at the screen.

The newsreader reported that a thirty-one-year-old Melbourne man, Michael Wentworth, disappeared on the fourteenth of February while visiting Hanging Rock. Despite air and ground searches in the area, the police, aided by many volunteers, were unable to trace him. Wentworth repeatedly insisted he'd been at a farmhouse in the area at the time of the search. The police sergeant in charge of the case disputed Wentworth's claim that he left an SOS on the main track.

Rebecca shivered. *February the fourteenth!* She also realised the described area wasn't far from where the willy-willy assaulted her car.

Missy's demand for more food temporarily diverted Rebecca's attention from the television. Then spooning slowly, she turned back to the screen. Her stomach shrank involuntarily. She shuddered from the high-pitched ringing in her ears.

Although the news item was lengthy, she remained dissatisfied, doubting the interviewer's explanations. She wished she could jump into the television and question Michael Wentworth herself.

The television station's website showed several photographs of Hanging Rock along with information on the police search. It inferred that a truck driver thought he'd come across a lunatic when he saw a man in the middle of the road, running towards his vehicle. Facebook posts declared Michael Wentworth was either a freak or a lying publicity seeker. Rebecca scrolled further on and noted the details of a planned press conference. *I just have to go to that.*

Rebecca got lost in an unfamiliar suburb, but finally found the advertised venue. She then faced two security personnel wanting her press pass. She pouted excessively and then smiled pleadingly into their eyes. Ramblings about a *connection* to Michael Wentworth left them bemused, but after some girly-begging, they relented and let her through.

Rebecca imagined an instant bond; a lightning-strike moment where everything would become clear as soon as she entered the room, but when Michael looked up, it was only to nod at the obese man on his left. As she scrambled into a seat at the back of the assembled group, she was invisible to him.

Seated behind a table at the front were two men; their chairs pulled closely together. A man of about forty tapped his notepad with podgy fingers as he leaned over Michael Wentworth. There was an air of control about this large man and he had the appearance of a manager – perhaps an agent.

Michael Wentworth's tan looked out of place. His hair stuck up like dry grass, as if he had run his hand through it many times. His shoulders were erect, but the young man's chin dipped towards his chest. With feet entwined, his clean shoes occasionally slipped against one another making a short sharp sound. He frowned so deeply that his left eye almost closed. His right thumb drummed against his leg as he waited un-enthusiastically. After the two men exchanged words, the older of the two pulled at his ear, nodded and then sipped from a plastic cup before speaking to a woman who stood nearby.

Around the stark room, journalists began to chatter. Two photographers jostled as they tried to get a perfect shot. One tripped and he mumbled continually as he retreated to a spot near the wall. A senior journalist waved his arm trying to attract the attention of the men at the front. He accidentally clipped the person next to him on the side of the head. She stood up, scowled at her attacker and moved to a vacant seat. Two young reporters whispered as they took turns to scribble on a pad. One suddenly laughed loudly, causing people to turn around.

The woman, standing to the left of the table, held a microphone in one hand and a clipboard in the other. She bobbed down to speak to the two men, then stood up and switched on the microphone. She paused for a moment, before finally blowing into the microphone and speaking, 'Excuse me. Your attention, please. It's time to wind up. Quiet, please.'

As the MC checked her watch and adjusted the microphone, Rebecca realised she'd missed most of the interview.

The sound of shuffling feet on the wooden floor mingled with an occasional cough, and when the noises ceased, the MC asked for a final question. Pulling her bulky handbag closer to her chest, Rebecca watched Michael Wentworth intently. He tucked one hand under his leg and leaned forward. His eyes darted over the assembled group before focusing on the woman with the microphone.

'Will you be publishing your story?' asked one reporter who balanced a laptop on his knee.

Before Michael could answer, Rebecca jumped up and asked, 'How come they couldn't find you?'

Heads swivelled instantly. Unintelligible comments jumbled together. Rebecca sat down quickly, trying to appear indifferent to the stares. Michael turned to the person beside him and made dismissive gestures with his hand. His glance towards Rebecca showed a tiredness of spirit. He didn't respond to her forced smile.

The MC leaned over and spoke to the agent before saying into the microphone, 'I'm sorry, Miss, that question has been covered, and unfortunately we've run out of time for any others. Thank you all for your questions. A prepared statement will be available from the website. Good afternoon. Thank you.'

Michael Wentworth walked with his hands dragging at his pockets and followed his agent out a side door. Pushing past the reporters, Rebecca hurried after the men and burst through the doorway. She found them talking quietly in the hall.

'Please, I missed most of the session,' she began. The scowling agent put out his hand to stop her. Rebecca continued, 'Michael, can

I ask a few questions about your story?'

Michael leaned forward and glared at Rebecca. Stabbing his chest with his forefinger, he spoke emphatically, 'My story! I'm sorry, but I'm sick of telling *my* story. Do you think I'm some sort of a freak too?' His strained voice screeched, 'Talk to the police, talk to the doctors. What about talking to the other journalists out there?' He pointed towards the door, jabbing at the air in frustration. He turned away and whispered, 'I'm not telling it again.'

Rebecca stood with her mouth open. Finally, muttering an apology, she edged past him, catching a glimpse of his sad blue eyes before he looked away.

TWO

Three months previous in a Melbourne pub, Michael's friends from his university days were planning to go for a day's surfing. Jock and Patrick were eager to catch a few waves. Owen was a beginner, but still looking forward to a day in the sun after a week of working in artificial office light.

'Sorry, guys, can't make it this time,' said Michael.

'Getting too old for it, Mick?' Owen asked sarcastically.

'Put on weight, have we? Wet suit a bit small?' Jock teased, as he put his empty beer glass in front of Michael. 'Your shout, mate.'

'Same again?' Michael stood up. 'And no, I haven't gained any weight. You, on the other hand …'

Jock wobbled his stomach like a belly dancer, making his mates and the people nearby laugh.

When Michael returned with four fresh beers, Owen tried again, 'So what's the excuse for not coming to the beach?'

'I'm driving out to Hanging Rock on Saturday. I'm determined to go and don't want to put it off again. Not even for the joy of spending time with you three losers.'

As the other two moaned, Owen asked, 'Hanging Rock? Haven't been there. You want some company?'

'Hang on, guys,' interrupted Jock, as he held out his mobile, 'Megan and I've a fancy dinner all set up. She tells me it's Valentine's Day.'

'Shit, thanks for reminding me,' said Patrick. 'I'd be in big trouble if I'd forgotten. Erin's already dropped hints.'

'I'm not tied down,' said Owen. 'The Rock sounds okay.'

'Sorry, mate,' said Michael. 'I need to do this on my own. Anyway, you'd just have me at the nearest pub. No fun in that when I'm driving.'

'Bloody hell, anyone would think we don't deserve a beer after slogging away all week.'

'I didn't say that.' Michael grinned and lifted his glass. 'Cheers.'

So, on the day his mates headed to the beach, Michael drove to Hanging Rock. On the way, he thought about his conversation with his grandmother, Wilma Irma Warren, the evening before she died.

Although Grandma Wilma was weak and not able to concentrate for long, she insisted Michael should hear the full story of his great-great-grandmother Irma and her two friends who went missing. She meandered through a description of long dresses and irritated schoolteachers while she fiddled with the hem of the bed sheet. After an extended pause and several sips of water, she explained there was an old secret that she wanted to pass on. He'd heard other relatives talk about Irma, but the finicky detail in Grandma's version puzzled him. There didn't seem any reason for her fussing. It all happened so long ago.

She squeezed his hand. 'Please, you must remember it. One day it might be important.'

He wasn't likely to forget such a surreal tale, but wondered how small details like shiny blue hair ribbons, bone-handled silver cutlery and two large bay-coloured horses were relevant. Over the next few weeks, visions of eerie hollows and vast towering rock stuck with him. He checked out various websites then decided to see the mysterious Hanging Rock for himself.

Grass prickled Michael's ankles as he stepped towards the base of Hanging Rock. The rock felt rough and cold against his palm. When he looked up, he was momen-tarily blinded by the sunlight as it glared out from behind the lofty height. He returned to the sealed path. *One hundred years ago. Can't imagine facilities would've been that great. I wonder if the little hut was there then.* He looked back at a white painted building with a red roof.

Michael commenced the climb to "The Hanging Rock". Boisterous teenagers raced past. Half way up, two men acknowledged him as they caught their breath. At the top of the stairs, Michael ducked under suspended rock and stood in the cool shade. He nodded to three women who were discussing whether to continue or go back down for lunch. After they moved away, he took some pictures of the imposing structures.

Hours passed as he roamed in and out of the curious formations. He took a tourist leaflet from his bag and scanned the information. Noises from the café and picnic areas had faded a while ago and

Michael felt pleasantly alone. He sat and checked his phone. Patrick's text message about "bloody awesome waves" made him smile. Yeah, but you can't beat a good workout climbing rocks, he texted back. Then he ate his sandwiches before continuing to explore.

Rough volcanic rock grazed his fingers as he gripped the ancient edges and pulled himself up to yet another level. He peered into deep hollows and stared up at the steep-sided formations. A passing aeroplane looked like a hyphen in the sky. Five rosellas landed on a tree a few metres away. Their crimson feathers contrasted with the white trunks of the majestic gums.

Michael was pleased when he came across a flat area near "The Saddle". He had enough of steep in-clines. He leaned against a rock and admired the view. A breeze sounded like whispered messages as it whistled through the gaps. He took his water bottle from his bag and tried to imagine schoolgirls in long dresses climbing between the rocks. *Grandma's story seems ridiculous.* He closed his eyes and visualised the bitumen path as a narrow track. *Surely few people would climb all the way up here in the 1900's.* Harsh squawks of cockatoos roused him from his daydreams.

He sipped lukewarm water and remembered how Grandma became obsessed with minute details when she told him the story of long ago. *I wonder if any of it's true.* He stood and looked across the paddocks that stretched into the distance. A remote farmhouse was only a brush stroke of white. Here and there, a half-filled dam broke up the monotony of straw-coloured grass. A few distant cows, like smudges on a painting, sheltered under far-off trees.

Michael noticed the shadows of clouds racing across the landscape. The wind increased and moaned through the crevices behind him. He looked at his watch. *It's stopped. Flat battery?* Anyway, he thought, it must be time to head home. A short, sharp shock stabbed his neck. He snapped his head around and glared over his shoulder. A small rock tumbled onto his foot. He felt uneasy. *Definitely time to leave.*

On the steep descent, his toes battered against the end of his sneakers. His tired muscles ached. He turned around for another look at the mysterious monolith. A chilling wind whipped his face, threw dust into his eyes and made him cough. Leaves scrambled across the ground. He stumbled and slid down the last two metres of a leafy path.

Michael stood up and glanced around, hoping no one had seen his clumsiness. Then he brushed off the dirt and headed down the track. He was surprised that he was no longer on the bitumen path. *When did the bitumen end?* He paced along the track for a few more metres. *Did I take a wrong turn?*

He sat on a small rock and checked directions on the leaflet.

There were only two options: up the stairs past the overhanging rock or on the sloping path. Both led from one bitumen path, which was supposed to be under his feet. He stared in the direction where the café should be. The absence of buildings freaked him out.

He scurried down to the flat grass. *The café where I got the sandwiches … Where is it?* He turned and looked to his left. His pulse increased. He stood still, but his eyes were working overtime. *Shit.* They darted to the right. More bush. His eyes travelled over the broad expanse of ferns. He blinked furiously because the edges of his vision were blurred.

Did I come down the other side? He checked the leaflet again. *I can't have.*

He listened for the sounds he heard earlier: people chattering as they climbed the steps, cars coming and going. *Nothing.*

Michael squatted down. He stared at his sneakers and noticed that one shoelace was longer than the other. He shook his head and tried to form rational thoughts. *All I have to do is find the bitumen, then the buildings … the car park … my car.* He stood up. *Right, first the path.* He frowned. The signposted path should have been in full view.

Sunlight skimmed across the tops of the trees, soon to sink into a spectacular sunset. Shadows of the rock crept across the grass, eating up the daylight. An irritating wind blew around his body again, pushing into his back. He jiggled his backpack into place. He still didn't understand why he couldn't see any buildings.

Grabbing his mobile phone from his pocket, he started punching buttons. *No connection.* He shook it violently. 'Bloody phone. Now what do I do?' he said, as he shoved it back into his jeans.

Mentally retracing his movements proved futile. He felt sick. His heart pounded. 'Bloody rock! Shouldn't have bothered coming here.' He moved away, flinging more insults. A bird flew away in fright.

As he continued his search, the bush crept into night. He became infuriated. *Where is everything?* A full moon appeared. *Thank goodness.* Michael closed his eyes. *I'll have to keep looking. Some water first.*

When he reached the base of the rock again and still couldn't find the sealed pathway, he was at his wit's end. His brain turned to mush. Moments later, he yelled, 'Can't find anything. How will I find my frigging car?'

Malevolence appeared to have slithered around him and he felt threatened. Then he realised he hadn't seen anyone else since seeing tourists at the summit. *They must have found their cars.*

As the moonlight fell through the trees, creating intimidating shapes on the towering rock, Michael thought he heard someone laughing. He stumbled into the spaces between the walls. His frantic voice echoed. No one answered. His mobile phone still wouldn't respond. *This is ludicrous!*

After deciding he would have to stay the night, he climbed into a cave-like shape of some overhanging rocks and kicked away several stones. *Tomorrow it will all seem like a frigging joke. It'll be okay tomorrow.*

Still baffled, he put on his jacket and cap, folded his arms tightly across his chest and leaned back against the cold stone. His ears strained. His eyes were sore from trying to see in the semi-darkness. Unfamiliar sounds made him shrink further back into the concave rock. Every time he thought of the eerie wind that slapped his face earlier, a strange sensation shot up his spine. *The whole thing is ridiculous.* Michael swallowed repeatedly. He wriggled his body and tried to find a comfortable angle for his head.

Imagined footsteps made him leap to his feet. 'Here,' he yelled. 'Over here.' No one called back. Michael walked several metres down the track and squinted into the night's greyness. He wandered back and sat hunched against the chosen rock. His mobile remained blank. Worry forced hunger away. He placed his backpack across his chest and tugged his jeans over his ankles. He moved a stone from under his leg and shut his eyes. He visualised calm waves washing over soft sand, but anxiety replaced it with crashing surf.

A sound of bushes being disturbed made him stiffen. He called out, but again, no one replied. When his eyes battled to stay open, he tugged his cap down over his forehead and tried to stop worrying. During the night, he slipped sideways onto the rough ground. Sleep was shallow and restless. A small wet patch next to his mouth dried slowly.

Michael woke early. He sat up and rubbed at a sore spot on his shoulder. His phone still didn't respond to frantic prodding. He swallowed the last mouthful of water from his bottle. After stretching, he swiped at bits of gravel on the back of his jeans and set out for his car. It would be easier to spot the landmarks in the daylight, he encouraged himself. 'How stupid, I won't be telling this story in a hurry,' he said to a lizard on a sunny rock ledge.

Michael wandered for two hours, weaving through the bush, tracking across small clearings, spasmodically returning to the path near the rock. He couldn't recognise anything. He called out often. He hiked over long grass and around prickly tea-trees; sure something recognisable would pop up behind the next bush. It didn't.

Anxiety strangled his thought processes. Bewildered, he yelled, 'I must be totally insane.'

All the buildings had somehow vanished. *Bloody rock's still here. No signposts. Where did the bitumen go?* His dehydrated body felt ready to collapse. He rested in the shade and tried to figure out a plan.

THREE

Michael Wentworth had obviously told his story to many people and Rebecca presumed it would be easy to track them down. She checked through some newspapers and then the television's website again. If I ask enough questions, she thought, it shouldn't be too hard to work out a logical reason for my feelings. She divided her notebook into sections with clearly marked headings.

> Woodend Police Station – Sgt Angus McKay
> Dr Millhouse – GP
> Kyneton Hospital – Dr Pendath Miralithan
> Dr Sylvia Carstairs – Psychologist

Rebecca's investigative plans were cut short by a constable at her local police station.

'Your name, Miss.'

'Rebecca Hannah.'

'Do you have a report number?'

'No, but it happened in Woodend.'

'Woodend? That will make it difficult. Are you a relative of this person?'

'No, but ...'

'Authority of some sort?'

'No. I'm interested in the disappearance of ...'

'Ah, a reporter.'

'Not really, I'm just fascinated ...'

'Look, Miss. We can't go giving out police information without the proper authority.'

She stomped out of the station and flung her empty notebook across the front seat of her car. After sending imaginary daggers at the police station door, Rebecca lectured herself for becoming frustrated at the first hurdle. *Surely others will be more helpful.*

Finding any professional who was willing to overlook identity security proved unsuccessful. She resorted to looking up Wentworths on line and, after many disappointments, she got through to a J&J Wentworth's voicemail.

'The Wentworths are not receiving calls at this time. Please respect our privacy and refrain from calling again.' There was no beep, so no opportunity to leave a message. However, Rebecca smiled as she scribbled down the address. *Just maybe they are Michael Wentworth's parents.*

Gently brushing aside Missy with her foot as she opened the fridge for some milk, Rebecca jumped at the sound of her mobile.

'Hi, Kyls.'

'Hi, Bec, what's up? You haven't returned my calls.'

'Sorry, I've been busy.'

'Too busy for your favourite sister?'

'Kylie, may I remind you, you're my only sister.'

'That doesn't matter; I'm still your favourite.'

'Certainly are.'

This greeting was standard patter. The sisters had few arguments and fewer secrets from each other. Kylie, three years older, was married with a two-year-old son, Thomas, who Rebecca adored.

'So, why haven't you called?' Kylie asked again.

'As I said, I've been busy.'

'Doing what? Another project? Or a fabulous new boyfriend?'

Rebecca hesitated, 'Well ... he is quite good looking, but he wouldn't speak to me.'

'What? Sounds complicated.'

Kylie was surprised when Rebecca explained she was following up on a weird feeling that had something to do with a recent news story.

'Do you know him?'

'Nup, never even heard of him before this.'

'You said he wouldn't speak to you, so you must have met him.'

'I went to his news conference.'

'Really? What did he say to you?'

'Not a lot. Well, nothing really. I was late and missed almost all of it.'

'Typical.'

'Well anyway, I found an address on the internet that I can check out.'

Kylie chuckled. 'I'm sure they'll have some champagne on ice for you.'

'No need for that.'

'Well, do you think they'll welcome you? They're probably sick of all the attention.'

'Yeah, I thought of that, but it's the only lead I have.'

'Well, good luck then.'

At the home of J&J Wentworth, the shutters were down and the carport was empty. No one answered the doorbell. When Rebecca peered over a rattly side gate, a dog from next-door started barking. She stumbled as she stepped back with surprise.

A woman appeared from behind the dividing hedge. 'Shut up, Rocky!' she yelled at the dog. A smile emerged from her angry face as she asked, 'Are you looking for the Wentworths?'

Placing her hands on the top of the diosmas, Rebecca shuffled closer. 'I'm looking for Michael Wentworth. The guy who went missing. Is this the right place?'

'Yes, that's him all right. I'd say it's a strange how-do-you-do.'

'Would you know when someone will be home?'

'They won't be. They've packed up and gone.'

Damn! Rebecca tried again. 'Do you know where they went?'

'No. With so many reporters hanging around, I don't blame them.' Rebecca could see the woman checking her out. 'Are you another one?'

'No, not a reporter. I'm trying to find out a little more about his disappearance. I want to speak to him.'

'Well, you're out of luck. They've gone.' She pushed at her glasses. 'People think he's lost his marbles. Personally, I do think it's odd. Have you read the papers? He comes back after three months with some fanciful story about those girls who disappeared all those years ago. Goodness me. Everyone knows *that* was just a rumour started to increase tourists. Poor Janet, she's pleasant enough, but this? We've been neighbours for over five years now, you know. Jack ... well, Jack will be wondering what hit him. He raised a son with proper values. Now he's gone potty.'

She finally took a breath and Rebecca jumped in, 'So do you know anyone who could tell me something more?' She gave a sugary smile and added, 'anything at all.'

The woman leaned over the hedge. Rebecca felt in-timidated by her close examination.

'I suppose you don't look dangerous. You have a nice smile,' she said, as her eyes narrowed for better vision.

Rebecca stood up straight and grinned. 'Thanks.'

'Well then, you could try his grandmother.'

'Grandmother?'

'Yes, she lives in the next street.'

This is too good to be true, thought Rebecca. 'Won't she have gone too?'

'Doubt it. They've kept her out of it. Do you know, she trots around here every other day. Well, she did before he reappeared. She used to sneak in here to wait until it was clear. They didn't want her talking to those reporters. Rose rattles on to me, of course. Not that I don't like a good natter you understand.' Her painted-on eyebrows went up. 'No, she won't be with them.'

She took another breath and Rebecca asked, 'Do you think the grandmother would talk to me?'

The woman pursed her lips, thought for a moment then nodded slowly. 'Perhaps. You seem like a friendly girl.'

Rebecca felt like laughing. 'What did you say her address was?'

Pushing her glasses into place again, the woman smirked. 'I didn't. Have to be careful, you know. Can't be giving out personal details to just anyone.' She leaned over the hedge, looked up and down the street, paused, then put her hand up to her mouth. Rebecca leaned closer and squinted, trying to imitate the woman's serious face.

'If I tell you, you won't go upsetting the applecart will you?' she whispered.

Rebecca whispered back, 'Of course not.'

The woman straightened her back and forgot about the self-imposed vigilance. 'Very well then, she's in Phillip Court, number twenty-two. It's easy to find. She's mad about cats. You can't miss them.'

'Thanks, Mrs ...'

'Mrs Jackson.'

'Thanks, Mrs Jackson. I must get going.'

'Okay, dear. I'm never one to hold anyone up by rabbiting on.'

Rebecca sidestepped towards the car as she called out, 'Of course not. Thanks again.'

Mrs Jackson was right. Driving up Phillip Court, Rebecca saw the first cat immediately. A large metal one curled around the letterbox of number twenty-two. On the red front door was a smiling yellow cat with a polka-dot bow. Rebecca grinned as she pushed the button, which sent the door chimes into a frenzy. The door opened and a short, softly curved woman smiled through the security screen.

'Hello.'

'Hi, are you Mrs Wentworth?'

'Yes, what can I do for you?'

'I believe you're Michael Wentworth's grandmother. I'm interested in his disappearance. I wonder if you might help me.'

Mrs Wentworth looked past Rebecca. 'Mmm, are you on your own? Are you a reporter?'

Rebecca hesitated.

'Well? Are you or not?'

'Sorry. No, I'm not.'

'What is it you want?'

Rebecca hesitated again. She realised the real reason might seem far-fetched and considered making up a more plausible story, but she couldn't think quickly enough. Taking a deep breath she said, 'I was driving home from Woodend a few months ago and, at the spot where the sign points to Hanging Rock ... I can't explain it properly, but I experienced something weird.' She shivered involuntarily. Mrs Wentworth leaned closer. 'I went all clammy. It was eerie and, well, crazy. Especially as my car stopped for no reason. *And*, a willy-willy appeared out of nowhere. Then, three months later, I saw your grandson on the news. His experience and mine seem to have happened simultaneously. I haven't been able to stop thinking about it. I don't know what it means, but a strange feeling of being connected just won't go away.'

Mrs Wentworth watched Rebecca adjust her large bag that kept slipping from her shoulder. She consid-ered Rebecca's story before asking, 'What's your name?'

'Rebecca. Rebecca Hannah. My friends call me Bec.'

'What a shame. Rebecca is such a pretty name. Now, you're definitely not selling anything are you, Rebecca Hannah?'

Rebecca shook her head and frowned as she spoke, 'I know it doesn't sound very plausible, but I can't get the experience out of my head. Please, will you just talk to me?'

Mrs Wentworth unclipped the door and pushed it open. 'Come in. You can tell me the whole thing. If I can help, then I will. Anyway, it's afternoon tea time and I think it's always better to have someone to share cake with, don't you?'

'Yes, of course.' Rebecca let the door shut behind her and watched Mrs Wentworth turn the latch. 'Thank you so much. I won't stay too long.'

Several cat pictures surrounded Rebecca. Some were glossy photographs while others were bold carica-tures. A large blue one, similar to the cat painted on the front door, peered out from behind a turquoise brick fence. Mrs Wentworth remained at the front door and watched Rebecca as she examined the pictures in the hallway.

'Fascinating cats,' said Rebecca. *Weird colours.* 'Do you have any real ones?'

'No, my Bessie died last year. That's her in the yellow frame. I decided not to get another, but some days I miss not having a cat to spoil.'

'I have a cat – Missy.'

'Really? What colour?'

'Grey and white.'

'How lovely. Now, would you like tea or coffee, dear?'

'You don't have to do that. I don't want to be a nuisance.'

Mrs Wentworth chuckled as she directed Rebecca to the lounge room. 'No bother. I've already boiled the kettle. I was just about to have my afternoon cuppa. Did you say coffee or tea?'

'Coffee, if it's all right.'

'Yes, but it's instant.'

'That's fine.'

Rebecca stepped into the lounge room and noticed several photographs of Michael. After a while, Mrs Wentworth reappeared. A tray held dainty cups and some chocolate cake.

'Please, sit down. Have some cake, Rebecca. It's the type I usually baked for Michael, but he's away just now.'

'Do you know where he is?' Rebecca sat on the edge of the couch.

After she folded two paper napkins, Mrs Wentworth placed one on a plate with cake and passed it to Rebecca. 'My guess would be down the coast at his uncle's holiday home.'

Rebecca took the plate and put it on the table. 'Do you think he'll return soon?'

'I don't know. They said they'd be in touch. My son Jack, and his wife Janet, are doing what they can. They've gone with him, you know. Dear Michael, he's still coming to grips with what happened.'

'I can imagine.' Rebecca felt a little awkward and concentrated on eating the cake without dropping crumbs.

Mrs Wentworth kept glancing at Rebecca, sizing her up in between each sip of tea.

The chatter from the radio filtered through the silence. Mrs Wentworth offered more cake. Rebecca replied, 'No thanks. I'll just finish my coffee. I shouldn't take up too much of your time.'

'Well, you can't go yet. You were going to tell me something about Michael,' said Mrs Wentworth, as she poked her finger into the chocolate icing and then licked it clean.

'I only saw him at the news conference, and that wasn't very enlightening. I was hoping you'd tell me something that might help.'

Putting her cup down, Mrs Wentworth said, 'I don't know how I can help. They haven't told me everything.' She grinned. 'You see, I can be a little too chatty at times and they don't want me spilling the beans to the wrong people.' She leaned over and patted Rebecca's arm. 'I'm a little naughty sometimes. I tell stories from the past and extend my visits. It's entertaining to see how my daughter-in-law finds different ways to encourage me to leave.'

'Why does she do that?' Rebecca couldn't imagine this pleasant woman annoying anyone.

'Janet keeps to a schedule. I'm more inclined to do things on the spur of the moment. Go with my feelings. You know, leave the dishes to pull out some weeds. Then leave the garden and ring a friend because she just popped into my mind.'

'I'm like that too!' Rebecca exclaimed.

'Thought you might be. Turning up to talk to an old woman in the middle of the day. Why aren't you at work?'

'Tuesday's my day off. I work Thursday nights instead.'

'I see. And you came especially to see me?'

'Yes. Well, no. Not really. I have to be honest. Mrs Jackson gave me your address. Said you might help. I didn't know what else I could do. But you're a very lovely last resort – and, this cake is yummy.'

With a slight twitch of her lip Mrs Wentworth said, 'Flattery will get you everywhere.' She took another bite of cake and then finished her tea.

After a brief silence, Rose's face became serious. She spoke quietly, 'I worry about Michael. He was such a sensitive little boy. He had several invisible friends. I wonder if it's true what they say about spirit children. Anyway, I often babysat when he was tiny. Then, when he was older, he would come here after school.' She continued while Rebecca drank her coffee. 'His other grandmother, Wilma, wasn't interested one way or the other in his invisible friends. She could be rather mysterious when she wanted to be. Chatty sometimes, other times all bound up in silence. *She* had a connection to Hanging Rock.'

'Holy shit!' Rebecca's eyebrows shot up.

'Manners, please, Rebecca.'

'Sorry.' Her hand shook as she placed the cup and saucer back on the table. 'What's her connection?'

'Well, they say she was one of the girls who went missing from the rock.'

'What, Michael's grandmother?'

Rose shook her head. 'No, not Wilma. I should have said Wilma's grandmother. Irma.'

'Wow!' Rebecca could feel her heart rate increasing. 'Mrs Jackson mentioned something about some girls being lost. And, they kept referring to them on the news. I was too busy concentrating on figuring out why I felt involved. Of course, I didn't catch on that one was Michael's relative. Did they find the girls?'

'They found Irma a few days later. Never found the other two.'

'That's really weird.'

'There are plenty of theories. Naturally, there is some doubt about it. It was a very long time ago.'

'But ... now he went missing at the same place.' Rebecca rubbed her forearm. 'I have goose bumps again. Did you know her very well?'

'Not Irma of course, but I did know Michael's Grandma. We met at family gatherings. She was a flamboyant character. Tried to be stern, but it never quite came off. I must say she was always spectacularly dressed.'

Settling back on the couch, Rebecca asked, 'Please tell me some more. I don't remember any of the reports saying Michael had a prior connection to the place.'

'Not Michael, dear. Only his great-great-grand-mother. I think that's right. Let's see, yes, Wilma's grandmother was Irma Leopold. I wasn't told much really. They always said it was a secret.' She paused. 'Perhaps not a *secret* exactly, but they certainly didn't raise the subject willingly.'

'You've got to tell me more. About Irma. And the other girls. Maybe there's some relevance.'

The teacup rattled in its saucer as Mrs Wentworth pushed them away from the edge of the coffee table. Rearranging herself in the chair, she sighed. 'I don't know how that could be. At least, not to you. Anyway, I'll tell you what I remember. Apparently, Irma refused to talk about the whole thing. She said she couldn't remember anything and cried all the time. I can understand that. Two of her friends disappeared. Then the authorities badgered her with questions.'

'I guess if she was the only survivor, they'd have to ask her what she'd seen,' Rebecca said.

'Yes, I suppose so, but ... it seems she was made to feel responsible. Anyway, her parents took her off to Europe.'

'That must have been something else, back then.'

'They would've gone by ship. I don't know anything about her time in France, but she returned to Australia, very much in style.'

'What do you mean?'

'She married a French Count – Conte de Latte-Marguery.'

Rebecca's eyes widened. 'That would make her a Countess.'

Mrs Wentworth brushed crumbs from her skirt. 'Yes, but it didn't do her any good. Their marriage failed. Two years later she was married again.'

'Another Count?' Rebecca asked cheekily.

'No ... not many of them in Melbourne,' Mrs Went-worth responded with a grin. 'However, the family still brags about her second husband's success in property.'

So, Michael has a family connection to Hanging Rock, thought Rebecca. *Very interesting. But it still doesn't give any clues about my experience.*

Mrs Wentworth stood up and moved towards the kitchen. She turned and said, 'You know, I've remembered something else. Michael was quite inquisitive after he visited Wilma before her passing. He asked me what I knew about her. I told him stories I'd heard about her youth. Her husband. That sort of thing. We also talked about her connection with Hanging Rock, but I know little of the day Irma's friends disappeared, of course. I'm sure he went back to see her the night before she died. Yes, I do believe he did.' She nodded as if confirming her recollection. 'The week after the funeral he asked for my scrapbook on Hanging Rock. I've got boxes full of newspaper clippings, you see.'

Rebecca shifted forward on the seat. 'Mrs Went-worth, may I have a look at it?'

'Of course you can, but please, call me Rose. I'd like that better.' She smiled as she walked over to the bookcase. 'Let's see, it's here somewhere. Yes, there you go.'

With butterflies in her stomach, Rebecca opened the large book. A faded picture fluttered to the floor. She carefully picked it up.

Rose peered at the newspaper clipping. 'That's nothing to do with Hanging Rock. Pop it in the back. The pieces you want are in the middle somewhere.'

There were several clippings on events held at Hanging Rock. One detailed a council meeting voting on the restoration of a toilet block. Another was of the 1965 race meeting, and there was an article announcing the upcoming visit by the Governor General in 1966.

Disappointed by the lack of anything relevant, Rebecca turned another page and found a photograph of several schoolchildren at a picnic in 1969: *"Local students study Hanging Rock"*.

'Ah, this looks interesting.'

'Is it what you're looking for?'

'I don't really know,' said Rebecca. She scanned the article. 'So far it's just saying the kids went for an excursion. Hang on – *"Mr Bentley, the Science teacher, will expect his students to write an essay on the unique rock formations after their visit. However, the teenagers were more interested in the tale of the girls who went missing from the site in 1900"*. I would be too, wouldn't you? Rocks are so boring. Science certainly wasn't one of my preferred subjects.'

Rose sat down next to Rebecca, trying to read the small print. 'What else does it say?'

'There's a footnote. *"February 14th, 1900. After a school picnic that went horribly wrong, Irma Leopold – who survived the ordeal – was unable to shed any light on the disappearance of her friends, Marion Quade and Miranda St Clare. All three young ladies were boarders at Appleyard College. To this day, the mystery has remained unsolved"*. Look at that. Fourteenth of February.' Rebecca shivered. 'Oh, goose bumps again.'

Rose rubbed Rebecca's arm. 'It certainly is a coincidence – all these things happening on Valentine's Day. Peculiar.'

Rebecca looked up quickly and nodded. She re-read the article. 'It mentions Michael's Irma.'

'Yes, the article must have struck me at the time. I've pasted bits and pieces in scrapbooks for as long as I can remember. Probably should go through them. I'm sure most could be thrown out.'

Rose watched as Rebecca turned more pages and scanned pictures

After a couple of minutes, Rose leaned back and said, 'Rebecca, I fear you'll begin to think me strange.' She twisted the rings on her fingers. 'Like many others, I suppose.'

'What you?' Rebecca grinned and pointed to her chest. 'Look who you're talking to. Remember, I'm the one who can't let go of a fascination for someone I've never met.'

'True,' the old lady smiled, 'but I'm talking about some of those newspaper clippings on Hanging Rock. I collected them before I met Wilma, long before Michael started asking questions and now you pop up with the same interest. What do you think of that?'

'I suppose it's just what it is.'

Rose thought for a moment. 'Yes, but how do you come to be so accepting at your age?'

'I'm odd, remember.'

They chuckled and nodded at each other. Rose boiled the kettle again and soon all that remained of the cake were some crumbs. Finally, Rebecca left Rose reminiscing over her newspaper clippings and promised to return the following Tuesday.

Later, tucked up in bed, with a purring Missy at her feet, Rebecca made some notes.

> Michael related to Irma – OMG!
> Irma rescued from Hanging Rock … lucky!
> Countess!
> Rose's collection of HR stories. Mmm.

She scribbled her feelings on a fresh page.
> Me? What is the connection?
> Confused? … you bet!
> Must continue to search.
> Rose is such a dear. Can't wait to visit again.
> Must take cake.
> ???????????

Hoping for a dose of reality, Rebecca visited her sister the following Saturday. She felt reassured by the warmth of Kylie's hug. Then, holding Rebecca at arm's length, Kylie scrutinised her sister's face. 'Are you okay?'

'Yeah, fine. And you?'

Kylie pushed uncombed curls behind her ears. 'Yep, going okay.' She accepted Rebecca's kiss. 'Just a little tired. I never sleep soundly when Luke's away.'

Stepping back to let Rebecca through the doorway, Kylie pulled her t-shirt down over her narrow hips and walked into the kitchen.

'When's he due back?' asked Rebecca.

'Next Thursday.'

'Not too long. So, how's my cheeky nephew?'

Kylie chuckled, 'You should've seen him trying to do a forward roll. Arms and legs were going everywhere.'

Rebecca placed a packet of biscuits on the kitchen bench and followed Kylie through to the family room. Thomas sat surrounded by toys. His feet kicked at the blocks, while his hands rubbed his eyes.

Kylie let out a deep sigh. 'Thomas is so tired, but he won't go down for his afternoon sleep. Listen to the grizzling.'

Rebecca stepped in. 'Who's making all this noise then?' she asked, bending down.

A broad smile covered Thomas' face. He jumped up, stumbled over the blocks, and hurried to his aunt. She scooped him up and planted kisses on his cheeks. 'So, where have you been all my life, young man?'

Thomas giggled and wanted to get down immediately. 'Brec, play with truck.'

Kylie rolled her eyes and headed back to the kitchen.

Making silly noises, Rebecca pushed the big blue truck around on the carpet. She banged it into the scattered blocks while Thomas snuggled into her legs. By the time Kylie came back with coffee and biscuits, Rebecca was twisting Thomas' dark curls around her finger as he slept on her lap.

'I don't know how you do it,' whispered Kylie, as Rebecca placed Thomas in his cot.

Rebecca put her arm around her sister's waist and grinned. 'Auntie magic.'

'Well, I could do with a bottle of it.'

They returned to the family room. Kylie pushed aside a pile of clean laundry and sat on the sofa with her legs tucked under her body. Rebecca relaxed back into the seat next to her sister and sipped coffee.

After she ate a biscuit, Rebecca reached for another, but Kylie grabbed the packet. 'Not until I hear all about this new *friend*.'

'Look, I haven't met him yet,' Rebecca said, as she thought of the tingling in her stomach when Rose showed her photographs of Michael.

'Okay, then tell me about your *not* friend.'

Glancing at the biscuits, Rebecca said, 'If that's the price I have to pay, I'd better get it over with.'

'What about this Michael then? Is he gorgeous?'

Kylie handed over a biscuit and Rebecca snapped it in two.

'You saw him on telly. What do you think?'

'Come on, Bec, you know what I mean. Is he serious boyfriend material or what?'

Rebecca shook her head and gripped her bottom lip with her teeth. She stood up and thought about the press conference where she was out of her depth. 'It isn't about that, Kyls. Really, it's not. I want to find out more about him, yes, but I want to unravel the synchronicity of it all. His disappearance, my trip, the feelings I had when I saw him on the news.'

Kylie patted the seat beside her. 'It's all right. Relax. You've told me all that weird stuff before. I want to hear about the bloke himself.'

Rebecca sat down on the couch and sucked on the chocolate biscuit. 'He's taller than me. Blue eyes, some freckles – cute bum. Yep, I'd say I like the package. I can't wait to meet him properly.'

'Well then, I can't wait to hear about it.'

They talked until Thomas came from his bedroom, dragging his pillow. 'Brec play with Tommy.'

Rebecca played with Thomas for a couple more hours until it was his bath-time and it was time for her to go home to Missy.

FOUR

'You know, you do look like a reporter with your hair tied back and those dark sunglasses,' said Rose, as she showed Rebecca into the lounge room where afternoon tea was already in place.

'Maybe I should have a notepad and start by asking some probing questions,' laughed Rebecca, as she slipped her sunglasses into her bag.

'I doubt I have anything new to tell you. The newspapers have covered most of it.'

Rebecca agreed, but felt that her connection must be personal, not the speculations that were splashed across pages of newsprint. 'I'm not sure what I'm after exactly. I'm just working with hunches.' Rebecca watched Rose pour the tea. '*Weird* hunches ...' She shook her head. 'They either get me into trouble or, at the very least, waste a lot of time.' She reached out for the hot drink. 'Have there been any real reporters hanging around?'

'No, not here. There've been plenty at my Jack's place, but I've avoided them. Anyway, tell me about you and Michael.'

'There's nothing to tell.' Rebecca shrugged. 'I haven't met him. Well, I did. Kind of. At the press conference. I caught up with him and his minder in the hall.'

'That would be Michael's so-called agent. He's a friend of a friend who thought he could help with all the media attention. Apparently, he's good at minding other people's business for his own benefit.' Rose paused. 'Sorry, I interrupted, go on.'

'I thought he must be something like that. He wasn't very friendly. He practically threw himself between us. I'm afraid I made Michael angry. He told me quite clearly that he wouldn't answer any of my questions. I didn't like him much.' Rebecca added quickly, 'The agent, I mean. Not Michael.'

'I see. Tell me more of why you are so keen to know about Michael.'

Rebecca moved her bag away from her feet and settled back into the couch. 'It's to do with feeling connected to him and Hanging Rock. When I saw Michael on the news ...' She paused, shook her head and then continued, 'This will sound a little crazy, but, I've always been one for believing we don't know anything about the ultimate possibilities of the universe. Most people dismiss what they don't understand. Then they refuse to believe anything at all.'

'Humph, I know a few of those.'

Nodding her agreement, Rebecca said, 'My sister is always on at me for following my hunches. I do tend to get side-tracked easily.'

A soft chuckle from Rose encouraged her to continue.

'The day I went to Woodend, I mean, what was that all about? By the way, I ended up buying a fussy little brooch. The woman tried to convince me it would bring me luck. Another stupid impulse. I suppose I could re-gift it. But the bag I bought is okay. I've used it already.'

'Rebecca, that's not relevant, surely. Tell me the bit about your intuition.'

'Sorry. I've already told you about my car and the willy-willy.' Rose nodded. Rebecca continued. 'Well, it was on the way to Macedon. I felt I needed to go down the road to Hanging Rock, but it was the wrong direction and, to be honest, I was terrified.' Rebecca's stomach churned as she recalled the panic of being on her own and not in control. 'I really can't understand why I couldn't stop shaking when I watched your grandson being interviewed. It all seemed related somehow.' She took a deep breath and let it out noisily. 'That's why I want to talk to him.'

'By golly! I'll have to get Michael to meet you.' Rose's voice then lost its excitement. 'He's had a hard time accepting what happened. I know it seems odd, but it did happen. That needs to be acknowledged at least.'

Rose came over and sat beside Rebecca, patting her leg gently. 'Like you said, some things can't be explained. One just has to accept them and move on the best you can.'

'Yes, that's what I tried to explain to my sister, Kylie. She's not big on the paranormal.'

'Oh, I see,' Rose replied with a grimace.

Rose got up from the couch and stood looking at a picture of Michael, aged about seven. 'I was disappointed when Janet returned to work. A little old fashioned of me I know, but in the end I was grateful Michael spent time with me. He was such a lovely little boy.' Rebecca noticed freckles across his cheeks. A smile emerged as Rose said, 'He spent an entire week during the school holidays dressed up like a pirate. The sand pit was the ocean and my poor cat was a very frightened captive. He made her walk the plank. Good thing there wasn't any real water.'

Rebecca imagined Missy, who always hid from Thomas, hating being a pirate's playmate too.

Rose chortled when Rebecca told her of the time she wore gumboots to work for a week because she dreamt the florist shop would be flooded. Lifting her feet off the floor, jiggling them up and down for effect, Rebecca added, 'The week after that my shoes and socks were soaked when a large vase fell off the counter.'

Rose laughed heartily. 'Thanks, Rebecca, I needed a laugh.' Then after a long pause, she spoke quietly, 'I still worry about my grandson. You always do. Doesn't matter what age they are.'

Realising they were sitting in the dark, Rose switched on the light and invited Rebecca to stay for dinner. After squabbling over whether it was too much trouble for Rose, they compromised and Rebecca rang for pizza – her shout.

'I haven't eaten pizza for a long time. I don't buy it for myself, but Michael used to drop in with one occasionally. Super Supreme, always Super Supreme,' said Rose.

'I love pizza, but I always feel a little guilty. Mum never let us have junk food,' said Rebecca, as she rolled her eyes.

'Good heavens, it's a lovely treat. She doesn't know what she's missing.'

'Exactly.'

They chatted endlessly until eight-thirty when, after a promise to return the following Tuesday, Rebecca left feeling she had a new friend. She also felt calmer. The anxiety that knotted her stomach had subsided for the first time since the trip to Woodend. It was as if a piece of the puzzle had fallen into place.

The week dragged with Rebecca getting on everyone's nerves with questions on what, or if, they'd seen any further news on the Hanging Rock saga. Kylie said it was a seven-day wonder; forget it. Rebecca's mother sighed and professed she must have been touched by a goblin while pregnant with her second child. Her dad pragmatically detailed the few items he'd heard, but agreed with Kylie that Rebecca should get on with her life – it had nothing to do with her.

Rebecca put her arm around her father's middle. 'But, Dad, this *has* got something to do with my life. I just haven't figured it out yet.'

'Put your energies into that gift shop idea. You said you were going to look for a place to rent. Have you started?' Feeling guilty because she hadn't followed up on their previous discussion, Rebecca made excuses and left.

FIVE

Michael let his mobile phone slip from his hand. He watched it hit the ground. He sat motionless for a few seconds then pushed at the phone with his foot. He wanted to toss the lifeless device into the bush, but despite his frustration, he wasn't about to discard his only potential lifeline.

As he pulled keys from his pocket they caught on the stitching. The thread snapped and the keys jolted against his thumb. Holding the keys at arm's length, his eyes narrowed as he glared at the brass front door key and then at the thick black plastic of his car key. Michael hoped they too wouldn't disappear. They were the only reality in this nightmare. Proof that his car did exist. Proof he wasn't going insane.

He dropped the keys. They clinked together as they landed between his feet. Michael wondered if anyone else heard the rattle of metal. He let his head fall onto his folded arms. The keys appeared to wink back at him. Now only fifty centimetres from his nose, they appeared large and intimidating. He noticed a tall piece of grass poking through the hole of one key. Odds of it falling in that precise position made him consider the random coincidence of nature. An involuntary laugh of derision emerged. 'Where *is* my bloody car?' he shouted, as he flicked a weed with his finger. Then he stood up and covered the keys with his foot.

He cursed his useless mobile again. He knew it was charged. It worked yesterday when he replied to several texts from his mates about perfect beach conditions. Now, the screen remained blank.

Saturday had started out as a means to an end. Scouting around Hanging Rock to get the feel of his grandmother's revelation was interesting, but it was now Sunday and he thoroughly regretted his trip. Surfing would have been safer. Even if he ended up having one too many beers, anything would have been better than this!

He brushed his forehead with his palm, then moved his foot and stared at the keys again. The tall piece of grass was flattened and the brass key had dug a small hole.

Michael bent down slowly and picked them up. He pulled the last piece of grass from the keyhole and threw it away. It blew back against his shirt. Seeing the fragile piece of leftover grass clinging to his shirt made him curse again. Would nothing, even the simplest thing, go to plan? He took a few steps towards the rock. He changed his mind and turned around. His attention returned to the piece of grass still stuck on his shirt. He flicked the dried stem off and watched it flutter towards the ground. When it landed, he sat down next to it and put his head on his bent knees.

Why is nothing the same? How can things just disappear? He lifted his head and shouted, 'What's happening?'

A woman's voice penetrated his thoughts. 'Hello.'

He jumped to his feet. 'Shit! You gave me a hell of a fright. Where'd you come from?'

Michael peered at the elderly woman who appeared reluctant to come too close. Her eyes were red, as if she'd been rubbing them. *Has she been crying?* She held a battered bucket and a faded scarf. Baggy trousers stopped above her bare feet. A cotton shirt billowed around her waist and made her look like a character from a black and white movie.

What happened next nearly scared the freckles off his face. The old woman dropped the bucket and threw her scrawny arms around his neck. Her wrinkled face puckered into shape and she planted a firm kiss on his cheek. She then grabbed his arm and jabbered, 'You're him. You must be. My prayers have been answered. Finally. Thank you, God.' She jerked her head up and down repeatedly. 'I'm so very pleased you're here.'

'What are you talking about?' Michael eased himself away from the unwanted attention. 'I'm just a bit lost. Can't find my car. Can you help me?'

She finally released him, although she stood close and tapped his arm several times as she repeated, 'I don't believe it.'

Michael stepped further away. 'Listen, if you just point me towards the main road, I'll be on my way.'

The woman grunted and looked into the distance. She turned back and went to touch him again, but she shook her head and announced, 'Young man, the way out can't be found.' She marched around him, looking him up and down. Michael was slightly amused. *Who is she?*

'How did you get here?' she demanded. 'Are you on your own?'

'Yep, just me.' Michael spun around and faced her. She stood still, but continued to stare at him. 'You see,' he said, 'I'm a little confused. Can't find my car. Probably stolen. You know what it's like?'

'If I may say so, it is quite uncommon for anything to be stolen around here. There are not too many of us. Certainly no one that can drive a car. It is too new for most.'

'What? No. My car isn't new. Anyway, which way to the main road? Maybe I can flag down someone for a ride into town.'

Squinting into the sun, Michael looked closely at the woman. Wrinkles spread across her tanned face and her long grey hair was tied back. If he couldn't find any clues to his location, what was this person doing here?

'Are you lost too?' he asked.

'No, I'm quite at home here in this place. I've spent too many years walking the tracks to be lost. However, I *am* very glad to see you. You've been sent for a reason. I'm Marion Quade.'

'Michael, Michael Wentworth.' He pointed to their surroundings. 'This place is something else. It certainly doesn't look the same today as it did yesterday. I can't even locate the buildings.'

Marion nodded her head slowly.

'But, don't worry,' Michael said, 'I'm sure someone will be looking for me. I'll be out of here in no time.'

'Ah, Miranda and I said *that* for many years.'

Michael frowned. He was surprised the old woman didn't question his concerns. *Maybe a bit of dementia.* But, there was someone called Miranda. Maybe, he thought, they live at a nearby farm. Or ... perhaps she's wandered away from a picnic group. If that's so, they can't be far away. He tested this notion. 'Hello,' he yelled. 'Hel ... lo.'

'There's no one to hear you, Michael. Except maybe the Aborigines, but they won't answer.'

Michael swivelled one hundred and eighty degrees for a cursory glance in case someone, Aboriginal or otherwise, might be watching them.

'Is the main road that way?' Michael pointed in the direction he thought he had driven yesterday. It seemed like a lifetime ago.

'Yes, I do believe the horses came that way.'

'Horses? What horses?' He now wondered if any of their conversation made sense. 'Look, what if we go together? Show me the way and then you can get back to your friend. If we don't find my car, I'm certain I can hitch a ride with a truckie sooner or later.'

Marion wound her scarf around her hand, filling in time as she formed an answer. 'I'm not sure where you think you are, but there are no motorised vehicles here. Only a few folk in these parts had some before. Wally Carrington owned a lorry to cart his sheep on auction day. He used to sell a carcass to our cook before he left town.'

She let the scarf unwind; the end touched the ground before she lifted her hand again. Shaking her head, she said, 'I haven't heard of Wally since time became distorted.'

Michael felt uncomfortable with Marion's continual inspection as he tried to process this peculiar information. 'But the truckies travel this road all the time. Nearly blow you off the road. I passed at least a dozen on my way up here.'

Looking him up and down several more times, trying to make assumptions, she asked, 'How old are you? When were you born?'

Michael was now certain he was dealing with someone with a confused mind, perhaps senile, and opted to humour her.

'I was born in 1982.'

Her face went ashen and Michael thought she was going to faint. He stepped towards her. 'Here, hang on. You okay?'

'Yes. Yes. That's it. More time lost. No wonder you talk of things I don't understand.'

'Time lost? Now *I* don't get it.'

'Well, no matter, you should come with me. You look like you need something to eat. I have some soup on the stove.'

'Soup sounds good, but I'd rather you show me the way to the main road.'

Michael jumped when Marion yelled, 'NO! You *have* to come with me.' Her attitude changed again. She smiled and touched his arm. 'Please, you must come with me.'

He was worried about the woman's strange ramblings. She confused him even more when she said, 'Don't you see, if your car disappeared yesterday, then it won't be there today. It's been swallowed by time. Please, come and have something to eat.'

Michael hesitated. She didn't make any sense. However, he was desperate for help. 'If I go with you, can I use your phone?'

'Phone? I guess you mean a telephone. No, I don't have one.'

'What about a mobile?'

Marion frowned. 'Mobile? I don't know what that is.'

Michael thrust his hand into his pocket. '*This* is a mobile.' He held out his open palm.

Marion peered at the small object. 'What does it do?'

Michael stepped closer and spoke softly, 'It's a telephone you can carry.'

'My goodness, where are its wires?'

'That's why it's called a mobile. No cord. Radio. It's a mobile phone. Obviously you don't have one.'

Marion stepped away from Michael before speaking. 'You have to come with me. It will do you no good to keep looking for your car.'

Michael's hand folded around his mobile. His shoulders sagged and his arms went limp. He closed his eyes. *How did I get into this mess?* He opened his eyes and found Marion watching him carefully.

'Come with me. You can rest. Eat something,' she pleaded again.

'No, thanks all the same.' If she doesn't have a phone, there's no point going there, he thought.

'Won't you come with me, Michael?' asked Marion gently.

'No,' he said, more forcibly. 'I have to get back to Melbourne. I'll find the main road - if I can't find anything else.'

'It can't be found. Not yet, anyway.'

Michael was annoyed this bizarre woman wouldn't help him. He glared at her before moving away. The stones crunched beneath his feet.

'I'll find it without you,' he yelled back over his shoulder.

'You cannot find what is not there,' she called.

'Of course it's there.'

'When you realise it isn't, come back to me.'

Michael let out a deep breath. He stopped and turned around. Marion hadn't moved. Loose strands of hair were blowing away from her face. She waved her faded scarf.

'Just keep on this track for about two miles and you'll find my house,' she explained, pointing back behind her. 'You won't miss it. There is nothing else.'

He thanked her, and added quietly, 'I'll find my car somehow.'

Michael watched her walk away. To make sure he could locate the exact spot again, he ripped the hem from his t-shirt. 'I suppose I'll have to come back and check on her,' he complained, as he marked several trees on his way through the bush.

No matter which way he went the tourist buildings were nowhere in sight, but from every position, the rock towered above him. He felt insignificant.

'Damn you, rock. What have you done with my car?' he shouted, as he stalked through the endless scrub.

After forty minutes, he rested. *No way out? The old woman must be mental.* He tugged at the frayed edge of his t-shirt. *Of course there's a way out.* He felt numb. *Patrick would've woken up this morning and wondered where I am. Unless he stayed at Erin's. But then again, he'd probably just think I stayed the night in Woodend.*

Michael was supposed to have dinner with his parents on Saturday evening. He imagined his mother brooding over a glass of red wine and his father telling her to calm down. By now, they would be anxious. *They'd ring the flat first. Then what? Maybe they'll ring the police.* He hoped so.

As he tried his phone again, he thought, but ... if I can't find the car park, will they be able to find me? He shoved his phone into his backpack. 'Come on, Dad, Patrick – ring the bloody cops.'

He stood and raged to the empty space. 'Ring 'em! At least *your* phone will work. Just ring them! Tell them where I am. Tell them to come and get me. Just ring them.' The three words became a chant as he retraced his steps and followed the pieces of his clothing. On reaching the last piece, he stopped and looked down the track. 'I hope she really does have a house.'

SIX

'You came back.'

'I couldn't find my car or even the bloody road.'

Marion drew in a quick breath, but ignored the swearing. 'I did explain that to you several times.'

'Yes, I know, but it was there yesterday.'

'And look at you. What happened to your under-shirt?'

Michael tilted his head, sighed and wrapped his arms across his stomach. 'I had to mark the way with something.'

'Good for you. Would you like some soup?'

He nodded. 'Yes. Thanks.'

'Have a seat. It won't be long.'

After placing his backpack on the floor and hanging his jacket on a chair, he stood for a moment and watched Marion stir the soup.

He noticed the dining table, chairs and the old dresser were solidly built. A worn rug filled the space between an oddly covered couch and the table. A ceramic rabbit, similar to his mother's collection of animals, sat on a small table with legs that appeared to have been burnt. A lamp with cracked glass caught his attention and he walked over and picked it up. The wick was well-used and the lamp was almost out of oil. He absentmindedly straightened a carved wooden picture frame.

'Who's Miranda?' Michael asked.

Marion clattered the ladle against the pot, but didn't answer.

'Have you been here long?'

Marion shrugged. 'Many years. Sit down, the soup is ready.'

'It's rather remote. Why didn't you move to town?'

There was an awkward silence. Marion served the soup into the bowl in front of Michael. Then, turning away, she said, 'For the exact same reason that you're sitting here eating my soup.'

He ate two mouthfuls of soup before the spoon slipped from his grip. He said, 'You ... you really believe there's no way out?' *She must be joking.* He retrieved the spoon and continued to eat the soup. He couldn't think of anything to say.

Marion leaned on the kitchen bench and watched him intently.

'What? What's wrong?' he asked.

'I apologise. I do know it's rude to stare,' said Marion, as she wiped her hands. 'I haven't seen anyone else but Miranda for so long, I suppose things are bound to be somewhat different from when I was fifteen.'

'Different?' Michael shrugged.

'Yes. Your clothes are unusual.'

Michael looked down at his torn t-shirt. 'I don't generally wear a ripped shirt.'

Marion chuckled. 'I hope not.' She sat down across the table from Michael. Looking at his hands she said, 'You obviously don't do heavy work.'

'No, I work in a government office.'

'Doing what?'

'I T.'

'What's that when as good as is done?'

Nervous laughter escaped from Michael. 'Not heard of computers and Information Technology?'

'I'm sure young people these days have their own language. No, I have no idea of what you speak.'

Michael's head sagged onto his chest. *Where do I start?* As he fumbled for words, he was surprised when Marion jumped up and pulled his jacket off the back of the chair. Fearing he was about to receive another bout of unwanted affection, he leaned away from her.

'The fastening, how does it work? Where are the buttons?'

'What? The zip?'

'Zip?'

Marion stood mesmerised as an amused Michael moved the zip up and down several times. 'Surely you know what a zip is.'

'I've never seen one. How fascinating.'

'Don't you have one on your ...' Michael paused, '... trousers?'

'No. Look, I have buttons.'

Michael turned his head away, but Marion insisted on showing him the three buttons and four buttonholes on the front of her trousers. As she passed her finger over the fourth buttonhole, she added, 'I lost it in the bush.'

In the end, Marion played with the zipper while Michael finished his soup.

Michael then said, 'Velcro is the latest thing.'

'What's vel cro?' She jumped as a size twelve sneaker landed on the chair beside her. She reached out and poked the heel. 'How strange.'

'Not really,' he replied. Her eyes widened as Michael flipped open the two tabs. 'That's Velcro. It's one word, by the way.'

'Let me do that,' she insisted. 'Please.'

Michael removed the sneaker and passed it to her. They both ignored the odour of synthetic footwear.

'Isn't that clever? Miranda would have loved it.'

Michael took his jacket from the table and held out his hand for his shoe. 'Who's Miranda?'

Marion didn't answer. *How much should I tell him?* She got up and pushed in the chair. *I mustn't scare him away.* Then she walked out the back door.

Michael didn't want to sit alone so he followed her outside and up to a small wooden outbuilding. He held the door open while she lifted a piece of tin off the top of a large drum and retrieved a small bucket of grain from its depths.

'Not much left.' She stepped around Michael and strolled a short way to a chicken enclosure under a large fig tree. Three hens and one rooster greeted her with noisy enthusiasm as she scattered the grain across the small pen.

'A lot of work went into this,' Michael commented, as he wound in a protruding strand of wire. 'Are they hard to keep in?'

'We have to keep the foxes out.'

'Foxes, of course.' He straightened a piece of rusty tin and then pushed a stake, which was holding the tin upright, a little further into the ground.

Michael dutifully followed the old woman back into the house. *Why is she avoiding my questions?*

'Do you want some tea?'

'Yes, that'll be good,' said Michael. 'White with one, thanks.'

'White? One?' Marion frowned. 'Ah, milk ... sugar I suppose.' She shrugged. 'You'll have to make do with black. We've never had fresh milk. You can have lemon, but the sugar finished some weeks ago.'

Michael shot a questioning look towards her. *Finished? You haven't bought more?* He said, ' Black on its own will do.'

While Marion busied herself with the tea making, Michael looked closely at the unusual couch. Drab brown arms contrasted against the loose covering. Large red and purple flowers clung to bright green ivy that criss-crossed the fabric, but half had faded into a dull grey. The overall effect was appalling. As he sat down and settled into the uneven padding, the covering crinkled under his legs. He tugged at the corner of the cloth. Michael then shifted along the couch. It seemed necessary to choose between the bright section and the faded end.

Questions rushed through his mind as he struggled to be logical. *Why does she insist there is no way out? Why is she so out of date? Surely she isn't just poor. Why no telephone? A hermit perhaps. But someone must know she's here. And ... who's Miranda?*

Marion joined him on the couch and they sipped their hot tea. After a few minutes, Michael heard her sniff. He peaked sideways. Marion was crying. She dabbed at her tears with a cloth. Michael looked away. He shifted in the seat before he glanced at her again.

'You okay?' he asked.

'It's the relief,' Marion answered.

'Relief? From what?'

She sniffed again. 'I feel my time is near and I want to be buried properly. Now you're here and I'm no longer alone. I'm ever so pleased.'

'Who's Miranda?' he asked again, unable to digest her answer rationally.

'She and I spent all these years – whatever the number is – together. We survived together.'

'She lives here too?'

'Lived.' The word was more a breath than a real word.

Michael wondered if he should ask anything else about Miranda. He drank his tea slowly. Marion continued to sniff. In between drinking her tea, she wiped more tears from her cheeks. She placed her hand on his arm and looked purposely at him. 'I want to be buried next to her.'

He gulped the last of the tea down. 'Who buried Miranda?'

'It was me. We dug our graves many years ago. It took us several weeks. We decided they needed to be dug while we were strong enough.'

He didn't know what to say, so he stood up and extended his hand for her empty cup.

'One time when I was very sick, I lay in the dirt, hoping to die,' she explained.

'What? You mean in a grave?'

'Yes, I was sure I was going to die.'

'Surely you went to a doctor!'

'No, no doctors. No one else.'

'Then, if you've been here for a while, how *did* you survive without medical help?'

'Fortunately we remained mostly in good health. I do remember another time. It was winter. I had a fever. It was the first time we saw an adult Aborigine. Usually it was just the piccaninnies.'

'Piccaninnies?' He placed the cups on the kitchen bench and

returned to the couch.

'Yes, the children. Anyway, this other time, I wanted water and little else. When Miranda went to feed the chickens, she saw a man standing at the end of the yard, waving his arms. He pointed to the shed, cupped his hands and pretended to drink from them. Then he faded into the tall grass beyond the fence line. Miranda called to him, but he was already gone. She found some liquid in the bowl we use to feed the chickens. I felt so ill anyway, there was nothing to lose. I sipped that awful concoction over three days. After that, I began to feel better. Needless to say I recovered.' A small ironic laugh escaped as Marion shrugged her shoulders.

'Do you know what it was?'

'No. And it wasn't the only time they gave us help.'

'Really! Did you speak to them?'

'We couldn't. Their language was different. Well, the piccaninnies' words were and the older ones never got close enough for us to find out.'

Michael left that train of thought and asked, 'Where is Miranda buried?'

Marion stood up and stretched her back, then left the room, indicating that he should follow. She led him to the far side of the lemon tree. She bowed her head. Michael sensed her sorrow. He stood by a mound of dirt and read the inscription on a small plank of wood.

Miranda   Born 1885
Died in a time unknown
A friend through it all

The date puzzled him. He fumbled for something to say. His voice came out in a quick burst, 'When did it happen?'

'Two pages ago.'

'Two pages? What?'

Marion shot him an unreadable look. Michael wandered over to the hole that stretched out alongside Miranda's grave. The soil was firm and gritty, but sev-eral edges had tumbled in.

Marion said, 'I will go soon.' Then she tottered away.

He sensed she wanted to be alone so he took the opportunity to check out the yard.

He rounded the corner of the house and came across a vegetable plot. Pumpkins were dying back. Carrot tops and a few lettuces were in good shape. He couldn't identify the vine that spread across a shaky frame. Dead tendrils and withered leaves covered some grapevines.

Past the end of the vines, he turned again and saw the small shed. The enclosed chicken run was a lot quieter now. He assumed the other small structure was an outside toilet. An old apple tree grew beyond the cleared area.

It had been a long day, he was still hungry and tired, but he wanted answers. He couldn't understand Marion's insistence that there was no way out. *There must be. If she's been here for a while, she must know the way. Otherwise, how has she survived?*

The kettle was boiling and the pot of soup simmered on the edge of the stove as Michael entered. Marion could recognise his uncertainty. She still remembered how that felt.

'Sit down. Do you want more soup? You can have some bread with it.'

'Thanks. Do you only eat soup and bread?' he asked kindly.

Marion gave a burst of sound that was the beginning of a laugh. 'Not always, but our supplies are running out. I get by on whatever is around. Fish are difficult to catch, but the hens are reliable. Soup keeps me going. I do the best I can.'

'Is there anything I can do?'

'Not today. Are you tired?'

'Yes. I didn't sleep much last night. I was cold and uncomfortable.'

'And frightened?'

Michael nodded. 'I think I'm going mad.'

'You will think that for some time yet,' said Marion softly.

They were silent, both lost in dark memories. Michael's so new. Marion's from long ago. The meal was finished in silence.

'You said it's two pages since Miranda died. What did you mean?'

'We have no way of accurately telling the time.' Marion shrugged. 'When we remembered, we marked off the days on a home-made calendar.'

'Then you've been by yourself for two months.'

Marion sighed, 'Probably a little longer. I threw the pages away. It seemed pointless.'

Michael nodded, but was too tired to make further comment.

Marion noticed his drowsiness. 'You should sleep. Come this way. You can have Miranda's bed. The bed-clothes are clean.'

Michael followed Marion into one of two rooms leading off the main room. Against the sidewall was a single bed with a small table beside it. She offered him a sleeveless shirt and left the room.

He frowned as he turned back the bedding. Under a grey blanket, two sheets covered a mattress and a wire base. *A mattress can't possibly be that thin.* Good job I'm tired, thought Michael.

Before he fell asleep he hoped that tomorrow he would find the main road. *Perhaps I can convince Marion to come with me.*

SEVEN

As the early sun filtered through the trees, Marion tiptoed across the cold floor and peeked through the doorway at Michael sleeping. His feet stuck out over the end of the bed. His hair was like a bunch of straw. Stubble covered his young face. One of his arms suddenly flung itself over the covers and Marion sprang back. When his breathing turned into a soft snore, she leaned against the doorjamb and resumed her observation.

She had little knowledge of men. She had no siblings and most of her older cousins were female. Other adolescent males, such as the yardman and gardener employed by her mother, acted like immature fools in their brief encounters with her.

Marion enjoyed her father's company and, on the evenings when she was home from school, would expect him to answer her neverending questions. Mr Quade would place his newspaper on his knee, take a long puff on his pipe, and proudly share his vast knowledge.

It was accepted behaviour, when entertaining, that after dinner the men would retire to spend time with each other. Women would gather in another sitting room intermingling housekeeping tips with the latest gossip. Young children were sent to bed. Unless someone particularly objected, her father would allow Marion to join the men in the smoking-room while they talked of politics and business. It was at her father's side she learned that knowledge was boundless.

However, her father's friends were not young and handsome. Here was a man that was both. She watched the rise and fall of Michael's broad chest. Her sight travelled along the blanket as she built an impression of his strong legs. Marion's hands slipped around her waist, caressing the softened stomach of old age. She trailed her fingers across her diminished breasts, up her neck and onto her flushing cheeks.

Michael rolled onto his side. Marion didn't move. The sheet no longer covered him and his shirt rode up to his waist. Her eyes widened and a smirk of pleasure formed. She took a small step forward, her hand felt for the doorknob. Yes, the freckles went all the way down his back. She continued to stare at his firm buttocks.

Suddenly, Michael turned over. The covers fell to the floor. He took several short shallow breaths and made grunting noises. Marion froze. Michael moved his head, but remained asleep. Narrowing her eyes, Marion looked over the athletic body. *Yes, very strong.* She licked her top lip.

Curls of dark hair started below Michael's navel, thickening at his groin and diminishing into soft golden shafts on his long legs. She looked at his penis and felt her face grow warmer. She placed one hand on her cheek and leaned forward for a closer look. *Well I never.* Michael moved again. This time Marion tiptoed from the room.

She sat on her bed admonishing herself. *Fancy standing like a schoolgirl staring at the body of a houseguest.* She grinned as she remembered the moment the covers fell to the floor. She stood up and sighed. *Where are my manners?* She determined she needed a long walk to get rid of the excitement at seeing a naked man for the first time.

Miranda had often teased her with details of the male physique. Miranda embarrassed Marion with her descriptions of her four older brothers' antics. It seemed they were forever without clothes: frolicking in the dam, chasing each other at bath-time and running through the first summer rains as it poured down on the dry outback soil.

As Marion dawdled along familiar paths, she could feel her face flushing again. She remembered a dishevelled kitchen maid at school returning from the stables, scurrying past them on the lawn, looking far from disappointed after a few minutes with her young man. However, information was sparse and whispering schoolgirls were hardly experts.

She wandered back to the house, stood by the lemon tree and took a few deep breaths. A slight smile turned into a grin as she recalled Michael's body. She tried thinking of something grim as she opened the front door, but the smile snuck across her face again. She went back down the step and stood by Miranda's grave. 'Goodness me, Miranda. What am I to do?'

By the time she composed herself and re-entered the house, Michael was fully clothed and standing over the fire with a piece of damper stuck on a fork.

'Morning, Marion.'

Marion picked up a frying pan and, keeping her eyes from Michael's face, said, 'Good morning, Michael.' She still felt flustered, but asked, 'Did you sleep well?'

'Yep. Didn't think I would.'

She cracked some eggs into the pan. 'I understand, but you do get used to things.'

Michael almost burnt the toast as he thought of his difficulties. 'I don't know about that. I'm totally confused. You said you've been two months on your own ...'

Marion poked at the eggs.

'I mean, you said there's no way out. But that's ... well, of course there is.'

'It's hard to explain, Michael.' *There is no explanation.*

'I was hoping you could tell me why I couldn't find the café. I'm sure I wasn't in the wrong place.'

'Like I said, it's all very hard to explain.' *I mustn't tell him too much, too soon.*

Michael pushed a fork into another piece of bread and held it over the coals. *Why is she being so evasive?* 'If you've been here for years, why do you keep saying there is no way out? You can't possibly live completely alone.'

Marion stopped what she was doing. How do I ex-plain when the answers only bring more questions? she thought. 'We went to the rock many times, but we always came back here.' *I must stop him from leaving.* 'Is the toast nearly done? I must eat something. The chickens have to be fed.'

Michael gave up. *She must be crazy.* He thought of the times he strode between the rock and where the car park should have been. He remembered how many times he searched for the bitumen track. *Shit! Maybe I'm going crazy too.*

Only the scraping of cutlery on the plates broke the silence as they ate the eggs and toast.

Marion kept her head bent, not meeting Michael's pleading eyes.

Once he'd washed the dirty dishes he offered to feed the chooks, but Marion refused, stating that routine got her through her day. 'Anyway,' she said, 'the chickens don't know you.'

Michael stood at the back door and watched. The noise from the hens and the attentive rooster increased as Marion rattled the seed in the feed tin. He was surprised she'd left the shed door unlatched and when she returned to the house, he offered to secure it.

'There isn't a lock,' she answered.

'A rock will do. It'll keep out the foxes.'

'There is no need,' said Marion. 'I have to leave it easy to open.'

'You *have* to?'

'The little ones can't open a locked door. They mightn't be able to shift a large rock either.'

'Right. What do you leave for them?'

Marion gripped the frame as she manoeuvred herself through the doorway. She stopped and looked back at Michael. 'It is *they* who leave something for *me.*'

Bewildered, he asked again, 'But, earlier you said there was no one. Now you're saying the Aborigines are around all the time. Are they the ones that bring you supplies?'

Marion shrugged and turned away. 'Not always. But many things have appeared. The shed has been good to us.'

Michael followed her into the living room that was still gloomy, despite the morning sun. Marion pushed at the fire and the water in the kettle sprang to life.

'Tea is nearly ready. Have a seat.' Marion pointed towards seven chairs. 'One was used as firewood. We weren't up to chopping that day. The chair was damaged, so it broke easily. At least we don't need to keep the house warm just now.'

Michael frowned. He hadn't thought about the uneven number of chairs. He was still trying to work out why her information didn't make sense. And, often contradictory.

Now he felt compelled to ask, 'Do you need some wood? I could chop some for you.'

'Perhaps you can. They left some branches yesterday.'

'Who ...?'

Marion rushed to lift the overflowing kettle from the hot hob. She poured the tea and Michael tried again, 'Who left the branches? Was it the Aborigines?'

He waited for answers, but she stood, dabbing at the stovetop, without speaking. Michael was fed up with trying to get information from Marion. He turned his back on her. 'I'm going out to look for my car again.'

'It's no use, it won't be there.'

'It's there somewhere. I just have to take the right track.'

'There is no right track.'

'I'll find it.' He gulped down the hot tea, scalding his throat.

Preparing to leave, Michael applied sunscreen to his face, carefully covering his ears. Marion stopped wiping the table. She watched intently as he squeezed the white cream out of the tube and rubbed it across his cheeks. When he returned the tube to his backpack, she couldn't contain her curiosity.

'What are you putting on your face? It looks sticky.'

'It's sunscreen.'

'I beg your pardon?'

Plonking his bag on the chair, Michael pulled out the tube again. He passed it to Marion who took it gingerly. She turned it over and squinted at the labelling. 'SPF thirty-plus, apply twenty minutes before going into the sun.' With a look mixed with confusion and distrust, she asked, 'Why?'

'Don't you wear a hat when you go outside?'

'Miranda did and I use it sometimes.'

'You look very brown. Don't you worry about skin cancer?'

She replied with a long and questioning no.

Michael sighed, 'Look, I'm going to find my car. Might be gone for a while. As for the cream, it just stops the sun from burning the skin. Slip, slop, slap and all that.'

Marion rolled the tube around in her hands again before relinquishing it. Fancy being able to stop the sun from burning, she thought.

Michael left Marion washing the dishes. She felt sure he was here because of her prayers, and maybe he had brought magical powers with him. 'Perhaps the cream will take my wrinkles away,' she said with a chuckle, as she put the last dish in the cupboard.

At the edge of Miranda's grave, Michael paused for a moment and read the inscription. 1885. *That's impossible.* He tried to link the date with the little information Marion disclosed. Born 1885, echoed in his mind as he stamped over fallen barbed wire. *128 years ago. Was Marion also born in 1885? No way. But they had lived together.* He snapped off a leafy twig and brushed the flies from his face. *It's all a load of bullshit!* He walked on, battling with the impossibility of it all.

He reached Hanging Rock and rested in the shade of surrounding gum trees. He should have already passed the buildings. *Where the hell are they?* Despite Marion's insistence that the main road was impossible to locate, he was sure he would find something today. *What's she not telling me?*

After fifteen minutes of climbing, he stopped and peered over the edge. Despite sunglasses, his eyes squinted against the glare. There was no sign of activity – nothing to indicate that any tourists had come to the rock.

Michael stroked his chin. *Need a shave.* He stepped over the uneven rocks and found an alternative viewing spot. *Where's the bloody road?*

The breeze stirred the tops of the trees and danced across the undergrowth. Native grasses dipped and swayed. Silver ferns shook like hundreds of tutus. The view of far-spreading bush was magnificent. Sheltered gullies protected the smaller plants while the majestic Mountain Ash stood proud. Snow Gums at Camels Hump were visible, but Michael sought man-made structures. *A road. A building. A frigging car park would be great.*

He wandered aimlessly for over twenty minutes, feeling as if a fog had seeped into his brain. Six screaming corellas flew over. He looked up at them and stumbled. After he regained his footing, he sat down and let his legs dangle over the edge of a steep rock. A kangaroo jumped across a narrow track. Two more followed. Several small birds darted across the sky and some butterflies twisted and turned through the bushes with miraculous agility. Even as he watched nature going about its business, his confusion made it impossible to enjoy. He kept sighing and licking his dry lips. His head turned with every sound, hoping it was made by another human.

His stomach felt empty, and he walked away from the rock, promising to return each day until he found the way out. *No way am I being stuck here like Marion!*

He built an SOS sign with stones laid out across the sandy track. Someone would be missing him by now. On Saturday, Jock and Patrick would've been scrambling to get ready for their night out, but Owen would have stopped in for a beer, eager to tell his surfing stories. On Sunday, they all must have been curious about his absence. *How long does it take to become a missing person?*

He trudged the two miles back to the old farmhouse, not noticing anything until he reached the clearing in front of the lemon tree. 'It's all right for you guys,' he yelled at magpies that flew high above him. 'You get a good look from up there. I bet you can see my car.' He cursed at the flies. 'Bugger off,' he said, grabbing his sunglasses off his face with one hand and smacking his other hand across his eye sockets, dislodging the insistent flies. Slowing his step as he reached the rickety verandah, he sighed, 'Here we go again.'

Michael pushed open the door. Silence surprised him. The unexpected stillness turned his annoyance to concern.

He heard soft whimpering. 'Marion?' Turning towards her bedroom her saw her lying on the bed. He asked casually, 'You okay in there?'

Marion sat up, but fell back with a cry of pain.

Michael stepped towards the room and called out, 'What's up? Can I help?'

'I just need to take some rest. I'll return to better health in a moment.'

Michael could see Marion rubbing her hand across her chest. He felt uncomfortable about entering her room. With his hand on the doorframe he asked, 'Can I get you a cuppa?'

She turned onto her side and smiled weakly at him. 'Some tea? Yes, that would be wonderful. Thank you.'

Michael busied himself with the fire and making the tea. Getting a kettle to boil on a wood stove certainly took longer than switching on an electric jug.

He returned to the bedroom and found Marion sitting on the edge of the bed. She smiled as he entered. 'Thank you, Michael. I'm glad you're here. Glad you've arrived in time. I was beginning to wonder if anyone would come.'

She doesn't look so good. I hope I can get out of here and bring some help before it's too late, he thought. 'Here you are. A hot drink might help. Is there something I can put together for lunch?'

'Give me a moment. I'll finish the tea and prepare lunch.'

'No, that's not necessary. I can find something. You stay here.'

Marion tried to stand, but resigned herself to sitting on the edge of the bed. 'There's soup on the stove. You can add some fresh herbs from the garden if you wish. There's bread left from breakfast. I'll make some more this afternoon.'

Michael added some chopped parsley and chives to the soup and, while it warmed, he examined the con-tents of a cupboard. Several plates, some with chips or cracks, bowls, and cups without saucers, were neatly stacked at one end. Two saucepans, one frying pan and several other cooking utensils sat on top of wrinkled paper at the other end. Space directly under the bench was empty apart from a banister brush with so few bristles one could almost count them. He took the bread from a large clay pot on the bench.

By the time he served the soup, Marion was sitting at the table looking only slightly better than when he arrived back. He placed the bowls of soup on the table and sat down next to her.

Marion watched Michael dunk his bread into the broth. She said, 'Decent bread is impossible without a yeast. This is really just a damper, but it cooks quickly.'

He didn't mind the soggy bread, and he hoped he hadn't embarrassed Marion. 'Can't you buy self-raising flour? Where's the nearest shop?'

'There is nothing else.'

'Nothing? You've said that before. Do you mean no one close by?'

'I mean nothing. No persons, no stores, nothing.'

Still not completely sure of her sanity, he asked again, 'Then where did the flour come from?'

'It came from the homestead. We have a bag of it that remains half full.'

'A homestead? You just said there is no one else.'

Marion sighed. She found it hard to explain to herself, even more difficult to someone else. 'The homestead was a burnt-out building we came across. It may seem strange to you, but when I feel better, I'll explain it the best I can.'

He dipped another piece of bread deep into the hot soup and then stuffed it into his mouth. It hurt his already scorched cheek, but he ignored the pain and chewed vigourously.

After he finished the soup, he went outside and chopped up a small dead tree that lay next to the shed. The axe was dull and his muscles ached. When he'd cut up the last branch, he sat on the chopping block and considered his dilemma. Keys in his pocket proved his car was there somewhere. How to find it was the problem. *It'd better be sooner, rather than later.*

His shirt was wet through and, as he finished stacking the logs, the comforts of his flat were at the forefront of his mind. *A hot shower, shampoo, deodorant and a fluffy towel would be good.* He wiped the dripping sweat on his sleeve and looked around.

The shed. Now was his chance to check it out. He peered into the small space. He saw nothing extraordinary. *Why do I get the feeling Marion's not telling me everything?* Several tools hung on nails and a lopsided shelf was empty. He kicked the dirt floor with disappointment. He stood the axe against the wall and then carried a couple of logs in to Marion.

'Are you feeling better?'

'Yes, thank you. And, you're just in time. I'm going to start the bread.'

'You said you'd tell me about the shed. It seems important. Is it because of the children?'

'In a way.' *I wish I knew how to answer his questions without frightening him.* 'Bring some more logs please; we need the fire to be going well.'

Michael was sure there was more to it. *Why is she stalling? I have to know what I'm up against.*

When the damper was in the oven, Michael offered to make a fresh pot of tea. Marion insisted it was her duty, but she did let him empty the teapot into the garden.

The aroma in the kitchen made Michael's stomach rumble in anticipation. He sat patiently while she washed dishes. Finally, he blurted out, 'Marion, I have to have some answers.'

She stopped wiping, dropped the cloth into a basin and came over to where he sat. 'Yes, Michael, I will try, but it isn't easy. You may ask questions to which I have no answers. We, Miranda and I, asked many questions, but there was no one to tell us anything.' She sat down. 'You've already experienced the disappearance of the buildings. So, how does one make sense of something that is beyond intellect as we know it? What do you say when things are not as they should be? I will try, Michael, but who knows the real reason behind the questions? I have no understanding of why this happened.' She touched his arm. 'Or how.'

Michael watched Marion closely. Her eyes narrowed. She twisted a strand of hair around her finger. She seemed to be trying to make sense of something before she spoke again. He placed his hand gently over her fingers and said, 'Can't you tell me what you do know? I'm here in this place too. Perhaps we can work it out together. Please, Marion, you must tell me.'

Marion let out a deep sigh and shook her head. *Will he believe me?* She stood for a moment, reconsidered, and then touched his shoulder before sitting back down next to him. 'It was such a long time ago.' She took a deep breath and released it gradually. 'Like you, we came to the rock for one day. Then ...' Marion fidgeted with the hem of her shirt. 'This was the only place we could find. In the beginning, Miranda and I assumed we would be found. Days stretched into months and then, of course, years.'

'Years? How many? Miranda's grave says eighteen eighty-five. That can't be true.'

'There is no way of knowing the time really. It doesn't seem to be the same here.' Marion sighed. 'The only clock we found didn't work.'

Michael interrupted, 'My watch isn't working either.'

Marion said in a distracted voice, 'Your watch?'

'It doesn't matter. Go on. You were saying about how long it's been.'

'Yes, so many years, but you have to understand there are not any clear-cut answers. Like the shed and the children. Finding the other homestead confused us even more. Then there were the coins.' She sighed. 'I understand your confusion - it's how we felt too. But I believe you've been brought here for a purpose.'

'Purpose? That's a bit rich isn't it? Aren't we just talking about finding the way to the main road?'

'No, young man.' She stood up and went to the kitchen. 'If it was just a matter of finding our way to Woodend, Miranda and I would have done that by now.'

'I don't understand. If it isn't about finding the way, what is it about?'

Marion pulled open the oven door. The aroma wafted across the room.

'That smells really good,' Michael said.

'It won't be too long before you can have a piece. In the meantime, are you positive you want to know everything? It may surprise, even shock you.'

'Doesn't matter. I have to know.'

EIGHT

'Hi, Puss-Puss.' Rebecca juggled her handbag and a strawberry cheesecake in one arm so she could ring the doorbell.

Rose took the cake with murmurs of delight. 'I love cheesecake. Now be a sweetheart and take the plates to the lounge room while I make some tea, or would you prefer coffee?'

Circling the room, Rebecca peered at various trin-kets and paintings. A small yellow caricature of a cat was prominent. 'Yes, coffee please. Can I help? I love this picture. Is it the same artist who did the one on the front door?'

Rose poked her head through the opening. 'Thanks, I can manage. The kettle's boiled. And yes, it is the same as the one on the front door, and some of those in the hallway. They're Michael's.'

'Michael's! Your grandson? Really?' Rebecca stepped back into the hall and looked closely at the paintings.

With a tray full of cups and cake, Rose entered the lounge room. 'Yes, I think he's quite talented.' She put the tray on the table, sat down and spooned sugar into her tea. 'He wanted to study art, but Jack, bless him, suggested he do accountancy. Said Michael could do art in his spare time.'

'He has a good eye. He's very marketable.'

'Maybe. So far Michael only paints for family, and sometimes, friends.'

Rebecca joined Rose in the lounge room and sat down. She considered the plum-coloured cat with grey patches in the picture that hung near the front door. 'Does he have any more? I could ask if my boss would stock a few in her gift shop.'

'Do you really think they'd sell? Michael would be delighted. I don't have any others, he might have. Now there's another reason to introduce you both.'

Rebecca paused and poked a knife into the cake. 'I'm beginning to think the cat thing might be the best option at first.'

'We'll see. Anyway, the cake looks divine. Can you cut me a piece, please?'

'All right, but you have to promise to talk about Michael and when he returned from Hanging Rock.'

Rose frowned and put down the plate she was holding out. 'I was hoping to delay it for a bit longer. I like your company, Rebecca. If I tell it all at once, you'll not visit me again.'

Surprised by Rose's comments, Rebecca thought about it before speaking, 'What if I promise to bring cake again next week?'

'And the following week?'

A slight chuckle preceded Rebecca's reply, 'Can I come without cake? I'll have to do more exercise otherwise.'

'I suppose so.' Rose grinned and held out the plate again.

'Then it's a deal.'

Once Rose had eaten her cake, she put the plate on the table and settled back into her chair. 'Michael came to me straight from the hospital. He didn't return to his flat because the media was camped out there, and more outside his parents' home.

'That twelve or so weeks was a terrible time. My friends were worried about me. They suggested I should carry on as normal, but that was impossible.

'The police asked so many questions. Just in case they missed something, they said. Obviously, the police thought someone wasn't telling the truth.' She fiddled with her rings as she continued, 'it was Patrick who raised the alarm after Janet rang him Sunday afternoon. Michael would never let his mum down like that. Just not turn up for dinner.'

'Patrick? I haven't heard that name before.'

'Patrick was Michael's flat mate. A likeable fellow. I met him when he dropped Michael here once. The police interrogated him several times. He may have tattoos and an earring, many young people do, but it's ridiculous to imagine him harming Michael.

'I guess the police had nothing to go on. He hadn't touched his bank account. They couldn't trace his mobile. You can't blame them for not finding anything. Michael said nothing would have been visible to them. He said something about being in the wrong time.'

'Wrong time? In what way?'

Rose frowned. 'I don't know. I found that an odd thing for him to say.'

They refilled the cups and waited for the hot liquid to cool.

'How long did they search for Michael?'

'Quite some time.' Rose frowned, as she recalled the trauma. 'Patrick rang Hanging Rock first. Staff at the café remembered

Michael buying some sandwiches and water, but that was all. The police weren't interested until Jack insisted they do something. By then it was Tuesday. They found the car, but not Michael. We were all frantic. They took the car to the station. You know, testing for blood and DNA. Patrick was adamant that Michael wouldn't have switched off his mobile by choice. He'd been overseas recently and Patrick said he even had a phone thingy that roams.'

'It's called global roaming.' Rebecca tried not to smile.

'Oh?'

'Your mobile works anywhere in the world,' Rebecca explained.

'Well, there you go. Modern technology.'

'So the police gave up?'

'Not before ground searches and everything, as you probably saw on the news. They had the police dogs out sniffing for clues. Even helicopters. Nothing showed up. Nothing. I do find that hard to understand. I mean, Michael was in the exact place everyone was tracking over. He said he put stones in the shape of SOS. How come they didn't find those?' Rose looked at Rebecca and shook her head slowly.

Rebecca shivered as she remembered the odd feeling she had when watching the first news story. She also remembered expecting to recognise something when the television report showed helicopters swooping low over the trees. Her mouth went dry. She drained the last of the coffee from her cup. 'I don't know, but it's scaringly familiar somehow. You believe him don't you?'

'Most definitely. He isn't insane like some people try to make out. Something strange, even wonderful happened. We just *have* to believe him.' Rose sat motionless and stared at the cup in her hands.

Rebecca now understood how hard the disappearance must have been for Michael's family. Breaking the silence, she asked, 'I imagine his parents had to consider a funeral.'

With a huge sigh as she placed the cup and saucer on the table, Rose said, 'No, not a funeral, but it was suggested we have something for him.'

'Like a memorial service?'

'Even that seemed too final. Without a body, it was hard to believe he was dead. There were many discussions about whether to have a service or not. Janet didn't want a public event. The media were still causing problems. On the other hand, Jack felt it was the only way to get on with life. I knew he was just trying to cover his grief by doing *something*.' Rose paused and rubbed her hands together as if she was cold. 'I kept wandering between their house and mine. I only avoided the photographers and those other chaps by going into Doris Jackson's house first.'

Rebecca imagined the two elderly women peeking out through the curtains with Mrs Jackson giving directions in minute detail. Rose sat quietly. In the silence, the background sounds of children playing next door and a noisy vehicle driving up the street were amplified.

'Do you see those albums on the sideboard? They're my photos of Michael. I turned the pages every day, looking at my grandson. Aged three. At ten. Twenty-one. I was hoping for a message. I could only see smiles. I refused to believe he was gone. When days turned to months, it seemed rather hopeless. The authorities said the file wasn't closed, but unless new evidence was presented, they wouldn't spend any more time on it. I mean, they hadn't found *any* evidence. Except for the car, obviously. They came to a dead end. They called off the search.'

'That must've been hard to take,' Rebecca said.

'You accept it when you see a missing person reported on the telly, but not when it's your dearest grandson.'

Even though Rebecca knew the outcome, she felt distressed. Rose's eyes misted over for a few moments before she gave a half smile and continued, 'It was a miracle when he turned up. I shan't forget it. Such pandemonium when we got that phone call. What a time that was. Jack and Janet went to the hospital immediately. Then, when they brought him home, my goodness, I was so relieved. He was very brown from working outside.' Rose's voice became a whisper. 'But he had such a terrible vacant look in his eyes.'

Rebecca wrapped her arms around Rose. 'Let's finish the story for today. I don't suppose you want pizza?'

This made Rose laugh. 'After so much cheesecake, I should say not. Perhaps we should have something healthy.'

'I'm not even hungry.'

Shadows formed across the carpet when Rose turned on the lamp. A car door slammed and the frogs started evening choruses.

'Rebecca, you make me feel more cheerful. I'm glad we've become friends.'

As she drove home, Rebecca thought of Rose's remark. The idea of a new friend pleased her. Someone to chat with – to share an afternoon. Someone other than her boisterous friends. The age difference certainly didn't seem to matter. *Probably a good thing.*

She thought of her grandparents. She felt sorry she hadn't been close to them. In her mind, Nan and Pop were grandparents who sent packages and amusing notes all the way from Bristol. She'd only visited them once. It had been fun, but brief.

Her maternal grandparents were domineering interlopers her parents kept at arm's length. Kylie and Rebecca trembled each time Grandmother sprang from the car. She always rapped on the glass panel of the front door despite there being a working doorbell. Grandfather spoke over anyone who didn't share his opinion. After a quick kiss, the sisters would disappear behind the closed door of their shared bedroom. Both grandparents died within months of each other when Rebecca was eight, and only her mum cried.

Meeting Rose Wentworth made Rebecca realise what she had missed.

Tuesday had always been Rebecca's most relaxed day of the week. She could sleep in. Occasionally, breakfast was coffee and sultana bread at the corner café after a swift twenty-minute walk.

When her friend Nicky's hospital roster allowed, they would stroll around the lake chatting about the comical stories and sad happenings in Nicky's ward. Rebecca's indecisive customers also made amusing topics.

Sometimes Kylie and Thomas joined Rebecca. Thomas would giggle as he bounced up and down in his stroller. Brec runs funny, he would say, commenting on Rebecca's non-running style as she tried to keep up with his co-ordinated mother. She'd forgive him later when he sat on her lap and drew circles in the froth spilt from her cappuccino.

Missy always enjoyed Rebecca's presence and would often sit on her knee as she answered emails. The ring tone of Rebecca's mobile would have Missy appearing in an instant, demanding attention by swiping at moving fingers as she stood on Rebecca's lap. The impatient cat would twist around Rebecca's feet as she made the bed, then Missy would climb up on the doona and purr herself to sleep.

Before Rebecca started visiting Rose, she would often dawdle through Tuesday mornings knowing she had all day to get things done. Now, that was not an option. So, she hurried through her chores, planning to be in her car heading for Phillip Court at a quarter to two.

Rose was waiting at the open door and she tugged gently on Rebecca's arm. 'Come in, my dear. Good, you've brought afternoon tea. I was too excited to bake. Come in, come along.'

'What's happened?'

'I'll tell you in a minute. Follow me. Bring your cake.'

Rose scurried into the kitchen, where she directed her guest to the prepared tray. Rebecca carefully removed blueberry muffins from a bag and followed Rose back into the lounge room with the tray. Rose plopped herself into a chair and said, 'Can you pour the tea, Rebecca? I'm sure I'd spill it.'

'How come you're so excited? It must be good news.'

Smiling so broadly that the lines around her eyes multiplied, Rose said, 'I've received a letter from Michael. He sent me a cat. Look.' She pulled an envelope out of her pocket and waved it around. 'This time it's purple and the grass is mauve. What do you make of that?' She held out a small card.

From the description, Rebecca expected a monstrosity. However, it was a skilful portrait of a plump tabby surrounded by tall grass with dominant seedpods. The unnatural colours highlighted the intricate patterns of its fur, created by an artist with exceptional ability. Rebecca hesitated to return it. She wanted to understand the emotions the artist instilled in the mournful expression, and hadn't noticed Rose was talking.

'Rebecca, where are you? Away with the fairies? Have you heard anything I said?'

'Sorry, Rose. I was admiring the painting.'

'So it seems.'

'This picture is wonderful.'

Rose paused, still unsure if Rebecca was listening properly. 'Now where were we?'

Rebecca looked up quickly. 'You were going to tell me what was in Michael's letter.'

'That's right. I did think of ringing you, but I knew you were coming around today.'

'Talking of phones, why didn't Michael just ring?'

'Can't send that over the phone, can he?' Rose grinned at Rebecca as she pointed to the card.

'Right, let's hear what was in his letter.' Rebecca was now literally sitting on the edge of her seat.

'Yes, of course.' Rose removed the letter from the envelope, flipped it open and read, *"Hi Gran. Hope you're well. We're all going okay. Don't worry about me. I'm gradually coming to terms with my strange adventure. I know you would say it was all for a reason. It probably was, but I haven't worked out what yet. Marion said that she would make sure there was a happy ending for me. She appreciated my help. So, the vibe is that all will be well. Grandma Wilma was also involved. I'll tell you more about that later. It's all good. Mum and Dad are doing OK. They send their love. We'll be home soon. Love, Michael".* There, isn't that a relief.'

'Read it again, Rose.'

'Here, you may read it for yourself.' She sat down next to Rebecca and handed over the letter.

The writing was neat and evenly spaced; just a hint of anxiety, but Rebecca felt butterflies race around her stomach as she started reading. She read it three times, looking for a clue to something unknown. Rose hovered, as if waiting for her turn to read it for the first time.

'There's a lot in that letter,' Rebecca finally said.

'Certainly is.'

'I suppose his Grandma Wilma's involvement is because of Irma?'

'Suppose so.' Rose held out her hand for the letter. She took it from Rebecca, folded it carefully and sat looking at it.

Blowing on the hot liquid, Rebecca sipped cautiously. 'Who's Marion?'

Opening the letter and scanning it through again, Rose said, 'He told me something about an old woman that died. Yes, that would be Marion. After that he was on his own.'

'So, this Marion died. Surely that isn't what he helped with. Maybe that's why he was so traumatised.'

Rose's head jerked up. She said forcefully, 'No. Michael wouldn't do that.'

'No ... sorry, Rose, I didn't mean he killed her. Maybe he ... what I thought was, maybe he ... I don't know, helped somehow.' Rebecca couldn't put her thoughts into words and she tried to unscramble the inference. 'I just meant ... perhaps he looked after her at the end.'

'It was, I think, yes, that's it.' Rose nodded. 'Also, it was about the woman being scared of not being buried. She didn't want to be eaten.'

'I don't blame her.' Rebecca sighed with relief. She hadn't intended to upset Rose. 'Then he probably buried her.'

Rose looked at Rebecca and nodded again. 'Yes, you're right. I remember now.'

'Glad it wasn't me,' said Rebecca. She tried to imagine having to handle a dead body. 'Yuk, not something I'd want to do.'

'No. However, that's behind him now.'

Rebecca shivered unexpectedly. 'Oh, something just crawled down my spine. It's really weird. Something like that always happens when I'm talking about Hanging Rock.'

'Dear me, do you know why?'

'I haven't a clue,' said Rebecca. 'Do you have any ideas?'

'Perhaps it'll fall into place when you meet Michael. He says he'll be home soon. That'll be nice.'

'No wonder you were excited when you got his letter.'

Rose struggled to stand, but grinned as she tucked the letter behind the yellow frame on the mantle. 'Yes, it seems he'll be okay.'

She nodded with the pleasure of her thought. 'It'll be lovely to have him back.'

On returning home, Rebecca changed into her pyjamas, poured a large glass of water and turned on the television. During the ads, she recorded more brief thoughts in her brightly coloured notebook.

> Where did Marion come from?
> Why couldn't she show him the way?
> He's coming back soon
> Why do I still get those feelings?

The media finally moved on. Kylie's seven-day-wonder had extended to three weeks, but she had been right about normal people getting on with their lives. Unlike Rebecca, who still found it difficult to concentrate on her everyday chores.

Her fitness level dropped and the housework suffered as she became fixated on gathering information. *There must be something to explain this weirdness.*

Rebecca tried to remember exactly what Mrs Jackson had said about girls going missing at Hanging Rock. No new leads appeared from her enthusiastic research on the internet.

A cold shiver slithered across the base of her neck as she recalled the first television report. After skimming through the recent newspaper articles again, she speculated on Marion's apparent link to both periods. However, it was her own connection to Michael that interested Rebecca most, and now she couldn't wait to meet him.

Rose said he was returning on Saturday and she would make sure he was there 'for cake' this coming Tuesday.

NINE

Abandoning the idea of working on the computer on such a lovely Sunday, Rebecca headed to the park for much needed exercise. She strode purposely, twice around the lake, trying to form constructive questions for the upcoming introduction to Michael Wentworth.

Sitting in a busy café, distractedly drinking coffee, she couldn't get through the usual slices of sultana bread. She kept thinking about what she could say. *I felt a connection when I saw you on TV. Sounds so stupid.* She decided to ring her sister.

'Hey, Bec, you're not usually this nervous with men.'

'I'm not nervous.'

'Of course not. How come you went twice around the park then? You hate jogging.'

'Kylie, I don't jog.'

'So, now you're nit-picking. Definitely nerves.'

'No.'

'No? Well, what about the lack of appetite.'

'Ah.' Rebecca felt caught out.

'Got you. Definitely nerves.'

'All right, so I'm nervous. Kyls, you still haven't answered my question.'

'What was it again?'

'The introduction speech.'

'Right.' Kylie paused. 'How about, I'm Rebecca, Queen Bee of the Weirdos. I'm longing to quell your fears by learning all your fascinating secrets. Please let me take you in my arms and ease your troubled mind.'

By this time, Rebecca was giggling. 'Stop it.'

'No I won't. You're being such an idiot. Your wonderful Rose will have told him all about you. You won't need to explain yourself at all.'

'Shit! Now I'm not nervous at all. Just totally petrified.'

'Oh well, Tuesday's a few days away. Think of the weight you'll lose.'

'You're no help at all.' It was Kylie's turn to laugh as Rebecca changed the subject. 'By the way, how's my precious nephew? Can he say my name properly yet?'

'Probably, but I think you'll be stuck with Brec for a long time.'

'That's fine, I guess. When can we catch up again?'

'Luke's back tomorrow, so I'll be making the most of that. I'll ring you next week.'

Their conversation continued for several more minutes before Rebecca said goodbye. She picked at the cold piece of toast. Kylie was right; Rose would have briefed Michael about me, she thought. However, after the disaster at the press conference, Rebecca wasn't at all sure she'd come out in a good light. No matter what Rose said to him.

The following Tuesday Rebecca detoured to a shop for a magazine rather than knock on Rose's door before she could settle her nerves.

'Come in, my dear. You're a bit later than usual.'

'Sorry, Rose, I didn't mean to be. I guess I'm a little self-conscious today.' She looked through to the kitchen. 'Is Michael here?'

'No, not at the moment. He went around to his parents for some business clothes. He's going back to work next week. But don't worry, he'll be in soon.'

A car pulled up outside and a door shut. Rose peeked around the curtains. 'Yes, here he is.'

Rebecca placed her bag on the floor and flicked her hair out of her eyes. Michael entered the room and she was relieved to see him smiling. Rose received a generous hug before she introduced Rebecca and discretely went to the kitchen.

Michael held out his hand and said, 'So you're Rebecca. Gran's told me a lot about you.'

Rebecca brushed her damp palm against her skirt, and then shook his hand. 'It's Bec. Nice to meet you.'

'Right, nice to meet you too, Bec,' he said and smiled again.

She stepped back and knocked her leg against the glass coffee table. 'Ouch.' She rubbed the throbbing spot. 'That hurt.'

'You okay?' A cheeky smile accentuated appreciative eyes that were taking in her leg.

She straightened her skirt. 'Thanks, I'll be fine.'

Michael waited until Rebecca was seated, then sat beside her on the couch. 'What's this all about then?'

His blunt question caught her off-guard. Rebecca knew she had asked to meet him to talk about Hanging Rock, but thought she would be the one asking the questions. Her eyes turned towards the kitchen door. She fiddled unnecessarily with her watch while Michael folded his arms and waited. Finally, she said, 'It's about Hanging Rock. I thought your grandmother might have told you something.'

'Yes, she did. Something crazy about a *connection*.' An emphasis on the last word made it obvious he didn't believe what he'd been told.

'I admit it doesn't make sense, but I can't help that.' Rebecca moved closer to the end of the couch.

'Mmm, I wonder. Not just after a story are you?'

She turned and looked straight at him. 'Of course not!'

He shrugged his shoulders and stared back. 'There've been cleverer ploys to get an exclusive interview than sucking up to my grandmother.'

Rebecca drew in a quick breath and folded her arms. 'What a mean thing to say.'

Michael looked away. He tilted his head forward and frowned. He placed his hands on his knees, then glanced at Rebecca several times before saying, 'I'm sorry. I'm out of line. But I've experienced the complete range of idiot reporters trying to get a different angle.' He took an audible breath and leaned back. 'Look, I think we best start again. I'm sure there is more to it than Gran's version. Anyway, I'd like to hear it all from you. Then maybe I can judge for myself.'

Rebecca watched him closely as his shoulders relaxed and his hands stopped moving.

'Gran says you two spend Tuesdays together; eating cake.' He smiled. 'I'm glad she's got someone else to fatten up except me.' He patted his flat stomach and laughed.

He's not so scary after all, Rebecca thought.

'Are you two getting along okay, or do you need some food to break the ice?' Rose called, as she entered the room with afternoon tea on the familiar tray.

'Gran, you wouldn't know what to do if we said no to your food.'

'That's true. Let me pass you some coconut slice. Made this morning in this very house.'

Taking a piece and leaving it on her plate, Rebecca wondered how to explain herself to Michael without sounding like a fool. *It would be easier if he weren't so hot.* Her wandering eyes spotted the tabby cat painting. 'I just love your art, the cats, especially the colour you use. The unnatural colours really work.'

Picking up his mug of coffee, he wandered over and looked at his painting, as if seeing it through someone else's eyes. 'Thanks. I really only do the cats for Gran. Don't I, Gran?'

'Yes, dear, and I feel very honoured.'

'What else do you paint?'

Michael settled into the chair opposite Rebecca. 'Did. When I had time.'

'You should find time. If your other work is as good as the cats, who knows what you could achieve. People love cats. I'm sure they would sell well.'

He placed the mug on the table, leaned forward and asked, 'And what do you do in your spare time?'

She spent all her spare time lately on trying to work out why she felt connected to him and Hanging Rock, and, as she searched for a reply, he eyed her curiously. Rebecca put off answering his question by taking another mouthful of coffee.

'Gran said you were the one who accosted me in the hall the day of the news conference.'

Rose nodded her head, but as Rebecca spoke, she started shaking it.

Rebecca sat up straight and looked him in the eye. 'I certainly did *not* accost you. Not by *any* stretch of the imagination.'

Holding up his hand in an action of apology, he looked at his grandmother and then at Rebecca. 'You're right, and I was rather rude. Derek suggested the media session. I hated every moment of it. The reporters were like vultures and unfortunately, I probably came across badly. Definitely unco-operative.' He tipped his head sideways and forced a smile. 'I do remember our rather brief encounter. I'm sorry for yelling at you.'

Smiling her acceptance, Rebecca put down her mug and waited.

'You seem to know something about art. Do you paint too?' he asked.

'No, but I'm interested in all types of artwork. I like going to the galleries in St Kilda.'

Michael smiled and shifted forward in his seat. 'Me too. The one in the main street recently advertised an exhibition of self-portraits. Did you see it?'

'No. I've been busy lately.'

'You mean going to news conferences and accosting innocent blokes,' he laughed.

Rebecca rolled her eyes and pulled a face. Rose chuckled.

'I felt a compulsion to talk to you. I've no idea why I get goose bumps every time I think about it. It's just that my own experience, on the way to Mt Macedon, seems to have taken place the same day as yours.'

'You'll have to explain it all clearly. Gran's obviously forgotten some of the detail.'

'It was as if the elements were taking over, demanding my attention for some reason. When I found out that it coincided with your experience,

I thought talking to you might help me sort things through.'

Michael closed his eyes and entwined his fingers. One thumb rubbed against the other. His grandmother watched him. She glanced at Rebecca whose tightly clenched hands were evidence of the sudden tension in the room.

Finally, Michael opened his eyes, but stared down at his shoes. 'It's true you know. All of it. And, it's just like you said, the elements interacting with some unknown force.' He looked at Rebecca. He looked dejected and spoke quietly. 'But I don't understand how there could be a connection between the two events.' He rubbed his hands over his upper arms in a frantic motion.

'I'm sorry,' Rebecca whispered, 'I didn't realise it was so painful.'

An agitated grunt escaped from Michael as he looked up. 'I struggled so much there.'

Rebecca trembled and covered her mouth with her hand.

'I thought I was going insane. Every hour of those three months was a nightmare.' He jumped to his feet, folded his arms and turned away from them. Rebecca stared at his back until he spun around and spoke again. 'If I tell you everything then you will become my accomplice. Even Gran, who is sympathetic to other realms of possibilities, doesn't know everything.'

Rose shifted in her chair as Michael apologised. She wanted to go to him, but she fiddled with a serviette and stayed where she was.

'The story itself is not shocking. Quite an ordinary one in fact.' He shrugged and sat down. 'Just someone getting lost and being found three months later.' Michael held out his hands, palms up. 'It's the parallel timeframes that'll simply blow your mind.'

Rebecca watched his face closely. His mouth was grim and his blue eyes were unfocussed. She leaned forward to try to catch what he was saying. She almost tumbled onto the floor. Michael snapped out of his reverie as Rebecca recovered by grabbing the arm of the chair. He smiled at her clumsiness.

'Once you know, there is no going back. No way to unknow,' he said.

Rose gathered up the empty mugs. Making as little noise as possible, she left the room. She peeked in from the kitchen, waiting to see what would happen next.

Michael sighed, 'Well, are you prepared to risk your sanity to resolve your goose bump theory?'

Letting out a short sharp laugh, Rebecca said, 'Goose bump theory, I like that. It certainly is a good description. Yes, I'm sure my sanity will remain intact. But I have to warn you, it's dicey at the best of times.'

He stood up and extended his hand. 'Well, let's not threaten it today. Perhaps we can make it another time, somewhere else. Maybe over coffee. Is there a café you go to regularly?'

She took his hand and stood up. She released it reluctantly and said, 'Yes, a couple in fact.'

'Done. I'll get your number from Gran.'

After helping with the dishes, Rebecca hugged Rose and promised to visit next week.

Michael stood next to Rebecca's car door and arranged to meet her on the weekend. They exchanged goodbyes as she unenthusiastically turned the key in the ignition. He remained in the driveway and watched Rebecca until the car turned the corner. She nearly clipped the curb because her eyes were fixed on Michael's image in the mirror.

Goosebumps of a different kind accompanied the anticipation Rebecca felt as she checked her hair. She stared into the bathroom mirror. She couldn't see anything different about her reflection, but she recognised that her life was changing.

She often daydreamed about Michael. His softness when he spoke to his grandmother showed a caring nature. The way he sat with one hand tucked under his leg was charming.

They agreed to meet for lunch at Beldon Café. It wasn't Rebecca's usual haunt, but she wanted to go somewhere that was certain to be busy.

Rebecca could tell he was checking her out as he followed her around the tables and fussed over where to sit. She was glad she'd chosen navy trousers and a light blue cardigan. They made the best of her long legs and generous curves.

'Right, food's ordered,' said Michael. He shifted the salt and pepper from the middle of the table, and smiled. 'I hope you enjoy the prawns.'

Rebecca angled her head towards another table, 'Theirs looks okay, lots of salad.'

'I'm still getting used to being able to eat what I want again.'

'Really? Wasn't there much to eat?'

'Bread and soup mostly. Lots of soup made of whatever was in the vegie garden. I ate rabbit for the first time. Marion caught fish several times. I was okay at finding the worms. Her fig jam was pretty good.'

'Rose said you had eggs for breakfast, so obviously Marion had chooks. Didn't she eat any of them?'

'Marion said she tried to kill one, but it wriggled so much she let it go. Apparently she didn't have the heart to try again.'

'Well, that'd put me off.'

Michael shuddered as he remembered the ordeal of chopping the head off a rooster. 'You have to be desperate.'

After a moment of silence, he eyed the pie on the plate being set down on another table. 'Maybe I should've ordered the Guinness pie.'

Rebecca laughed. Michael had chosen a fillet steak with apple pie to follow.

Their meals arrived and conversation was mostly about the food. Michael caught Rebecca watching him eating the wedges with his fingers. 'What?' He grinned. 'They're the perfect finger food. Here, have one.'

'Exactly,' she agreed, as she accepted the crispy potato.

He finished off the last piece of pastry and sat back. 'Good choice, Rebecca. This place certainly knows how to make apple pie.'

'I don't know how you can eat all that and stay so slim. I'd have to run around the lake sixteen times a day.'

'You run?'

'No, don't even jog really. But I would have to if I finished off such a huge piece of pie too often.'

Rebecca felt her face flush as he put down his spoon and looked her over. 'You look pretty good to me.'

'Thanks.' Quickly changing the subject, she asked, 'How's Rose?'

He stroked his chin. 'She's fine, but I worry about her. Mainly because she worries about me. I'm okay most of the time, but Gran notices things.' He frowned and lowered his voice, 'I become reflective at odd times. Some days those three months seem like a dream.' He shook his head unhurriedly, as if trying to explain something to himself.

Rebecca wanted to hug him. To tell him everything would work out somehow, but she smiled and said, 'I'm looking forward to hearing about it.'

'Yeah, sorry. Not quite up to it today. Perhaps next time.'

They agreed to meet the following weekend and lingered over their goodbyes.

TEN

The first few days at Marion's farmhouse were hell for Michael. Every task took ages. Cooking was difficult without electricity. Except for an open window, there was no cooling system. There were no modern cleaning implements.

He started marking off each day on a homemade calendar. At least that was something he could resolve. The year caused Marion much anxiety.

'Twenty thirteen, how can that be? I was born in eighteen eighty-five. My body tells me I've aged considerably, but not anywhere near a hundred and twenty-eight years.'

She didn't wait for an answer. She walked out of the house and down the path towards the fence-line and stared towards Hanging Rock. *How can it be?*

Michael couldn't fathom it either. He was still coming to terms with Marion's insistence that they were living in some sort of time warp. She believed their timeframes were inexplicably entwined – all wrapped in a unique landscape.

Each morning he set out for the rock. Most days he spent time in the cool shade, pondering the why and how. As he leaned against a rough surface, aged by the passing of millions of years, the clammy fingers of cold reached into his body. The longer he sat there, the more he felt possessed. When he woke from his dream-like state, he was always eager to leave for the warmth, but dreading not being able to identify reality, yet again.

On the walk back to the farmhouse, perspiration dripped from under his cap, proving he was still alive – although in which era he couldn't be sure. Marion's theory on a parallel existence was far-fetched. Surely it was one time frame or the other. *Is Marion in my time? Am I in hers? How is either plausible?*

One morning, while he wandered around the bush, a summer thunderstorm hit. A torrent fell in a few short minutes. His first reaction was to seek cover, but there was none that would sufficiently prevent the relentless rain from attacking his body. He stood in the open and accepted nature's punishment. He held his arms towards the blackened sky and acknowledged the battering of the rain and the insults of the thunder.

What is the message? His arms fell to his side. *How can I find the answers?* He tipped his head forward allowing the stream of water to rush over his forehead and down his nose. He held his breath as long as he could; like a drowning man.

Every limb felt like stone. He visualised ancient marble statues: David and his slingshot, Venus de Milo. *Is this what I've become? Immobile. Incomplete.*

Seconds later, his chest heaved as he gasped for air. Every nerve of his body cried out for oxygen. He bent over and sucked furiously. His tears fused with the rain.

After the downpour, when his senses calmed down, he walked sluggishly towards Marion's home. He shook the excess water from his hair like a dog. When the sun reappeared, he stopped in a clearing and stripped off. Wringing out his clothes and laying them over the bushes, he then balanced his sneakers across small rocks. He jumped up and down to get warm. His flaccid penis responded with ridiculous movements. Suddenly self-conscious, he stopped and replaced his wet underpants. He held his t-shirt above his head, and raced down the track making the fabric flap like a sail. He yelped when he trod on a sharp stone, then he hobbled until his foot recovered.

Waiting for his clothes to dry, he drew noughts and crosses in the sand and inwardly laughed at his pretence of not knowing the next move. The thin cotton shirt dried, but his jeans, socks and shoes remained damp, so Michael hobbled back wearing only the t-shirt and damp underpants. He kept to the soft edge of the path, but still had to stop several times to brush grit from his bare feet.

He refused to do anything for the rest of the afternoon. He ignored Marion, her food and her best efforts to explain that it wasn't all bad – this existence where time was unpredictable.

The next day, Marion showed Michael her treasure chest. It was a large trunk with metal reinforcements on the corners, which matched a heavy keyless latch. She explained they'd used most of the old clothes, several lengths of material and countless linen items found in the trunk.

She offered Michael a pair of brown socks. He refused them politely saying that he'd rather go without than wear uncomfortable, heavily darned woollen socks. Marion then held out a stiff collared shirt that reached past her knees. He took off his t-shirt and put on the striped shirt. He paraded in front of her and although she laughed at his eccentric antics, she was pleased to have his body fully covered.

Marion trimmed the long cotton shirt so it fitted easily into Michael's jeans. The stiff collar reminded him that he should be at a desk four stories up in a government office block staring at a computer screen. He hacked off the collar with large scissors and didn't miss either the collar or his workplace. However, as he thanked Marion, he thought of the modern technology plugged in at his desk. He pulled his mobile from his pocket.

'Can you tell me about that please?' Marion asked, as he plonked it down on the table.

'Can't show you much. The bloody thing doesn't work.'

'Michael!'

'Well, it doesn't. It should. I charged it the night before I came to Hanging Rock.'

'Charged? What did you charge?'

Marion wanted to know all about the new type of telephone. He patiently explained modern communications and mobile phone applications, but she became tired of imagining something that wouldn't work.

He showed her the items in his backpack. She was like an astronaut on another planet as she soaked up the information. The water bottle proved to be an object of intrigue. Marion popped the top up and down relentlessly. She was astonished by the magic of plastic and curious of the never-ending products it could produce. She inspected the fabric of Michael's backpack with interest and tried all the zips. Marion constantly uttered words of amazement, saying she wished Miranda could have seen these modern delights. She considered a purse-sized packet of tissues was less impressive, but took some for future use.

Captivated by the capabilities of Michael's camera, Marion was astounded how the cameras of old could have become a tiny box of buttons. She inspected it in minute detail.

'It's digital,' he explained. 'Got it duty free.'

He ignored her frown and flicked the button on the side. 'Look here.' He grinned in anticipation. 'This is Singapore. The greenery is phenomenal.'

Marion peered at the small screen. She was amazed at the spreading trees and brilliant colours of the bougainvillea. Michael pressed the button and the next photo appeared.

'How did you do that?' she asked.

'See this button.' He carefully explained how to view other pictures.

'Can I try?' Marion was delighted and alternated between the purple blossom and the view of a flower stall on the side of the road.

'If you keep pressing you'll get more,' explained Michael.

'What in heaven's name is that?' asked Marion, as she tapped the button again.

'Let me see. Oh that,' Michael chuckled. 'It's the side of Owen's head. I was making sure he has some brains. I was proved wrong.'

'I don't understand.'

'Marion, I'm teasing. I was fooling around with the camera. Look, can you see this. It's the interior of an aircraft.'

Marion was awestruck. She wouldn't let go of the camera. Michael patiently explained that millions of people used air travel to visit family, attend business meetings and have holidays in far off places. She struggled to comprehend how one could fly to Paris in such a relatively short time.

'Hang on; you can look at the others later. I want to take a picture of you. I'll take some of the house as well. When I finally get out of this place, I want to be able to show people where I've been.'

She reluctantly handed over the camera.

'Smile.' He pressed the button. 'Now, come and see yourself.'

She sat down at the table and he leaned over her shoulder. Michael flicked the tiny switch and waited. The screen sprang to life and her image filled the screen. Marion stared at it, unsure she liked her picture.

Michael took the camera from her and snapped a picture towards the front door. When Michael tried to show her the image, it became pixelated. Marion grabbed the camera and tapped the backwards button. Her photo appeared for a moment ... then the screen went black.

'Fix it, Michael. Make it work. I want to see more.'

No amount of tapping, battery turning or fiddling would encourage the camera to create pictures for Marion to see.

Marion wasn't forthcoming when Michael asked questions. How, was rarely answered.

Michael had seen rabbits scampering across the small open piece of land between the house and the chook pen. *Marion said she didn't have a trap. So who supplied the rabbit for their dinner? Was it the invisible children?*

On one occasion, a strange meaty soup simmered all afternoon on the stove. Apparently, a kangaroo jumped right into the pot. It might as well have, as Marion gave no explanation.

The fresh eggs that Marion cooked reminded him of the occasional Sunday morning in Grandma Wilma's kitchen. Saturdays he liked to do something active, often hiring a kayak for a day on the river with Jock or barracking for anyone playing against Patrick's football team. Most Sunday evenings he dreamed of being an artist instead of returning to his desk and resolving another problem.

As he crunched on toasted damper, he thought of the grainy bread, spread with Vegemite, he invariably ate in his car on the way to work. He dipped a piece of Marion's unleavened bread in the soft egg yolk to make it more palatable.

In the middle of March, Michael gave up walking to Hanging Rock every day. Instead, he explored the surrounding bush. Once, he became disorientated in thick scrub. It was the only time he thanked the rock for being there.

That night, lying in the bed that squeaked at every twitch of his body, he relived the fear that gripped like a noose around his neck. He curled his knees up, wrapped his arms across his chest and thought of home. 'Patrick, for God's sake, you'd better not be sitting in a café sipping fucking lattes. Get the police. Get some-fucking-body looking for me.'

'One more bloody day to live through,' complained Michael, as he crossed off the thirty-first of March on his makeshift calendar. *Or is it already April?*

'Please, Michael, one more day should be a blessing.'

'How can you say that?' He dropped the pencil and glared at Marion. 'I've been here for forty-five days. Don't know if anyone is even looking for me. I've lost hope of getting back.'

Marion folded her hands on her lap and looked at the thinning skin on the back of her hands. Michael rose from the table and stomped towards the door.

'Then why are you still looking?' asked Marion.

Turning back to face her, Michael said, 'There has to be a way. If I got *into* this, there has to be a way *out*.'

'We've never found it.'

'I'm going to. I have to.'

'Yes, Michael, but that's what hope is.'

Michael opened the door and leaned against the doorjamb. 'Well, I've not got much of it left.'

'It could take a while.'

He glanced out the doorway, then back at Marion. 'Forty-five days I've been here. Forty-five days. That's longer than Jesus spent in the wilderness. He at least had a purpose. What's bloody mine?'

'Michael!'

'I'm sorry, Marion. But I can't take much more.' He stood up straight, ready to leave.

'You won't have to wait much longer, I'm sure of it.'

'How can you be sure of anything here?'

'You're right. Almost everything is uncertain, but not death.'

Michael let go of the door. 'Death?'

'Yes, death, Michael. Mine is imminent.'

'Now you're scaring me.'

'I don't mean to. Please don't go. At least, not right now. Come here. I want to explain.'

Reluctantly, he sat down opposite Marion.

'I've shown you Miranda's grave.'

'Yes.'

'And mine, next to hers.'

'Bit off-putting isn't it?'

'We all have to die, Michael.'

'Yes, but the grave sitting there, waiting. Doesn't it freak you out every time you go by?'

'What?'

'Don't you think it's weird, having a grave ... waiting?'

'No, it actually calms me. Especially now that you're here.'

His eyes widened. 'Me?'

Marion reached out and touched his arm. 'Yes, I believe you've been sent to finish this. Whatever it is.'

'The saviour of mankind.'

'Michael!'

'Sorry.' He had the decency to look contrite, but he wished Marion would get to the point. It reminded him of sitting through an intense weekly meeting. His boss always appeared reluctant to part with all the information, releasing just enough to keep all the lab-rats content to go back to their screens for another day.

'Michael, are you listening?'

'Sorry.'

Marion rolled her eyes and tapped her fingers on the table. 'You keep saying that.'

Michael folded his arms and said, 'You said I was sent to finish this saga. Sooner the better, I'd say.'

'I'm unwell. I know I'll die soon.' She ignored Michael's attempt to interrupt. 'It is my wish that you bury me next to Miranda. Do you know, I'm sure you will then find that blessed car of yours.'

After clearing his throat, Michael could only offer, 'Really?'

'For your sake, I hope so. I've been praying for your release from the burden Miranda and I have had to bear.'

'I thought you said you gave up praying,' Michael teased.

'Mmm, well, now I've started again.'

ELEVEN

Most nights Marion and Michael talked long after the need for lamp light. She found it hard to comprehend freeways and computers, and impossible to imagine ladies of all shapes and sizes cavorting in small pieces of fabric next to men with bare chests on the beach. She blushed when Michael explained unmarried women were bearing children without shame. Michael found her stories of her life 'before Hanging Rock' an appealing way of absorbing social history. However, she continued to evade his questions on her life with Miranda.

A few days later, after the evening meal, Marion removed a 1942 calendar from the cupboard next to her bed. She often took it out and wondered at the unfamiliar pictures. Residual smell of ash brought back memories of the day she found it. Without looking at it, Marion remembered the small details. Like the trim on the calf-length suit of a woman in a brimless hat, and the motorised vehicles carrying only one person. *How wasteful.* Her stomach did somersaults when she realised Michael might be able to interpret the pictures. Perhaps she could learn of the war in which Pete died.

'Michael, when did you say you were you born? Was it nineteen forty-two?'

He came towards her, shaking his head, a wry smile across his face. 'That would make me seventy-one. Do I look that old?'

'No, but then who can tell in this place?'

'It was nineteen eighty-two.'

'I was close. Only one number out,' she laughed. Her smile turned into a straight line as she asked, 'Do you know much about nineteen forty-two?'

'Um, middle of the Second World War. Time of my grandparents. Anything in particular?'

Marion stopped moving. Her mouth opened, she closed her eyes for a second as she struggled with the news. Then she opened her eyes and said, 'Second? *Second World War?*'

'Yes.' Michael nodded deliberately.

'Will you tell me more? I have this calendar. It's dated nineteen forty-two, but I'm afraid it's rather burnt. A *second* world war, dear me. When was the first one?'

He guided her onto a chair, took the scorched pages from her quivering hand and sat down next to her. Starting from January, he turned the coloured pages over, trying to remember his history lessons.

'The First World War was nineteen fourteen until nineteen eighteen. It was terrible. So many lives lost. One of my great-uncles never came back from the Somme in France.'

'Then boys from Woodend probably signed up. Goodness, I hope they survived.'

'It was an especially brutal war.'

'Dear me, how horrid. When was the second one?'

'Nineteen thirty-nine until nineteen forty-five.'

'Poor Peter,' whispered Marion.

'Who's Peter?'

'Look at November. *Pete died.*'

They looked at the bold red ink. The poignant words stood out on the blistered page. For Michael, the futility of war and the heartbreak caused to so many, touched him in a way he hadn't previously experienced.

'Was there a third?'

'No, not as such. There've been many smaller wars all over the world. Now we're fighting the Taliban in Afghanistan.'

'Afghanistan? Surely the British resolved that problem before ... before your current year?'

'I don't know about any resolution back then, but they're still fighting. It's an international war now. Many nations are involved. Australia has troops there, but there's talk of withdrawal.'

'How can that be? It's so far away. It would take so long to ship all the men. All the horses. My goodness me.'

'There is so much more to explain. They don't fight with horses any more. They fly the men in. Drop supplies by parachutes. From helicopters.'

Michael then had to explain what a helicopter was.

After sitting for a while to absorb the new information, Marion crossed the room to the dresser and returned with four coins.

He took the offered coins and asked, 'Where did you get these? They're current coins.'

'Nineteen eighty-nine. That is the year, isn't it?'

'Yep.' He put the coins down. 'Look, I've got more.' He pulled out his wallet, ignored the notes and tossed a few coins on the table. Marion picked them up and turned each one over. Amazed that they were similar to the ones she'd found, she placed them on the table in a row.

'Where did you get them from, Marion?' He picked up the dollar coin and examined it.

'I found them in the bush.' She paused, sat down next to Michael and asked hesitantly, 'When did we have the war with America?'

Michael almost dropped the coin. 'With America? No, they're our allies.' He put the coin down again and asked, 'Why did you think we went to war with America?'

'The dollar coin. Australia uses pounds.'

'Ah, not anymore.'

Marion became more confused. Although she was pleased America hadn't invaded Australia. The conversation shifted from the coins to modern concerns. She couldn't fathom global warming, graffiti sounded disgusting and the final straw came when Michael told her about the New York World Trade Center disaster. She put her hands over her ears and demanded he stop making things up. 'The world couldn't possibly get itself into such a mess,' she said, as she left the room.

She retreated to her place of consolation. Michael left her under the lemon tree until the cool air reached in through the front door. He called to her and she ambled in, arms wrapped across her chest and her eyes directed towards the floor. There was no doubt the information shocked her, but he thought it was something other than the difficulties of the modern world.

'I'm sorry to give you so much bad news, but lots of good things have happened too.'

'I know. I love your stories about electricity, plumbing, and the transport ... how wonderful it all sounds.' She put her hand on his arm. 'It's not just the bad news, Michael. I feel so ... so isolated. No, that's not quite strong enough. Miranda and I were protected from all those troubles, all those wars. We haven't had to watch men march off to battle, never to return. How terrible that must be. I can't imagine those happy young soldiers in the back of that truck on the calendar, fighting for their country. I wonder if they all returned safely. They were all someone's child. Dear, oh dear.'

She perched on the edge of the chair then turned the pages to December. 'Don't you see, we were protected from the miseries, but we also were separated from everyone and everything joyous. Look at this scene. Mother carrying a Christmas cake to her family. The father has a cigar and probably a port. There are children's toys on the carpet. All those celebrations and love we missed. For what? Can you tell me why? What did two fifteen-year-old girls do to deserve this?'

She began to sob openly. Michael had no idea what to do. He was still trying to believe everything she'd told him. *Was it all true? Could it be true?* He sat still. His eyes followed the grain of timber up and down the table. When Marion's sobbing became irregular sniffs, he chanced his luck and offered, 'I'm really sorry, Marion. I don't know how to help. I certainly don't have the answers. Whatever caused you to be here, it looks like it's done the same to me. I'm sure glad I'm not here on my own.' He placed his hand on Marion's shoulder and held it there for a moment. He thought of his own grandmother and felt tenderness towards the woman who, for some reason, was sharing this odd existence. He leaned over and embraced her, holding her tightly until she whispered, 'Thank you, Michael.'

She levered herself up, went into the kitchen and set about making some tea. Noisy preparations broke the silence and not for the first time Michael wished his mobile phone worked. They drank their hot tea with few words spoken. In silent consent, they withdrew to their bedrooms.

They followed each other around through daily chores, exchanging snippets of information. Marion found it hard to imagine skyscrapers and watched intently as Michael sketched box-like buildings on scraps of paper. She was delighted to hear that women in Australia were now in prominent positions and laughed at the term, "glass ceiling". Medical advances overjoyed her and she never failed to be impressed with his descriptions of shopping centres where one could buy everything under one roof.

Michael chuckled when he heard of the restrictive rules governing young women. He wondered how he and his friends would have reacted in those times. They spent hours digesting stories, becoming unlikely friends.

After an interesting discussion on the benefits and pitfalls of modern education, Marion asked, 'Have you any knowledge of what happened after we went missing? There must have been repercussions. Was there something in the paper?'

'Probably, but you disappeared, when did you say, Nineteen hundred?'

'Yes, it was.' Marion became thoughtful. 'I would like to know what happened to Mother.'

Michael said, 'I'm sorry, Marion, but that was a long time before I was born.' He fiddled with an empty cup, pushed it further along the table. 'Hang on; my grandmother had some clippings on Hanging Rock. Now, what were they?'

Marion leaned towards him. 'Please, Michael, try and remember. Anything would be something.'

Michael thought about Rose's scrapbook, unable to recall any useful detail. It suddenly struck him that there was a similarity between Marion's insistence that she disappeared while at a picnic in nineteen hundred and Grandma Wilma's fanciful tale about her grandmother.

He stared at the side of Marion's head. *Really? You've honestly come from that same picnic. No way.* He wanted to touch her. He looked down at his lap. *What did Grandma say her grandmother's name was? Eileen? No ... Irma. That was it.* He stood up. *Think, Michael. What else did Grandma say?* He gripped the back of the chair. *Something about a bag.* His head spun.

Marion's voice broke into his thoughts, 'Michael, what is it? Are you all right?'

He sat down again. 'Marion ...' He shook his head, unsure of which of the dozens of questions that were almost out of his mouth to ask first. 'You said you went to a picnic, didn't you?'

'Yes ... back in nineteen hundred.'

'Was that when you ...? Was that when you ended up here? Was an Irma with you? Marion, was that ...?'

Marion interrupted, and tapped Michael on the arm as she answered, 'Yes, yes, Michael.'

Michael sprang up. He pulled at his hair. 'Oh my God!'

'What?' Marion struggled to stand.

Michael took hold of her hand and helped her up. He stepped closer. He stared into her face, not knowing what he expected to see. She frowned and stepped back. Michael let go of her hand, looked down at the floor and then back into Marion's eyes. 'I wonder ... do you know anything about a tapestry bag? Did you have one by any chance? Does a bag with the letter M surrounded by pink roses have something to do with you?'

Marion went pale, grabbed his arm and said, 'My bag? What do you know about my bag?'

'It was *your* bag?' Michael felt hot, then shivered. His mind went into overdrive as he tried to recall all the details his grandmother told him. *It is all true. Now I'm involved.* He felt faint.

'How do you know about my bag?' She shook his arm gently. 'What did Irma do with it? Tell me. Tell me what you know.'

Michael put his hands behind his back. He paced and tried to think clearly. 'I'm trying to remember ... She said it was mostly red and green cross-stitching with, I seem to remember her emphasising, *six* pink roses. I was surprised at how much detail she insisted on telling me. I'm not big on sewing, so I drifted off a bit. But, ... a chain for a handle – a gold clasp. The initial M was definitely yellow. Grandma said she had the tapestry bag at one time.'

'*Your* grandmother?' Marion eased herself down onto a chair. 'How did she get it?'

Michael stopped pacing. 'It seems *your* Irma was *my* great, great grandmother.'

Marion put her hands to her face, 'You're related to Irma Leopold?'

Michael grinned. 'Absolutely.' He started to relax.

'I can't believe it.' Marion narrowed her eyes and stared at him. 'You ... Irma. Goodness!'

'It's true and I believe it's somehow connected to all this ... this situation.'

Marion stood up again and, as she moved away, muttered about Irma and long-ago memories.

Michael said, 'Please stay. Talk to me.'

Suddenly, she gripped her chest. She ignored Michael's pleading and staggered towards her bedroom. As Marion reached the doorway, she turned and whispered, 'It's all too much right at this moment.'

Michael was confused. Was Marion ill or just reacting to his revelation? He was sure they'd discovered something relevant. *Why won't she talk about it?* He wanted to call her back. *If she was Irma's friend, it must be important.*

Marion closed her bedroom door.

With a glass of water in his hand, he sat at the table trying to work out what to do next. *Damn! It has to be worth discussing.* He put his forehead on the table. *Think Michael, think.* He drank the water, then stood up. *Doesn't she want her questions answered after all?* He tapped each corner of the table as he strode around it. *What did Grandma say?* He recalled the tale of the lost girls. *Marion is apparently one of those girls. What does that mean? How is it even possible?*

With his mind in a jumble, he sat on the couch and stared at Marion's door.

Later, on his way to his bedroom he heard Marion crying. He placed his hand on the brass doorknob, hesitated, but didn't enter. He realised that he'd obviously struck some sort of chord. *A bag started all this? No way.*

The next morning Marion's eyes were still red from crying and Michael felt too uncomfortable to say anything. He avoided eye contact, and for the first time, took his breakfast outside and sat on the verandah step.

'Michael,' Marion spoke just loud enough for her voice to carry. He turned and watched her walking towards him, dodging the uneven planks. 'Can I talk to you, please?'

'Sure, here?'

'No, I need to sit in comfort.'

'Okay, but I warn you, I need one of your teas,' he said, trying to ease the tension he felt.

'Come inside. I'll make the tea.'

They sat on the couch. Michael tucked one hand under his leg and waited.

'You've asked many questions, most of which I've avoided. I wanted to be sure that you needed to know what I'm able to tell you. The link between your grandma and me has proven there is a special reason you're here. So, it's time to tell you the whole story.'

TWELVE

Michael said Rebecca reminded him of his gran. That must be a good thing, thought Rebecca, as she dropped her mobile phone into her bag. They'd agreed to meet at her flat on Saturday morning and then go for brunch.

He arrived early and presented her with a painting of an orange puppy surrounded by black and grey daisies.

'I believe you're a dog person,' he said, as Rebecca thanked him with a hug.

'I love dogs.' She circled the puppy's large ears with her finger and tried to work out just how he used the paint so effectively.

'Have you ever owned one?'

'A dog? Nearly.'

He laughed. 'What does that mean?'

Rebecca told him she once brought home a lost dog. At the age of seven, she couldn't resist her neighbour's new puppy and forcibly removed the cute animal from behind their gate. She thought her parents would let it stay.

Michael pretended to take the painting from her and they laughed over her childhood precociousness.

Before they left for the café, Michael questioned her aspiration to own a gift shop. For a moment, he sounded like her father.

She crossed her arms over her chest. 'It's still in the planning stage.'

'What's in place so far?'

'Dad and I've collated a rather large file full of figures. I've made a list of likely stock and looked at a few suitable buildings, but there are so many things to consider. The finance scares me. I'd have to get a loan.'

Michael tapped her on the hand. 'I'm sure you could do it. But

...' His eyes sparkled as he commented that a person who wore odd socks because they couldn't decide between pink and green, may not be considered a good credit risk.

Deliberately changing the conversation, she badgered him about getting his art into commercial venues. 'What are *you* scared of, Michael?'

'What do you mean?'

'Your gran said you did accountancy instead of studying art.'

'Yeah, then I moved on to my current job. It hasn't been wasted. I'm financially secure.'

'And what about your dream?'

'Dreaming doesn't pay bills.'

'No, but three months, Michael. Didn't you reassess your plans? Didn't it teach you something?'

He paused. 'Lots of stuff. Stuff I'm hopefully never going to use again.'

'Like what?'

'Chopping wood for one.'

'Is that all? Lots of people chop wood.'

'I know, but it's a killer on the back. The worst was the toilet. Pans and digging. Revolting. It was the one chore Marion happily handed over. Give me modern toilet facilities every time.'

'Yuk, too much information.'

'You asked!'

'I know, but tell me something a little more ... amusing.'

He laughed and stroked his chin. 'Shaving. Now that was something else. You should've seen my one and only attempt at that.'

'Why, what happened?'

'Obviously my whiskers kept growing. No electric shaver. Not even a disposable.'

Rebecca frowned. 'I suppose she didn't have any.'

He smiled. 'Exactly. Anyway, the only cutting implement capable of trimming a beard was a pair of scissors. They were beasts. About thirty centimetres. Quite tough to use. The mirror was a small hand one. I think you'd call it a part of a dressing set.'

'I know the sort. You often get them at antique shops.'

'So, there I was – with this mirror leaning against a book – trying to trim my whiskers with these bloody great shears.' He grinned with the memory.

Rebecca started giggling.

'I got one side done. Then my hands started to shake.'

He acted out the scene. He waved his hand around as if snipping off bits of his nose while making stupid shapes with his mouth. Rebecca held her cheeks because her face hurt from laughing.

'It wasn't *that* funny.' However, he was laughing heartily as well. 'It certainly wasn't at the time. There were great gaps on the left. The piece under my nose was longer than any other bit. Marion tried to trim it, but we were scared I'd end up without a nose, so we left it.'

'W-what happened then?' Rebecca laughed.

'I just let the bloody lot grow. Funny how it sort of evened out in the end.'

Rebecca could see a faint mark from the uneven tan on his clean-shaven face and wanted to touch it. They were quiet for a moment before she asked again, this time more gently, 'So, when are you going to do your art full-time?'

He took a deep breath and let it out slowly. 'One day.'

Leaning over and resting her hand on his, Rebecca asked again, 'How long are you going to wait? Didn't your experience show you that anything can happen in an instant? You said as much yourself. You learned there's stuff more important than money. About life, about yourself, how you coped, how you came through it all. It must have altered your perception of life.'

He stared at their joined hands, 'Maybe ...'

'And it seems you remained relatively normal,' she added with a chuckle.

'Look here, smart arse, if you're going to be rude ...' Michael laughed and ran his finger up Rebecca's arm and flicked her ear, 'you can pay for all our coffees in future.' Jiggling his keys, he looked towards the door. 'And you can start with this next one.'

The July week was wet, but Sunday turned out to be sunny, although cool – the perfect day for being outside.

Michael walked briskly through the park towards Rebecca. 'Hi, you look too good to go jogging.'

She rearranged her scarf as she greeted him with a grin. 'Sorry to disappoint, but I don't jog.'

'I thought you said you ran around this lake all the time.'

Placing her hands on her hips, she pouted like a child caught out with a lie. 'Kylie calls it a "jalk", just to annoy me. Stupid word. It's probably an accurate description though.'

'Well then, shall we get jalking?' Michael grinned and waved his hand in the direction of the concrete path. 'Let's go. I'm hungry, but we'd better do some exercise first.'

His long strides were enough to keep up with Rebecca as she hurried along, trying to breathe evenly.

'Kylie's your sister, right?'

'My favourite sister.'

'Really, you haven't mentioned your other one – ones.'

'Nup, there's only Kylie.'

He raised his eyebrows, shrugged his shoulders and said, 'I'm an only child.'

'That's a shame. I couldn't imagine life without my sister.'

'When can I meet her?'

Rebecca stopped and faced him. 'Well, funny you should ask. My sister's rather insistent. In fact, she said she would stop by later – at the café. She wanted to meet you, too.'

'Really? I suppose now's as good a time as any.'

They continued to walk energetically around the lake, stopping occasionally to watch children feed the ducks. Rebecca spoke to several of the mothers as they kept an eye on their children.

Michael chuckled, 'You look like you want to take them home with you.'

'No, but I wouldn't mind borrowing them for a while,' she said as they walked away from a pram that had a cute bundle of pink wrapped up against the cool breeze. 'I did that once.'

'What, take one home?'

'Certainly not. Just borrowed one for a bit. I went into a deli after work and ended up looking after a four-month-old baby for another customer.'

His eyebrows shot up. 'How come?'

'The woman needed her hair cut. I babysat and she got a new hairstyle.'

Michael walked on ahead, glancing back over his shoulder with a smirk on his face. 'Only you, Bec.' He stopped and held out his hand. 'Come on, slacker. We shouldn't keep your sister waiting.'

She kept hold of his warm hand until he released it in order to open the door of the café.

'So this is your café.' Michael settled himself into a seat facing the park. 'Awesome. You can watch all the people … running.' He waited for Rebecca's reaction before he took a mouthful of water.

Pulling a face at him, she picked up a serviette and folded it into a small square. 'Michael, you haven't told me exactly why you went to Hanging Rock.'

He leaned forward and crossed his hands in front of the empty glass. 'That was supposed to be the easy part. I was going to research information my grandmother gave me. Thought I would start at Hanging Rock. You know, get the feel of the place.' He fiddled with the glass. 'Certainly did that.'

'Why that particular day?'

'No reason. Just that I'd put if off before. Nearly did again.' Michael sat back and watched a couple of kids trying to control their dog. 'I almost went surfing with my mates. Anyway, I didn't. I went to Hanging Rock instead.' He picked up the menu and propped it between the salt and pepper shakers. 'And now, after that, it's sometimes hard to get through the day at work. Seems so pointless.' He paused and shifted the cutlery. Looking up he said, 'But thanks to your encouragement I've started painting again.'

'Excellent.' She felt pleased she'd helped him. 'Have you done anything special?'

'Yep, I've nearly finished one of the farmhouse. Hanging Rock's in the background. It's a challenge to get the atmosphere right. I've made several other sketches in my notebook. I'm trying to record the scenes before I forget the details. I feel relaxed when I've got a pencil or paintbrush in my hand.'

'Great. I'm glad. I bet they're brilliant.'

'The painting's turned out okay. I'm quite proud of it actually.'

'I hope you'll show it to me.'

'Sure. When I've finished, I'd appreciate your opinion.' He paused and looked directly at her. 'Maybe some of the drawings will help work out your incident. I wonder what the connection might be. Have you thought of one?'

'I've been over and over what happened to me. Even after talking to you and Rose, I can't say that anything relates to me.'

'So you still don't know why?'

Rebecca shrugged. 'I've got nothing.'

Michael picked up the menu again. 'Shall we order or should we wait for Kylie?'

Looking at her watch, Rebecca said, 'She should be here by now. Maybe Thomas held her up.'

'Sounds like he's a handful.'

'Not really. I think he's great. His giggle is absolutely contagious. I love playing with him. Kylie's a great mum.'

'Is that me you're talking about,' said Kylie, as she tapped the top of Rebecca's head.

Rebecca jumped up and gave Kylie a hug. 'Kyls, you're here. Grab a seat. Where's Thomas?'

'Sorry, Bec. Luke's mum rang and when I said I was going to lunch, she offered to take him. I wasn't about to say no. It's ages since I've had a day off.' She sat down and grinned at Michael. 'I guess you're the fabulous Michael?'

Michael looked at Rebecca, raised his eyebrows, then turned to Kylie and smiled. 'That'll be me. I've heard a story or two about you and Thomas.'

This time Kylie raised an eyebrow at Rebecca.

'All good, I assure you, Kyls. Shall we order?'

After their food arrived, Kylie asked, 'So, Michael, I guess a steak burger's better than stewed rabbit?'

Rebecca glared at Kylie. Michael put down a chip and glanced at Rebecca before answering, 'Mmm. Especially when you've chips with it.'

'Had you eaten rabbit before?' Kylie asked.

'No,' said Michael, 'and it's not something I'll bother cooking for myself.'

Kylie shook her head and sighed. 'I'm amazed by your experience. How do you explain it?'

'Kylie!' Rebecca squeaked.

'It's okay, Bec. Everyone asks that.' Michael took a sip of water and picked up another chip. 'See, I don't really have any answers. Dr Carstairs reckons I fell and hit my head, wandered into Marion's place and dreamt up the whole bloody lot.' He took a bite of the chip.

Kylie frowned and stabbed into a piece of tomato with her fork. 'The newspapers' conclusions were even stranger.'

'Perhaps Michael doesn't want to talk about it,' said Rebecca, as she glared at her sister again.

'Look,' said Michael, 'I realise it sounds a bit dodgy, but Bec's right. Can we change the subject? Tell me about Thomas. Bec says he's a handful.'

'I did not!'

Michael grinned and offered her a chip. Rebecca was pleased the awkward moment had passed.

Kylie pulled a photograph from her bag. 'He's not really. Just hard to keep up with some days.'

After finishing their meal over every-day chatter, Rebecca and Michael said goodbye to Kylie and walked back to Rebecca's flat.

Missy broke the initial silence by leaping onto Michael's knee without warning. Rebecca scrunched her knees up under her chin as he placed the cat on the couch. Rebecca stroked her cat's back, but Missy jumped down and headed for the other room.

After brushing cat hairs from his jeans, Michael sat up straight and tucked one hand under his leg. Aware that the mood had changed, Rebecca waited silently.

'Bec, I think it might be time for you to hear about Miranda.'

'It's not because of Kylie is it?'

'No, not really.'

'I'm sorry if she put you on the spot. We're rather alike; Kylie and I. Questions come easily.'

Michael chuckled, and then became serious. 'I just don't feel comfortable talking about it in a public place. You know, people overhear things, and then they think they have a right to give their opinion. I've had enough of strangers offering solutions.'

'I can imagine.'

'So, do you want to hear more about Marion or not?'

'Of course. I'd love to.'

'I've told you about my time with Marion, but her time with Miranda is much more interesting.'

Rebecca put her feet on the floor. 'I didn't exactly find yours boring.' Shifting the cushion that sat between them, Michael moved closer. Rebecca was tempted to snuggle into him, but waited patiently for him to speak.

'I spent three long and, what appeared at the time, traumatic months with Marion. Months that taught me so much. I now appreciate my family more. As well as those losers I call my friends.' His laugh came out as a snort. 'Everyday things like instant hot water, fresh milk, proper bread, electricity, definitely electricity, and shit loads of other things. Marion and Miranda didn't have those things. Even in the nineteen hundreds, their proper time, things advanced, but nothing reached into their existence. I'm not sure how that happened, but do you realise they never saw a movie, had running water, visited shops, and ... they never had a steaming hot cappuccino.'

His eyes were smiling as he held up a lukewarm mug of instant coffee. Rebecca squeezed his arm and smiled back.

'You see, I suffered, but they missed out on a part of life that we take for granted. My three months were nothing. They lost a life-time.'

'So, tell me all about it. I'm ready for anything.'

'Get comfy, 'cos there's a lot to tell.'

THIRTEEN

Marion and Miranda helped each other to stand. Miranda sobbed uncontrollably and welcomed Marion's embrace. Marion trembled as she stroked Miranda's mess of tangled hair. After her struggling breath became even, Miranda asked, 'What happened?'

'I'm not sure. The wind knocked me over. I'm sure my arm will be bruised.'

'My leg is quite sore.'

'What an ordeal. It was frightening. Here, take your ribbon. Mrs Appleyard will be furious if you return without it.'

'Thank you.' Miranda tucked the ribbon into her pocket and wiped away the last of her tears. 'Look at your dress, Marion. Brush off the twigs. We must find the others. I don't like being here anymore.'

'This place is awful.'

'Come on, move quickly. Irma should still be here.'

They wriggled through the small opening where Marion had tossed her bag towards Irma. There was no sign of either Irma or the bag.

'Irma must have gone for help.'

'She's taken your bag.'

'I hope she doesn't think she can keep it.'

'Why did you throw it?'

'I wanted Irma to have proof. You know, that we ... that she ... I had to do something. It was all so strange. I felt like I wasn't in control. My legs were moving by themselves. Then the wind came out of nowhere. The dust ... the moaning sounds ... the creeping shadows ... how do you explain those extraordinary things? Who would believe her?' Marion paused before adding, 'I thought we might die.'

'Me too. It was horrid.' Miranda shivered with the memory of the vicious wind that had tossed them like autumn leaves onto the ground.

'Well, it's over. Now hurry up. They'll be looking for us.'

'Wait for me, Marion. I must get my hat.'

They climbed down through the rocks, repeatedly calling out, expecting that someone would answer them.

'Where are they?' Miranda asked when they reached the leafy pathway at the base of the rocks. 'They can't have gone already. The horses wouldn't have been harnessed yet.'

'They must be here somewhere. Picnic baskets would have to be packed up and Miss McCraw would insist on the cutlery and linen being accounted for.'

'Do you suppose we fainted, Marion?'

'Perhaps, but if so, why didn't they find us? Surely Edith and Irma would have shown them where we were.' Marion scrutinised the surrounding area. 'Where is everyone?' She listened for familiar sounds of horses or noisy schoolgirls.

Miranda waved her hat in front of her face, trying to create a breeze. 'Mademoiselle won't leave without us.'

'I hope not.' Then, as she paced down the track towards the flat ground, Marion yelled over her shoulder, 'Do hurry up.'

'I think they've gone without us. Mrs Appleyard won't be at all pleased.' Miranda licked her dry lips. 'They will come back for us won't they?'

Marion turned and nodded to her friend. 'But they might not have left at all.'

'Well, where are they?'

'It is quite the impossible thing. I can't see the racetrack. I do think we must have come down the wrong way.'

'I don't think there is another way.'

Marion was already walking back up the slope. 'We must find them. Mrs Appleyard will blame Miss McCraw if we don't go back with them.'

They tried several smaller tracks, but all were dead ends. Marion slipped several times as she attempted to climb to a higher spot. Miranda tied her hat on firmly and helped Marion as she clambered down again. After two hours of searching, they were exhausted. They stopped at a creek, sipped from cupped hands and dipped their stockinged feet into the cool water. Marion stood in a clearing wondering what to do. When she suggested it was time to start looking again, Miranda refused to put her shoes on wet stockings.

'I really think we need to keep looking.'

'I really think it's a waste of time,' said a sulky Miranda. 'We shouldn't have to, Marion. *They* should be looking for *us*.' She stood up and went to walk away. 'Ouch! Oh, my foot.' She sat down on a log and brushed pebbles from her stockinged feet.

'You're wasting valuable time,' said Marion. 'Put on your shoes. Hurry up, they won't wait all day.'

'It seems they haven't waited at all.'

Marion stomped away. Miranda followed but stopped and picked a flower.

'Come on, we need to keep walking.'

'Where are you going?'

'Maybe we should walk to the main road.'

'It's too far.' Miranda stopped again. 'We should wait here. It's decidedly more pleasant. They'll find us soon. We're expected back at school for supper.'

'Don't talk of supper, I'm hungry.'

'So am I, and we are to have those currant buns I like so much.'

'Oh yes, so we are,' Marion added absently as she continued to pace up and down the path.

'Marion, please come and sit with me. It shouldn't be much longer. Someone will come for us.'

Before the sun dipped below the horizon, Marion suggested they return to the rock. On the way, Miranda slipped and ripped her stocking. She grumbled about her grazed knee and insisted on resting every few minutes.

'Come on. Stop complaining,' said Marion for the fourth time.

'But, Marion, it hurts.'

'I know, but we need to find somewhere safe for the night.'

Miranda instantly forgot about her bloodied knee. 'Safe? How can we be safe here?'

Marion hugged her friend. 'I don't know what to think. However, one thing I do know is that we can't stay out here. It will turn cold later. We need some sort of cover.'

Miranda grabbed her friend's arm. 'I'm too frightened to go back up there.'

Marion turned and stared at the rock, calculating which parts were accessible. 'I'm afraid also, but we have to. Please, Miranda.'

Miranda twisted her hair around her fingers. 'Very well then, but not where we were before.'

'We can try further along, but we will have to hurry. It's going to be dark soon.'

As malevolent shadows turned into eerie darkness, they huddled together in a hollow of a rock. It was hard to get comfortable. Marion moved several times before she felt reasonably satisfied. Miranda wriggled beside her, removing several small stones that dug into her bottom. They slapped at hungry mosquitoes. Marion resorted to pulling her skirt around her shoulders. It made her feel a little warmer and kept the biting insects at bay. Miranda refused to copy this most unladylike behaviour. If Mr Hussey found her with her undergarments on show, she wouldn't be able to bear the shame. It would be even worse if the pompous Police Sergeant Bumpher saw them. She pushed her shoulder into Marion's and hoped the insects would soon stop biting.

Night noises kept them awake. When the mournful sounds of distant dingoes reached the cavernous rock, they huddled even closer. Miranda suddenly shrieked and accidently hit Marion as she tried to dislodge an insect from her neck.

The girls had just drifted into a restless sleep when an owl hooted. They were instantly awake. Marion stood up and stepped out of the hollow. Miranda jumped up and tugged on Marion's dress. 'Stay here. Don't go anywhere.'

They pushed aside more pebbles and arranged themselves against the rock wall again. Miranda brushed off imaginary dust from her skirt. She played with her hair and tugged at the ends.

Marion grabbed Miranda's hand. 'Do stop that and sit still. It's most annoying.'

'I don't think I shall be able to sleep.'

'We must try. It will make the night pass quicker.'

'Could you sing something?' asked Miranda.

Marion cleared her throat, then changed her mind. 'I certainly don't feel like singing. Perhaps you could.'

'No. I'm much too upset to sing.' Miranda wiped away a dribbling tear and leaned her head on Marion's shoulder. 'I've only slept outside once before.'

'I've never slept outside,' Marion said. 'Father believed camping was only for when one couldn't afford to sleep in a bed.'

Miranda said she was sure Mademoiselle would agree and jabbered about the time she'd gone mustering with her father. 'I wasn't scared at all. Johnno made a fire. Another man played his guitar. Dad was next to me and I fell asleep almost at once. Riding all day does make one feel tired. Mum said I could only go for one night. Johnno rode back with me the next morning. I wish he was here now.'

Marion rubbed Miranda's hand and hummed softly. Rustling bushes caused her to stop. She hoped whatever was making the noise would go away. Towards dawn, deep sleep provided relief, but all too soon the day began with screeching cockatoos.

'Miranda, are you awake?'

Miranda blinked repeatedly as she sat up. The ordeal of the previous day and the distress of last night flooded back. 'Oh, Marion, I was hoping it was all a dream.' She rubbed at a red spot on her wrist.

'No,' said Marion. Her lip quivered. 'I'm afraid it wasn't, but someone will find us today.'

'I hope they jolly well hurry up. I want to go home. Just look at us. What a frightful sight we are.'

Marion agreed and they spent several minutes trying to neaten their clothes and re-tie their hair. Reluctantly, Miranda removed her torn stockings and pushed them into her pocket. They left the rock and returned to the clear stream. They felt better after they drank some water and splashed their faces. The coolness relieved the itch of the mosquito bites.

'I'm hungry.' Miranda stared at Marion, turning the statement into a demand.

'What do you think I can do about it? I'm awfully hungry too.'

'I'm sorry, but what *shall* we do?' Miranda paused before adding, 'I guess they'll come looking for us again today.'

'Of course they will.'

'Even though it's Sunday? Won't everyone be in church?' queried Miranda, trying not to form a frown that may cause wrinkles. She patted her hot cheeks, and pulled at her uncombed hair again.

'I shouldn't think Sergeant Bumpher will be. Mrs Appleyard will insist we are fetched.'

'I don't want to spend any more time here. Maybe we can walk to a farm?'

Marion peered into the distance then looked back at her friend. 'Yes, if you are willing to try, but I don't know which way is best. Perhaps we should go towards Woodend.'

'It's better than staying here. This place gives me the creeps.'

The two girls held hands and hurried along, calling out every so often. Every now and then they would nervously glance at each other. If she's not scared then I don't need to be, they thought simultaneously.

The sun, high in the February sky, was relentless. Marion tucked her dark hair under her scarf and wished she had taken notice of Miss McCraw's suggestion to wear her hat. Heat was already making her skin blotchy. They found a wild gooseberry bush and ate all the yellow fruit, but they were still hungry. Miranda now didn't like the fact that they had moved so far from the rock. 'They won't find us,' she said repeatedly.

'It was you who wanted to find a farm.'

'I know, but we've walked so far.'

Marion sighed and strode away from Miranda. 'Let's go back then. Your whining is annoying me.'

Running to catch up, Miranda cried, 'I don't want to be here anymore.' She grabbed Marion's arm. 'Please, can't we just go home?'

Marion lost her temper. 'Of course, Miss Miranda. I'll call the carriage for you. The chauffeur will be happy to drive you wherever you want to go. Step this way into the shade. I'll attend your every wish.'

Miranda started blubbering, which only increased Marion's anger. 'Don't start crying. It won't do us any good.'

'But, Marion, I'm scared.'

Once that was said, there was no taking it back. Marion wrapped her arms around Miranda and tears flowed down both faces. Marion was frightened, confused and hungry, just like Miranda.

They dawdled back to the rock. Darting willy-wagtails startled them. They screamed as a large lizard scurried across the path. Miranda's fingernails dug into Marion's hand, but she didn't pull it away. They spent frustrating hours, wandering around the area where the picnic had been set up. When Marion suggested they may have to spend another night at the rock, Miranda's lip trembled and her mood darkened.

'Will we go back to the same place, Marion?'

'I think that will be best. It seemed safe enough there.'

After sweeping the remaining stones from the hollow with leafy branches, they broke off fern fronds and tried to make the ground more comfortable. Their fingers blistered and added to their woes. Miranda copied Marion and pulled her skirt around her shoulders – she didn't care who saw her drawers this time.

The sounds of the night were less threatening, but insects still bit them. Miranda leaned against Marion and hummed softly. As they dozed, they fell sideways and ended up huddled together like newborn kittens.

In the morning, their neglected stomachs ached. So, despite their fear, they decided they would have to travel further away from the rock in the hope of reaching a farmhouse. Marion suggested writing their initials in the sand near where the horses had been tethered. When they couldn't decide on the exact spot, they drew arrows on the narrow track, hoping to direct rescuers.

After almost an hour of walking in the hot sun, the sight of fence posts excited the two girls. The fact that the posts leaned at various angles and the barbwire lay tangled in the grass, didn't register. Fence posts meant a farm. That in turn meant safety. Someone would help them. They would be going home. Despite feeling weary, their pace quickened.

'Hurray,' squealed Miranda when a farmhouse came into view.

'Yes, yes,' agreed Marion. 'Quickly, let's get out of this scorching sun. I feel I shall suffer terrible burns and with Mother's birthday party coming up I shall be a sorry sight in my best dress.'

With fresh energy, Miranda skipped beside Marion and asked, 'Can I come to the party, or is it just for adults?'

'I'm sure Mother will let you come. Although we will have to amuse ourselves after supper.'

'Do you mean I can stay?' Miranda stopped skipping and took Marion's hand.

'Yes, if you want to.' She dropped Miranda's hand and stepped away. 'Now hurry up, I want to get out of the sun and ask for something to eat.'

'I hope they have sweet buns.'

'Just hurry up.'

FOURTEEN

They reached a lemon tree that shaded most of the front of the house. The shabbiness of the verandah and peeling paint on the front door was obvious. Marion knocked politely then stood back expectantly. She knocked more urgently the third time. When there was still no answer, they walked around to the back of the house. The two girls called out several times in case they were considered impertinent for not waiting to be greeted at the main entrance. Long grass grew against the back of the house. Weeds struggled between the stones of the path and several fallen branches from a gum tree lay against an unpainted outhouse.

'Hello,' they yelled in unison. Marion knocked on the back door then opened it cautiously. Flies swarmed around a dead carcass that spanned the doorway.

'How disgusting. Oh, my stomach.' Miranda bumped into Marion as she stepped away.

'What an awful smell. Don't you dare be sick.' Marion peered into the dark room. 'Hello, anyone there?'

'There's no one here. They wouldn't put up with that terrible smell. Let's leave.' She tugged on Marion's sleeve, trying to stop her from moving any closer to the heap on the floor.

Swiping at Miranda's insistent hand, Marion called out again. When no one responded, she held her nose, stepped over the decomposing animal and into the house. In doing so, she disturbed the flies.

'Now look what you've done.'

'Do stop fussing, Miranda. Follow me. Let's see what we can find.'

'I'm not going in there. The smell is sickening. How can you bear it?'

'I'm holding my nose.'

Scattered rubbish and animal droppings littered the room. Miranda held the door open while trying to look anywhere but at the flies and their meal.

'It's dead. It won't hurt you,' said Marion.

'It's horrid.'

'Surely you've seen dead animals before, Miranda? Doesn't your father kill cattle?'

'I've seen hundreds of dead animals, but they don't smell like that.'

'Forget the smell. I'm going to see if there is anything to eat. I'm so hungry.'

'So am I, but you look.' She moved a little further away. 'I'll keep guard out here.'

'That's all right for you. You're happy to leave me with the smell.' Marion kept hold of her nose and took shallow breaths.

'I can smell it from here anyway. Just see if there is anything we can eat. I'll faint otherwise.'

Miranda continued to stand outside the doorway. She flapped her hand in front of her nose. Although the smell was overwhelming, she couldn't help glancing at the dead animal.

After searching through the few shelves in the kitchen area, Marion discovered two unlabelled tins, but couldn't find a way to open them. There was weevil-infested flour and plenty of tea leaves in two jars that stood on the end of a bench. When she could no longer put up with the smell, she joined Miranda outside.

'We shall have to remove the carcass.'

'I won't touch it.'

'How can we prepare any food if we don't get rid of that animal first? Could you eat while that smell fills your nostrils?'

'Ugh.' Miranda's bottom lip dropped. 'No, I couldn't, but is there anything to eat anyway?'

'All I found were tea leaves and some flour. We can have a better look after we shift that horrid mess.'

They walked away from the doorway and breathed in fresh air.

'We can light a fire and have some tea. I saw a pot we can use, and there are matches on the stove. There must be some clean water somewhere. Come on, Miranda, let's look for a spade or something.'

During their search, they found a shovel leaning against a large water tank on the side of the house. A dented bucket lay on its side under the water tank's brass tap. Further along, Marion pushed some weeds aside with her foot and uncovered a prostrate tomato plant.

'Miranda,' she called, 'look, tomatoes.'

She pulled a bright red fruit from the straggly plant, removed a black spot with her fingernail and wiped the tomato on her skirt. 'There's plenty,' she said, after locating another plant. She bit into the tomato and chewed vigourously. Juice trickled down her chin. She pushed the rest into her mouth and snatched another from the same bush.

Miranda tripped in her haste to reach the ripest fruit. She grabbed Marion's arm, steadying herself before twisting off a tomato. 'Oh, I'm so hungry,' she said, as she tried to pick off a piece of leaf. She shoved the whole tomato into her mouth. Seeds oozed from between her lips and fell on her dress.

Marion picked tomatoes and dropped them in a pile on the ground while she continued to eat. She shoved a third tomato into her mouth, ate rapidly and wiped the dribbling juice on her sleeve. Miranda accidently ripped a plant from the ground. She ate with her eyes closed, savouring the sweet taste.

The two girls continued to step between the plants in their search for more tomatoes. They pulled up weeds and tossed them aside as they went. They chewed more sedately on the fifth one.

Marion poked at a seed on Miranda's lip. 'You've missed a bit.' She giggled and wiped her mouth on her sleeve again in case she too had left some behind.

'Thanks, Marion. Oh, I'm beginning to feel sick. I think I ate too quickly.'

'I've had enough. I need a drink. I do hope there's water in the tank.'

After struggling with the tap, Marion washed the bucket and placed the tomatoes in it. She knelt down and drank with cupped hands from the tap until her thirst was satisfied. Miranda wanted some tea, but the smell prevented them from entering the house. She avoided the wet soil under the tap and sipped from her hands as Marion controlled the flow of water.

They sat under the lemon tree and Marion wondered aloud what they should do next. Miranda asked what one was *supposed* to do in these circumstances. Marion suggested one would normally have servants or parents to rely on. Miranda grumbled that she didn't want to look at another tomato – ever. Then finally, they returned to the vegetable patch, retrieved the shovel and headed for the back door.

Miranda shuddered at the thought of the task. 'You can do it, Marion,' she said.

'It has to be done. We might as well get it over with.'

'I think you should dig a hole first.'

'*You* should dig the hole.' Marion thrust the shovel at Miranda. 'Marion!'

'If I have to shift the mess, you can, at least, do that.'

Miranda snatched the shovel and stomped away from her friend. She started digging beyond the vegetable garden. When the hole was deep enough, she strode back and handed the implement over. 'It's done,' she stated petulantly.

Marion took the shovel and went inside. Maggots wriggled in the rancid goo on the shovel as she carried it out. For a moment, she thought her stomach would lurch its contents into the hole, but she took a deep breath and looked up to the sky.

Miranda held the door open and made obtuse noises each time Marion walked by. Marion sprinkled sand across the remaining smear of smelly liquid and then took the shovel back outside.

The odour lingered and Miranda wrinkled her nose as she took several steps inside and waited for Marion. As Marion re-entered the room Miranda said, 'Perhaps the owner will return.'

'I don't think so. Who would live like this?'

'I surely couldn't.'

Marion opened the jar that held the tea leaves. 'I think we should try and light a fire. After we've had a cup of tea we might feel like walking back to the rock.'

'Oh no, not so soon,' Miranda folded her arms and said, 'I'm much too tired.'

'All right. I guess we can stay here for a while. We can go back later. It should be cooler this afternoon.'

Miranda grabbed Marion's hand. 'I don't want to go back to the rock. I hate that place.'

'We have to. They'll be looking for us.' Marion pushed Miranda's hand away.

'Yes, but they'll find the marks we made in the sand. We don't have to go. They'll come here.'

Marion put the lid on the jar and moved the container along the bench. 'I guess they will.'

Miranda screwed up her nose again as she stepped around the sandy patch on the floor. 'It still smells.'

'The sand will dry out soon. Then we can sweep it away.'

They ventured into a bedroom, and even though it was mid-afternoon, the two girls found it hard to see much at all. They pulled open the heavy drapes and revealed reasonably clean lace curtains. A single bed with a brass bed-head had a bare mattress that held the sickly smell of old sweat. A side table with carved legs had one central drawer. Miranda found a large journal with a few torn pages and flicked through it before returning the book to the dusty space. 'It's really quite lovely.'

'Then this room can be yours,' said Marion.

'No!' Miranda shoved the drawer in. 'I meant the table. I guess the bed-head is lovely also, but I won't need any of it for long. I'm going home as soon as they come for us.'

'Of course we are.' Marion put her hand on Miranda's shoulder.

'Let's see what's next door.'

The other room had similar curtains and a double bed with a plain wooden bed-head. A huge trunk with brass fittings stood in the corner. A large wardrobe, without a door, filled the opposite wall.

'Look, there are coats in here,' Miranda said. She pushed aside a man's coat. 'See. A woman's jacket; lovely shade of blue, and look at the small one. Maybe they'll come back for them.'

'I don't think so. They seem to have taken everything else.'

'Surely one wouldn't leave without one's coat.'

'Only if you were in a hurry.'

'Or it was hot.'

'Never mind the coats. What's in here?' said Miranda, as she opened the door of a small bedside cupboard. 'Well, I never.' She shifted a small notebook. 'Look, a lady's companion.'

Marion peeped over Miranda's shoulder and saw a nail file, hairbrush, comb and a hand-mirror without glass, arranged on a tray.

Miranda picked up the brush. 'I need to tidy my hair. There are so many knots.'

'I want a bath,' said Marion.

Their attention turned to the trunk. Without sufficient light, it was hard to determine what was in the vast space and when Miranda turned over a few layers, the odour put her off further investigation.

'At least this looks clean enough,' said Marion, as she prodded the mattress. 'We can sleep here; if we decide to stay.'

Miranda nodded. 'I think we should. It's more comfortable than rock.' She grinned and nodded again.

'Yes,' agreed Marion, 'but hopefully only for one night.'

Miranda groaned, sat down on the bed and started whimpering. She gripped her knees and rocked back and forth. 'Oh dear,' she repeated between sniffles. Marion held her friend's shoulders. Miranda leaned her head on Marion's chest. Marion battled with an urge to cry too. 'Mirry, don't cry. Please. They'll find us.'

'I don't want to sleep by myself,' said Miranda, as she clung to Marion.

Marion gently removed Miranda's fingers and stroked her hair. 'I agree with you. We can both sleep here.'

Looking up through damp lashes Miranda said, 'We should sleep in our petticoats. My dress is rather grubby.'

'Mine is too. How simply awful. They'll be frightful to clean.'

'What are we going to eat for dinner? I'm so hungry and I don't want any more tomatoes.'

'We may have to,' said Marion.

'Didn't you find some flour? Can we cook something?'

'Dry your eyes. Let's have another look in the kitchen.'

They returned to the main room and opened a cupboard door.

Marion took out a dusty frying pan. 'I've been thinking about how to use the flour. If we pick out the insects we could make some sort of pancake.'

'Ooh, yes. Pancakes.'

'I shouldn't think they'll be perfect. I haven't made them before.'

'Never mind, I'm sure they are only flour and water.'

'I think they usually have eggs and milk, but we'll have to make do.' Marion inspected a crumpled box of matches. 'Have you ever made a fire, Miranda?'

'Yes, but not in a kitchen. My brothers often make campfires. If you're rounding up stock, you have to stay out for several days. Making a fire is the only way to boil the billy. They tried to show me how, but I was slow and they took over.'

'We must try.' Marion bent down and looked at the cold ashes. 'It's extremely grubby. It certainly hasn't been cleaned out.'

'I think you can leave those bits. It will help once the fire is going. First, we need some dry twigs and then some wood. We can use this paper from the floor.'

They gathered dry twigs and found a small pile of chopped wood on the verandah. Once the fire was crackling, they filled the kettle and sat on the front step, picked the weevils from the flour and waited until the water boiled.

With cups of hot black tea beside them, they attempted a batch of pancakes. They threw the first three away, but ate the next batch as soon as they were cooked. They pulled away burnt edges, gobbled down the remainder, and when their stomachs felt full, returned to the front step.

Miranda looked into the distance and asked, 'Marion, do you think we'll be found soon?'

'We have to go back to the rock.'

'But, Marion, won't they see the arrows and come here?'

'It would be nice to think so.'

'What if they don't?'

'That's why we have to go back.'

As the day darkened, they lay on the bed and slept soundly for a few hours. Then they tossed and turned until early morning.

'Marion, are you awake?'

'Mmm.'

'I need to go to the bushes again.'

Marion yawned and stretched. 'I don't.'

'But you have to come too.'

'Go by yourself. I don't want to see you pee.'

'Please come to the back door *at least*.'

'Maybe you should use the outhouse.'
'I'd rather go in bushes just now.'
'We should look at the outhouse.'
'Later, Marion. Please, hurry up; I don't want to wet my drawers.'
'All right, I'm coming.'

After a breakfast of leftover pancakes, the girls set out towards the rock.

'Stop dawdling,' said Marion. She waited for Miranda to catch up. As she turned to continue walking, she screamed and jumped backwards. Miranda bumped into her and the two girls almost fell over.

'Watch out. There's a snake.' Marion grabbed Miranda's arm. They watched the lazy snake wriggle across the path. 'How horrible,' whispered Marion.

Miranda shuddered. 'I don't want to be here.'

They huddled together until the snake slithered away. Then they scampered along the path and only stopped hurrying when they were close to the rock. To their surprise, they were unable to find the toilet block.

'Was it here yesterday, Miranda?'

'I'm not sure.'

'It mustn't have been. Otherwise we would have visited it.'

'It was here the day before,' Miranda said without conviction.

'Well, it isn't here today.'

'That's really odd. *And*, really annoying, I hate going in the bushes.'

'Stop complaining, Miranda. You didn't want to use the outhouse this morning.'

'That's different.'

'I fail to see how it is. Anyway, I'm worried that it's something else that's disappeared.'

'You mean like the racetrack? Things can't just disappear. Are you sure we're in the right place.'

Marion looked up at the rock, back down the track where they came from and nodded. 'Yes, *we* are in exactly the right place. It is everything else that isn't.'

Miranda glared up at the rock. 'It's that rock. I just know it's that rock. It's terrifying and I want to leave at once.'

'Let's go to the stream. There's no one here anyway.'

They hurried away, calling out occasionally. At the stream, Miranda asked, 'Why isn't Sergeant Bumpher looking for us?'

'Perhaps he's given up.'

'Don't say that, Marion. They can't just leave us out here.'

'Well, they obviously can't find us.'

'But we left those marks in the sand.'

Marion was also bewildered. She was sure Mrs Appleyard would insist on a search party. *Mother would have demanded it. Miranda's parents could afford to pay a fortune to find her. The local men, perhaps even schoolboys, should be scouring the bush, searching for clues. Why isn't that happening?*

They wandered along the edge of the stream. Marion removed her shoes and paddled her feet. Miranda splashed water over her face. They both stared through the trees, imagining a rescuer.

'Come on, Miranda, let's go back to the farmhouse. We've been here long enough.'

'But, Marion ...'

'Miranda, I don't know.'

'I didn't ask anything.'

'I don't have the answer anyway.'

Marion stalked off and Miranda followed. The silent walk back to the house didn't improve their mood.

Marion looked through the kitchen cupboards again. Miranda stood at the end of the bench and fiddled with a large serving spoon.

'I'm sorry, Marion,' said Miranda quietly.

Marion gently shut the cupboard door. She sighed. 'I'm sorry too. I just don't have any answers.'

'I don't understand.' Miranda banged the spoon on the bench. 'I ... don't ... under ... stand.'

Marion took the spoon and slid it across the bench. Then she put her arms around Miranda and held her tightly. 'Neither do I,' she whispered. 'Neither do I.'

FIFTEEN

The unknown age of the flour concerned them, but as they hadn't suffered any ailment from the previous batches, they picked out the tiny insects and made more pancakes.

After the meagre meal, they removed the velvet curtains from the front window to allow more light to enter the room. Once they had taken them down, rolled them up and stuffed them in the bottom of the bedroom cupboard, dusty net curtains were fully exposed.

Marion washed down the kitchen workspace. Miranda started singing *Ta-ra-ra Boom-de-ay* using the broom as a dancing partner. Marion imitated a hula dancer as she flicked a cloth at the dust on the dresser.

They located eight chairs in various parts of the house and placed them around the freshly cleaned table. After removing animal excrement and a bird's nest from a grubby couch, they were disappointed to discover severely ripped fabric and missing padding. They pushed the couch into a corner of the room, declaring it too far gone to bother with.

When the sunlight faded, they prepared for bed. The two girls slept for a few hours until Marion woke up shivering. She prodded Miranda. 'I'm cold.'

Miranda groaned and turned over. 'What did you say?'

'I'm cold.'

'Just go back to sleep.'

'I can't. I'm too c-cold.'

Miranda forced her eyes open. 'What do you want me to do about it?'

Marion pushed gently on Miranda's arm. 'G-g-et a coat. Please.'

'You get it.'

'You're closer.'

Miranda sat up. 'It's too dark to see.'

'Please. I won't be able to get back to sleep. I'm too cold.'

'All right. I'll try.' Miranda fumbled her way through the dark. 'Ouch! That was my toe.'

'Can you find a coat?'

'Ouch! Yes. Oh! It feels awful.'

'Bring the coat. I hate being cold.'

'Who's whining now?'

'Pass it to me. Please.'

The coat was warm, but prickly. They scratched relentlessly and hoped it was the wool rather than crawling insects that tormented them.

'Wake up, Miranda, it's morning.'

'Oh, I'm so stiff. I couldn't straighten my legs because my feet would stick out.'

'I was hot.'

'Hot? I thought you were cold.'

'That was last night.'

Marion let the coat tumble to the floor as she stretched her legs over the side of the bed. 'The early mornings are quite chilly and the coat is impractical. Are there any blankets in the trunk?'

Miranda yawned. 'We could use one of those purple curtains. Then we don't have to rummage through those revolting smelly things in the trunk.'

'Splendid idea. Now, I need a drink. Thank goodness there's water in the tank.'

'We won't need it all. I'm sure they'll find us today.'

'I hope so. Let's leave for the rock straight away.'

Miranda frowned. 'I need to eat first.'

'We can take a tomato with us.'

'Not another tomato. I wish we had something else.'

'We can look for something on the way to the rock. Perhaps we'll find some more gooseberries. Come on, Miranda, let's go before it gets too hot.'

'Why isn't anyone here?' Miranda leaned against a tree and shut her eyes.

'It's early.'

'But it's such a popular spot; I would expect someone to be here.'

Marion stared up at the rough rock face. 'I'm convinced something odd has happened to us.'

Miranda sat down on a small rock and whimpered for several minutes. Marion stood with her hand on Miranda's shoulder and didn't bother to wipe away her own few tears. 'Come on, Miranda, let's try further along.'

Miranda stood up and kicked the monolithic structure. 'Blast and curse you!'

'Coo-ee,' Marion yelled through a gap. 'Coo-ee,' the rock answered.

After three hours of sitting, wandering, standing and yelling the girls were depressed. Then after sitting some more, they walked away – back to the farmhouse again.

'What will we do if they take a long time to find us? I mean what if it's two or three weeks?'

'Heaven forbid, Miranda, the police will find us. We didn't walk that far. And we left the arrows.'

'Remember Jimmy Watkins? He was missing for five days and they found him dead.'

'Hush, he was only four.'

Miranda sniffed and Marion thought another bout of tears would start. However, Miranda rose from the spot under the lemon tree and said, 'We need to make a bonfire. If we make enough smoke, they'll be able to see us for quite a distance. If Sergeant Bumpher has given up, perhaps a farmer will see it.'

Marion was unsure. 'Is that advisable? The risk of it escaping would be quite high.'

'Well then, you could stand on the roof and wave your scarf,' said Miranda with a laugh.

'Oh yes,' said Marion, eager to join in the fun. 'You could do a handstand. That would attract attention.'

'What? On the roof?'

'Most definitely. Or, you could ...'

Miranda finished the sentence, 'just build a bonfire.'

They concluded the task was beyond them.

They skirted the house and removed more weeds from around the tomatoes. Marion was delighted to uncover small strawberry plants. In a little over an hour, they also found some limp cabbages and drying runners of pumpkin plants. Grapevines straddled a sturdy trellis and dried tendrils of an unknown vine clung to a structure at the end of the trellis. The grapevines and strawberry plants were dormant, but they picked two large pumpkins and carried them inside.

'Are they ripe enough?' questioned Marion.

'They look exactly like the ones in our garden.'

'Can you make soup with them?'

'Of course.'

'I mean do *you* know how to make pumpkin soup, Miranda?'

'I've seen our cook cut up the pumpkin and boil it.'

'Let's try. I'm starving.'

The two friends made a watery soup, and although they pulled faces as they ate it, their attempt pleased them. Then, once again, they removed weevils from the flour.

'It's a waste of time,' said Miranda as they walked towards Hanging Rock. The top of the rock was visible over the trees and Miranda shivered as she said, 'I don't trust that rock. It's evil.'

Marion put her hand through her friend's arm and tugged gently. 'We must keep looking. It's our only chance.'

They walked the rest of the way without their usual chatter. Miranda sighed each time Marion called out. They broke off twigs and scratched more arrows. When they reached the trees near the water, they disagreed on whether to go to the rock or stay at the stream.

'We could still hear any horses or someone shouting if we stay here,' said Miranda. 'They would be calling out, wouldn't they?'

'I suppose so, but their voices mightn't carry. No, we have to go to the rock.'

'I hate that evil rock,' she said again.

'Come on, Miranda. Once we've looked around, we'll come back to the stream again.'

Miranda followed reluctantly, but when Marion peeped in through the towering walls and called out her name Miranda giggled at the echo. She shouted, 'Sara, Sara,' and smiled as the name bounced back.

When they reached the end of the clear path Miranda said, 'We shouldn't go any further. There could be another snake.'

Marion took her hand. 'Next time we should walk towards Woodend. If they've stopped looking for us, we'll have to get to Appleyard College by ourselves.'

'It's much too far.' Miranda shook her hand free.

'We might come across another farm with people.'

'What if we get lost?'

Marion sighed. 'We seem to be lost already. Certainly nothing is quite as it should be.'

Twenty yards down the path, thick undergrowth stopped their progress. Marion tried to push through the grass, but her dress caught on a shrub. Miranda stood on tiptoes; she dared not move. 'Please, Marion, don't go any further.'

Marion pulled her dress off the branch. 'There really should be a pathway. The horses were tethered just near here.'

'Are you sure?'

'Yes. This part of the rock was visible when we first arrived.' She turned around and tried to explain properly. 'Yes, I'm sure. Can you see that tall rock? I remember thinking it looked like a face. The round hollows are the eyes. See, Miranda.'

Miranda agreed it looked like a face, but said, 'It can't be the same place. There's no room for a carriage.'

Marion stepped onto a flat rock and gripped the edge of a higher one. 'I can't explain that. But I know it's the same place.' She grunted as she climbed onto the next level. 'I'm going to see if I can recognise anything from the top.' She pulled herself up onto a ledge and looked down. 'Are you coming?'

'Maybe.' Miranda climbed up and stood next to Marion. 'You can't see anything from here.'

'Then let's go higher.'

Marion clung onto the edge of a rough stone and levered herself up. When she climbed as far as she dared, she called out, 'It's lovely up here. You can see for miles.'

'I'm not coming any further,' Miranda said, as she moved her foot off a shaky rock. 'Can you see the road?'

Marion turned and looked in the direction she thought the road should be. *I can't believe it. Where's the road? I'm sure we came that way.* 'No, the road isn't there.'

'Well, can you see another farm?'

Marion held onto a jagged edge and swivelled around. 'No, there is nothing that way either.' She squinted into the distance. *The road should be there.* She pointed to the south and tried to convince herself that she was correct.

'What can you see, Marion?'

Marion leaned back against the hard surface. 'Nothing but bush.' She squatted down and shut her eyes. 'Nothing,' she whispered.

Miranda now sat by the stream and refused to walk any further.

Marion's emotions flicked back and forth between anger and confusion when she couldn't locate the racetrack. She stormed back to Miranda, yelling as she approached, 'The racetrack's definitely gone.'

Miranda looked up from watching a stick float by. 'A few days ago you assumed it was on the other side of the rock.'

'I did, but that is not so. I didn't see it when I climbed to the top. It has simply disappeared. Just like the toilets. Tell me, how is that possible?'

'It isn't. Did you see another farm within walking distance?'

'No. There was only bush. Even the little farmhouse we've found wasn't visible.'

'Did you look in the right direction?'

'Of course I did. It simply wasn't there. I didn't see *any* building. There's nothing but thick bush.'

'There has to be *something*.' Miranda shoved her hand into the stream and flicked water into the air.

Marion watched the fallen drops turn to ripples. *Does she think I'm making it up?* The back of Marion's neck stung from sunburn. Her feet ached. Blood spotted her right hand from where she caught it on a bramble. 'Come on, Miranda,' Marion yelled. 'I'm leaving.'

'Wait! I'm coming. Wait!'

Marion trudged towards the farmhouse. A little way down the track, she turned and held out her hand to her friend. 'I'm sorry, Miranda. I guess I shouldn't be so irritated, but nothing is as it should be since the picnic.' She tugged Miranda's hand. 'Let's hurry. I'm hungry. We'll get the fire going again and heat the soup. I'll make some more pancakes. We'll feel better then.'

'I wish we had something else to eat,' Miranda said.

'Yes, I do too,' said Marion. 'We can search the rest of the yard in the morning.'

Two pigeons flew out of a tree. Miranda jumped. Marion closed her eyes and imagined eating them for dinner.

When they came across a sandy patch, Marion bent down and drew a circle, explaining to Miranda, 'This is the rock.' She made another circle away from the first one. 'The farmhouse is here.'

Miranda bent down and put a cross in the sand. 'We are here.'

'Yes. So the road back to town is supposed to be … about … there.'

'But it's not?' asked Miranda.

Marion stood up and brushed the makeshift map away with her shoe. 'All I could see were the tops of trees. They stretched far into the distance.'

'You must have been able to see the road.'

Marion started walking. 'No. Not even this track.'

'Are you sure?'

'I'm going back to the farmhouse,' Marion yelled over her shoulder. 'I hope it's still there.'

Marion stopped and waited for Miranda. 'I believe it will be.'

Early the next morning, Miranda woke to the sound of Marion's muffled sniffing. She lay still, wondering what she should say. A loud sob made her turn over and put her arm across her friend's waist. 'What's wrong?'

Marion sat up. She continued to cry.

'Please don't cry, Marion.'

'I didn't mean to wake you.' Her tears gradually stopped. 'I was thinking of Mother. She'll think I've deserted her.'

Miranda ran her tongue over her dry lips. 'No she won't. You would go home if you could.'

Marion got out of bed and went to the window. She rubbed dust from one panel and looked out. 'Somewhere out there is home. Appleyard College is only a carriage ride away, and yet we seem separated in a strange manner. I'm sure we would find nothing else – no matter how far we walked.'

'We can go to the rock again,' said Miranda. She was concerned with Marion's distant stare and her resigned attitude. 'I won't complain. I'll look after you this time. Cheer up. We can go to the rock later.'

Marion turned back to Miranda and said, 'Somehow that sinister rock has changed everything.' Her smile was weak and forced. 'We won't go today. Perhaps someone will find the arrows.'

Miranda was relieved not to have to spend the day walking.

Soft grass under the shady lemon tree made a comfortable spot to pass away the time, but every so often the girls would stand up and wander down to the fence posts.

With eyes shaded by her hand, Marion wondered if shapes in the distance were people finally coming to rescue them. Eventually she gave up and flopped back down onto the grass.

Miranda also thought she saw something move in the distance. She clapped her hands and made sounds of delight as she hurried away from the lemon tree. Marion jumped up and dashed after her friend.

'Is it someone?'

'I'm not sure now. At first it did so look like a person.'

'Damnation! Excuse my French, but damn!'

Marion returned to her place under the tree. Twenty minutes later, so did Miranda. As she picked at the grass she asked, 'What's going to happen to us, Marion?'

'We're going to be found.'

'When?'

'I don't know when.' Marion faltered. 'I ... I just don't know.'

Miranda started crying. Despite a valiant effort not to, Marion gave in and wept too.

'Are you asleep?' whispered Marion.

Miranda sighed. 'I was until you spoke.'

'You can't have been. I said it very quietly.'

'What do you want?'

Marion rolled over and faced Miranda. 'I think we are going to be here a while.' Miranda gasped. 'I know, Mirry. But it seems that way.' Marion stretched her legs and straightened her petticoat. 'I've been thinking. We need to search the yard. Who knows what we might find.'

'I agree, but did you have to wake me up to tell me that?'

'You weren't asleep.'

'Yes I was.'

'Well then, how did you hear me?'

SIXTEEN

Attached to the back of the house was a structure that wobbled when Marion leaned on the doorway. Miranda ducked under the spider's web and stepped into the dusty space. A glassless window at the far end of the building let in light. Against one wall was a sturdy bench with a grubby ceramic bowl. A large oval tub hung on a crude nail to the left of the doorway.

'This looks promising. We should be able to use it for bathing.' Marion took hold of the tub in both hands and lifted it down. Two spiders ran out. She yelped with surprise and dropped the tub.

Miranda screamed and rushed outside. She peered back into the building, admonishing her friend. 'You frightened me. I thought there was a snake.'

'No, only a few spiders and they probably got a bigger fright than we did.'

'I'm going to find a stick before I go back in there. There might be more.'

'I'm sure there will be. But, if we want a bath, we will have to continue. Let's see if the hand basin is clear of spiders.'

A dead rat and some chewed up paper filled the bowl. Miranda pushed at the dried carcass with a stick until it flipped out of the bowl.

'We should fetch some water before we do anything else,' said Marion, as she dusted her hands on the back of her dress.

Marion used the bucket. Miranda filled a kitchen pot with water from the tank.

'Be careful, Miranda, don't spill it. Slosh it around the basin. I'll wash the tub.'

Marion watched the dust disappear into the water. Then the water trickled through the newly uncovered holes onto the ground around her feet. 'Oh dear, there are too many holes.'

Turning to see what Marion was talking about, Miranda missed the bowl completely and water slopped down her dress. She put the pot down on the bench and groaned.

'Don't worry, I've a little left.' Marion poured the water into the bowl and put the bucket down. 'Look, the basin is watertight.' She hugged her friend and patted her back.

'I'm sorry, but this is so awful.' Miranda stepped out of the embrace and walked outside. 'We have such a lovely bathroom at the college. We have two bathrooms back home. One near the kitchen for the men and one upstairs for Mum and me. You can fill the bath right up and lay there for hours.'

'We'll just have to wash from the basin, that's all. At least it's bigger than the one inside. We can boil some water and take turns. I'll let you go first.' Miranda still looked miserable, so Marion spoke cheerfully, 'Let's go and see what else we can find in the yard. Maybe we'll find another tub.'

Sticking close together, they came across a dilapidated chicken coop surrounded by a fence. They stood with their fingers through the wire, peered into the shadows and tried to see if there was anything suitable beyond their reach. They also inspected the toilet. The door hung by one hinge and gaps in the planks meant there was reduced privacy, but thankfully, the pan was empty. Just beyond the house yard, in a barren paddock, they found a water trough partly covered by a fallen windmill.

'This will do admirably.'

Miranda sighed, 'I'm longing for a bath.'

Marion tested the weight of the trough. 'I hope we're strong enough. It's quite a distance to the house.'

Miranda picked up a small plank and tossed it away. 'Will we be able to have a warm bath?'

'There's sufficient wood, but not many matches. Have you seen any more boxes?'

'No.' Miranda gripped one end of the trough and pulled it sideways. 'Let's drag this back, then we can look for some.'

They managed to get the trough up to the back of the house, but in doing so Marion ripped the hem of her dress and Miranda bruised her hands. The idea of a cold bath in a dirty trough wasn't appealing, and after a struggle to get it through the door of the washhouse, their hard work for the day was finished.

Miranda spat on her finger and rubbed at the dirt on Marion's cheek. 'We must look like orphans. Can you imagine what Mrs Appleyard will say?'

Marion folded her arms and lifted her chin. 'Just what do you think you are doing, Miss Miranda? What *will* your mother think, Miss Marion? Please tidy up and present yourself at my office *at once.*'

Miranda was about to cry at the reference to Appleyard College, but Marion pulled such a face she laughed instead. The two girls poked fun at their teachers and school friends, as if nothing were wrong at all.

They washed their face and hands in the recently cleaned bowl, threw the dirty water over the vegetables and returned to the main room.

'We need a bunch of flowers for the table,' said Miranda.

'That would be lovely. See if you can find some.'

Miranda hesitated. 'Come with me.'

'All right, but I'm not walking far. I think I shall go to bed soon.'

Miranda sat down and leaned on the table. 'I'm so very tired too. Perhaps I'll look for the flowers tomorrow.'

'Do you want a tomato? I'm too tired to light the fire.'

'What day is it, Miranda?'

'It's Friday.'

'Are you sure?'

'No, not really.'

'How long have we been here?'

'Maybe, ten days.'

'No, it's not that long. I'm sure it's more like six days.'

Miranda turned her back on Marion before sulking out her reply. 'Well, why did you ask me then?'

'I wanted to know. Mother's party will be soon. I don't want to miss it.'

'I think you will. It's been at least ten days and no one has come yet.'

'No, I told you it's only six,' Marion said more firmly.

'Well, if I'm right you will have missed your mother's birthday party already. So there.'

'Don't be so horrid, Miranda.'

'I don't really care if you have.'

Marion glared at Miranda. 'You don't mean that.'

Miranda threw the hairbrush on the bed. 'I do.' She then walked out of the room.

Marion sat down on the bed and hung her head. She hadn't meant to upset Miranda over such a silly thing. *Does it really matter how many days we've been here? What can I do about it anyway?*

After stomping through the house and slamming the front door,

Miranda realised she'd over-reacted.

A few minutes later, the girls forgave each other. They promised not to argue again and hugged before sitting down to warm pumpkin soup.

As the light of the late summer's evening faded, Miranda numbered lines, twenty to twenty-eight, on a page torn from the journal. 'We can start from today and mark off each day. We'll be back home by the end of the month.'

'I hope so, Miranda. I'm already tired of playing house.'

Spread across the floor of the main bedroom were scarves, socks, trousers, skirts, dresses, undergarments – along with single blankets, various sheets and towels, all tossed from the trunk. Pillows in various stages of decay sat separately. Pieces of linen, cotton fabric and lace covered the bed. In the kitchen, the bench held pots, pans, crockery and cutlery. No more food. No matches.

In the small shed, a row of nails held a rake and a perished hose. A spade and an axe stood behind the door and on the shelf were some well-used small implements. Still no matches.

They shoved the items back into the trunk, tidied the kitchen and resigned themselves to having a cold bath.

It took all afternoon to clean the bath and fill it enough to bathe. Marion sat on the front step with a bowl of weevil-ridden flour while Miranda undressed. There were agonising screams when the cold water hit bare flesh. Miranda complained about having to use an 'awful' towel but, when her ablutions were finished, she felt fresher and more comfortable. She took over the task of picking out weevils while a considerably less vocal Marion bathed.

Then they changed the bathwater and washed some linen. Three towels and two sheets were first, along with a piece of fabric that may have been a tablecloth. It was small, white and with a row of delicate lace down one side. Two tea towels and four pair of tatty drawers were next. When everything was hanging over the chicken coop fence, they soaked one of the velvet curtains. The water turned purple, and when the curtain finally dried, it was six inches shorter.

Another portion of flour became tasteless pancakes, but this time they wrapped them in cabbage leaves.

'Revolting,' said Marion with a grimace.

'I hate greens,' added Miranda.

Another two days passed.

Marion stared out the back door. She thought of her mother,

Woodend and the college. Walking to the open front door, she frowned and thought of Hanging Rock, the buildings that were no longer there, and the impossibility of their circumstance. She shut the door softly.

Miranda sat in the middle of the floor surrounded by clothes and linen pulled out of the trunk.

'I hate doing nothing,' said Marion. 'I'm going outside. Perhaps I'll look at the garden again.'

Miranda folded a towel, looked up and said, 'Don't go any further than that.'

'You'll be okay here, won't you?'

'Yes, I'll sort through and see what's useful.' She was determined to find something else to wear.

Miranda tried on a few shirts, a pair of baggy trousers and squeezed into a sweater that made her arms itch. Looking rather like a scarecrow, she abandoned the sweater and was about to go and show Marion her new outfit when Marion came running into the house, squealing with delight.

'I've found matches. Mirry, Mirry, I found matches.'

Miranda stumbled across the room, trying to hitch up the long trouser legs.

'Look, Miranda.' She placed six boxes on the table. 'They were on the shelf in the shed. We can have a hot bath now. Yes. Yes.'

'But we looked there.'

'I know. We must have missed them.'

Miranda sat down and let the trouser legs tumble over her feet again. 'No, that isn't possible. Remember, I took down the hammer and couldn't hang it back up. I left it on the shelf. There definitely weren't any matches there then. So, where did they come from?'

Marion spent most of the evening trying to figure out how the matches appeared. Miranda chatted on endlessly about the sandwiches they ate at the picnic and the sweet buns one could buy in town.

During the night, there was a brief summer shower. It watered the newly weeded garden and freshened the air.

The following day Miranda surprised Marion with her decision to wear the baggy trousers. 'I'll have to take them up and make a belt. They're too difficult to take in.'

'I can't imagine you wearing men's trousers.'

'Marion, there is nothing else. The woman's clothes are too small and much too fussy. I shall wash my dress to wear when someone takes us home. I don't want to spoil it beforehand.' Miranda frowned and pointed at Marion. 'Look at your dress. You've torn the hem already *and* you're ruining it in the garden. What will your mother say when she finds out?'

Ignoring the reference to her mother, Marion said, 'I know. It's hard to dig in the garden without soiling my clothes.'

'Very well then, you should choose some trousers too. I found a sewing box in the back of the wardrobe. There are buttons, needles, pins, a little lace and many threads, although the big scissors are hard to handle.'

'Oh, Mirry. What are we going to do? I want so much to go home.'

Another bout of tears led to both girls feeling miserable all day.

Miranda proved she had taken notice in Mrs Parrington's sewing class by stitching neat hems on a pair of trousers. She sewed all afternoon and, when Marion came in from finishing her self-imposed chores, she displayed her handiwork.

'Look, Marion. Look at my new blouse.'

Marion let the back door bang as she carried a pumpkin through to the kitchen bench. She was surprised to see her friend twirling around, one hand on her hip and the other hand raised elegantly in the air.

'Why, Miranda, you look most appealing. Who would have thought a girl could look so attractive in men's clothing.'

A binding of blue satin replaced the collar. Miranda had shortened the sleeves and cuffed them immaculately. A small blue bow, held firmly in place with neat stitching, decorated the pocket. The shirt hung over the trousers hiding a belt made of a long piece of cloth.

Miranda stopped twirling and accepted Marion's inspection. 'You need to decide now which shirt you'd like. The grey trousers should be long enough, even for you.'

'I can't sew. *And* I don't have time. The vegetable patch needs a lot of attention.'

Holding two shirts out, Miranda said, 'I wouldn't expect you to. You fuss around in the garden all day. I'll do the sewing.'

Miranda's casual inference to what was hard work offended Marion, but she took the shirts. 'They look so, I don't know, so crumpled. This one has a torn pocket. And they smell awful.'

'I'll wash them once I've finished sewing. Which one do you prefer?'

'This one will do.' Marion tried on the blue one. 'I don't have to have the ribbon and bow, do I?'

'No, I'll leave the collar ... and the sleeves. It will save you from being sunburnt again. I'll remove the cuffs to make it more comfortable – and more ladylike.'

Marion handed over the shirt to Miranda. 'Yes, thank you, I'd like that very much.'

Miranda loved pretty dresses, jewellery and all the feminine trappings. She couldn't wait until she was considered old enough to wear her hair up with diamond clips her father had promised to buy. Raised with four older brothers, she longed for female companionship of her own age. She was delighted to escape the harsh outback and took every opportunity to be more like the elegant Mademoiselle Diane De Poitiers of Appleyard College.

Marion on the other hand, worked hard to emulate her father, Irwin Quade, a barrister. Her lack of interest in feminine pursuits appalled her mother, Ida. Marion was indifferent to her extravagant bedroom and disinterested in the latest clothes sent by English relatives. She was one of the few that enjoyed Miss McCraw's mathematics class and delighted in the challenge of studying French. Marion was a voracious reader and seemed to remember it all.

The two girls complemented each other and became friends on their first day at the College. Miranda was an introspective dreamer, while Marion a strong-willed, promising academic.

SEVENTEEN

Hot days and cool evenings dragged on endlessly. Marion tended the garden while Miranda stayed indoors. Both young women often stood on the verandah and stared into the distance. They hoped to see Sergeant Bumpher, or a local farmer who perhaps, noticing the smoke from the chimney, would investigate. However, there was no one.

'Miranda, come quickly, come quick.'

Miranda dropped her stitching and hurried outside. She was disappointed to find Marion alone. For a few brief wonderful moments, she thought someone had come to rescue them.

'What, Marion? What are you yelling about?'

'Look what was in the shed.'

Miranda peered at the object in Marion's hands. 'What is it?'

'I think it's a rabbit.' She pulled aside the damp bark and let Miranda take a closer look.

'Yes, it's been skinned,' said Miranda, as she gently poked the meat. 'But who put it there?'

'Come on, come inside with me.' Marion pushed Miranda with her elbow, edging her inside.

'Did you see *who* left it? Why didn't they introduce themselves?' Miranda held the door open and stared across the yard, looking for any sign of movement. 'We must find them. They can take us home. Why didn't you stop them? Are they still there?'

Miranda continued talking until finally Marion demanded she stop. 'Miranda, I'll tell you if you just stay quiet long enough for me to do so.'

'All right, but I'm really cross. We should go and look for them.'

'There were only two piccaninnies.'

'Piccaninnies?' She immediately let go of the doorknob.

Marion kept glancing back at the door as she walked towards the kitchen bench. 'I was weeding around some carrots I found.'

'The rabbits will eat them,' Miranda snapped.

'No they won't. I've put some wire netting around the garden.'

'Well, I don't really care what the rabbits do. Tell me about the children,' begged Miranda.

After placing the rabbit in a large pot, Marion sat down at the table. Miranda refused to sit and gripped the back of a chair. 'Please, Marion, what happened?'

'I was weeding the garden, as I said, when I saw two little children run from the shed. I called out for them to stop, but I suppose they didn't hear me. I wondered what they'd been doing.'

'You should have followed them.'

'I was going to, but they ran away before I had a chance. I went to the end of the yard, but then I realised that if I tried to find them you'd be on your own.'

Miranda's anger started to abate. 'I guess if there are small children there must be parents.' She sat down. 'Marion, now I'm frightened.'

'I'm a little worried too. When I saw the children, I didn't know what to do. I knew you'd want me to go after them, but ...'

Miranda shuddered. She peeped out the back window. Her eyes searched the bush beyond the yard. She pulled firmly on the door.

'Come away, Miranda. I'm sure they've gone.'

After dicing pumpkin and placing it in the pot with the rabbit and hot water, Marion reconsidered the incident. 'Miranda, I've had second thoughts. If the Aborigines were going to harm us, they would have done so by now.'

'I hope you're right,' said Miranda. She took the fork from Marion and pushed at the rabbit.

'Father said there are many kind Aborigines. They just aren't always given a chance.'

Miranda's head shot up as if she were going to argue, but she sighed and said, 'If they left us this rabbit they mustn't be going to hurt us.'

'I agree,' said Marion. She replaced the lid on the pot.

As they waited for dinner to cook, Miranda asked quietly, 'Why hasn't anyone come for us?'

'I don't know.'

'If there are Aborigines here, why isn't there anyone else?'

'I don't know.'

'Why don't the Aborigines take us home?'

'I believe they can't.'

'There must be something we can do, Marion.'

'But what?'

'I don't know,' Miranda said, as she sniffed away a threatening tear. 'We have to think of something.'

Marion returned to the stove and looked in the pot again. She tested the softening meat with the fork. 'We will have to go back to Hanging Rock again.' She replaced the lid.

'It's such a long way.'

'I know, but it's the only thing we can do.' She stared at the pot, resisting the urge to lift the lid again.

'Marion, how far do you think it is?'

'It's about as far as Appleyard College is to the main road. It must be two miles at least,' replied Marion, recalling what her mother once said.

'Two miles? No wonder it takes so long.'

'Don't you want to go, Miranda?'

Miranda nodded. 'I suppose we must, but I was sure that someone would've found our marks on the track and come here.'

Marion sighed, 'I can't work out why there aren't a lot of people looking for us. We haven't seen one person.'

'My father would've sent Johnno.'

'Johnno? You talked about him the other night.'

Miranda nodded. 'He's Dad's foreman. I know he'd send Johnno. He might even come himself.'

The pot boiled over and Marion grabbed the lid. Miranda snatched a rag and pulled the pot to the side of the stovetop.

The next morning, dressed in their recently laundered dresses, the two girls walked to Hanging Rock again. They were disheartened to discover rain had washed away their arrows. They scouted around the area close to the rock. No one answered their calls. When the sun was high in the sky, Miranda refused to move from the flat grass under the shade. Despite the agreeable weather, no one was picnicking at Hanging Rock.

Marion wished she were able to study the formations more closely. Even though Hanging Rock had lost its innocent appeal, the mamelon intrigued her. She thought about the information gleaned from a library book on the day before the picnic. The formidable formation of volcanic walls was at least five hundred feet in height at the highest peak and millions of years old. She shivered as the clouds shifted and formed a sudden darkness over the rock face.

'Miranda, this is an interesting place. I wish I had more information.'

Miranda pulled the most hideous face. 'Surely you don't mean that. This is a terrifying place.'

With a deep sigh, Marion agreed. 'But if we hadn't been swept up with that awful wind, and ended up … lost, then I would have liked to study this place some more. Do you know that back in the eighteen thirties, a Major Thomas Mitchell named it Mount Diogenes?'

'I don't care what it was called. I wish I'd never come here and I don't want you to talk about it.'

'Don't put upon me so much. I certainly would rather not be stuck here, but … it is a very interesting place.'

Miranda hurried off leaving Marion gazing up at the rock.

Marion found her sitting near the stream where, on the day of the school picnic, they saw two young men watching them. After several minutes of silence Marion spoke, 'Don't be cross with me, Miranda. Think of this spot by the water. It's lovely here; so calm and peaceful.'

Haunted eyes looked back at Marion. 'I sincerely wish I had stayed here and talked to those chaps instead of going up into the rock.'

'I felt compelled to climb into the rock,' explained Marion. 'I remember you not saying a word, just climbing higher and higher. Edith kept screaming at us to come back. I was in a daze.'

'Yes, I felt like I was in a trance too. I wish … dear me, why can't we just go home. I do so want to go home.'

'Don't be disheartened. Someone will come soon. I'm sure they will. Come on, let's gather stones and make some more arrows. Rain can't wash away stones.'

The girls arranged stones into their initials and arrows. Both girls held as many pebbles as possible and built more arrows on the way. By the time they reached the fallen fence posts, their dresses were grubby again.

Miranda finished two sets of clothes for each of them. She shortened trousers, altered shirts and made under-blouses from the tops of old dresses. Knickerbockers were stitched from full skirts and they giggled as they tried on the brightly coloured undergarments. With a burst of laughter, Miranda suggested Gwendolyn from Belle's Fashion Shoppe in Woodend's main street would keep them in the back room for her special clients.

The grapevines sprouted and they discovered an apple tree not far from where the water trough had been. Carrots and cabbages did well with Marion's attention and she discovered onions and spinach growing next to the washhouse. Her hands looked like those of Walter the stableman and she wished for some of her mother's hand cream.

Marion spent several evenings trying to get comfortable on a wooden chair. A folded blanket provided some relief, but her eyes kept sneaking to the distasteful couch. She wondered how she could turn the couch into useful seating. *Surely something can be done to improve it.* They'd picked off the debris, but were unsure what to do with the damaged upholstery and the irregular padding. Marion chose to tackle one thing at a time.

'What on earth are you doing?' asked Miranda, when she came back from the outhouse.

Marion's arm stretched under the tweed covering. Bits of padding were all over the floor. She stood up and blew some fluff from her lip. Miranda picked a piece of kapok from Marion's hair.

'I'm trying to make this couch bearable to sit on,' she said, as another piece of padding fell to the floor.

Miranda chuckled. 'I hope you can get it back together.'

'So do I.' Marion frowned. 'I've sponged off the bird droppings and if I can spread out the padding, the seat should be comfortable enough.'

'It might be comfortable, but the material is stained and terribly torn. Look at it.' Miranda poked her finger into one hole, then another. She was tugging on the edge of a third when Marion hit her arm.

'Don't do that. You'll make it worse.'

'Well,' said Miranda, as she turned away, 'I won't sit on it.'

Marion ignored her friend and continued to spread the padding as best she could. She admitted that Miranda was right about the damaged cover. She rummaged through the trunk and found a suitably sized piece of material. After tacking the material to the back of the frame, Marion stood back and admired her efforts. She disregarded the tweed arms. Half the couch was now smattered with bright colours. It looked cheerful and made her smile. Marion thought it didn't matter that the other half was faded. She liked the overall effect.

Marion was wriggling on the couch, testing the comfort, when Miranda emerged from the small bedroom, pulling a mattress across the floor.

'What are you going to do with that?' asked Marion.

Miranda stopped and let the mattress plop to the floor. 'Look at you sitting in the middle. You have cheerfulness on one side, misery on the other. What is *that* all about? Is it a choice?' She pointed at Marion. 'What will you choose?' Her hand dropped to her side. 'What will I choose?'

Miranda fell on top of the mattress and lay looking up at the ceiling softly chanting, 'Purple or grey, purple or grey.'

Marion jumped up, turned around and stared at the couch. 'In heaven's name, Miranda, what are you going on about?' She turned back to Miranda. 'Anyway, I'm not changing it. I like it.'

Raising herself into a cross-legged position, Miranda said, 'Of course it can stay. It will be nice to have somewhere more comfortable to sit.' She patted the mattress. 'Come, have a good view of your work, Marion May. Let's make a decision.'

As they sat on the mattress and looked at the couch, Miranda stared at the side of Marion's head waiting for an answer. She poked Marion's thin arm, continuing to say purple or grey until Marion reacted.

'Stop it, Miranda. You're hurting me.'

Miranda rubbed the spot her finger had been prodding. 'Sorry, Marion.'

Marion pushed her friend's hand away and scowled. 'Don't do that either.'

Letting out a deep sigh, Miranda said, 'We need to keep going back to Hanging Rock on the weekends. It's the most likely time for people to be there.'

Miranda's suggestion surprised Marion and she challenged the idea. 'But we don't know what day it is. How can we know when to go?'

'We can go on a different day each week.' Miranda's head bobbed repeatedly. 'Then we might get lucky.'

'So, you say we should go once a week to Hanging Rock?'

'Yes.'

The brief silence was broken when Miranda asked again, 'Purple or grey, Marion?'

'What are you talking about?'

'The couch.'

'What about it?'

'You sat in the middle not choosing one or the other.'

'I sat on the couch!' exclaimed Marion.

'Well, I know. But don't you see; it might be a long time before we are found.'

Marion gripped her friend's arm. 'We might never be found. Never. Never. Have you thought of that?'

'No. I don't want to think that.' Miranda shook her arm free.

'We must. For some reason they can't find us.'

'I won't believe that. They'll keep looking. Or, someone who isn't looking will find us.' Miranda hit the mattress with her closed fist then rolled onto her back and lay still. After a while, she poked Marion again and said, 'In the meantime we must choose.'

Marion lay down beside Miranda and looked at a cobweb in the corner of the ceiling. 'You said that already, Mirry. I don't understand. Choose what?'

Turning over and facing her friend, Miranda said, 'Mum always says we have a choice in being happy or not. Like when it rains on your birthday and you've planned an outside party.'

'Like Mother's.' Marion said, as she sat up.

'Yes, like that. You can stay inside being miserable because you can't play Hide-and-Seek in the garden or you can be happy and play Pin-the-Tail-on-the-Donkey. The birthday cake remains the same. It's up to you. That's what Mum says.'

Marion leaned over and kissed Miranda on the cheek. 'You're right. I'll sit on the grey side of the couch so I can see the bright colours. Let's choose to be happy.'

'But we have to keep trying to find our way home.'

'Yes, of course. Once a week. On different days.'

'And we might still cry sometimes.'

'I'm sure we will. I miss Mother.'

They sat quietly, thinking of home.

After a few moments, Miranda poked Marion on the arm again. 'I like wearing these clothes. Look how we can sit cross-legged. Mademoiselle wouldn't like us doing that. Do you know Marjorie called Petunia a tart when she found her sitting like this on the front lawn at lunch time?'

Both girls giggled.

'It is comfortable, isn't it?' said Miranda.

'Yes, and I can bend over and remain respectable.'

'They're rather hot. I might make some out of the old petticoats in the trunk. I'll have to work around the torn bits, but the material is much lighter.'

'What about a pattern?'

'I'll just follow the shape of the trousers.'

'You are clever. I wouldn't have thought of that.'

Miranda intended to remove the kapok from the mattress and add it to the couch, but as Marion had already completed the repairs, she changed her mind.

She refused to believe they would *never* be found – Marion was wrong about that. However, if they were to be here for a while longer, then she wanted some privacy. Separate bedrooms would be much better.

She tugged the mattress closer to the front door and leaned it against the wall.

Daylight was disappearing and, as they hadn't found any way to light the house, all activity had to cease. Bedtime came early.

'What are you going to do with the mattress?' Marion asked, as they lay in bed.

'It needs airing. I'm going to put it in the sun and, hopefully, it will become fresher.'

'Why?'

'I'm going to sleep in the other room.'

Marion rolled onto her side and propped her head on her bent arm. 'There's no need to do that. I'm happy to share.'

'But you snore, and I wake up. It's better to use both rooms.'

Laying down again, Marion said, 'You were too scared to even have me leave the room. What's changed?'

'Your couch.'

'My couch?'

'Well, Mum's theory.'

Marion thought about it for such a long time that Miranda fell asleep before Marion answered, 'Oh, that.'

EIGHTEEN

They continued walking to Hanging Rock one day a week. Each time they left the rock, they checked the arrows. They were their symbols of hope.

The supply of pumpkin was almost finished. They hoped the saved seeds would prove fruitful. 'If we're still here next season.' They wished lemons were more useful.

Many hours were idled away under the lemon tree. They talked about family and friends they missed, giggled over antics of the past, and tried to guess what was happening in the world to which they no longer belonged.

A fresh batch of carrots was almost ready to harvest, but the grapes were still forming. Several days went by with little to eat. Then Marion came back from the shed with a portion of meat and several rough-barked branches with red fruit attached.

'What are they? Can we eat them?' asked Miranda.

'I don't know what they are, but I've seen several of these pale-leafed trees near the rock.'

'It's the Aborigines helping us again, isn't it?'

'I suppose so. The fruit was with the meat.'

'I guess we can trust them by now.'

They peeled away the waxy skin and discovered white flesh covering a hard nut. After tasting a small portion, neither became ill, so the next day they consumed the remaining fruit.

'It's lovely, Miranda. Tastes a little like a peach.'

'I hope you can find those trees again.'

Miranda sat in the mellow afternoon sun with her eyes closed, trying to ignore the events of the last six months.

The food supply gradually improved. The tree beyond the fence posts turned out to be an almond tree. The apple tree was flowering and a sparsely leafed tree eventually bore oranges. The vegetables thrived.

Marion and Miranda enjoyed another rabbit stew with stale damper soaking up the liquid. However, they were missing familiar meals.

Marion discovered a recipe book in the trunk, but with so few ingredients, she found it difficult to create anything but the simplest of dishes. Miranda did most other household chores. She hated the cooking lessons Appleyard College insisted the students attend. Mrs Featherstone was adamant that a lady should know how to cook so she could keep an educated eye on her staff. Miranda concluded that this was easily overcome by employing the right housekeeper.

Miranda's thoughts turned to the sumptuous food her mum organised with Bridget. She remembered the beef pie – flaky pastry with generous chunks of meat – chicken soup, sago pudding with cinnamon cream, and crunchy bread with freshly churned butter. Sunday roast with crispy potatoes – delightful.

Currant buns, trifles and sponge cake crossed Miranda's mind. Devilled sausages, bacon and eggs for breakfast – the thought made her mouth water.

When she heard cackling, she assumed she was still daydreaming of eggs on hot toast with mountains of butter. On hearing a second burst of chicken-talk, Miranda opened one eye and peeped around. Her second eye opened twice as quickly and twice as wide.

'A chicken!'

Deciding the chicken wasn't a mirage, she jumped to her feet. She walked with her arms outstretched. 'Shoo, shoo, chicken,' she began gently. She tried to move the bird towards the back of the house. 'Marion! Marion, come here and help. Quickly, Marion.'

Marion shoved the spade into the soil and stomped over the pile of dead weeds. *What is so urgent?* Miranda was usually reluctant to work outside, continually complaining about the dirt. She often refused to help trim the grass, despite the threat of snakes.

Marion's mood changed the instant she rounded the corner of the house. A hen stood perfectly still. Its beady eyes stared at Miranda. Marion walked slowly forward, flapping her hands in an attempt to help move the chicken into a corner.

'Where did you find it?' Marion whispered, as she edged alongside her friend.

The hen observed its adversaries before it scampered between the two startled girls.

'Get it, get it.'

'Quick! Run!'

'Catch it!'

The chicken ran. The girls tried to grab it. It squawked as it raced around the fig tree and past the vegetable garden. Its wings flapped. Its feet hardly touched the ground.

Marion stood between the trunk of the fig tree and the coop waiting for the unsuspecting bird to come her way. She jumped out from her hiding spot and grabbed at the hen. The chicken slipped through her fingers and scuttled away with one less feather. Marion dived at the chicken again. She fell flat on her face. Miranda was trying to catch her breath when the little hen came towards her. She stuck out her leg. The bird ran across it. Miranda fell on her bottom and watched her prey disappear behind the shed.

'Bother,' shouted Miranda. 'It's got away.' She looked down at her clothes. 'How awful. I'm filthy.'

Marion spat the pieces of grass and dirt out of her mouth. She stamped her feet and cursed the chicken. Clucking triumphantly, the hen strutted into view. Frustratingly out of reach.

After watching the hen search for food for several minutes, Miranda remembered that her father's cattle would walk miles for fresh grass. Similarly, the college's cats responded to food in an instant. 'Have we got any food for the chicken?' she asked.

'What do they eat, Miranda?'

'Wheat. Grain of any sort. Scraps.'

'I could gather some scraps from the vegetable garden.'

Miranda shook her head. 'Perhaps there's something in the coop.'

They left the bird to roam freely and gingerly entered the chicken yard. Marion swiped at the long grass with the spade. Miranda brushed away a thick layer of spiders' webs with a broom. They crouched down and searched through the small coop. A large drum, standing at the back of the coop, held a substantial quantity of grain. Marion half-filled a small tin and attempted to attract the hen by rattling the grain, but the bird didn't lift its head.

'Let's sprinkle some grain inside the yard,' said Miranda.

After an impatient wait, Marion asked, 'Why doesn't it want it?'

'We should make the trail longer so it finds it quicker.'

'Yes, let's do that. Do you think it came from here originally?'

'It must have. Dad said there was a huge drought down south; that is, around these parts. Many sheep farmers walked off their properties. Then prices of lamb went up and people bought more beef. Good for our family in Queensland, but not for sheep farmers.'

'I guess the poor little chicken has been scratching around in the bush ever since. It's lucky to have survived. I'm sure there are foxes in the bush.'

'Then it is lucky. I wonder how long it's been wandering around.'

'Quite some time if you look at the state of the house,' said Marion.

'But the chicken isn't very old, so it can't be too long ago. Look.' Miranda tapped Marion's arm. 'Look, it's pecking at the grain.'

It took several more minutes before the hungry hen ate its way into the coop. They sprang into action and squabbled over the task of securing the wobbly gate.

After they returned to the kitchen, the two girls washed their hands and celebrated their success with a cool lemon drink.

'Are we going to eat the chicken?'

'I've been thinking about that,' said Marion. 'What do you think?'

'We'd have to kill it. And clean it.'

'That means pulling its feathers out.'

'Could you kill it, Marion?'

'No. What about you? You're the country girl.'

'I'm certainly not going to kill the chicken.' Miranda shivered. 'All those innards. It's disgusting.'

'Then we can't eat it.'

'Maybe it will lay an egg.' Miranda sighed, 'I was dreaming of bacon and eggs.'

'There's no bacon, but if the hen co-operates we might have an egg tomorrow.'

The next morning when Miranda went out to see if there was an egg, the red hen met her at the door.

'Oh no, Marion, the chicken has escaped.'

In the end, they presumed the hen wouldn't wander too far from the ready-made source of food. Miranda put aside her objections to manual work and helped clear the grass in the chicken enclosure. There were many squeals as they dealt with the numerous resident spiders and small lizards. The coop leaned slightly, but it had a decent roof and a long roosting perch. The girls stretched wire across the many holes and poked pieces of wood into the larger gaps. They shifted the drum of grain to the shed, leaving little room for anything else. With broken fingernails and numerous scratches from their two-day effort, the young women finally declared the chicken run finished.

Lucky, the newly named hen, was content in its new home and eventually produced an egg. A couple of days later, they were surprised to find a black hen scratching at the wire, trying to get to the feed. They opened the gate and it strutted inside. Over the next week, the brood of fowls grew to five hens and one rather scruffy rooster.

Several years after Marion and Miranda settled into a life of routine, the landscape dried out, shrinking and splitting under brittle grass.

Clouds almost forgot to rain, even in winter. The water tank echoed as Marion banged on the corrugated metal. They hardly dared to use even four inches of water for their weekly bath.

The battle with the weather took another turn when the streams swelled with an over-abundance of rain; flooding across the pathways. They grew tired of sloshing through puddles. Washing took forever to dry. It was a battle to keep enough wood covered to use for warming the house. A light fall of snow covered the top of Mt Macedon. Icy rain accompanying vicious winds kept them indoors for weeks.

One dry year – when the grass crackled under their feet and the air seemed hot enough to make one's breath smoulder – a spread of smoke covered the horizon. They watched as fierce gusty winds pushed the smoke parallel to the edge of their yard, but thankfully, several miles away. A second fire threatened to come closer. They could see the flames over the tops of the trees, swallowing the leaves without a care. They filled the bath, the bucket and the basin they used for the dishes, and waited. Fortune favoured them. The wind changed and blew the snapping fire back across Mt Macedon.

Days were mostly slow moving, but the years evaporated swiftly. After many calendar pages were written and many more forgotten, Marion and Miranda realised they'd missed their birthdays again, and another Christmas.

'We can't celebrate Christmas now. It's too cold. It must be May or, if we've calculated wrongly, June.'

'I suppose it must be. Your birthday is the eighteenth of June, isn't it, Miranda?'

'Yes. It would be nice to have a party.'

'Well, let's start a calendar again. We'll just have to guess at today's date.'

'Mum always celebrates her birthday with her sisters. Marion, I remember how jolly her last one was. Aunt Jane gave her some perfume and I ended up with a half-empty bottle of Lilly of the Valley. The scent reminded me of a garden.'

Marion pressed three daisy-like flowers between two pieces of paper and weighted it down with a log. She made glue out of flour and water. The flowers clung insecurely on cardboard torn from a book in the trunk.

'How lovely,' Miranda said, when she received the gift. 'I'll keep it on the dresser.' She kissed Marion on the cheek. 'Thank you.'

They spent the evening reminiscing over parties they attended. High on the list was the Mayor's celebration for his injured son who returned from the Boer War. Streamers hung across the streets of Woodend. Everyone participated in the singing and dancing. Marion admitted sneaking some sherry from the supper table. Miranda confessed to having three dances with the good-looking Bert.

The young women traipsed off to bed in a good mood, both with their special memories to ease them into peaceful sleep.

They no longer wore their dresses when they walked to the rock. It didn't matter what they were wearing when the miracle of rescue occurred.

Miranda refused to accept no one would find them. She always spoke of *when*, but then contradicting herself, asked Marion, 'Do you think we will be found?'

On most occasions, Marion would simply answer yes, but one time she found the repetitive question so maddening she decided to be honest.

'Miranda, it has been so long. I don't think it will happen.'

'But it's still possible.'

'I'm not sure. There's something odd about our situation. I can't explain, but it's been ever so long.'

'Marion, we don't know how long it's been. We could have got the pages mixed up.'

Marion hated to upset her friend, even though the unwanted barrage was irritating her. She admitted to herself they mightn't be found, but there was always a smidgeon of hope, so she resorted to her usual answer, 'Yes, Miranda, one day we'll be found.' Her deadpan voice didn't stop Miranda from asking again.

'But do you *really* think so?'

'Stop it,' Marion shrieked. 'Stop asking. We have to think so. Otherwise we might just as well give up and die.'

'Marion, I don't want to die. I want to go home. I want to get a new dress. I want to have Bridget's roast beef. I want to see Sara. I don't want to die. I just want to go home.'

Marion felt like screaming again, but knew it wouldn't achieve anything. She sighed, 'For goodness sake, so do I. I would love to have a hot bath without having to spend so long carting water. I want to get some sturdy shoes. Is Mother keeping well? We've missed so much history. Is Mr McLean still Premier? I want ... I want to know so many things. I also want you not to go on about it. It just makes it worse.'

Marion stormed off to the chickens. She stood with her fingers entwined in the wire mesh. It was true. She wanted to go home, but she didn't know how that could happen.

Because of Miranda's latest inquisition, Marion considered the question thoughtfully. *Will we ever be found?* It was improbable. Her heart pounded as she bore this confronting realisation. If that were true, if people had stopped looking for them, then they would have to find their own way out. But, thought Marion, there's something else. Something that isn't just about *them* not looking, or *us* not finding. Some puzzle which doesn't have an explanation. She remembered her father saying that there is an answer to everything. *Well, Father, I'd like to discover the answer to this one.*

'Here chickens, chick, chick,' she called, waving a stalk of grass at them. They rushed over, but strutted away in disgust. Walking around to the gate, she pushed past the rooster and collected two eggs. 'Ah, breakfast. Thanks girls.'

NINETEEN

After a tiring day with a new shipment to unwrap and check, Rebecca was hoping for a quiet Thursday evening. Closing time couldn't come quickly enough. During the evening she secured the sale of an expensive tea-set and an excited teenager parted with pocket money for a china duck to add to her collection. As Rebecca adjusted the ornaments to fill empty spaces, someone tapped her shoulder. She turned slowly and was surprised to see Michael.

'Oh, hi.' She automatically straightened her jacket.

'Hi. Thought I'd drop in and see where you work.'

Rebecca glanced around and spotted Jan, her boss, talking to another customer. 'Cool! It's been quite busy. My feet are killing me.'

Michael pushed up his sleeve and checked his watch. 'Not long, it's nearly eight o'clock.'

'Thank goodness. Thursdays seem to go on forever.' She fiddled with some photo frames. 'Do you want to look around?'

'I had a quick look while I was trying to find you. You've got some awesome stuff.'

'Did you want something in particular?'

He lowered his voice, 'Yep, and I'm hoping you'll help me.'

'Of course, what are you looking for?'

Michael grinned and leaned closer. 'I was rather hoping you'd come for coffee when you've finished here.'

Dropping her head to hide a smile, Rebecca said, 'That'll be great. Ten minutes?'

He smiled back. 'Good. I'll wait outside.'

'Okay, see you soon.'

Peeking out through the window display, she watched him walk up the street.

Jan came up behind Rebecca and saw Michael's tall slim figure. 'I guess that's Michael?'

Rebecca spun around. 'You made me jump. Yep, that's Michael.'

'Sorry. He certainly lives up to your description. Very well in fact.'

Rebecca grinned to cover her embarrassment. Jan was amused when Rebecca requested the morning off to attend the news conference in May. Jan thought it was an odd way to 'find a fella'.

Jan shooed Rebecca towards the back room. 'Off you go. I can finish up here.'

'Are you sure?' But she moved towards the cupboard that held their handbags.

Turning over the sign that declared the shop was closed, Jan chuckled, 'I can see you're itching to go. I'll lock the door behind you.'

Rebecca ran her fingers through her fringe and tightened her ponytail. She squirted some perfume from a sample bottle onto her wrist. 'Thanks, Jan, see you tomorrow.'

'Have a good evening.'

Michael was waiting on the footpath near his car. He stepped towards Rebecca as she approached. 'You ready for a decent coffee?'

'As long as I can sit while I'm drinking it.'

'Do you know somewhere close?'

'The café around the corner isn't too bad. Their coffee's strong and Jimmy makes a mean toasted sandwich.'

'Right then, Jimmy's it is. I guess you haven't had dinner?'

Shaking her head, Rebecca said, 'Just an apple and a cup of tea at six o'clock. What about you? Have you eaten?'

As he opened the door to the welcoming aroma of coffee, he said, 'Yep, but I can always go an egg and bacon sandwich.'

Once they ordered, Rebecca continued to sigh over the relief of sitting.

Michael spoke softly, 'I find it difficult to sit all day, staring at that god-awful screen.'

'Really? Most days I'd give anything to be able to sit for even five minutes.'

Without commenting, Michael shook his head and said, 'I cursed at being stuck out there in the endless bush. Now ...' His mouth twisted and he paused before continuing, 'today at lunch time I walked around frantic streets and wished for some peace and quiet.'

Rebecca noticed Michael's jagged nails and wondered if they were the result of manual labour or if he picked at them when he was nervous. When he became aware of her gaze, he put them under the table.

'Does that mean your day didn't go too well?' she asked.

Michael considered his answer. 'Before I went to Hanging Rock, I probably would've said it was okay. I mean, nothing went *wrong*. My boss even complimented me on how efficiently I resolved a particular problem.'

Their order arrived and Rebecca started eating. Michael twice picked up his cup and put it down before adding two spoons of sugar. Stirring the liquid slowly, he looked up. 'Bec, it was such an experience. I didn't ... and still don't understand why it happened. But the whole thing has changed me.'

Rebecca swallowed another piece of toasted crust. 'I bet, and you're coping so well.' Her voice turned to a whisper. 'How did it change you?'

Michael took his time to place the teaspoon in line with the edge of the saucer. 'Mostly a change in attitude. Some of it's hard to put into words.' He shifted the spoon again. 'I can't be bothered with people who complain about not having stuff. I mean, one of the guys at work was going on about a lack of credit on his card to pay for some concert at two hundred dollars a seat. Someone else complained her iPad was playing up. Shit – so what?' He lifted the corner of the toast and stared at the bacon. Then he grinned, and said, 'I keep getting the feeling of wanting to sit by myself ... and contemplate my navel ... or something equally stimulating.'

The change in sentiment caught Rebecca off-guard. She laughed and almost choked on a piece of cheese. He poured some water and offered it to her.

'What will you do about it?' Rebecca finally managed to ask.

Michael sighed and picked up his sandwich. 'It's taking some time to come to terms with it all.'

'It sounds like it's made you restless.'

'Totally.'

'Well, I'm here if you want to tell me more.'

'Thanks.'

TWENTY

Marion thought that something beyond the ordinary had engulfed them.

Their attempts to re-create the moment when they fell into a lost world failed. They occasionally crawled through the same gap where they last saw Irma and sat and waited for something to happen. Once, a gust of wind spiralled around them in haunting whispers. Miranda's fingernails left imprints on Marion's fright-induced damp palms. The wind ceased and a cloud of dust settled, but nothing else changed.

Tumbling rocks narrowly missed them another time. They were petrified and scurried down the slope carefully avoiding the loose stones. It was only when they reached the safety of the flat grass at the bottom that they dared to stop and look back at the crumbled mass.

Miranda wouldn't go the following week and Marion didn't bother on her own.

The bush beyond the unused paddocks revealed little. There were plenty of wild flowers, small creatures, a disinterested wallaby or two, but no evidence of human habitation. They found wild honeybees and a seasonal patch of mushrooms on subsequent outings. Trampled grasses made their well-travelled tracks easier to follow. Many times, they stopped for lunch, ate the packed damper and apples, and sat listening to the sounds of the bush before heading back home.

Marion thought it was time to find out what was beyond their usual boundaries. Armed with boiled eggs wrapped in cabbage leaves and a couple of apples in the bucket, they set off in the opposite direction from Hanging Rock. Lizards scurried away from their feet. They munched on the apples as they walked through unfamiliar bush. Later, they rested and ate the eggs.

'Can you hear running water, Marion? Stand still. Listen.'

'Yes, I can. A river. How wonderful.'

They hurried towards the sound of rushing water and were overjoyed to find a creek that tumbled over rocks and fell into a small pool right at their feet. Marion rolled up her trousers and paddled into the cold water.

'Come on, Mirry, this is delightful.'

'Is it cold?'

'Yes, but it's beautiful. Maybe I'll have a swim.'

'Marion, it's not dark enough.'

'I don't care. I'm hot from all the walking. Anyway, who is there to see us?'

Miranda stood at the water's edge with her arms folded.

'Look at you, standing there all hot and bothered just because of some silly old rule that doesn't exist here. Anyway, I've always thought that it is ludicrous that men can swim in the daytime and women can't.' Marion walked out of the shallows and removed her shirt and trousers, flinging them away so they landed on dry grass. 'Forget all that.' She returned to the river, scooped up water and let it dribble down her body. 'It's delightful. You'll enjoy it.'

Miranda stood in the refreshing water for a few minutes, hurried to where Marion's trousers were and removed her clothes. She lay down in the water a little way from Marion and splashed water over her naked body.

At first, Marion couldn't look at the pale skin of her friend. Then she peeped at the soft lines of a girl who had turned into a woman. Miranda's eyes were closed and her hair floated away from her face. Marion continued to admire the slim waist, the gentle curve of her hips and the cluster of pubic hair. Entranced by the beauty of the female shape, she placed her hands over her own breasts and considered the transformation that until today was mostly unacknowledged.

Miranda was now on her feet, dancing around in the shallows, skipping over the small rocks and splashing water towards Marion. 'Come on, Marion. It's just as you said. Delightful.'

Marion removed her drawers and camisole and together the two girls splashed around in the water. They lay in the deepest part of the creek until they shivered.

Later, with their teeth chattering, the two girls dressed. Marion left off her wet undergarments and felt uncommonly bare.

'We must come here again,' said Miranda.

'Mmm,' replied Marion, as she wondered if they would be punished for their wickedness. Mother told her that a lady never let anyone see her without clothes. *Well, what more could happen to us?* Mind you, she thought, someone is looking after us. Hadn't the chickens appeared and then hatched more every other year? And, there were the items that mysteriously appeared in the shed. 'God bless the shed,' she said, not realising she had spoken aloud.

'What? What about the shed?'

'I was just thinking about the shed. It's been a blessing.'

'We know it's the Aborigines who leave the food.'

'Yes, but the matches and the chicken feed that never runs out. How does that happen?'

'So many peculiar things happen. What about the tea?' asked Miranda, as they wandered back home.

'Who knows? I'm just glad it does.'

The pleasurable feeling stayed with them for hours.

The stream became a much-visited location. When the sun raged on the roof and made the house unbearable, they stayed at the stream as long as they dared. As the gentle autumn days moved into early winter, they enjoyed lazing on the rocks.

On one such placid day, while Miranda paddled around in the shallows, Marion walked further up-stream. She saw fish swimming around; some were large enough to eat.

'Miranda,' she yelled to her friend, 'do you have any sort of pin on you?'

'Pardon?' Miranda called back, as she shuffled through the water.

'Shush. Stand still. Don't frighten the fish.'

'Fish?' She hurried out of the water. 'Oh yes. Look!'

'Do you have a pin?'

Miranda stepped gingerly across the ground. 'Yes, it's holding my shirt together. The button fell off. Why?'

'May I use it?'

'What do you want it for?'

'The fish – I'm going to try and catch one.'

'Can I help?'

'Yes, pass me the pin. I'm going to use my belt.'

She tied the safety pin onto the belt with her hair ribbon. A berry became the bait. It took quite some time before the odd fishing equipment was effective.

They laughed at Marion's success, and planned to dig for worms next time.

On another day, when it was too cool to swim, they wandered along the banks of the stream in the other direction. They moved away from the soft ground of the water's edge, intending to walk the shorter way back to the farmhouse. Miranda picked wildflowers. Marion swung the bucket in time to her soft humming. When they had walked for ten minutes, they were surprised to find a windmill, some fence posts and the remains of a small outbuilding. Pieces of timber lay across the track.

'That's astonishing,' said Marion. 'I don't remember seeing this. Do you?'

Miranda stared at a pile of bricks. 'Are you sure we've come this way before?'

'Many times. We come this way when we spend too long at the swimming hole.' Marion watched the wind-mill spin. 'I wonder how we could use this.'

Miranda tugged on Marion's shirt. 'Do come on, if there's a windmill, there might be a house.'

Excitement built as they hurried along an uneven brick path. The path ended abruptly at the charred re-mains of a large homestead. They stood silently, disappointed at finding a pile of bricks and charred timbers.

'Oh dear, there's been a fire.'

'Everything is burnt. I was hoping to find something,' cried Miranda.

'We still might. There's a lot of rubble, but perhaps *something* might have survived.'

'I meant I was hoping to find some *one*.' Miranda stood with her arms folded. She scanned the devastation and squinted back towards the windmill.

'Mirry, I'm sorry, but I don't think we will.' Marion touched Miranda's arm gently. 'Cheer up, you may find something pretty.'

They trod carefully around the cold charred timbers and damaged possessions. Marion disregarded the crushed stoneware, but was interested in a partially burnt book caught under distorted tins. Miranda pounced on a triangular piece of blue glass and a cracked ceramic rabbit. A glint of silver had her dropping the glass and pulling a mirror from the rubble.

'Look, Marion, a mirror. I'm going to keep this.'

Marion dusted ash from the book and walked over to Miranda. 'Does it have a reflection?'

Miranda twisted the decorative mirror around. 'Reflection? Of course. It's a mirror.'

'I just wondered. There have been so many strange happenings I wondered if we're not really living.'

'What a funny thing to say. Anyway, whatever has that to do with a mirror?'

'Ghosts, Miranda. Ghosts are said to have no re-flection.'

'Good heavens, I'm certainly not a ghost. Have a look, Marion. See if I've been living with a ghost all these years.'

They took turns at looking in the mirror. Both exclaimed how 'simply dreadful' they looked.

'My hair, it's awful,' said Miranda, as she passed the mirror to Marion again.

'Ugh. I look like Aunt Ruthie. Perhaps I should cut my hair.' She extended her hand towards Miranda. 'You can keep the mirror. I don't want it. I found something much better.'

Miranda reclaimed the mirror. 'What have you found?'

'A book. Look.'

'It's burnt.'

'Well,' said Marion, a little put out, 'there are many chapters that aren't damaged.' She picked at the cover. 'I'll be pleased to have something to read.'

'I hope we can carry everything,' said Miranda.

'It depends if they'll all fit in the bucket.'

'My pieces are quite small. What do you have?'

'Not much apart from three books, so I guess we won't need to find a horse and cart.'

They both giggled at the unlikely occurrence.

Moments later, Miranda squealed with delight. Marion let the length of wire she was considering fall to the ground and hurried to where her friend was jumping up and down.

'Look, a lamp. Oh, this is the best piece I've found. A light. Hurray.'

'It's lovely, Miranda, hardly damaged at all. Now we just need some kerosene.'

Miranda dropped the light and stomped away. She called back to Marion, 'I thought I'd found something worthwhile.'

Marion yelled at her, 'It didn't break, did it? I just meant we need some oil of some kind. Please, pick it up and put it with the other things.'

Miranda's mood didn't improve until Marion found some plain hair slides and offered them to her more egocentric companion.

At the far end of what once would have been a handsome home, stood a small brick room that endured the fire. A warped door remained closed, but it didn't take more than a hearty shove before it collapsed.

'My goodness, my goodness.'

'Heavens be praised,' Marion whispered in amazement.

The thick stone construction had kept supplies safe from the fire, safe from animals, and now it was theirs.

'Rice, Marion, we have rice.'

'And more flour. Without weevils, I hope. And, what's in this tin? Sugar. Hurray.'

'This one has powdered milk. Disgusting.'

'It's better than no milk, Miranda. We can make pudding.'

'And cakes. Fancy that.'

Marion taste-tested a speck of salt. 'Yes, definitely salt. Here's some dried fruit. Very dry. Don't know if it will be safe to eat.'

'Now we really do need that horse and cart.'

That set the two girls giggling. They remained animated as they sorted through jars of pickles and preserves. Some had a crust of mould clinging to the top of the contents, but it all added to the merriment of discovery. Marion unearthed a long rope and two hessian bags from under a wooden box of empty bottles.

'Let's take as many things as we can today and come back tomorrow. What will you take, Miranda?'

'I want to take the mirror and the clips you found. I'll be able to see to do my hair nicely.

'Don't you want to help take some food?'

'Of course I do, but some of my collection will fit in my pockets. What will you take?'

'The rice. I think that should be first. And the books, of course.'

'We can't carry the rice, Marion. The sack's too big.'

'We'll have to drag it.'

'What if it tears?' Miranda asked.

'We'll have to be careful.'

'I don't want to go right now. Let's keep looking.'

'No. We have to get going. It'll take us some time. We have to get home before dark.'

'What a shame we can't use the lamp, Marion. Are you sure there is no oil in the bowl.'

'No, I shook it. Fortunately it didn't break when you dropped it.'

'I'm sorry. I was just so disappointed.'

'Never mind. Pick up the mirror. I'll carry the bucket in my spare hand.'

The two women dragged the sack of rice until their hands refused to grip the corners. Marion tried to carry it for a while, but she staggered under its weight. They then reverted to dragging it again. After many stops and by risking a short cut, they reached home before the sack ruptured.

With stomachs full of boiled rice and their heads full of anticipation, they slept soundly and woke an hour after sun-up.

'Miranda, time to get up. We have to be going.'

Miranda's hand instantly went to her head. Last night, with moonlight glimpsing through the window, she was able to see her hair clearly for the first time since being at the farmhouse.

Marion was trying to work out how they could carry the many containers of food from the homestead. The wooden box would be useful, but she couldn't remember if she'd seen any sheets of tin or flat timber that might work as a sled.

They followed the track made by the dragged sack and arrived at the back of the burnt homestead.

'Let's look at the remains of the outbuildings,' suggested Marion. 'We might find something useful for the garden and we need something to carry the food on.'

There were spades, rakes and a hoe, all burnt beyond use. Marion put aside a tin of nails. As she kicked aside more rubble, she spotted a wheelbarrow leaning on a crumbling section of an outside wall. The wooden tray was gone, but the metal wheel and frame survived.

'Miranda,' Marion yelled. 'I've found our horse and cart.'

'What? Where? Surely not.'

'As good as. Look, a wheelbarrow. It's a shame we didn't have it yesterday, but we can take all the food home today.'

'How wonderful, and I can take this little table.'

'You can't really want it. It has burnt legs.'

Miranda retorted, 'The top isn't burnt.'

Marion was calculating how much would fit on the wheelbarrow. 'We have to take the food first.'

'That may be so, but I'm coming back tomorrow.'

'Tomorrow is our day for going to the rock.'

Miranda's eyebrows shot up. 'The rock? Who wants to go to that stupid old rock when we can come here? Really! This is the closest thing we have to going shopping.' She stood with her hands on her hips, glared at Marion and dared her to disagree. 'If you think I am going to that silly old rock where nothing ever changes, well, you are mistaken. I'm coming back here until there is nothing, but nothing, left. So there.' Miranda stalked back into the remains of the homestead, picked up the items she left behind yesterday and placed them in the bucket.

Marion silently agreed. She chuckled at Miranda's unnecessary outburst as she knocked the remaining pieces of the burnt tray off the wheelbarrow.

Marion's hands were filthy, but that was nothing new. It's very different from wearing gloves every time one leaves the house, she thought. *I'm not sure that I don't prefer this life after all. Gloves and hats, corsets – thank goodness we got rid of those horrid things. Rules about this. Rules about that. What a blessed relief to be on one's own.*

Making choices for oneself. Not worrying about what Mrs Appleyard said. Not fretting about whether someone would tell Mother that I giggled through morning prayers.

Marion lifted the end of a piece of charred timber. *I just need to find something flat. A sheet of tin should do.* She dropped the timber when it disclosed nothing suitable.

After she tugged a warped piece of tin from under other rubble, she stood on it, pulled the ends up and then laid it on the wheelbarrow frame. She placed the wooden box on the tin, filled it with containers of food, wrapped the hessian bags over the top and tied it all securely with the rope. The bucket was full of Miranda's knick-knacks and five slightly twisted spoons Marion found under a seared sheet of roofing.

She was about to call to Miranda when a bunch of papers blew across the rubble and became stuck against the leg of the wheelbarrow. Noisy flapping caught her attention and she discovered several coloured pages that appeared to be a diary. There were pictures of people, of buildings and city streets opposite a monthly calendar. Scribbled across the blank sections of the diary were shopping lists, notes and reminders of upcoming birthdays. Marion smiled at the thought of someone anticipating Nellie's birthday on the first of February. How lovely, she thought, the pictures will make a pleasant distraction. She was about to tuck the calendar under the rope when she noticed the date on the cover.

Miranda found her sitting amongst the ash and rubble; her head down. 'Marion, what are you doing? Your trousers will be filthy.' When Marion didn't answer, Miranda touched her friend's shoulder. 'Marion, what's wrong? Are you all right?'

Marion looked up at Miranda with troubled eyes. 'I'm nearly sixty.'

'Sixty? What are you talking about?'

Waving the paper, Marion said in a whisper, 'It's dated nineteen forty-two.'

'What is? Let me see.' Miranda pulled the calendar from Marion's grip and turned to the front page. Sure enough, the year of nineteen forty-two was clearly vis-ible on the scalded page. 'Nineteen forty-two? How can that be?'

'I don't know. This world of ours is crazy.' Marion stood up. 'Let's go, Miranda. It's too weird.' She grabbed the calendar from Miranda and shoved it under the rope. Her shoulders strained against the weight of the load as she lifted the handles of the wheelbarrow. Her face became expressionless. 'Let's go home.'

Miranda grinned. 'You mean home, as in home to Mum and Dad.'

Marion dropped the wheelbarrow. She spun around and faced Miranda. One hand was on her hip, the other one shook as she rubbed her chin. 'Don't be so stupid, Miranda.' Her eyebrows furrowed with irritation. 'Haven't you worked it out yet?' She wrapped her arms around her body. 'We won't ever get back. Never. Don't you understand that? Never.' Marion pointed to the pieces Miranda had gathered. 'Now put them in the bucket. We're going home. To the only home we have. The only home we are destined to have ... ever.'

Miranda picked up the bucket, and in defiance, grabbed the leg of the little table.

'You know, there is no need to be so bad-tempered,' Miranda said as they traipsed through the bush.

There was no answer from Marion. She pushed the load doggedly, her head down and a scowl across her face. She refused to accept Miranda's persistent offers to take a turn.

'What did I do? I didn't find the calendar.'

More silence. More shoving and grunting.

'Perhaps it was a misprint.'

'Umph.'

'Well, what else can it be?'

'Umph.'

'Nineteen forty-two? Does that mean we have lived all those extra years without knowing it? That's not possible, is it, Marion?'

Marion didn't answer.

Several times Miranda hurried ahead. She then waited for Marion to catch up. She smiled at her friend, hoping for communication. Marion looked away. The charade continued until Miranda became tired of it.

The bucket bumped against Miranda's leg and she had to stop to retrieve a bottle that toppled to the ground. When they reached the fence posts, Marion put down the wheelbarrow and stretched her back. Miranda waited some paces off, not caring for Marion's mood. Marion licked her dry lips and watched Miranda pick a thistle and blow the seed head away.

'Listen here, Miranda, why do you ask all these questions of me? I don't know the answers any more than you do, but let me tell you this. Nothing, I repeat, *nothing* is unusual in these parts. How can anything be what we were used to? I simply don't know.'

Miranda tossed the weed away. She opened her mouth to speak, but Marion continued.

'Remember when you said we should choose to be happy. Well, right now I choose to be angry. I choose sad, miserable and frustrated. I am wretched and confused. If you want to choose happy, you jolly well have to be happy on your own.'

She took up the weight of the wheelbarrow and pushed on, right up to the back door. Miranda followed without replying.

Marion again rejected Miranda's offer of help with the food. Miranda carried her pieces to one end of the table and tried to stay out of Marion's way. Marion let the door slam each time she carried an armful of jars into the house. She placed them on the other end of the table with a bang. Miranda washed her new trinkets and watched Marion through half closed eyes. Marion grunted repeatedly as she dragged the flour and sugar bags across the floor. Miranda rearranged the knick-knacks on the dresser quietly.

Marion sighed and a hint of a smile emerged as the last jar of pickles was placed in the cupboard. Miranda grinned with relief and left the room.

Marion thought of rice puddings and currant buns. She recalled the recipe book in the trunk. Then she remembered the books she'd found. *It's a shame we don't have a light. It would be rather pleasant to read before bed.*

Marion flicked through one book. Some pages were missing, others damaged, but written words they were, nevertheless. They would be something to enjoy later. With her sombre mood lifting, she made a rice pudding with powdered milk and sugar. A handful of sultanas completed the treat.

'That was lovely, Marion,' Miranda said carefully. It was difficult as Marion was rarely in such a temper.

'It was tasty,' Marion agreed.

After a brief silence, Miranda voiced a question with trepidation, 'Can we go back tomorrow?'

Marion lifted her head and looked at Miranda. Her eyes had no sparkle, no life in them. 'No.' She paused. 'Well, maybe.' She stood up. 'What do you expect to find? Surely we've been over it all.'

'We can't have uncovered everything. Do let's go again. We might find some kerosene. It would be wonderful to have some light.'

Marion answered with exasperation, 'Kerosene would've exploded in the fire.'

Miranda's lip trembled. She picked up her empty plate and stood up. She sniffed and wiped her hand across her eyes.

Marion turned towards her bedroom. 'We can go if you wish. I'm going to bed. I'm so tired. The wheelbarrow was very hard to manage.'

'I offered.'

'I know, and I'm sorry. I'll be better in the morning.'

'And we can go to the homestead?'

'Yes.'

TWENTY-ONE

Miranda was up and ready to leave for the homestead before Marion stirred. She prodded Marion awake. 'Come on, sleepy-head, have you forgotten we are going to the homestead?'

Marion stretched. 'No, but it's still early.'

'You should get up. I've put some wood on the fire. The kettle's boiling.'

'What!' exclaimed Marion. She couldn't help being surprised at Miranda's effort so early in the day. 'Why the hurry?'

'I want to go shopping again. You never know what we will find.'

Marion laughed as she walked to the kitchen. 'Miranda, you are surprising.'

'Now hurry up.'

Incessant badgering made Marion speed up her morning ablutions. It wasn't long before the two women, armed with the wheelbarrow and its unstable tray, headed down the track made by their previous endeavours. This time Marion allowed Miranda to struggle with the wheelbarrow while she walked ahead with the bucket in her hand.

The air was hot and smelled of eucalyptus. The bush surrounded them with the noisy cacophony of cicadas, bees and magpies. They followed the haphazard markings of the dragged rice sack and wobbly wheelbarrow until the track ceased. The two women stood in shock.

'But ...? Marion ...?' Miranda let go of the wheel-barrow.

There was no evidence of the remains they searched through yesterday. No burnt timbers. No brick footpath. No storeroom.

'Are you sure we are in the right place?' asked Miranda.

Marion pointed to the marks on the ground. 'Yes, it's the right spot. We followed our tracks, and look, the jacaranda; it was near the front entrance – where I saw the coloured glass.'

'I remember the tree,' Miranda whispered, 'but how could the homestead disappear overnight? What can have happened in such a short time?'

'A short time?' Marion frowned and looked around again. She stared at the tree as if it too might disappear. 'You're right. It must have to do with time. But where does it go?'

'I don't know, but it's not fair.' Miranda strode around, picked up several stones, and tossed them as far as she could. She yelled, 'Take that you horrible, whatever you are. Take that ... and that ...' She threw another stone into the distance. 'Why? You could have left it *one more day.*' A pebble flew out of her hand. 'Take that!' She almost fell over with the ferocity of her throw.

Marion thought of the broken glass, which yesterday, lay near the jacaranda. It would have made a pretty edge for her garden. Now it was gone. Everything had disappeared into a time and place no longer accessible. A vortex had enveloped them, filled their immediate needs and then, while they were sleeping, evaporated. Perhaps taking everything back to 1942.

She reflected on how it was possible. *Does that mean, while it sat in a pocket of our time, people in 1942 were without a piece of reality? What failed to happen in the moments when time was here instead of in its proper place?*

Were chunks of the homestead owner's life turned into a hiccough? A little piece of their week wouldn't have made any sense. Had anyone noticed? How did they react when it reappeared?

Marion supposed that the whole mystery of Miranda's and her existence must be about time. Somehow, time had aborted reality. Time should tick by regularly, one minute by one minute. People should age predictably, not bounding over years like a fully-grown kangaroo.

As Marion contemplated the impossibility of time, Miranda finally stopped throwing rocks at invisible monsters. She sat down in the middle of yesterday's ashes trailing her fingers in the soil. *Why has the building disappeared? Why couldn't it remain so we could come again and again?* After several minutes of reflection, she clapped her hands, stood up and re-moved the dust from the seat of her trousers.

Marion remained under the jacaranda tree. She placed her hands across her stomach, slowly moving her fingers across her hips and rubbing the muscles at the tops of her legs. Yes, she felt older. Signs were definitely there. But, the age of fifty-seven. She was now older than her mother was when all this began. Marion brought her hands to her face and felt for the tell-tale lines of any wrinkles.

'Marion, Marion,' called Miranda.

Marion sighed, 'Yes, Miranda, what is it?'

'Can we go to the creek?'

'I guess so.'

'Come on then, let's go now.'

'Right now?'

'What's wrong? Don't you want to go to the creek?'

Marion wished the endless decisions would go away, no matter how small they were. 'All right, let's go, Miranda. There is nothing for us here.'

They left the makeshift wheelbarrow, deciding it was too difficult to manage. It didn't even matter if invisible forces swallowed it too. Marion picked up the bucket. It couldn't be replaced.

They reached the water's edge and immediately paddled into it. Miranda was chirpy as she swished her feet at the self-made waves. Marion was still sombre and Miranda's cheerfulness surprised her.

'Marion, I wonder what will appear next? It's ever so exciting.'

Stepping out of the cold water, Marion asked, 'Exciting? Do you really think so? I thought you wanted to go *shopping* at the homestead. I thought you were disappointed.'

'I was angry. Very angry at first. There were probably other things under the rubble. I mean, we didn't even take everything out of the storeroom. Wasn't there more food?'

'I left a few bottles of indistinguishable food, but not much else.'

'Well then, nothing to worry about.'

Marion couldn't work out Miranda's sudden change of attitude. 'You don't seem bothered now.'

Miranda twirled around; arms out like a ballerina. Smiling at Marion, she said, 'No, I'm not. I *was* very upset. Then I thought of all the things that appear when we need them. Somehow. Who knows?' She spun around again and faced Marion. 'But, don't you see, it won't while the homestead is here. So, I thought, good, that's gone, now we can look forward to something else.'

Despite her low mood, Marion couldn't help but smile. Trust Miranda to think about receiving another gift, she thought. *Maybe something will appear that would solve the riddle of the calendar. That would be exciting.*

After a miserable start to the day, they dined in style again and went to bed with full stomachs. However, Marion couldn't sleep. She kept thinking about the homestead and how it had been there one day, but not the next. *If the calendar is from the time of the fire, is it a sign for us? Is it the current year? Have we really been here that long?*

Marion thought about the pictures on the calendar. *The women have such different clothes. Slim skirts. Shorter, too. They look so glamorous. The buildings. I wonder which city it is. Probably Melbourne. Streets full of strange vehicles. Goodness, where are the horses? They must get frightened. And, the soldiers. Australia doesn't usually have many soldiers walking the streets. Certainly not in Woodend. There was Malcolm, the butcher's son. He joined the army. People said he wasn't much good for anything else. They said it would give him discipline. Keep him out of trouble. Soldiers? Perhaps there was another war. The Boer War would be over by 1942. Surely.*

As she finally drifted into a restless sleep, the perplexing pictures continued to float through her dreams.

Marion found it impossible to interpret the scraps of information in the pictures. Seven soldiers looking out from a truck moved her greatly. The man at the front held a cigarette in one hand and gripped the edge of the vehicle with the other. In the centre, two likely lads had their arms around each other and waved happily. This was the April picture. May was of a young woman, dressed in dark trousers and a silky blouse, draped over the bonnet of a sleek car. *Ah! She's wearing trousers. I must show Miranda that one. Have the glossy vehicles replaced all the horses? What would happen to my Maggie? Will she be sold and replaced by a smelly motorised vehicle?*

May the twenty-third declared, "Peter leaves". The announcement of Cecile's birthday on the fourth of August stood out. A large asterisk marked September twenty-sixth and Charlie's name appeared at the bottom of October with "apple pie" next to it.

Marion chuckled and thought of Maudie making something more elaborate than apple pie for her mother's birthday. *Are they still alive?*

She was dismayed to read the frantic red markings on November's page. "Pete killed! Bloody War!" She stared at the words. She touched the writing and tried to imagine the pain of the family's loss.

She turned back to the pictures of April. *Smiling lads, ready for anything. Who was this Pete? Was he in the picture? Whoever he was, he only left in May. In November, he was dead.*

Who took the time to mark his demise this way? Someone who never wanted to forget the way they felt at that moment. A grief stricken wife? A heartbroken mother? Would a man record such a thing? No, a father would probably be out drinking with his mates. With other men who'd lost their sons.

Marion cried out, 'Bloody war.'

She let the calendar flop shut and placed her head in her hands. Had Australia succumbed to invasion? The horror of the thought made her tremble. What was happening in the world to which she no longer belonged?

She flicked over the pages again. December captured a picture of a family around a Christmas tree. The ash-marked page concerned Marion as she looked at the fashion of both the clothes and the room. *Was it a glimpse of the future? Were these the people who once lived in this farmhouse? Are Miranda and I floating around in a bubble of time, landing at the whim of nature?* It's too much to take in, she thought. *Why me? Why us?* She drifted in and out of morose thoughts as she brushed the pages with her fingers, trying to remove as much grime as possible.

Deep in thought, she jumped when Miranda called her name. Marion shot to her feet. Her eyes flicked right and left, searching out the room. She gripped the edge of the table as the smell of burning oil reached her.

Light shimmered in front of Miranda's face making her hair luminous. Marion's breath came in short gasps. Miranda's voice floated to Marion's highly alerted ears, 'Marion, isn't it wonderful?'

Marion closed her eyes and breathed evenly.

Miranda didn't understand Marion's reaction. 'It's what we need, isn't it? Light for the evening.'

Marion opened her eyes and stared at the lamp. She spoke hastily, almost a command, 'Put it down on the table.' She sighed and softened her voice, 'You gave me quite a scare. It looked most eerie in front of your face.'

Miranda placed the lamp on the table, then clapped her hands like a small child who had just opened a birthday present. Marion leaned over the lamp and watched the flame. She wanted to touch it. 'Where did you find the oil?'

'I didn't,' Miranda chuckled. 'I was shifting things on the dresser. I picked up the lamp and felt the liquid move. I didn't say anything to you in case I was wrong.'

'You'd better turn it out and leave it for later.'

'I don't want to turn it out in case it won't light again,' whispered Miranda.

'I suspect it will have a mind of its own, no matter what you do.' Marion looked out the window before turning back to Miranda. 'It *will* be pleasing not to have to go to bed with the sun.'

Miranda turned down the wick and watched the flame disappear. 'I shall be extremely cross if it doesn't light again.'

Night after night, the lamp ignited. Like so many other mysteries they encountered, the provision of oil was unexplainable. A crack in the glass gradually crept across its width, but it didn't hinder the interminable flame.

Most summer nights they spent outside, filling time with idle chatter and companionable silences. The gentle light of the moon sought out their limbs as it filtered through the branches of the lemon tree. It was a treat to be able to lay on a blanket outside in the semi-darkness, waiting for drowsiness before retreating to their hot bedrooms. Sometimes, the need to reject the endless biting insects spoilt the pleasurable twilight.

However, on winter evenings, they struggled with the inconvenience of dark rooms when they weren't sleepy enough for bed.

Now, with the lamplight making shadows flicker across the wall, Miranda and Marion rejoiced in being able to sit inside, watch the sun disappear into the distance and not have to prepare for bed.

'Do you want me to read to you, Mirry? Some of this book survived the fire.'

'From the homestead?'

'Of course.'

Miranda put down her stitching. 'What's its title?'

'This one is so burnt that the front page doesn't exist.'

Miranda picked up her sewing, unable to get inter-ested in the book. 'Why did you bother to keep it then?'

'Well, there were only three. I didn't have a library to choose from.'

'I guess not.' Miranda leaned over, trying to read the title of the book on Marion's lap. 'And that one?'

'*Middlemarch* by George Eliot.'

'Is he any good?'

Marion shoved the book in front of Miranda's face. 'She.'

'A woman?' Miranda frowned, and asked if it was true.

'Of course. What were you doing when we read her other work? Remember we studied *The Lifted Veil?* You really should have paid more attention.'

Miranda pushed the book away. 'Marion, don't be so rude.'

'Sorry, Miranda, but really, you should have known that.'

'Perhaps, but I'd rather read poetry. I remember one of Banjo Paterson's poems.'

'Do you? Will you recite it for me?'

Miranda put down her needle and thread, stood up and with a curtsy started ...

'Twas Mulga Bill, from Eaglehawk, that caught the cycling craze;
He turned away the good old horse that served him many days;
He dressed himself in cycling clothes, resplendent to be seen;
He hurried off to town and bought a shining new machine;
And as he wheeled it through the door, with air of lordly pride,
The grinning shop assistant said, "Excuse me, can you ride?"

An awkward gap in her recitation lapsed into giggles.

'Is there any more?' asked Marion. The poem made her think of her grey mare stabled at home. *How I'd love to be able to saddle Maggie and ride out for the day.*

'Quite a lot more, but I can't remember the rest. It finishes with Mulga Bill saying he would rather ride a horse because he fell off the bike.'

'It's very amusing,' laughed Marion. 'I'm sure you didn't learn that at Appleyard College, did you?'

Miranda giggled, 'No, you're right. My brothers taught it to me. Their books were more entertaining than the ones we had. It's a long time since I thought of it.'

'You've done well knowing that much. Do you remember how awful they were to Sara when she wouldn't memorise the one we were studying?'

Miranda didn't answer immediately. *Of course I remember.* She thought about Sara, and that particular day, often. The picnic was to be so much fun. A day away from the restrictions of the college. A chance to romp around the bush. Miranda couldn't believe it when Sara hugged her and said she wasn't allowed to attend.

Miranda placed her hands on her cheeks and shook her head, devastated at the memory. 'It was more than that. She wanted to recite her own poem.'

'Of course, that was it. Mrs Appleyard refused to give in.'

'So did Sara.'

Marion waited a moment before asking, 'Would you like to hear some from one of the books now?'

'What's the third one? Is that one written by a woman as well?'

'No, John Stuart Mill wrote it. *On Liberty*, I have no idea what it is about.'

'Is it complete?'

'No. Many of the pages have scorched edges. *On Liberty*. Sounds like just the story we need.'

'Yes, but I'll keep stitching.'

'A few pages are missing. I'll start here. "In order more fully to illustrate the mischief of denying a hearing to opinions because we, in our own judgement, have condemned them, it will be desirable to fix down the discussion to a concrete case" ... goodness, it is heavy going. Do you want me to continue?'

'I've drifted off, I'm sorry. I was still thinking about Sara. Her Valentine's card is the closest thing I have to a book.'

'Oh, I'd forgotten about her card. You've kept it all this time?'

'I must keep it – always. It was in my pocket at the picnic.' Miranda waved her hand in a flippant manner. 'I received so many cards. Some from chaps I know. My brothers' friends mostly. One was particularly amusing and some of their attempts to be romantic made me blush.'

'And Sara's card?'

'It's lovely. I'll show it to you later. She's stitched lace on the front. It has pictures of butterflies and pansies. I like pansies. They look like velvet. Don't you think so?'

Marion was thinking of her own three cards. One card from her mother with words of encouragement *to do well at school*, one with scratchy penmanship declaring love from *anonymous*, and the third card; a beautifully crafted declaration of *friendship forever* from Irma.

'I wonder if she is still at the school,' mused Miranda, speaking of Sara who was never far from her mind. 'There was some sort of problem with fees.'

Marion put down the dusty book, clapped her hands together to disperse the ash marks while saying, 'You do realise that Sara will be fending for herself by now. We've been here, how long?'

'Forty years – if you believe the calendar you found,' quipped Miranda.

'Well, no matter how long it's been, Sara's problem will have been concluded a long time ago.'

'You're right. It's terrible, Marion. There is so much we don't know.'

Miranda started to sniff. Marion left her seat and, with one hand on Miranda's shoulder, stroked her soft hair with the other hand. When the lamplight flickered, both women looked up, but after the stream of light steadied, they sighed and returned to their activities.

Miranda stitched lethargically. She occasionally wiped her hand across her wet cheek. Marion turned the pages of Mr Mill's work, snapping off charred pieces. She looked for a place to recommence.

"There is always need of persons not only to discover new truths, and point out when what were once truths are true no longer, but also to commence new practices ..."

Marion let the book sit on her knee while she contemplated the words. *New truths? Is that what we are living? Have we travelled into an originality of living? Are we still to discover the truth? What is the valuable missing element of our existence?* She pondered for many minutes until finally she thought to herself, Yes, we've commenced new practices – new for us. That, at least, is true.

She tried to read more, but the irregularity of burnt edges made it difficult. She sat quietly watching the shadows made by the clouds spreading their whimsical shapes in front of the moon.

TWENTY-TWO

To: bechan@hotmail.com
From: mwworth@iinet.net.au
Hi Bec,
Is Saturday still ok? If so, I thought we could go to Simpson's Gallery. The new one in St Kilda I was telling you about. We can have lunch if you'd like. Let me know.
Michael
ps – Still don't trust my mobile.

Rebecca sat, poised at the keyboard, ready to reply. She could easily type, yes, lunch would be great, and leave it at that, but she thought of Michael and typed –

tall, slightly skinny, loves apple pie, is nice to his Gran.

Her fingers kept moving as she thought of Rose and her obvious affection for Michael.

Wish she were my Gran.

Thinking she was becoming soppy, she held down the delete button. Then she recalled the day Michael entered the shop where she worked.

Great smile, BLUE eyes, freckles, muscles, f…… gorgeous!!!!

Rebecca had always wanted blue eyes.

funny, talented, polite, SEXY!!!

She grinned, as she thought of him in jeans.

Missy gave Rebecca a fright when she jumped up onto her lap. She felt slightly embarrassed as she deleted her musings and typed,

Yes, lunch would be great. see u at ten. bec

'Wow, you look great.' Michael smiled as he greeted Rebecca.

She laughed, adjusted her scarf and said, 'Thanks, I thought I'd try and look arty.'

'And just what makes one look like an artist?'

'Definitely a scarf. Maybe a beret.'

'No hope for me then. I don't own either.'

As Rebecca locked the door, she felt his eyes checking her out again. She took a little longer than necessary.

They wandered around the streets of St Kilda, undecided on which restaurant or café to choose. As they browsed, Rebecca considered cushions in an oriental-style boutique. She was surprised when Michael hugged a purple cushion made of velvet. He drifted away for several seconds before he raised his eyebrows at her and then tossed the cushion back onto the display.

The art gallery was in an old building with high windows. Either side of a huge wooden entrance door was lollypop greenery. Inside, French provincial chairs stood next to highly polished tables where art catalogues were creatively scattered. As they entered, the flamboyant owner greeted them. 'Come in, my dear things,' he said taking Rebecca's hand and winking at Michael. He enthusiastically described his newest artist and forced a brochure into Michael's hand.

'Rather over the top,' Rebecca said, as they hurried to the far end of the gallery.

'Yeah, you could say that. And it's probably all in here,' Michael said, as he opened the fancy brochure.

Spectacular watercolours of inner city life lined one wall. Michael explained how thick accents of black ink on the pale shapes captured the artist's message of strength. Rebecca liked the balance between the buildings and the people. However, she preferred the small delicate pencil drawings of birds hovering over nectar-filled flowers.

'Imagine getting those sorts of prices for your art,' she said, linking her hand through Michael's arm. She pointed to the plaque under a miniscule canvas. 'Fifteen hundred dollars.'

'One can dream.' He slipped his hand down Rebecca's arm and entwined their fingers.

Smiling at him, she said, 'One day, you'll see. You'll have your paintings on show. But you'd better find somewhere a little less pretentious and,' she dropped her voice to a whisper, 'I'd make a much more restrained manager.'

He reacted with a gentle squeeze of her hand and then led her towards the exit. Assuring the owner that they enjoyed his collection, but politely avoiding his efforts to secure a sale, they walked back into the street.

'Okay, Bec, what do you fancy?'

'The vegetarian place looked good.'

'Not today, if you don't mind, I'm still craving meat. What about Charcoal Grill Café?'

'Yep, that's fine.'

'Right, let's go. I'm starving.'

When Michael was tucking into his steak, Rebecca asked tentatively, 'Have you thought any more about why Marion was stuck out there for so long?'

He tapped the end of his fork on the table. His eyes shifted between his plate and Rebecca several times before he spoke. 'All the time.' He placed the fork across the plate. 'When I'm not trying to work out how and why I got to be there. One thing for sure though – if anyone wants to disappear, then that place has all the right qualities.'

'What *was* Hanging Rock like?'

He paused, picked up his fork again and put the last piece of steak in his mouth. Michael chewed slowly and considered his answer. When he'd finished eating, he wiped his mouth on the serviette and then said, 'The area is spectacular. The bush was definitely denser in Marion's time. The rock is interesting. Insanely formidable. So many levels. Lots to explore. No wonder it's popular with tourists. But,' he grimaced, 'as soon as the sun starts to make long shadows it becomes creepy. No, I don't like the place.'

'You obviously feel strongly about it.'

'Wouldn't you? I think it's bloody horrific after what it put me through.'

Rebecca placed her knife down and nodded. 'I looked it up on my computer. I can see what you mean. It does look spooky.' The fork slipped from her grasp and she listened to it rattle against the plate. 'You know, I still can't figure out why it means something to me.'

Folding his arms, Michael looked away. 'Let's forget about it for now.' Then he turned back and smiled, 'Coffee?'

TWENTY-THREE

The shed continued to surprise Miranda and Marion. Mostly it was just an ordinary building with a few tools. Occasionally the shelf contained food or vital supplies.

Each morning and afternoon on the way to tend the fowls, Marion checked the shed. Miranda's visits to the shed were sporadic, but she always felt hopeful as she entered.

Just when they thought they'd received their last surprise, another rabbit or a piece of kangaroo would appear. One time, some yellow soap materialised. They were delighted when seeds, discovered on the shelf, grew quickly in Marion's vegetable garden.

Sometimes they spotted a small dark child coming out of the shed. There were usually older children waiting at the end of the yard and they would all run off together, hand in hand, into the distance.

The first time Miranda saw a child she hurried towards him, calling for him to wait. However, the boy was much quicker and slipped away before Miranda reached the end of the yard.

Marion scolded her, saying she would frighten the child. 'Leave them be, Miranda, they won't harm us. They bring us food.'

'But, Marion, they must have parents. Adults could show us the way home.'

Marion already concluded that if the Aborigines were a means of escape, then it would've happened already. For some reason they were keeping an eye on the two women. With one hand, the universe had taken much away, but with the other, compensated them with unique nurturing.

Miranda was a little gentler in her approach in subsequent sightings. She would wave, call to the children and when they retreated, she would follow them to the end of the clearing, calling out for them to bring their mother next time. The children never looked back.

Marion watched them from a distance. As they scampered across the grass, she would raise her hand in a salute. She usually waited until the children reached the bush before she left what she was doing and investigated.

'They are beautiful children,' said Miranda, after one such visitation.

'Mmm,' was all Marion said in agreement.

'Did you want children?' Miranda asked, as she picked up her sewing and settled next to her friend.

Marion paused from her game of solitaire. 'Children? I hadn't really thought about it.'

'Mum said five was enough. Dad was glad he had four sons to work the cattle.'

'What about you, Miranda? Would you have had children?'

'Yes. Two girls and a boy would be perfect.'

'I don't think you can choose.'

Miranda giggled. 'No, I'm sure you can't. Although that odd lady at the bakery, you know the one that wears the long hessian apron, she says that if you drink ... I can't remember what ... anyway if you drink something particular, you will have girls and not boys.'

'I've never heard that. Can it be true?'

'I'm sure I don't know.' Miranda pointed to the five of diamonds that went on the six of spades. 'I like the name Bethany. That's what I'll call my first daughter. Bethany Clare.'

Marion moved the card into place and considered her reply. 'Mirry, to do that you have to have a man. We are decidedly short of that gender.'

Miranda threw down the stitching she was working on and hit the table. 'I know that, I'm not stupid.' Rubbing her hand, she declared, 'I was talking about when we get home. There'll be plenty of men who will court me. I will wait, but I'll call my first daughter Bethany.'

Marion decided that silence was the best reply. *Would I have wanted children if I lived a normal existence?* She liked the sweet smell of her cousin's new baby and his cute endearing face as he tugged on one's finger. However, the two noisy children that lived next door were enough to put anyone off wanting babies.

'Marion, what would you call your daughter?' asked Miranda, as she tapped on the table to attract her friend's attention.

'I'd call her after my mother, or perhaps my husband's mother.'

'I can't wait to have children of my own.'

Marion knew time had run out for both of them. 'Yes, but first things first.'

They suffered through the winters. They often wrapped themselves in blankets and huddled in front of the stove, only moving to put another log on the dying fire. They went to bed early and rose late, sometimes snuggling together, happy to stay under the warm covers until their bladders were fit to burst or their stomachs demanded attention. With the wind whistling around the old house, sheets of tin banged against each other. Loose pieces of wood shifted in the pile.

The two women hated the wind. It was even worse when the soil was dry and blew into their faces as they struggled to do outside chores. When strands of hair nipped at their cheeks, they remembered the evil day when the dust announced their emergence into this strange existence.

There was no consolation inside either. They tried to plug the gaps, but gusts still snuck in and tormented them. Curtains fluttered with cold shafts of air. Small ornaments would suddenly tumble over. It would all be too much. They would sit immobile, waiting anxiously for it to stop.

Summer rain was always welcome as the water level in the tank was a constant worry. Marion remembered her mother's lectures on water use. 'There's a drought going on. We must be careful. The farmers are losing sheep. Now be good and don't use too much water,' Mrs Quade would say.

Although austerity was still necessary for Marion and Miranda, the effort of filling the bath was more than enough to ensure frugal use of the water from the tank.

Marion liked the winter dawn when the air was cold enough to make smoke rings with each breath. Early flowering wattles pushed puffs of flowers out, making her smile as she touched the miniscule yellow balls. For her, solitary early morning walks became a habit.

Once, she spied some leaves that looked out of place in the middle of a clump of wild grasses and was delighted with her discovery. The potatoes formed the basis of a new garden bed and, with experimentation of their growth patterns, provided crucial variety to their diet. Another time she discovered golden mushrooms under some pine trees, but mostly she just enjoyed roaming the bush.

After three days listening to constant pounding rain on the tin roof, Marion became tired of reading her books of partial stories. Miranda refused to play cards after she lost so often and they were bored with the monotony of each other's company.

For Marion, it was a relief to get out of the house. She walked purposefully, striding along familiar narrow tracks. Bare feet no longer hampered her, as her soles were now tough. Every so often she stopped to inspect a plant in the hope it might be edible, or at the very least, pretty enough to take back to Miranda. She spotted a huge ant's nest and kept well away. A burst of flapping ravens startled her before she laughed and told them, 'Come back soon, my lovelies.'

On her return journey, Marion poked her toe at what she thought was a shiny stone. On picking it up, she was surprised to discover it was a silver coin. A further hunt revealed three more coins – one gold and two tiny silver ones.

She flicked off bits of dirt. *How interesting – something new.* Then she ambled back to the house. As she came through the doorway, she patted her trouser pocket and smiled at the amusement the coins would bring. She savoured the anticipation of disclosure.

After washing the lunch dishes, and with the coins in her cupped hands, she moved them through the soapy water and shifted the last of the dirt.

'Look at this, Miranda.' She held up the gold coin.

'What is it? Hold it out further.'

Marion stretched her arm over the bench.

'Money!' Miranda's eyes opened wider.

Pleased with Miranda's reaction, Marion closed her hand and dipped them into the water again. 'Seems so. I found four. The one I showed you says "one dollar".'

Miranda rushed over to the bench, holding out her hand. 'A dollar. Marion, are you sure?'

'Yes, it is handsomely engraved.'

'Where did you find them?'

'Just beyond the track, near where we found the mushrooms.'

Miranda took one of the wet coins. 'We're rich. We have money.'

Fancy getting excited about being rich, Marion thought. 'And just where do you think we can spend it?' she asked.

Miranda closed her hand around the coin and sat down. 'Marion, do you have to spoil it? I was just imagining what could be bought.'

Marion's eyes lifted and saw the disappointment on her friend's face. She considered if Miranda's wistful dreams and imaginings, which helped her through every endless day, were any more foolish than her own method of resigned acceptance. She admitted she liked the solitary life, loneliness bothered her less each season and she rarely dreamed of rescue. As she looked at Miranda's vexed expression, she chided herself for stamping on her imagination.

'I'm sorry, Miranda. I suppose we could buy many things.'

Miranda opened her hand and peered at the coin. 'How much do we have altogether?'

Marion sat down at the table and put out her hand. 'Let me see that gold one again, please.' She grabbed the coin off Miranda's palm.

'Why are you looking like that?' asked Miranda, concerned at Marion's deep frown. 'What's wrong?'

Marion drew in a loud breath as she stared at the coin. 'Don't you see what this means? This coin has a dollar on one side and is clearly marked "Australia" on the other.'

'Yes. What does that mean?'

'Don't you see? Do you know which country has dollars?'

'America.'

'Yes. Certainly not Australia. We have pounds, like in England.'

Miranda shrugged. 'So they're American coins.'

'It *says* Australia.'

'Oh dear, now I'm confused.' Miranda rose, walked around the table, stopped behind Marion and peered at the coins again. 'What do you think it means?'

Marion put the other coins on the table. 'Fifty; I think that would be fifty cents, and the two little ones, five; five cents.'

'But America, what has that got to do with them?'

Marion sighed heavily and laid the coins out in a neat row across the table. 'I'll explain,' she said gently. 'Remember the calendar?'

'The burnt one?'

'Yes. Remember, Peter died in a war, November nineteen forty-two.'

Miranda giggled a little. 'Bloody war. Yes, I remember.'

Marion ignored the inappropriate giggling and explained, 'I think the war must have been with America.'

'What!' Miranda picked up the gold coin and turned it over. 'Do you really think so?'

'It can only be. When a country invades another and wins, they obviously change things to their way. Therefore the Australian–*American* dollar. I would think that would be so, don't you?'

Miranda answered, 'Yes ... but ...?'

'So, I think Australia now belongs to America. Good heavens, so many things we don't know. I wonder what other drastic events have taken place.'

Closing her eyes a little, Miranda looked into space and said, 'I love Americans.'

'Really? How many Americans do you know?'

Miranda sat down opposite Marion. 'There was a man and his wife in Mr Horton's drapery shop once. I was there with Miss Parrington, picking up a bundle of fabric for our dressmaking class, and I overheard them talking. The woman was so elegant. Her hat was divine. They said hello to me. I loved their accent.'

'And you fell in love with every American because one said hello. Really, Miranda.'

Miranda shoved the chair out, stood up and threw down the coin.

'Well if they *have* invaded Australia, then I think you better change your thinking.' She glared at Marion and stomped off towards her bedroom.

If only I had the chance to form an opinion, thought Marion. She stopped the coin from rolling off the table. Moving coins around with her forefinger she thought, if one dollar was equal to one pound we could buy many things. *Fresh white bread for five pence, a dozen eggs for six pence. Not that we need to buy eggs. Milk would definitely be on the shopping list. Threepence a pint. Fresh milk. That would be a luxury.* Marion picked up the coins and counted them. *One dollar, fifty cents, a dollar fifty-five, a dollar sixty. One dollar sixty. That is almost two dollars. Two pounds!* Imagine, she thought, a schoolteacher only earns about three pounds for a whole week. Or so cousin Richie said.

She was all set to drop the coins into a jug on the dresser when she took a closer look at the largest coin. "Elizabeth II" was inscribed around the crowned head. *A new queen. How jolly.* She stood for a while and let it sink in. She wondered why an English queen would be on an American coin. How confusing. Engraving around the other rim left Marion gasping. "Australia 1989".

'I must be as crazy as a bedbug,' she said aloud. *1989! How can that be? Is that another portion of time we've been carried across? 1989. That would make me ... a hundred and four.* 'Miranda. Miranda! Do you know we're now a hundred and four?'

TWENTY-FOUR

'Mirry, come and get your dinner. You've been lazing around all day.'

Miranda yawned. She ran her tongue over her cracked lips. 'I don't feel like eating.'

'I've boiled potatoes to go with the meat.'

'When did we get meat?'

'It was there when I went to feed the chickens this afternoon.'

'We should cook one of the hens. There were no eggs again this morning.'

'I was worried about that, but some babies hatched yesterday. We can't have eggs *and* chickens.'

'What if we don't get eggs, Marion? We rely on them so much.'

Marion came over to the couch and knelt down in front of Miranda. 'I'm more worried about you than not having eggs.'

'Please, Marion, I'll get better. I just don't feel like eating today.'

'But you didn't eat much yesterday, or the day before. What about some rice?' All the gardening and wood chopping made Marion hungry. She looked forward to a meal of rabbit and potato. 'Come on, Miranda, try to eat something. Don't you want a piece of rabbit?'

'No, I think I'll go to bed.'

Marion placed her knife and fork beside her plate of hot food. She realised Miranda must be more than a little ill if she was retiring to her bed before the shadows reached across the side yard.

'Are you really ill, Mirry?'

'I don't know. I might have a fever.' She placed her palm on her forehead.

'What can I do for you?'

'I just need to rest. My stomach doesn't feel right and I feel a little giddy. Perhaps I could manage a tea. Do you mind?'

'Of course not. Get into bed and I'll bring it to you.'

Later, as she sat over her re-heated meal, Marion thought about her friend. What was she to do if Miranda was very ill? The thought made her shiver. She pushed the idea of living on her own into the back of her mind and cut into the rabbit.

Miranda spent three days in bed. It was a further two days before she felt able to complete her usual chores.

They sat under the lemon tree enjoying a brief moment of sunshine on an otherwise cold autumn day.

'I didn't think I would recover.'

'Are you completely well, Mirry?'

'I don't think so, but I will be in time.' She picked at the grass.

'I was anxious.' Marion reached out and grasped Miranda's hand. 'What would I do without you?'

'One of us will die first,' said Miranda, as she took her hand away slowly.

Marion relived her fear in silence. *What then?*

Miranda stood up and leaned on the trunk of the lemon tree. 'I hope I die first.'

'Miranda, don't talk like that.'

'Why not?' She shrugged her shoulders. 'One of us has to die first and I want it to be me.'

'Why you?'

'Because it will be better.'

'For you.' Marion stood up and faced Miranda. 'I don't want to be left alone either.'

'It's not just that. If you die first, Marion, I shan't be able to survive.' Miranda tapped her friend on the chest. '*You* are more able to do the outside chores. And … the chickens don't like *me*. Yes, I am going to pray that I die first.'

'Don't you dare.'

'What die first? I can if I want to.'

'No,' whispered Marion, 'I meant, don't pray that you'll die.'

They sat down, leaned against each other and considered the thought of dying. They shared the dread of managing a burial on their own, so they resolved to start digging two graves. Allotments were marked out next to the lemon tree and, when Miranda declared she was fully recovered, they started digging.

'I've had enough,' said Miranda, as she threw the spade down. 'I'm going to have a bath.'

'We haven't got far.'

'My hands hurt.' Miranda sat down on the front step. 'Anyway, I think we're wasting our time. Fancy digging one's own grave.'

Marion tossed another mound of soil onto the small pile then walked over to the verandah. 'If we don't dig together, whichever one of us is left will have to dig the grave alone.'

'Oh, I hadn't thought of that. Where would I put you while I finished all the digging?'

Marion said in a monotone voice, 'I would be dead.'

'I know. I know you would be. I just couldn't do it with you laying there … dead.'

Walking back to the partially dug graves, Marion made a half-hearted thrust into the soil with the shovel. 'Then we'll have to continue.'

'Not today. I feel ever so grubby. I'm going to have a bath. Will you help with the water?'

Marion stopped digging and shared the chore of carting water instead. Annoyed at the tedium of the task and the expectation of cooperation without consultation, Marion grumbled continually. Miranda waited until Marion tipped a final pot of boiling water into the trough, then she undressed hurriedly and shooed Marion away.

'Thank you, Marion May,' Miranda called, as she dribbled water across her chest.

Marion felt that a self-centred Miranda was better than no Miranda. Her mood lifted as she re-read her favourite chapters in the ash-marked books and waited for her turn in the bath. The weather was becoming colder and it would soon be more comfortable to use a bucket of hot water in front of the warm kitchen stove. The small washhouse was hardly cosy enough for disrobing on a chilly day.

'I hate doing this,' complained Miranda.

'Don't think about it. Just dig.'

'It's all right for you. You're strong.'

Marion grunted, 'You're strong too. You rode horses at home. Remember how much work you did on the family station.'

'Yes, but that was a long time ago. You know, Mum argued with Dad all the time about me doing chores fit for boys. They sent me to Appleyard College and expected me to learn how to be a lady. So much for that, I've ended up digging a grave. It's so unladylike.'

'Goodness me, but it will be even more unladylike to die without a grave.'

Dropping the spade, Miranda said, 'Well, I don't feel like doing any more today.'

Marion straightened her back and pushed her hair away from her face. 'You shouldn't just leave it to me. That's not fair.'

'Marion, you like digging.'

'What!' Marion glared at Miranda. 'I do not.'

'You're always digging in your blessed garden.'

Stepping out of the hole, Marion sighed, 'That's different. We have to have something to eat.'

Miranda tipped up her chin as she walked off. 'Pity we can't grow shortbread biscuits.'

'Miranda, come and do some digging,' called Marion, as she shovelled dirt from the depths of one hole.

'In a while, Marion, I want to finish writing this chapter.'

Marion was unable to comprehend what she heard. 'Chapter?' she queried. *Miranda knows how to get out of the hard work. I'll be glad when these ridiculous graves are finished.* 'Miranda, are you coming? My grave is deeper than yours.'

Miranda appeared with a book in her hand. Marion stopped instantly, as the next spadeful of dirt would have landed on Miranda's feet.

'I thought we were digging each other's grave.' Miranda pushed some soil with her shoe. 'I couldn't bear it if I've been digging my own. It would be too awful.'

'Awful? How? You'll be dead before you know which hole you're in.'

'Marion!'

'Stop complaining and come and dig. I've nearly finished my ... your grave. You will have to catch up.'

'Not today. I'm finishing off this story.' Miranda walked off, opening the book as she went.

Fed up with trying to convince Miranda to help, Marion left the spade in the hole and climbed out. She washed down and started to play a game of solitaire, happy to leave Miranda to sit hunched over her writing.

'There, I've finished.' The sound of the book being slammed shut startled Marion.

'Finished what?'

'*Middlemarch.*'

'*Middlemarch*? But that's George Eliot's story.' Marion raised her eyebrows and gathered up the cards.

'You said the book is missing the final pages.'

'Yes.'

'Now you have a conclusion.'

'You mean you've written an ending? How clever of you.' She paused, as she counted out the cards. 'When can I read it?'

Opening the book again, Miranda said, 'It might be a little silly.'

'I'm sure it won't be.'

'You see, I married off Dorothea and Lydgate.' She twisted the pencil between her fingers. 'Don't you wish *you* could have married?'

Marion gave up trying to find the ten of spades. 'Sometimes. What about you? I'm sure you would've had dozens of proposals.'

'I would very much like to be married, but I'll only agree to marry someone who is rich. Mum said it is hard when you don't have enough money.' Miranda put down the pencil and sat quietly for a moment before adding, 'I wouldn't have to wear trousers if I were wealthy. I would buy the latest styles, velvet in winter, and exotic brocade for evening parties.'

'What if you fell in love with someone who was poor?' Marion ventured to ask.

'I would never do that. I would certainly choose very carefully with whom I fell in love.'

Surprised by her friend's calculating pronouncement, Marion changed the subject. 'Do you often dream of the chances we've missed, Mirry?'

'Every night I build a new story where I am in a pretty dress being feted by handsome men in wonderful suits and top hats. It's the only way I can get to sleep.'

'I'm usually too tired to do anything but fall asleep.'

'It's all that digging in the garden.'

Marion tried to ignore her friends quip, but mut-tered under her breath, 'It's better than digging graves.' She shuffled the cards again and said, 'I wonder who you would've married. How about Boris? They live in that big house outside town *and* have pots of money.'

'Not Boris. *Boring Boris*, Sara and I called him.'

'Well, what about Edith's brother? He has striking eyes.'

'Good heavens, no. I wouldn't want to be Edith's sister-in-law.'

'That's horrid, Miranda.'

'Maybe it is, but she fusses so. Now if Sara's brother could have been around, I would definitely like to be her sister-in-law.'

Marion thought Lawrence was good-natured and amusing. It didn't bother her that he was related to Edith. But, by now he would probably be married with several children and working in his father's drapery store. All their friends would have married, moved away or forgotten them. They would be old maids. Even without knowing the correct year, she knew her body was wearing out. She'd become old.

She sighed and stopped her wishful thinking. 'I shall look forward to reading your ending, Miranda. Now let's prepare dinner. I hope you're hungry. I'm going to make potato and onion patties to have with spinach. Then we can have some fig and apple bread.'

TWENTY-FIVE

Rebecca was enthralled as Michael related the amazing story. She was bursting to hear it all at once. He told her to be patient, but it was like watching a serial on TV and having to put up with the ads.

On Saturday they watched a DVD. Rebecca was distracted when Michael drew letters on her knee. The word "later" made her look at him with a cheeky smile and she held his hand to keep him from ruining the film.

'Coffee or tea?' Rebecca asked, as she filled the electric kettle.

The kettle turned itself off as he came up behind her. His hands fondled her body until he found her breasts. She closed her eyes and enjoyed the soft pressure of his hands against her raised nipples. She tipped her head back so he could kiss her neck.

Rebecca turned around and lifted her shirt. He explored her bare flesh with his hands, making sounds of delight as he caressed her face with his lips. She responded with kisses of her own, not wanting the pleasure to stop.

'You don't want coffee then?' Rebecca whispered.

He undid his shirt and shook his head, 'Nup, not right now.'

She scrunched her t-shirt under her chin and cuddled into his bare chest. He played with her hair and tickled her back, sneaking his finger under her bra. She wanted to make the next move – to remove his clothes and explore his body, but she hesitated. Only because she wanted to be sure it wasn't just the "goose bump theory" hurtling her towards future heartache.

He understood her reservation and nestled against her, stroking her shoulders and making circles on her back.

TWENTY-SIX

With Miranda's safety pin fashioned as a hook and securely tied to a piece of twine, Marion spent the afternoon fishing.

She thought about Miranda's decision to stay home. Faced with a lethargic Miranda, Marion hesitated before leaving. Eventually she went by herself.

Previously, wandering through the bush, gathering pretty bunches of wildflowers, which would end up in various containers around their house, would have delighted Miranda.

One time, Marion threatened to stay at home after Miranda fidgeted like a child waiting to set off for a trip to a much-loved relative. 'Come on, Marion, let's go now. The chickens can wait.'

'Of course they can't. Let me finish this.'

'You are deliberately being slow. Hurry up, Marion. I love going to the creek.'

Marion scowled. 'I have to get my scarf.'

'Come on, come on.'

Marion also loved the time spent at the creek. She enjoyed the sensation of the cold water on her skin. Never once, after that first time, did she feel awkward about swimming naked.

Now, as she fished, she worried about Miranda. *Was Miranda becoming seriously ill?* Yesterday, she even ignored her habitual tasks and spent the morning listlessly watching the clouds make patterns across the windy sky. In the afternoon she took a nap instead of helping Marion pick fruit from the laden tree at the bottom of their yard. Stewed apple with a damper crust was pushed around her plate and left uneaten. *Yes, Miranda is poorly.*

With a fish in the bucket, Marion headed for home. She picked some wattle, which she hoped would cheer Miranda.

Marion watched with great anxiety as day after day her friend shrivelled beneath her clothes.

Miranda's much-repaired dress hung unattractively on her skeletal frame. She sat on the bed, stroked the thin material of the skirt and fiddled with the buttons before she removed the dress and handed it to Marion.

'Mirry, are you sure you're all right? You've lost a lot of weight.'

'Stop fussing, Marion, wouldn't every lady want to fit into the dress she wore at school?'

Putting her arm around her friend's shoulder, Marion said gently, 'We don't have to go to the rock to-day. You certainly don't have to wear that dress. It's way beyond its best.'

Miranda leaned against Marion's strong body. 'It is ages since we've been.'

'And it's even longer since you've worn your dress to the rock.' Marion noticed the seam on the sleeve had come apart.

'I know, Marion, but I want to go one more time.'

Marion was shocked at this request. They stopped going to the rock once a week at Miranda's insistence. In summer she complained about the heat and worried about sun damage to her fair skin. In winter, she always declared it was just about to rain and she didn't want to get her remodelled coat wet. The umbrella they found on the top of the wardrobe had a broken arm and mouse-nibbled holes.

Marion was more than happy not to go to the rock regularly, but she occasionally wandered in that direction and scouted around the base, staring at the pitted surfaces.

She had become used to the solitude, used to surviving, and resigned to her odd existence. She enjoyed the selfishness of seclusion, the pleasure of isolation, and she never tried to explain it to Miranda.

Marion shook herself out of her reflections and asked kindly, 'Are you even up to walking that far?'

Miranda took the yellowing dress from Marion, folded it and then laid it gently on the bed. 'Perhaps not,' she said quietly.

'Then let's leave it until you feel better.'

The stillness in the house was suddenly disturbed by a rushing wind. It knocked over an ornament and blew the tablecloth to the floor. Marion put her arms around Miranda. They stayed that way until the air was once again calm.

'It's all right, Mirry. It's all right, just an autumn storm on its way. We are due for one and the rainwater tank certainly needs topping up.'

They returned the dress to the cupboard and spent all afternoon reminiscing.

The rain came late that night, blustering its way across the welcoming soil. Quick slithers of puddles filled the edges of the vegetable garden before the ground accepted the wet. Flapping sheets of tin echoed noisily on the roof, but the house stood firm.

As the wind continued to moan, Marion thanked 'the heavens', while Miranda lasted only ten minutes in her own bed. She crept under the covers and snuggled up to Marion. She muttered long-ago learned prayers until she fell asleep.

The departure of the storm brought clear morning skies. Gum trees spread their distinct eucalyptus aroma through the air like a declaration of thankfulness.

Marion left Miranda sleeping and pushed the kitchen fire into wakefulness. She needed a cup of tea. *Thank goodness there are always a few more spoonsful in the stone jar.*

With two steaming cups of tea wobbling in the saucers, Marion called out, 'Good morning, are you well today?'

With a yawn and a stretch, Miranda greeted her friend with a smile, 'Yes, I think I am.' She got out of bed and stretched again. 'I feel quite well today. Did you sleep well?'

'Not really. I'm used to sleeping by myself.'

'I'm sorry, Marion; I didn't mean to spoil your sleep.'

'It's quite all right. I can catch up tonight. I was glad of company too,' she lied.

They tucked themselves back into bed and enjoyed the rare occasion of a morning with postponed chores.

'I had a wonderful dream, Marion.'

'Was I in it?'

'No. It was all about butterflies.'

'You're smiling, so I guess it had a happy ending.'

'It was lovely. There were two large crystal vases filled with roses. Then, one vase tipped over and instead of water spilling out there were dozens of beautiful butterflies. They flew around a tree that looked like our lemon tree, except it had diamonds hanging on it. Roses in the other vase grew even taller before they smiled and died. The butterflies came back and landed on the flowers that sprang back to life. Then the butterflies flew to the heavens.'

'Mirry, that sounds gorgeous.'

'I feel very happy today. I think we should have a party.'

'That sounds a grand plan. You must be feeling better. What do you want to eat?'

'Can you make a cake?'

'Not a proper cake.' Marion frowned. 'The sugar has finally run out.'

'I suppose pancakes and lemon will have to do.'

'I could turn pancakes into some sort of layered cake. There's a little jam and perhaps you could look for some berries for the top.'

Miranda declared she would make new party hats and find the home-made checkers board.

'First breakfast and chores,' said Marion.

Marion was pleased to see her friend active again. Miranda liked playing with the small china rabbit that she named Brisket. She often talked in whispers to a porcelain lady without a left arm. Dusting was usually completed with regular monotony – whether it needed doing or not, but it was some time since Miranda felt up to it.

Late in the morning, Marion jumped when the back door banged. She looked up from stoking the fire and was shocked to see a dishevelled figure, outlined by the winter sunlight, push through the door. The shock of seeing her friend so rumpled made her fumble the poker.

Honey clung to Miranda's arms and little globules of golden liquid were stuck in her grey hair. 'Look what I found.' Miranda stumbled across the floor.

'Goodness, what have you been doing?' asked Marion, as she hurried towards her friend.

Miranda's hair stuck out at the back, her shirt was twisted and her trousers were spotted with dirt. Honey dripped down the side of the bowl leaving a trail on the floor. Marion took the sticky bowl and ushered Miranda to the basin on the bench. 'Where did you get this?' Marion dabbed at the dust on Miranda's face and encouraged her to wash her hands.

'I found another beehive down where the path passes the jacaranda.'

'Bless you. Surely you didn't attack the hive without cover.'

'The bees seemed sleepy. I pulled my shirt over my head.' Miranda giggled. 'Remember how you did that with your skirt on the very first night.' Marion nodded with surprise. 'Well,' continued Miranda, 'I put my shirt over my head, peeked out through the button holes and poked the hive with a stick.' She pushed Marion's hands away from her face. 'The bees went everywhere; mostly up in the air. I didn't know bees were so noisy. I couldn't see much, but I could hear them around my head. I stood still and hoped they wouldn't sting me. I waited until they settled down. Then I scraped as much liquid as I could from the part in the tree. A broken piece is in the bowl too.'

Marion couldn't believe that Miranda risked being stung. Usually, anything resembling danger would be left to Marion.

'I thought we just had to have something extra sweet for our party.'

Picking at the sticky wax in Miranda's hair, Marion assured her that the honey was a blessing and she would attempt to make a cake.

'Now change your clothes. Then you can tell me more about your adventure with the bees while we have some lunch.'

After Miranda changed, the two women sat eating fresh tomato, carrot and parsley for lunch.

'I couldn't find any berries. I don't think it's hot enough. While I was looking, I spotted bees hovering around one of those spindly bushes. I was most surprised to see a hive. Fortunately I could reach it.'

'Weren't you afraid?'

'I did think about coming to get you.'

Marion's lips moved slightly at the corners. 'Why didn't you?'

Putting down her fork, Miranda turned and gave Marion a stern look. 'I just knew I could do it.' She grinned. 'It suddenly seemed a shame to waste all those tough years on the station.'

'Well done. I might get you doing more outside work.'

'No, I should think not. Honey doesn't hurt my hands.'

Although Miranda laughed, Marion thought she was holding something back. She touched Miranda's forearm. 'Is something bothering you?'

Miranda stared at the tiny pieces of parsley in the bottom of the bowl. She whispered, 'A little.' She peeped up at Marion without lifting her head. 'After I gathered the honey, I watched the bees for a while. They were busy, happy to go about their particular task, even though I'd disturbed them.' She took a long breath. Her chin lifted. 'It made me think of my dream. When I remembered those beautiful butterflies, I wanted to dance.' She pushed the bowl away and sagged onto the table, no longer looking at Marion. 'I wanted to be able to do things without feeling so tired all the time.'

As the lowering sun peeked out from the dense grey clouds and announced evening was on its way, Miranda demanded that Marion should put on her dress.

'I'm not wearing it, Miranda. It's so old. It probably won't fit me anymore.'

'You *have* to wear it.'

'No, I don't. I haven't put it on for … I can't remember for how long. I'm not even sure where it is. Besides, I'm more used to trousers now.'

Miranda put on her most shocked voice, 'You can't wear trousers to a party.'

'I have to every other party we've had.'

'You can't wear trousers this time. I won't let you.'

'Miranda, you're sounding like a spoilt child. What's got into you?'

Without another word, Miranda dropped the towel she held and stalked out of Marion's bedroom.

'Well, I never.' Marion pushed her hair behind her ears and

pinched her cheeks before returning to the kitchen. She hoped that Miranda wasn't going to spoil their plans by sulking.

Twenty minutes later, Marion was about to place the kettle back on the stove top when she stopped and stared at Miranda. She was stunned at the image that swept across the floor and twirled in front of her.

Miranda's hair was clipped up in a becoming fashion and she wore a dress Marion hadn't seen before. A pale blue bodice, with embroidery around a high neckline, sat over a velvet skirt that showed off her slim figure perfectly. Marion realised the velvet was one of the discarded curtains and the lace on the sleeves was probably the piece from the tablecloth washed all those years ago. 'Mirry, you're beautiful. When did you make it?'

'Do you like it?' She twirled again.

'It's ... it's wonderful. Come closer, let me see it properly. It must have taken you ever so long.'

'You sat there every evening, reading your books. I continued stitching.'

'I did wonder what you were making. I should've taken more notice.'

'It's all right.' Miranda adjusted the skirt. 'Are you sure it suits me?'

Marion touched the lace then pointed at the skirt. 'The colour is perfect. You look most elegant. Let's start the party.'

'Won't you now put on your dress?'

'Dearest Miranda, I'll stay as I am. You're the Belle of the Ball tonight.'

They played knucklebones with small smooth stones, checkers and snakes and ladders while sipping cool lemon tea out of the best glasses. They ate cold rabbit and pickle sandwiches, apple-layered pancakes and a sultana cake, soggy with honey. When darkness came, they danced amongst the flickering shadows of the lamp, swaying together slowly as they hummed long-ago learned tunes.

Miranda lingered near the stove and watched the embers fade from glorious amber and red to solemn black. Her fingers, crumpled with age, stroked the smoothness of the velvet, delaying the time when she would have to remove the only finery she owned.

'Come, Miranda, it's time for bed.'

'I don't want this day to end.'

'I know. It's been lovely, but you look very tired.'

'Can I sleep in your bed tonight, Marion?'

'You would sleep better in your own bed.'

'Yes, but it wouldn't be as nice.'

After receiving numerous kicks to her shin, Marion finally slipped out of her warm comfortable bed and into Miranda's cold one. No butterflies tonight; it must be hound dogs chasing her, thought Marion, as she rubbed the sore spot.

The next morning, Miranda lay in a motionless heap and whimpered. Waking with a start, Marion rubbed her eyes and sat up. She tried to decipher where the urgent mewing was coming from. Wrapped in a grey blanket she scurried through to the other bedroom. She was confronted with an acidic smell and vomit across the floor.

'Miranda, what's happened?'

A body wriggled beneath the bedclothes. When a mop of hair, tangled with hairclips, forced its way to the top, Marion could hardly recognise the ashen face and darkened sockets. Two eyes struggled to focus. 'Marion, I feel terrible.'

Stepping around the dried particles of food, Marion adjusted the pillow and gently lifted strands of Miranda's matted hair away from her face. The covers were splattered with the proceeds of Miranda's stomach, and stiff under Marion's touch.

'Stay still, Mirry, it's difficult to attend to you properly until I clean the floor.'

Miranda found it too exhausting to consider forming a sentence.

Marion mopped the floor and replaced the bedcover with the grey blanket. Then, after wiping Miranda's face and hands, left her to sleep.

Marion dressed, splashed water over her face and tackled the onerous task of washing soiled linen. When the wet bedclothes were hanging out to dry, she returned to the bedroom. She held her breath as she gently touched the blanket. 'Mirry, would you like a cup of tea?'

Miranda lay still, but whispered, 'Yes … please.'

The tea lasted one minute before it was heaved across the floor by violent stomach contractions. Marion jumped up from the foot of the bed and grabbed the tea cup from Miranda's shaking hand. Miranda slumped back on the pillow, distraught at the mess.

Marion took the cups back to the kitchen. She returned with a damp cloth and offered it to Miranda. 'I think you overdid it yesterday. All that food. You ate three pieces of honey cake.'

Miranda whispered, 'So delicious. So sweet.'

'I know, but you haven't been well for quite a while.' She handed over the cloth. 'Maybe the dancing was too much. And you had that encounter with the bees.' Marion nodded. 'Yes, I think you overdid everything.'

Pleased with the coolness of the cloth against her flushed skin, Miranda said, 'I felt … wonderful. Happy … so happy. The honey … was lovely.' In between the gasping words she dabbed at her lips with the cloth. Suddenly her stomach heaved again. The continual dry retching left her pallid and weak.

Marion forgot to eat. She tried to ignore the demanding chickens.

Watching her friend took up the remainder of the day. The emotional effort of wanting to ease her friend's discomfort, and not being able to do so, hung over her like a heavy coat on a hot day. By evening, weighed down with the knowledge of their impossible isolation, Marion was exhausted. She left Miranda sleeping and retired to the other bedroom. The bed was hard and unforgiving while Miranda's constant groans disturbed her.

Rising early after a night of worrying, and sleeping in broken hours that felt like minutes, Marion was saddened by Miranda's deteriorated condition. Her frail bones were now visible through opaque skin.

The left-over honey cake went hard and the pancakes grew mould. Marion survived on soup. She lost weight she couldn't afford to lose. Warm water with a spoon of honey was all Miranda could keep down. Six long days after she took sick, Miranda asked to be dressed in her new party dress.

'Why do you need your dress? I'm sure you're more comfortable in your night clothes.'

'Please, Marion. My party dress. Please.'

'Wait until you're stronger.'

'That's just it,' she wheezed, 'I won't be well again. My lovely dress ... want to wear it.' Her eyes closed. 'Before I die.'

Marion let go of the bedclothes she was straightening and said, 'No, you mustn't. I won't let you.' She hurried from the room feeling as if she had been crushed by falling rocks. Automatically drawn to the lemon tree, she picked a leaf, and with shaking hands, tore it apart.

She went back into the house and reluctantly helped Miranda into her dress. The dress that fitted only a short time ago now gaped around her bony neck. It took quite some time for the small buttons down the front of the bodice to be fastened and Marion was dismayed to see how much the effort of dressing exhausted Miranda.

'Mirry dear, is there anything else I can do for you?'

Miranda sat on the edge of the bed and fiddled with a button. 'I'm going home,' she took a deep breath, 'today.'

'You should stay in bed, save your strength.' Marion felt her fortitude waning. Her bottom lip quivered.

'The butterflies,' Miranda sucked in air, 'look how close.' Her breath came out noisily. 'Such pretty colours.'

'Don't talk. Here, lie back against the pillows.'

'I want you ... to see ... the butterflies.' She coughed so violently that her lips turned white. With determination she raised her hand and pointed. 'Blue ones ... on the bed.' Miranda smiled valiantly. 'Look ... aren't they ... pretty?'

Marion looked lovingly at her friend. Miranda was breathless, but enjoying the mirage that fluttered around the room. Marion's hand wafted through the air, as if waiting for the butterflies to land on her suntanned fingers. Why should I spoil the last moments of her time by explaining reality to her? thought Marion. *Haven't we lived without reality anyway?*

'See, Marion, ... gold ones ... like you ... best.'

When Miranda felt dizzy, Marion fluffed up the pillows and tucked her back under the covers. Miranda sipped more warm honey water and contentedly watched the butterflies come and go.

She drifted in and out of consciousness for several hours. Each moment brought a new heartache for Marion. Miranda's demand for them both to be ready for rescue at any moment was a most repetitive appeal. In her delirious state Miranda spoke to her mother about a new hat. She giggled with someone called Rachel for a few minutes before heart-wrenching coughing stopped the chatter. Her clipped sentences continued as she instructed her father to organise a party for her homecoming. Deep sighs accompanied hand waving. She mentioned Sara repeatedly.

Marion resorted to acting out the part of the recipient of Miranda's attention. She found the emotion of seeing her friend in such confusion more difficult with each character. Marion felt close to tears, but she straightened the bedclothes, sat on the edge of the bed, held her friend's frail hand and hummed quietly.

In one of her lucid moments, Miranda said, 'You've been a good friend. Hasn't it been most odd here?'

Marion couldn't trust herself to speak. Slight pres-sure on her hand made Marion smile gently as Miranda said, 'I tried to be happy. I wanted to be happy.'

'I know,' was all Marion could manage.

Miranda's next words came out in one breath. 'I'm going home today.' Then, with an involuntary spasm, she stopped breathing.

Marion withdrew her hand. She stood up and looked at the motionless body through dribbling tears. After shifting a stray hair from across Miranda's cheek, she left the room.

Marion wandered around the house. She remembered when they first met at school, how Miranda insisted on brushing her hair every night, and how ghostly she looked with the lamp in front of her face. Marion touched Brisket the rabbit, and picked up a chipped vase. She smiled as she replaced it on the table with burnt legs. She remembered how Miranda grabbed it with defiance as they left the homestead.

Night birds ceased their calling and started to hunt. Marion sat on the bright purple flowers of the couch and sobbed.

TWENTY-SEVEN

'How awful,' Rebecca said, as she fished a tissue out of her pocket. 'The poor woman. What did you do?'

Michael touched Rebecca's face; wiped away some mascara. 'I felt terrible. I didn't seem to be able to comfort her properly. She cried for ages. All I could do was listen. Marion said she had to tell me everything. I didn't really see the point. But now, I know it really is important to share your feelings.'

Rebecca smiled at him. 'You've made it sound so real. I feel like I've lost someone I've known for ages.'

Michael nodded and said, 'I understand how it would feel to lose your best friend, but most people have family or other friends for support. Marion was all alone after that. Imagine – no one. Bloody hell, it must've been tough.'

Rebecca hadn't experienced the permanent loss of anyone close. Imagining being completely alone, her tears welled again. Dabbing her eyes, she said, 'I couldn't bear it if Kylie died.'

Michael picked up a tissue box and thrust it towards Rebecca, saying with a chuckle, 'You'll need these if you start thinking of Kylie like that.'

After getting Rebecca a glass of water and drinking half of it himself, Michael said, 'It took a few days before I dared to prompt her for more. She usually took off after feeding the chickens in the morning. Sometimes she'd instruct me to do something for her. I assumed she wandered around the bush. She never suggested I could go too.'

'Why didn't you just ask if you could go? I would have.'

'Yeah, you would've, but I thought she wanted to be alone. I mean, she wasn't used to men.'

'Surely she'd want to find out everything she could from you?'

'Her questions were never-ending, but she didn't always want constant chatter.'

'Are you implying I'd be better at the talking bit?' Rebecca playfully punched him on the arm.

He pretended to be hurt and grabbed her hand. 'Well, maybe. I know stuff about everyone you come into contact with.' He grinned and added, 'but hey, that's one of the things I like about you – no secrets.'

They nibbled potato crisps and drank fruit juice as she heard more of Marion's story.

TWENTY-EIGHT

Tossing grimy soil over her beautiful friend left Marion emotionally devastated. A corner of the hand-stitched dress stuck out from beneath the plain cotton sheet and Marion thought of the night Miranda wore her new dress for the first time.

Although the afternoon was cool, perspiration dripped from Marion's forehead. Her arms ached from the effort of shifting the soil, but it was the turmoil that gnawed inside her chest which made her pause every few minutes. It took several separate attempts to com-plete the burial.

Marion then washed, changed her clothes and draped Miranda's hair ribbons across her shoulders. She stood next to the grave and started singing a song they learned in Religious Studies. 'Count your blessings, name them one by one, and it will surprise you what the Lord has done.'

She folded her arms over her chest and bit her lip. *What has the Lord done?* Her grief overshadowed any anger she felt towards a god who'd left them in a void.

Throwing a final shovelful of soil onto the completed grave, she repeated words she heard at her great-aunt's funeral, 'Dust to dust, ashes to ashes. Um ... bless you, Miranda. Thank you for being my friend.'

She bent down and placed a small wooden plaque on the soil, then straightened up. A picture of Miranda repeating Mulga Bill's Bicycle flashed through her mind. She chuckled and tried to remember the poem.

'Twas Mulga Bill, from ta, de, dum, with a cycling craze

He shooed away the good old horse that ... that ... was with him for days

He dressed himself in clothes, um something ... um ...

'That's not right. Sorry, Miranda,' she whispered, 'I should have paid more attention.'

She tied the ribbons to a branch of the lemon tree and watched them flutter in the breeze. Then she turned away and went and watered the garden. She would have to cope with the loss of Miranda with the same stoicism which got her through each step of this surprising life.

Marion missed Miranda with persistent melancholy. Marion realised it was Miranda who had prevented her becoming mute. Miranda's chirpy chatter filled the silence during meal time and her melodic humming, as she turned another unwanted item into a useful garment, provided an unspoken closeness. Marion even missed the scenarios Miranda built after the babbling questions of, I wonder what ...? Do you think ...? Who do you think ...? Now Marion wondered, what would Miranda do? What would Miranda think if I ...?

There was no one to admire the fish that took two hours to catch, no reason to pick a delicate creamy bush orchid or a bunch of rock fern, and carry them home in the bucket alongside dark berries. Miranda was gone. Even the kind unseen Aborigines couldn't change that.

However, as the days went by, Marion found she could be happy again. Walking through the bush remained a joy. She often talked to the ever-changing menagerie that wandered past on the way to its own challenge. Almost every day she would dress quickly and step out into the fresh air. Breakfast and chores were done later.

Because her days were filled with wanderings and gardening, the shelves of the dresser became a depository for dust. She swept the floor spasmodically. Meals were taken after hunger pangs crept to her stomach. Marion rarely used the magic of the lamp, preferring to go to bed with the sun so she could rise early.

Sometimes she would stay out all day. There was always water in the creek, or if she ventured in the other direction, a catchment of water in rocks. With the wind tugging at her coat and her hair flying behind her, she would spend the last hour of sunlight walking along familiar pathways through the bush she loved.

Marion stopped crossing off days on the makeshift calendar. She crumpled up the spare sheets in a period of despondency. *I don't need to count my days. One day follows the next. I do what I have to do.* Nothing else matters, she thought, as she let the crushed paper fall into the fire.

Marion noticed supplies were dwindling. Several weeks earlier the sugar had finished – it never reached below a few handfuls for all its years. It was odd that the fig tree had withered. She still had a pot of jam in the cupboard, but the branches, which usually shaded the fowls, had lost most of their leaves.

'Oh dear, I was really looking forward to more of your grapes,' she told the vine, as she touched its dead trunk.

Along with the dwindling supplies, Marion realised that her energy was diminishing quickly. One morning she felt a stab of pain in her right knee as she strode towards the creek.

'Old age. What a nuisance it is.'

Her white skin lay hidden beneath her clothes, but the exposed parts were deep brown. Marion's pale legs almost disowned the tanned feet, her arms were a patchwork of colours and her hands were spotted with the marks of a grandmother.

She sat with her fishing line circling around the rocks in the creek's edge, hoping a fish might like the worm dug from the muddy bank. When the bucket held the inquisitive fish, Marion gathered her things and headed for home.

The bush was dry. The grasses were silvery brown – ready to drop their seeds in anticipation of early autumn rains. There were few flowers to brighten the bushes. A pair of wedge-tail eagles broke the silence as they flew out of the tree tops; disturbed by the old lady sauntering along the gritty track.

The fish lay motionless under her wet scarf. Marion brushed the waist-high bushes with her fingers, continuing along the path at a slow but regular pace. She came to the area where the homestead had stood in a window of constrained time. All that was left was the jacaranda. How beautiful it looked as it reached out across the lonely space. Distinctive purple-blue bells covered the majestic limbs and provided a canopy which seemed to bring the sky within touching distance. Marion took one more look over her shoulder as she turned for home. She understood that the image was all in her heart, for jacarandas flower just before Christmas.

It was one of Miranda's evening rituals to attend to her hair and while Marion was permitted to use the brush and comb, it was imperative that they were returned to their rightful spot in the drawer of Miranda's bedside table. Some habits didn't change, even when they could.

'In you go.' Marion absentmindedly pushed the brush into the drawer, but it wouldn't slide across the wooden base. 'Away with you,' she said, but the brush dug into the end of a book. 'Oh, I remember,' she said, as she picked up the journal and flipped it open. Neat script filled almost every page. *Dear Mum,* the first entry said. *Please insist that Sergeant Bumpher finds us immediately. I would dearly welcome the opportunity to be gone from this place.*

'Good heavens!' Marion exclaimed, as her knees gave way. She sat on the bed and read the heartfelt poems and comments which were intermingled with begging letters. *Please, please, come and get me. I cannot bear the torment for much longer.* Each page was full of emotion. Reading the dark thoughts and poignant pleadings to unreachable persons filled Marion with regret.

'Mirry, I didn't know you were *so* unhappy.'

Marion assumed the annoying and constant questioning from Miranda was a habit. Make-believe stories of what would occur, once they were found, were Miranda's way of passing the endless time. Here was evidence that those annoyances were the outpouring of an underlying yearning that consumed her friend. While Marion gradually eased into a life of compromise, all those isolated years had been purgatory for Miranda.

My dearest Sara,

How I miss you. Do you still have my photograph? I hope you will not forget me even though I've been away for so long. I think of you every day. Please, I beg you, please remember me.

Marion closed the journal slowly and pushed it into the dark recess. The brush lay forgotten on the bed.

She leaned against the window frame and stared through the glass until dusk turned into evening. She remained there until she shivered with cold. No tears came, but Marion felt a darkness descend on her contentment.

Although the date was unknown to her, on the morning of the fourteenth February, 2013, Marion felt the magnetism of Hanging Rock grip tightly. She stood alongside a fence post and looked into the distance. Dust swirled around her feet and the far-off rock pulled at her curiosity. She shook her head and thought, no, it's no longer important. I'll not bother.

That night, her restless sleep was filled with dreams of deep crevices and tumbling stones. The soft light of morning was welcome. She dressed hastily, ate sparingly and fed the fowls.

Again she stopped at the boundary and looked to-wards the rock. Despite not being able to see it, the pull was even greater than yesterday and she knew she had to submit to its unnatural demand.

After dawdling along familiar tracks, Marion stood and admired Hanging Rock. The many contours fascinated her. She respected its majesty, but the wariness born from the memory of long-ago terror remained. She ambled around the base of the foreboding monolith, stepped over the spiky grasses and ducked under the stringy-bark trees. A sense of necessity clung to her as she traipsed across a small clearing beside the rock pools. It was as if she expected to find something important. Something unknown. Something that would only be evident when it was found.

Marion scooped a few handfuls of water into her mouth. She sat and leaned back against a tree, shel-tering from the glare and heat of the mid-afternoon sun. Thoughts returned to the day her new life began – a life in which every normal aspect of living had been whisked away in a cloud of dust.

Marion remembered seeing Miss McCraw moments before stepping into the place where the tearing wind lashed their delicate bodies. *Had she also been transported to another place? How would an elderly teacher with such delicate habits survive?*

Marion realised that Miranda and she had been closely nurtured by parents and teachers. Both families employed servants to cook, clean and tidy for them. A finishing school taught manners, deportment and French. All scholarly attributes, but useless in the face of reality. She smiled and felt proud of their resourcefulness.

Marion stood up, brushed down her trousers and thought about going home. *I don't know why I came.*

When she walked no more than five yards, movement caught her attention. She stopped and shaded her eyes. It must have been a wallaby, she told herself. She moved on, swinging the bucket by her side. It was still empty, but one never knew what could be found along the way.

There it is again. Too large for a wallaby. It must be a kangaroo. She stopped again. She took a closer look through the bushes to her right. 'Well, heavens be praised. It looks like a person.' She dropped the bucket and hid behind a bush. Her hand covered her open mouth. *Perhaps I'm dreaming.* Marion shook her head and rubbed her eyes. *No, the person has moved again. Looks like a young man.* She stood behind the bushes, trying to come to terms with her discovery. *Is it a mirage?* She blinked repeatedly as she watched him pull something small from his pocket.

The man sat down and stared at the ground. Marion crept closer. *He's definitely not a mirage.* She pushed aside a branch of the shrub. The man kicked at something. He stood up. Marion let go of the branch and stooped down. There was something odd about his clothes. His blue trousers were well-fitted and he wore only an undershirt. She straightened up slowly when he sat down again.

Marion thought of how many times she wished for someone to appear. But now, she was wary of this strangely-dressed person. *Where did he come from? How did he get here when no one else had?*

She sat down and bent her head so low it almost touched her bent knees. Tears threatened. She covered her mouth with her hand again; determined to remain silent. *Will I finally be rescued?* She leaned her chin on her hands. Her elbows dug into her thighs. *Do I want to be rescued?* She considered this for several moments and then she heard the man talking to himself, swearing at the elements. She stood up, but remained hidden. *I have to help him.* She reached for the bucket and then stepped from behind the shrub. Her pulse raced. Her mouth was dry. As she took a couple of steps forward she thought, I must find out who he is.

'Hello,' she called.

The man jumped to his feet. He looked surprised. Then his mouth opened slightly and his eyes expressed relief.

TWENTY-NINE

'Heavens, I bet you were glad to see her.' Rebecca hunched up her shoulders and then rolled her head back and forth trying to get rid of the stiffness in her back.

'Mmm ...' Michael closed his eyes.

'You're so brave. I would've been a mess.'

Opening his eyes and staring at her, he said in a weak voice, 'Brave? No. Shit-scared more like it. It was all totally insane.'

She watched him closely as he scrunched his eyes closed again. 'Michael.' She lightly touched his leg. 'Are you okay?'

He stretched his arms towards the ceiling, holding them up as he rotated his wrists. Rebecca was about to speak, but he brought his arms down and rubbed his neck as he focussed on something across the room. 'That's where I went in ... into a bloody dream world, Rebecca. Three months of a dream.'

'It wasn't a dream, Michael. You were definitely missing for three months.'

'Sometimes I wonder.'

'You only have to check out the police reports to know they thought it was real. You being missing I mean.'

Michael sighed. The reality was he knew it had happened, but as he was relating the details to Rebecca, he felt it drifting away. It was like going on a holiday to a far-away place. All the pictures are on the computer, probably one or two displayed on a wall or a shelf, but the actual *feeling* of the holiday goes. Someone could convince you it never happened if the proof wasn't there. He knew that his visit to Hanging Rock was a reality that he would have to tuck into a pocket of memories, but not just yet.

Rebecca convinced Michael to paint pictures of six abstract cats. She dragged a promise out of him that if the colourful art sold he would supply more cats, and some dogs. Jan was delighted to have original work by a local artist and displayed it prominently in her shop. The exposure contributed to it selling quickly.

Michael said it was Rebecca's fault they had so little time to spend together. His complaints weren't genuine as he welcomed a reason to paint more often. He delivered a further three cats and two dogs within a fortnight and gradually extended his range. A green giraffe, a gorgeous blue monkey swinging on an aqua-coloured vine and a smiling red elephant with a multi-coloured palm leaf created immediate interest. Owen stopped teasing Michael about the 'psychedelic squiggles of drug-induced beasties' when Michael's art proceeds subsidised a trip to the pub with Michael, Rebecca and her friends.

Meanwhile, Rebecca regularly visited Rose on Tuesdays. When the weather co-operated they strolled to a nearby park and enjoyed each other's company in the fresh air. Rose would often tell Rebecca about her friends. Fran and Audrey in particular.

'Three old biddies painting the town pink.' She chuckled, as she explained, '*Red* is unfortunately out of our league now. Fran's recently celebrated her eightieth birthday and caught up with Aud and me.'

Rebecca was astounded. The things they got up to. It made her look at them in a different light. If they could climb Mt Kosciuszko in their sixties, and later start a friendship club for elderly immigrants, she felt ashamed that she didn't fill her time with more productive activities.

'Well, dear,' Rose explained, 'When you don't have to go to work every day, you can be more useful. That's what life's about, isn't it? Being useful; helping others. What do you young things say? A journey. It's just that. And one should always have good travelling companions.'

Michael continued to share his experiences with Rebecca. Emotion would often sneak into his blue eyes as he recounted stories of his time with Marion. He tried to explain the utter hopelessness of the situation.

'A life without some sort of hope turns to despair. How Marion, and Miranda, did it, I can only guess. You know, they did absolutely everything for themselves. Apart from the Aborigines, who popped up when the women were desperate, they were all alone. They lost all their dreams for a normal future. They had no idea of the changes that were going on in the world. For instance, they didn't know if their parents were alive or dead. They had no notion of how their friends' lives were going. I guess there are people the world over who feel that every day. It must be awful. I certainly don't want to feel that again.'

Rebecca hesitated, but decided she wasn't about to start being cautious. 'Michael, don't you think you should take control of your future? What about that cubicle with the computer screen that you hate so much? Is that all you want?'

With a grunt of a laugh, Michael said, 'I hate that cubicle, as you so aptly describe it.'

'Then?'

'Then what?'

'It's really up to you. Remember, you've experienced the real feeling of lost hope, now's your chance for a life where dreams can come true.'

'You're right, of course. Stupid of me to stay there, but ... it's a huge step.'

'Life's full of huge steps. You just have to be brave.'

Placing his hand on Rebecca's knee, he smiled and said, 'And when are you going to take your own advice?'

'What do you mean?' she asked, putting her hand over his.

'Just a little matter of a gift shop of your own. I've heard you talking to your father. You have that file full of information. What about those hand cream samples you gave Gran? Are you brave enough or is it just me that has to take these huge steps?'

'Right.' She grimaced. 'Looks like it's decision time for both of us.'

When they parted, he hugged her tightly. She felt a special closeness as he kissed her gently on the lips, then whispered, 'Take care. I'll see you soon.'

Rebecca waited three days before calling Michael, but he wasn't home. She hoped that the remainder of his story might disclose the reason for her odd reactions. Rose told her he'd been a little distant and spent a lot of time painting. 'But, right now ... I think he's gone for a walk. His car's still here. He left without saying anything. That's not like the old Michael.'

'That doesn't sound good, Rose. And what about you? Are you okay?'

'Yes thanks. I'm just worried about him. I'm sure it's the memories. I guess he has to work through them all.'

'I agree. Last time we were out, we went past a fruit shop and he looked at the lemons for ages. He said they reminded him of the day he buried Marion. I didn't like to ask about it. I guess he'll tell me when he's ready.'

Rose took a while to speak. 'I dished up pumpkin soup last night. He apologised for not being able to eat it. He went to his room. His light was still on when I got up again about three o'clock.'

Rebecca knew pumpkin soup took him back to Hanging Rock. She'd been with him when chooks cackling at the local farmers' market stopped him in his tracks.

'Is there anything I can do, Rose?'

'You could come around and talk to him some more. Please, dear, at least ring again later. There really does seem to be something special between you two.'

Previously worried that she'd pushed him to think about things he wanted left alone, Rebecca now felt encouraged by Rose's sentiments, and promised to ring back.

'You're not angry with me, are you?' Rebecca asked Michael, as she entered Rose's home.

'No, why would I be angry?'

Michael had sounded a little cool towards her when she finally spoke to him on the phone. She assumed she'd been a bit pushy, but now she felt as if she placed too much emphasis on him not having been in touch.

'Well, not angry, but I thought you might've thought I shouldn't be telling you how to run your life, when I'm not much better.'

Michael's head tilted and a wry smile broaden into a grin. 'Really?'

'Well, yeah.'

He guided her through to the lounge room and indicated that she should sit next to him. He swivelled sideways so he could look directly at her. Rebecca put her head down and fiddled with her bag.

'Bec,' he said, touching her cheek, 'it's nothing like that. I just have to sort things out. I need time.'

Rebecca put her hand up and touched the same spot. He took her hand and rubbed his thumb over her knuckles.

'Telling you about Marion brought it back so vividly. I needed a break, but I still want you to know the rest.'

THIRTY

Michael took over most chores, but Marion insisted on choosing the vegetables for the soup pot.

'The soup diet, eh!' Michael exclaimed. 'That and wood chopping – guaranteed to reduce the waistline in sixty days or your money back.' He smiled broadly and patted his torso.

Marion felt slightly flushed as she recalled his sleeping body. He certainly hadn't looked like he needed to be on any diet.

Michael swept, dusted and cleaned at Marion's insistence. 'Just because I'm dying doesn't mean standards should slip,' she said. She didn't admit that she rarely dusted Miranda's shelves.

Marion was despondent. She could do little. When the aroma of the bush blew in with the soft evening breezes, her mind filled with memories of her long walks. The sun peeking through the lemon tree reminded her of the time spent with Miranda. She reminisced with Michael as they sat at the table over scant meals. She talked of the second grave under the lemon tree and the things she would miss.

It worried Michael – all her talk of dying, but he helped her make a sign similar to Miranda's. He wanted to even-off the old picket and smooth the edges. She'd argued against the idea.

'I don't want to upstage her,' she insisted.

They had long discussions about their predicament. There *were* no answers, only questions. Why Marion and Miranda? Why were they transported to a time that didn't pass in the normal way? Why was someone from 2013 caught in the same conundrum?

Most nights Michael fell asleep quickly after weeks of unaccustomed manual labour. Other nights, sleep wouldn't come. His mind raced. *What should I do? What can I do?* No answers ever came.

Marion reckoned there was a master plan.

Michael wasn't impressed. 'You mean by God?'

'I'm not sure about God.'

'You pray – surely you've asked him to show you a way out.'

Closing her eyes Marion said, 'You shouldn't expect God to do everything.'

Michael leapt to his feet. He spread out his arms, turning around as he spoke in a staccato fashion. 'Everything! But ... you ... have ... nothing.'

Marion wrapped herself in her arms, looked out the window, then brought her eyes back to Michael. 'My needs have been met. I've had my health and a wonderful friendship. This is a peaceful place, where dreams don't have to come true for one to be happy. Everything ... no, but nothing. No, you are wrong.'

'Bloody hell, Marion, if God showed you the way out, you may've had all that anyway.'

'Maybe it has nothing to do with God.'

He shook his head and sat again. 'Then what?'

'Somehow a little glitch has occurred.'

Michael jumped to his feet and strode to the open back door. He stared out across the long grass. He looked at the scrawny chickens and withered leaves of the fig tree. Spinning around to face Marion, he banged one of his hands into the other and said, 'Well, sure ... like mixing up time frames. How can you call it a *little* glitch when it's totally messed up our lives?'

Every part of Marion's burial was prepared, and she made Michael go over the list so many times it became annoying. He knew she kept altering the text of what she called "her blessing". God knows what she's written, he thought, realising he would be the one to read it.

One time he stormed off telling her that all that was missing from the list was a body. Not very tactful, Michael, he told himself, as he returned inside, sat down next to her on the couch and apologised for his selfishness.

'Thank you, Michael. I understand how difficult it must be for you, but I am doing the best I can.' A slight twitch of her lip showed her sense of humour. Marion touched him on the knee. 'I think you'd better start preparing for a solitary life.'

Wrenching his leg away as if she had struck him, he shoved his hands under his thighs and frowned. 'You're right. I'll have to, won't I? Shit!'

He began taking the bread making more seriously and eyed the chickens with scepticism.

'Are you going to co-operate?' he asked the current batch of hens as they scratched at the vegetable scraps. *Don't chooks stop laying as they get older?*

Each morning he was grateful when Marion appeared. She sat languidly around, asking nothing for herself. She instructed him, 'Keep watering the vegies. Make sure you're careful with the rainwater. Check the shed every day.'

Marion would spend much of the morning sitting on the deteriorating verandah step. She occasionally wandered around the yard and looked longingly into the bush.

As he scrubbed at a pan, Michael thought about the fragility of his own life. *Life is for living, learning, experiencing everything. Well, in a rational existence. Here, that's another matter. Perhaps a tomorrow where you wake up, but have to figure out if the timeframe is the one you were in the day before, might make you think twice.* All I can do is make the most of it, he thought. *Hey! I'm starting to sound like Marion.*

Marion always spent the late afternoon sitting close to Miranda's grave. As long as the weather was decent, she would drag a hessian bag out to sit on and let the softness of the evening envelope her. This was a private time and Michael left her alone.

Her movement from beyond the doorway caught Michael's eye as he sat with his elbows on the table and his hands curled under his chin. He wasn't surprised to see Marion sitting outside, but it was her excessive arm waving that made him stop daydreaming and focus. Marion was pointing to her right and then trailing her fingers through the long grass. Her head nodded occasionally. The leaves of the lemon tree danced above her head and the dappled light made shadows come and go across her grey hair. Sunlight shone on strands that had escaped from her ribbon-bound ponytail.

Michael rose from the chair and scanned the room for some paper. His mind was already plotting how to draw the scene. He found a pencil and the calendar on the table next to the couch, but writing covered both sides of the paper.

He returned to watch Marion as he etched the scene into his memory. He imagined watercolours blending the grass with the sky – delicate greens fading into soft blue. The sturdy trunk of the old tree needed ebony contours – to give the painting strength. He wasn't particularly good at drawing hands, so he would hide those. *One hand behind her leg. Perhaps the other in the grass.*

Marion sat straighter and smiled as if thinking of something pleasant. Yes, that's better, thought Michael. I must give bold lines to the body, but softness to the face. *Damn! There must be some paper somewhere.* He continued to mull over details of the proposed artwork, noting the changing light and its effects.

Finally, Marion eased herself up and gripped a low branch. Her gaze remained on the ground, but her right hand patted her chest. She shook her head slowly as she spoke to something unseen. She picked up the corner of the hessian bag and turned towards the house. Michael moved out of sight and pretended to be interested in the trinkets on the dresser. He turned as Marion pulled the door shut.

'Mosquitoes have risen for the night. They're a blessed nuisance.'

'Yep,' he said. 'Do you have any large pieces of paper, Marion?'

'I beg your pardon?'

'I just wondered if you have any paper.'

'There's the little book we used for the calendar.'

'No, I need something larger.'

'Let me think. We've used most of it over the years. Apart from that book and Miranda's journal, there are only a couple of old accounting books in the trunk.'

'Mmm, could be okay if there's nothing else.'

'What do you want it for?'

Michael picked up a china dog with a missing ear and examined it. 'If I have to stay here then I need to do something constructive with my time. I thought I might draw stuff.'

'Stuff? There's another one of your odd words. What will you draw, Michael?'

'Well, the house makes a good subject. Maybe the lemon tree.' He didn't think Marion would agree to be a subject.

'We haven't got any artist's paper, but let's see what you think of the accounting books.'

The trunk had been relieved of most items, but there were a few dusty books, a yellowing dress and a purple curtain in its depths.

'This one must have been the farm's ledger,' said Marion, as she banged the dust from pages full of handwritten figures. 'There are no spare pages.'

'This's the same sort of book, but it's nearly empty,' said Michael. 'It's better than nothing.'

Marion reached into the trunk and retrieved a small, decorated book. She flicked it open to reveal smudged handwriting. 'Cottage Pie,' she read. 'Scones, teacake. I remember this. It also showed us how to make jam, but it won't do either of us any good today. No blank pages for you – no ingredients for me.' She threw the book back into the darkness.

'This will have to do,' said Michael, as he struck the partially empty ledger against his leg. 'I think I'm going to sneeze.'

Several days later Michael came out from his room, yawning and stretching. He found Marion sitting on the couch wrapped in the curtain that was to be her shroud.

'Bloody hell, Marion. What are you doing?'

'Dying, Michael, and that's no excuse for your bad language.'

'What am I supposed to say? You're sitting there, dressed in your grave robes – you're supposed to be dead first.'

'I'm trying, Michael, really I am.'

He sat down next to her and took her hand, lightly tapping his thumb against her fingers. 'Please, don't joke, Marion.' He smiled compassionately and hugged her.

In the short time he had been there, he'd become fond of Marion. She reminded him of his grandmother. They had the same strength of character. Neither of them let him get away with much, but spoilt him a little as well.

Marion patted his back gently, responding to his affection. After a moment or two, she leaned away from his embrace, but kept hold of his hand. She realised how it would be to have a son, even a grandson, who would bring everyday happenings to one's attention. His eyes that hide nothing, his genuine smile, and the disarming way he laughed at her attempted humour, were endearing. She released his hand and pulled the curtain fabric firmly around her shoulders.

'Don't forget your promise.'

'I won't,' he said quietly.

'And keep your chin up, after I'm gone.'

A short sharp laugh escaped him. 'My *chin* up?'

'Yes. And you must remember everything that's happened.'

'I'm not likely to forget it.'

'I guess not.' She touched his hand. 'I'm glad you came. I've loved every minute of it.'

Michael turned his hand over and gripped hers. 'It's been crazy, but thank goodness you were here, Marion. I probably wouldn't have survived without you.'

After a brief silence she said, 'Michael, you must start looking for your car again.'

He sighed, stood up and looked towards the door. 'I don't believe you just said that.'

'I know, but you must. There is no need to start until after you've buried me. It will be useless until then. I feel it in my bones.'

'Maybe, but let's get you back to bed. You're shivering.' He extended his hand and helped her to her feet. She took time to stand and battled to put one foot in front of the other.

'I'm thirsty,' she said when they reached the bed.

'I'll get you some water.'

'No, not water. May I have some tea, please?'

Once Marion was tucked up in bed with two pillows behind her back, and the bedclothes clutched tightly under her chin, Michael returned to the kitchen. While the pot came to the boil, he chose the prettiest cup and saucer. Determined to do something special, he broke off a few fragrant flowers from the lemon tree and placed them on a tray.

Michael was anxious. He never knew anyone of Marion's age who was as lively as she was when he first arrived. Even his gran, with all her comings and goings, couldn't compete with Marion's daily activities. However, in the last fortnight Marion slowed down completely. He thought she must be extremely ill to go to bed during the day. Marion insisted her death was imminent. He tried to convince her otherwise. She told him it would actually be a blessing. Michael trembled at the thought of being alone.

Entering Marion's bedroom, Michael had to stop the tray from falling from his hands. Marion had let go of the bedclothes and slipped sideways.

Tea splashed over his sneakers. He didn't notice.

'Marion! Oh no!' He dumped the tray on the floor. He tried to prop her back against the pillows, but her inert body fell sideways again. 'Damn it, Marion. You can't die. I need you.'

With his hand gripping her arm, he leaned closer. 'Bloody Hell,' he whispered. 'Marion, please ...' He half-heartedly felt for a pulse, but he knew she was gone.

Marion's body slipped a little more. He shuddered and clenched his teeth. He removed the pillows and carefully pushed her shoulder until her body lay flat. He sucked in a long deep breath, lifted the tray and re-treated to the kitchen. Picking up the flowers, he sniffed them and then hurled them across the room.

THIRTY-ONE

He sat on the front step and stared through the cracks. Marion had died and it was up to him to deal with the situation. His mind drifted to the day he first saw her. Her unusual clothes that no longer seemed out of place, the battered bucket, which he now knew she kept by the back door, the faded scarf, her bare feet and unkempt hair. He smiled as he remembered her surprise at the zip on his jacket, her scorn of modern manners, her strength and subtle humour.

He looked up and spotted Miranda's plaque. It had tipped sideways – as if pointing to the hole in the ground beside it. The significance of the empty grave washed over him like an unexpected cold shower. He gripped his biceps, scrunched up his shoulders and closed his emotions in on himself.

He'd never been to a burial. Grandma had demanded a cremation and that was hard enough to endure.

Now, as he tried to think clearly about the task ahead, he felt stunned by the loss of his elderly companion. *Marion, dear God, why did it come to this?* His whole body felt immeasurably heavy. His lip trembled. His chin quivered in collusion. He rubbed his hands up and down his thighs and tried to breathe evenly. After sitting in a trance-like state for twenty minutes, he stood up, clenched his fists and staggered to the hole in the ground.

Alone. Totally … absolutely … fucking alone. Shit! He stared into the distance, beyond the struggling grasses, over the rusty barbwire that lay next to the rotting fence posts and towards Hanging Rock. *I'm alone now. Is that what you wanted all along?* Standing with his arms folded he dared something to happen.

His newly found determination faded as he turned back towards the house.

Considering the heap of soil that he would have to move, he asked silently, can I drop Marion into the cold earth and shovel dirt over her? His eyes began to mist over as he looked at Miranda's grave then back to the gaping hole. He shook his head and spoke aloud, 'But I have to. I can't leave her where she is. I have to do it. There's no alternative.'

He forced his body to relax as he shook the tension out of his hands. Standing by the bedroom door for several minutes, Michael looked closely at Marion. He'd never seen a dead person before. *She doesn't look much different from two hours ago.*

'Let's get on with it,' he said resolutely.

On his way back from fetching the shovel from the shed, he announced to the fowls, 'It's just you lot and me now.' This simple acknowledgement triggered his emotions and by the time he reached the house he was crying softly. He carried the shovel over his shoulder like a rifle. The back of his other hand wiped away increasing tears.

At the graveside, he thrust the shovel into the heaped soil, covered his face with both hands and sobbed. His sobbing lasted until the shovel fell on his foot. The metal top scraped against his sockless ankle. 'Hell!' He sniffed repeatedly while he examined the graze.

After standing at the edge of the grave for several minutes, he mentally ticked off Marion's list. *Wrap me in the velvet curtain. Don't forget the book. Read the blessing. Lemons.* He smiled as he remembered her instruction about placing her head at the end of the grave nearest the trunk – the same as Miranda. That way, Miranda and I can chat without yelling, she told him. Michael sniffed again and wiped his hand across his moustache. 'Well, Marion. It's time.'

He washed his hands and picked up Marion's shroud. Walking back into the bedroom he hesitated, took a deep breath and spread the purple cloth over her. The warm flaccid body was naturally unco-operative and it was difficult to wrap the body entirely. The first time he lifted Marion, a hand fell out from the covering and bumped against his leg. He shuddered and placed her back on the bed while he steadied himself. Only by divorcing himself from the emotion of it all, could Michael complete the process. He easily carried her through the house and out to the front yard.

I should have planned this better, he thought, as he placed her gently on the ground. Positioning her in the grave was cumbersome and he struggled to handle the body respectfully. The shroud kept slipping off and exposing parts of her body. Several times Michael stopped to calm his reactions. His throat felt tight as he covered her face for the last time. *That's the first bit over.*

Middlemarch was easy to locate. He thought of the many times he saw her reading the book. *She probably knew it off by heart.* Miranda's handwritten script was in the back, behind the partially burnt pages. Michael dropped the book carefully into the grave. It landed near Marion's waist and flipped open at a well-read paragraph.

He swallowed repeatedly and tugged at his beard. Then he went to the kitchen, drank some water and ate a piece of bread before returning to the graveside.

He felt nauseous as he began dropping the soil around her feet. Then he shovelled fervently while not looking where the rest of the soil fell.

As he tapped the back of the shovel across the finished grave, he felt emotionally exhausted. He leaned on the shovel and rubbed his hand across his forehead making several grubby marks.

'That's it, Marion. This's all I can do for you,' he said reverently as he placed the little wooden plaque on the mound.

Marion Quade
1885 – 2013
Gone to join Miranda
After an impossible time

Taking Marion's handwritten note from his pocket, he read aloud, 'Marion was proud to have accepted her life with dignity. Grateful for true friendship. Content with the solitude and thankful for peaceful surroundings. Satisfied with her efforts. Hoping for a better hereafter.' He crumpled the paper, stumbled to the back step and sat down. He licked at his gritty tears as he re-read the eulogy. 'Bye, Marion. I'm sorry I couldn't do more.'

Relieved the gruelling task was over, Michael suddenly realised he hadn't placed the lemons in Marion's grave as instructed. He leaned against the knobbly trunk and considered whether it was necessary. *After all, Marion won't know.* He looked at his neglected hands. He wiped them across the rear of his jeans and then forced them into his pockets. Five minutes of staring at the fresh grave made him reconsider. A promise is a promise, his father always said.

He picked six lemons; frustrated at the ones that were difficult to separate from the branch. He placed them at intervals around Marion's grave, then poked at them with his foot, cursing quietly when soil tumbled into his sneaker.

Knowing his efforts were inadequate, he crawled around the newly finished grave and shoved the fruit as far into the soft ground as possible. The freshly turned dirt became wedged under his fingernails and tiny particles clung to the hairs on his arms. Each time he pushed a piece of fruit towards Marion, he begged for her help in finding a way out of the misery he faced. The knees of his jeans were filthy and matched his hands.

As he stood up and banged his hands together, a waft of lemon scent came to him. He felt it was Marion thanking him for fulfilling her requests. He nodded, formed a tired smile and said, 'You're very welcome.' Then an anxious thought hit him. *Who will bury me?* He took a deep breath and let it out slowly. *When the time comes.*

Working methodically, he heated a pot of water and filled the basin in the washhouse. He tossed off his clothes, washed from head to foot and cleaned his teeth with a cloth on the end of a stick. He put on his night-shirt and dunked his dirty clothes in the water. Once he'd hung them up to dry, he made an omelette. With the house so quiet, he sat at the table, consumed his meal and contemplated how he would cope without Marion.

In an effort to ease his loneliness, he lit the lamp and pulled it close to the open ledger on the table. Michael made five sketches before he was sure he had the correct balance in his drawing. He wanted strength to show along with softness, both in the tree and in Marion. Satisfied with his work, he retreated to his bedroom.

For the next two days he did the chores that Marion had instilled in him - feed the chickens, fetch water, tend to the vegetables, chop wood and sweep. He didn't bother to dust.

On the third day, the hens didn't lay, he used the last of the dry wood, and rabbits burrowed under the wire and ate most of the remaining vegetables.

Michael picked at his broken nails and drew imaginary circles with his foot as he sat and contemplated the inexplicable nature of his situation. *What will happen to me?* It seemed that time here was running out. Winding down to the end like a bad movie. *One with an unexplainable plot and no plausible climax.* He made a grunting sound and considered who had been the main character. *Certainly not me.*

He felt cursed by events. Tucking one hand under his leg, he felt the rough cloth of the covering on the couch and looked closely at the pattern. Moving to his left, he sat over the faded grey section exposing the purple flowers. He grinned inanely. He wriggled further along and sat hunched up in the corner of the couch. He gripped the edge of the cover and muttered, 'Choices? Yeh, right.' Life in the tiny house, in the surrounding paddocks, felt artificial and time passed slowly as jumbled thoughts increased his despondency.

He woke with his head on the arm of the couch. He wiped the saliva from his lip, waited a moment then stood up and moved to the open door. The only sound he could hear was his mechanical breathing.

'A choice?' he whispered as he glanced back at the couch. Then his eyes passed over the graves, through the branches of the lemon tree and towards Hanging Rock. He shouted, '*You* don't give me any choice.'

He went outside and stood near Marion's grave. 'What should I do now?' he asked her. *I've done everything ... curtain, book, plaque, blessing, even the lemons.* He shook his head at how ludicrous he must have looked crawling around the fresh grave, poking lemons into the dirt.

Although there is one other thing. His eyebrows shot up. *Look for my car.* He grunted. He clenched his bottom lip with his teeth. *But, will it still be futile?* Wasn't Marion convinced the mysterious void would disappear once she died? *Why didn't I go immediately?* He was suddenly excited that he might be free at last. *Tomorrow, Marion, tomorrow I'll try again.*

Out of habit, he watered the remaining ragged vegies. 'After this you can bloody well die. I'm out of here tomorrow,' he told a struggling tomato plant.

The next morning was sunny, but a few dark clouds hovered on the horizon. He put aside his fear of disappointment and carefully prepared for his departure. The hens were noisy in their appreciation of extra food. 'This'll keep you going, but I'll come back for you, if it's possible,' he said, as he filled another container with water.

He washed the dishes, swept the floor and straightened the ornaments he knew had belonged to Miranda. He made the beds and gathered his few possessions. He slipped his phone into his pocket, filled the water bottle and pushed it into his backpack next to his camera, wallet and car keys. He folded his sketches and tucked them in the front pocket of the backpack. As he picked up his watch, the engraving on the back caught his eye. *To Michael with love – Mum and Dad.* His eyes watered, but he clipped on the watch, picked up his backpack and left the bedroom.

He held the front door open while he looked around the room. 'Well, this is goodbye,' he said, as he spotted Brisket and the one-armed lady. 'Think I've got everything.' He mentally listed his belongings. 'Ah, I should take something of Marion's.' Brisket stared back. 'No. What else is there?' He wandered around the house considering items small enough to carry. He found Marion's 1942 calendar on the top shelf of the bedside cupboard. 'Yes, that's it. That'll be perfect.' He rolled up the calendar and placed it in his backpack. He looked around the room again, crammed his cap on his head and set out.

At first he was stunned when there was no evidence of 2013, but the pull of the imposing rock was inescapable and he was enticed by the feeling of belonging. Following the pattern of investigation he had fallen into, he raced up the path, scuttled down stony slopes and ducked into small crevices even though he knew they led nowhere. The familiar formations seemed to smile at him and he felt unusually comfortable within the craggy shapes. He found it easy to leap across the gaping cracks he hadn't previously managed. The dark clouds lingered in the distance, leaving the rock bathed in sunshine. It seemed a happy place today and his optimism grew. He remembered the far-stretching scenes he saw on the first day: the farms with the dusty golden paddocks, the straight roads and the verdant patches of trees.

Standing at the highest peak his expectations plummeted far deeper than the rocks below. The view into the distance revealed nothing but continuous bush. No farms. No roads. No fences. Not even the house from which he had just travelled. He squatted down and closed his eyes. Every nerve quivered with defeat.

Marion's face appeared in his mind. She smiled and nodded. He straightened up slowly and breathed audibly. Maybe, he thought, maybe this is a blank canvas, a place ready to start again. The tension in his jaw increased. He rolled his head around and tried to think logically. His stomach turned over with anticipation. *Maybe Marion's prediction can still come true.*

As he swivelled to have a better view in the other direction, he fantasised about what would happen. *Car park comes into view. One blue Forester parked amongst several other cars.* He shaded his eyes. *Nothing.* He frowned and scoured the distance again. He moved to another spot. Two wallabies looked up at him, then hopped away. He saw the effect of the wind on the treetops, but no buildings. He sat down on the hard surface and hung his head. *Marion was wrong. Nothing is different. It's all still hovering in an inexplicable space in time.* The sun hit his back, but he felt cold. He shivered repeatedly. *Stuck. Stuck here forever. Bloody hell!*

In the late afternoon, he dawdled back to the farmhouse. He scuffed his feet and kicked at the small stones on the edge of the path. His temper built. By the time he stomped across the boundary of the farm, his anger climaxed. He cursed the kookaburra sitting in a gum tree, swore at the grass that dared to grow and punched the fence post just because it was there.

Ignoring his hunger, he started digging. Heaving dirt into a pile next to the other graves was easy work for someone in a rage.

Michael was unaware of the time he fell into bed. He didn't change into the sleeveless shirt that was his night attire. He didn't even wash his hands. What did it matter if he left dirt on the sheet? 'Tell someone who gives a damn!' he cried out, as his fist hit the pillow

THIRTY-TWO

Michael continued each day in a trance-like state. He tried to keep his food sources alive. He ate what was edible and cursed the plants that were determined to die. The chickens stopped laying. The shed supplied nothing.

He killed the rooster; it was tough. He pretended slices of yesterday's damper were waffles with maple syrup. When he had eaten the last chicken, and the bones washed clean by repeated cooking, Michael felt wretched. The grapevines had withered, the shade over the empty chicken yard was disappearing rapidly and two onions were standing defiantly in an otherwise barren vegetable garden. The shed still supplied nothing.

Michael decided not to enlarge the third hole under the lemon tree. He thought it unlikely he would finish his grave before he starved to death. 'Next week, next month, doesn't matter. I'm about to disappear from all timeframes,' he said to a magpie that watched him throw the shovel at the small pile of dirt.

However, he wanted to make his headstone. Although he wasn't sure if anyone could penetrate this mysterious vacuum and find his body, he wanted to leave some mark of his presence, just in case. He chopped into an old fence paling and, after a frustrating morning with the blunt axe, ended up with a simple block of wood similar to the pieces that stood at the head of the other graves. In deciding to smooth the edges of the oblong piece of wood, his nails became even more ragged and bruises appeared in his palms. His once delicate artistic hands ached from the continual pushing of a stone over timber.

'I don't care. Dead people don't need hands,' he said, as he wiped blood off his thumb.

In the evenings, he worked on the drawing of Marion. Pieces of charcoal from the cold stove added quality to the picture. He was annoyed with the blue ledger lines that spoiled his attempt to show the evening light on Marion's face. When he stooped over the table with his eyes close to the paper and a pencil or charcoal in his hand, Michael felt calm and peaceful.

Eventually he considered his artwork finished. He slid his initial sketches under the lamp, moved several trinkets and propped the picture of Marion up on the dresser. He stood back and admired the completed work. In the flickering light of the lamp, Marion appeared to come to life.

After another futile day at the rock, Michael prepared to track back to the farmhouse. Earlier, he pounded on the ancient stones and demanded it return him to 2013. The wind whistled through the gaps as if sniggering at his insistent pleas.

He removed his cap and crammed it into his back-pack next to his superfluous wallet, defective camera and an almost empty tube of sunscreen. The constant blank screen of his mobile tormented him. The water bottle was the only useful item in the pack and he filled it from a stream for the return journey.

At the farmhouse, he entered the unlocked door, threw the empty water bottle at the table and heaved his backpack across the floor where it landed next to the dresser. He slumped onto the couch and remained there until dark.

Working in dim lamp light, he tipped the tea container sideways and jiggled the last few leaves into a clean cup. He used the lukewarm water from the kettle and tried to figure out what he could eat. He couldn't be bothered restarting the fire. *Hot buttered toast with smoked ocean trout and feta cheese, or sautéed mushrooms in red wine would be great.* He tore a chunk from a piece of dry bread and nibbled half-heartedly. He downed the liquid in two gulps as he still wasn't used to tea without milk and sugar. After rinsing his cup and throwing the dishwater over the onions, he picked up the smooth block that was to be his headstone.

Michael Wentworth
198

He had considered printing something witty, but the paint he found amongst Marion's garden tools ran out as he tried to add his birth year. "The tomatoes didn't like me" seemed stupid, "gone and forgotten" rather pathetic, but he thought the single word, "trapped", would have been appropriate.

Michael wandered outside and stood under the moonlit lemon tree. He read Marion and Miranda's epitaph several times. The evening's air was cooling swiftly and he shivered as he fingered his unfinished headstone.

'One, nine, eight. Yeah, that means a bloody lot.'

He turned away from the house and heaved the piece of wood as far as he could. It plopped into the long grass. Michael just shook his head and went inside.

He played solitaire with the women's homemade cards, annoyed that he was continually unsuccessful. 'This time,' he said, as he dealt the cards into seven piles.

A strong gust of wind unexpectedly blew the door open and tossed the cards from the table.

'Damn!'

The curtains flapped noisily as the wind increased. The loose sheeting on the roof beat urgently. The back door banged. With each thud, he winced.

Michael fought to shut the front door against the might of the wind. Something hit the side of the house. He jumped and automatically let go of the door. The small table tumbled across the room. Two chairs tipped over. Outside a cockatoo screeched on its way into the distance.

'What's happening?' he cried, as he jammed the door shut again. It struggled against its hinges.

The glass in the window smashed and shards shattered onto the floor.

'Oh my god!' Michael's hands covered his ears.

The buffeting wind continued to moan. He swung around as the ornaments on the dresser clinked together and then danced off the end of the shelf. Brisket shattered. The drawing of Marion sent out a puff of charcoal as it blew away. The lamp fell over and its glass smashed. Fragments floated in the spilt kerosene. The flame ignited Michael's sketches. He tripped over the little table in his attempt to reach the dresser.

'Ouch! Shit!'

By the time he reached the flames, it had flicked embers onto the couch. The dull grey burnt first. The purple flowers smouldered. Then the old kapok caught alight. Burning pieces blew away from the couch. Michael stomped on the mat as the fragile threads caught. The dresser burnt fiercely. The wind laughed at the destruction. When the fire rushed towards him, Michael scampered out the back door.

He watched the flames gobble their way through the building. They licked possessions before consuming them. The fire moved on to take hold of the weather-board walls. It crackled and sniggered its way up the dry boards. The roof swayed. Then with an exaggerated sigh, it collapsed. Lurching timbers pushed the tank over. Water exploded from the warped metal. The rush ripped the remaining onions from the sandy vegetable bed. They bobbed along on top of the torrent as it forced its way across the cleared ground and into the long grass. Puddles sat around his feet, but Michael was compelled to watch. The fire gathered the remainder of the house in its grasp, held it tightly for a moment and then devoured it.

The wind died. The flames whimpered into coals without spreading beyond the yard. It was as if some force deliberately obliterated the farmhouse and nothing else. Standing near the empty chicken coop, Michael looked first at his hands and then at the remains of the building. Both were black. Two blistered fingers and a throbbing thumb were the result of his unsuccessful attempt to snatch his backpack from the flames. Congealed blood dotted his forearm. His beard felt thick with ash. The odour of singed hair made him feel sick.

For several hours, he sat on a rotting fence post that lay on brittle grass. He was empty of thought. He gaped at the blackened space. Every so often puffs of ash exploded into the air, breaking the monotony of his vacant stare. He sniffed occasionally and wiped away the oozing tears. When an owl flew above his head, hooting as it landed in the naked branches of the fig tree, he glanced up at it, shook his head slowly and returned his gaze to the pile of cooling ash. Finally, he stood up, ambled around the perimeter of the burnt-out house, and poked his sneaker at unidentifiable rubble.

'Shit, now what?'

With the mid-May evenings turning cold, Michael realised he could huddle in the hen house amongst the dried chicken droppings, or spend the night in the small shed. He dragged the drum out of the shed and forced the wobbly shelf from its support.

He slept fitfully, thinking of his bed in the flat he shared with Patrick. He longed for a hot shower and clean clothes.

His foot fell into a deeper sleep than the rest of him, so he got up and stomped around until the pins and needles were gone. As he limped around the ruins, he noticed the purple embers had faded into dusky charcoal. Flaky particles drifted around the area, carried away on the softening breeze. He rubbed his arms to create some warmth before returning to the confines of the shed.

He slept until the sun began to warm the small space. Michael woke, stiff from being curled up for so long. Coming out from the shed, he stretched into his tall frame and walked to the chicken coop. Shuddering at the murkiness in the bottom, he splashed water from the half-empty dish over his face. He pushed his hands through his beard and shook the water onto the ground before wiping his hands on his jeans. He put aside worrying thoughts of no food or drinking water and stepped towards the cooled blackness of the previous night's fire. He noticed a piece of paper caught in the wire of the chicken coop's fence. Its stark whiteness contrasted against a pocket of scorched grass.

'I don't believe it,' he said, as he flapped the paper to remove the ash. He gaped at the scrap in his hand. The edges were charred, but the centre of the paper was as white as his mother's best linen.

'No way,' he shouted in amazement. The paper clearly showed Marion's head and shoulders. 'Impossible.' He flapped the scrap again, removing more ash from the reverse side.

Remember to look for your car after I'm gone, Marion had said. As he cradled the drawing in his filthy palm, he realised he must keep trying.

He stepped precariously around the cooling remains. The metal bedhead was now a twisted wreck. A distorted lock was the only proof that the trunk had existed. The solid table, at which Marion and he had many intense discussions, wasn't distinguishable. Treading between the piles of ash, he found what he thought were the remains of Miranda's trinkets and, cursing strongly, kicked at a piece of pottery from the lamp that started the blaze.

Michael searched unsuccessfully for anything worth taking and then set out for Hanging Rock. He didn't have his backpack, cap or water bottle; they burned along with everything else. He tapped his jacket pocket that held his mobile phone and keys, lingered at the graves and said goodbye. 'Thanks Marion. Thanks for everything.'

He strode away, trying to keep his emotions under control. When he reached the boundary, he banged the top of a fence post with his hand and looked back at the blackened spot that had been his home in a strange pocket of time.

Further down the track, before it bent north, he turned again. All he could see was the tip of the lemon tree. He knew he couldn't return. 'Whatever happens today, I can't come back,' he said, before walking on.

There appeared to be less undergrowth surrounding the gum trees, but more gravel on the path. An outcrop of rocks, ten metres from the path, showed signs of covered-up graffiti. He blinked his eyes and dismissed the idea as ridiculous.

As he approached Hanging Rock, he spied a track to the left. He stopped. He could see shoeprints in the dry path – prints that were certainly not there previously. *Are they real?* Michael circled the indentations, leaning over and inspecting them. Then he swiped his sneaker over one. The sand moved, distorting the imprint – as it should. His stomach churned. Half of his mind was elated, the other wary of disappointment. He scurried along. He repeatedly scanned the scene. *Am I imagining the differences?*

Then he saw it. 'Fucking hell!' His hands shook. His throat tightened. He squinted at the small white building. *Doesn't look like a mirage.* He took a few tentative steps and swallowed repeatedly. *Really?* Then, when he saw the other buildings, he was convinced.

Michael sprinted across the cut grass. He leaped over a treated-pine barrier and picked up a handful of stones from the car park. 'Yes,' he shouted, throwing them in the air. He spun around with his arms out-stretched. 'Hey, everyone, I'm back. Yes.' He tugged his beard. 'Marion was right. She was right.' *But she had to die first.* 'Thank you, Marion.'

He stood in the middle of the car park and looked around. 'Hang on, where's my car?' *The car, Marion. Where's my car?* Michael rushed across the car park. He swivelled left and right as if the car might suddenly appear. He stood still and twisted his fingers together in anguish. Then, while walking towards the café, he realised his car would've been towed away. *I guess they wouldn't have just left it here.* He pulled his phone from his pocket. It remained blank. *Of course.* He scanned the open grass area again, turned towards the rock and let his eyes drift up the black path. *See, the bloody path is bitumen.* He grunted. *I knew it was.*

Although the buildings were in place, it was unusually quiet. There were no vehicles and no people. *Not again.* He raced to the café. The door was locked. *Shit!* Chairs sat upside down on the tables. A can rattled as it blew across the brick paving towards him. Michael kicked the can away. He hurried around the building and rattled every door. He tucked his hair behind his ears. *Bloody hell!* He washed his face and hands under a tap and gulped down cold water. The excess dribbled down his chest.

He jogged away from the café and along the road leading to the racetrack. Blustery wind continued to circle him as he ducked under the white rails of a fence and approached a row of small buildings. He tested every door. The stables smelt of rotting hay and manure. He felt like throwing up. The wind blew through his damp shirt and made him shiver.

Finally, he found a door that opened. Several plastic crates, many empty milk cartons and three beer bottles were strewn over a dirty floor of a small musty room. He sagged against the doorjamb.

Michael blew on his hands and rubbed them together. He sat down on a crate and closed his eyes. *Will this never end?* The door blew shut with a wallop. His eyes shot open in panic. He felt hot and cold at the same time. He rubbed his forefinger backwards and forwards across his moustache several times. Then he stood up, stomped on two milk cartons and marched out into the cool air.

The buildings, trees and even his hands seemed to have blurred edges, but he started to jog. The sound of crunching gravel seemed remote. Air blew up his nose. He dashed back towards the café.

The door of the Discovery Centre jiggled against his impatient pushing. He strode to the café and put his nose against a window. He scanned the empty space. He spotted a clock on the wall. *Seven thirty?* Automatically checking his watch, he was astonished to see the seconds ticking over. Twelve fifteen and ten seconds, eleven seconds, twelve seconds. 'Shit. It's working,' he said. He peered back into the café and spotted another clock behind the counter. *Yep, half past seven.*

He looked over at the empty car park, leaned against the wall and blew out a long breath. Someone should be here, he thought. *The kitchen staff would have to prepare. You'd think maintenance people would also start early.* He looked at his watch again. Forty-five, forty-six, forty-seven. He corrected the time on his watch.

He was about to lift a chair off a table when he spotted a small green sign stuck on the window. "Please note. This café will be closed on Mondays until further notice". He raced back to the Discovery Centre. A similar sign stuck out from under a myriad of advertisements on the notice board. 'So it's Monday,' he called out.

As he sauntered down the driveway to the main road, he wanted to laugh. His mind felt clearer as he made sense of the lack of activity. *Closed on Monday until further bloody notice.* He was relieved it was a Monday. *A 2013 bloody Monday.*

It was okay that the car park was empty. There was a legitimate reason for the locked doors and no tourists. He smiled and punched his right hand into the air. He skipped a couple of steps and grinned like a circus clown.

When he reached the boom gate, he playfully pushed on its arm. It bounced until his hands slipped and it smacked into his armpit. He leaned against the fence and waited for the pain to subside. He felt foolish, but grinned as he continued to rub the sore spot.

An aeroplane rushed across the sky. He almost waved to it. The familiar sound of far off traffic focussed his thoughts. *It's not over yet. I need to get home.*

Michael tucked his hair behind his ears again and strode the short distance to the main road. The signage gave him a choice – Woodend or Romsey. He drew in a deep breath and started running towards Woodend. He watched each shoe hit the bitumen. His jaw hurt as it jarred with every step. Two kookaburras flew from a fence post. The end of his shoelace flipped up with every step; he was mesmerised by it.

A truck, approaching from behind, blasted its horn. Every nerve reacted and Michael spun around. The truck blew its horn again. *Truck! Shit!* He held up his hand and started running towards it. He would have run into the truck if it hadn't stopped.

THIRTY-THREE

Rebecca felt overwhelmed by his story, but she believed him.

Sitting with her legs curled underneath her body, she ran her fingers along the arm of her beige leather lounge and thought of Marion's couch. She took Michael's hand and squeezed it.

'Thanks, Bec.'

'That's okay. Not much to thank me for really.'

'Yes there is.' His fingers tightened around hers. 'I've been over and over it in my head. So many times. Trying to come to terms with it. I've told bits of the story to other people. Most of it to the professionals. Some offered explanations. None of them feasible, of course. I don't think I'll ever understand it. But telling you, Bec, well, it seems easier to deal with somehow.'

'Troubles shared, troubles halved, they say.' She wriggled closer and put her legs over his lap.

He pulled her legs closer to his body; his hand remained on her thigh. 'That's true, but it's still such a puzzle.'

'But, Michael, surely you worked out how some things happened?'

'Some, yes, but for others there isn't an explana-tion.'

'Like the tea?'

'Yep. Marion said it disappeared one leaf at a time while she kept using it by the spoonful.'

'But that doesn't make any sense.'

Gently removing Rebecca's legs, he got up and volunteered to make another hot drink. Following him into the kitchen, Rebecca watched him as he switched on the kettle and rinsed the mugs. He took a teabag from a container, tore it open and tipped the leaves onto the bench. Running his finger through the fine leaves, he said, 'You can see how small a leaf is, then that's how come it lasted so long.' With a vacant stare, he added, 'that was Marion's explanation, I don't have another.'

'But, Michael, surely even tea leaves can only last months. Not all those years.'

He shrugged his shoulders and put another teabag into a mug. It was impossible for him to resolve Rebecca's questions and he realised Marion had been in the same position.

Rebecca didn't know what to think. There were so many emotions running through her mind. The story was incredible, but she knew it was real for him. She wanted to hold him close, so he knew she understood.

Michael carried the mugs of hot tea back to the sitting room and placed them on the low table. He sat close to Rebecca and gripped her hand. His eyes misted over. She smiled at him and he let go of her hand and placed his arm around her shoulder. Leaning into his body, she made herself as close as possible.

Rebecca felt melancholy, but excited at the same time. Although the knot in her stomach had loosened, it hadn't untied completely. Musing over his revelations she felt something important still had to be revealed. Rebecca thought her goose bumps hardly rated against Michael's three months in a time warp, but some part of the story that included *her* was incomplete. *Why do I feel this way? These peculiar sensations, what do they mean? Is it just my imagination working overtime?* She still had no clue to the answers.

'What did the truckie say when he stopped?' She had to stop thinking about herself somehow.

'Poor guy. I gave him a huge fright.'

'I bet.'

Michael chuckled and continued, 'He tried not to show how annoyed he was. Someone probably didn't get their supplies on time.'

'So he was pissed off.'

'Yeah, and even more when he had to drive to the police station again and sign something. After they concluded I wasn't completely insane, I made a written statement as well. I wasn't very popular with the truckie, I can tell you.'

Once they'd finished their drinks, she lay with her head on his lap and listened.

Bill Malloy changed his mind several times in an instant when a figure came into view on an otherwise boring road. One minute he was whistling along to music, the next, the airbrakes squealed as they struggled to stop the semi-trailer.

I should stop. No. Yes. He seems to need help. These jumbled thoughts dashed through Bill's mind, but in the end he had no choice – the idiot was running down the white line towards his moving truck.

The rig was still easing to a stop as Michael reached up to the step on the right hand side of the vehicle. 'Help me,' he gasped. 'Please, help.' He bent over and tried to catch his breath.

Bill opened the door and climbed down. He pushed Michael firmly away from the truck. 'Take it easy. What's the trouble?'

'I need help. My car's gone. I have to get to Melbourne.' Michael was now clinging to an arm that was trying to avoid contact.

'What car? How'd you get here then?'

'I left it three months ago. They've taken it.' Michael sucked in more air.

Bill was still trying to brush away flaying hands. 'Three months. Bloody hell! You left it three months ago and expect it to still be here.'

'I couldn't get out. Not until Marion died. Please help me.'

'Who died? Come on, mate, explain yourself.'

'Marion died, but it's okay, I buried her.'

'Wait a bloody minute.' Bill took a good look at the fellow who was now leaning against his truck. 'If you've killed someone, I'm not having a part of that.'

Michael squatted at the truck driver's feet with his head down. 'I didn't kill her. I think her heart just gave out.' He stood up and looked at Bill. 'Please. Just get me out of here. Please.'

The two-hundred-centimetre tall truck driver didn't like interruptions to his day - especially ones that caused trouble. He gripped Michael's arm and marched him over to the edge of the road. 'Pull yourself together, mate. Calm down and explain yourself a bit better or I'm going to leave you here.'

Michael slumped against the wheel. He pleaded with his potential rescuer again, 'No, please don't leave me. I've been here too long already. I don't want to stay another minute. You have to take me to town. Please.'

'Shut up just now.' The man rubbed the stubble on his chin before adding, 'right, get in and I'll see what I can do.'

Bill cursed as he paced around his rig. He unnecessarily tested the tension of the tie-down straps before swinging up into the driver's seat and starting the truck. 'Look, I'll take you to the police station in Woodend. You can tell them about the dead body.'

'What about the train station? I have to get back to Melbourne. My family will be wondering where I've been.'

Bill thought the police station was the obvious place for a fellow who knew something about a dead woman. 'Nope, I'll drop you at the police station. They'll sort things out.'

Michael didn't answer. He was enjoying the movement of the

vehicle as it gobbled up the road with ease. The open road was taking him home – *at last.*

Mesmerised by the swaying air-freshener that hung from the knob of the radio he let his mind drift for a while. He thought of Marion and the house by the lemon tree. Chickens, soup and damper came to mind. He shuddered as he remembered the half-dug third grave.

He looked around the cabin and grinned. An empty drink carton lay on the dashboard next to a well-worn cap. A solitary dried-up chip stuck out from a wrapper on the floor. Michael shifted around in his seat as he revelled in the small details. *Yes! 2013.* He pulled on the seatbelt, extended it out and let it snap back several times.

'What's it to be, mate? Police station? I don't have all day. Got a schedule to keep.'

'Sorry. Umm, perhaps you're right.'

The truck consumed the kilometres easily. *You're safe, you're safe,* the wheels seemed to say as the vehicle hummed over the smooth tarmac. *I'm going home. Sleep in a proper bed. Have a shower. And coffee. Ah, coffee.*

'Doing some sightseeing were you?'

Michael glanced sideways at the driver. 'Yeah. Supposed to be a day's trip. Three bloody months later and here I am. She was right, you know. Marion had to die before I could escape. I expect my car's been towed away. I hope it's at my parents'. Three bloody months locked in the middle of nowhere. Can you imagine what it's like to be trapped in time? Locked in a frigging void. Not able to extract yourself.'

Bill shifted in his seat. *I've picked up a weirdo. Wonder who Marion is? Or was? Well, I could take out this weedy bloke in an instant if he tries anything funny. The sooner I get to the police station the better.* He changed gears and increased speed.

Several more minutes went by in silence before Bill heard sniffing that turned into great gulps of sobbing.

Michael remembered Marion saying it was the relief that made her cry when he arrived. He now knew exactly what she meant.

Bill attempted to ignore the outburst, but it was impossible. His passenger could be insane, even dangerous. He fiddled with the two-way and contacted base.

'G'day, Sandra, Malloy here.'

'Bill, you've a problem?'

'I'm fine. Picked up a chap who needs help. Going to drop him at the police station in Woodend. I'll get you to check if they're open.'

'Stupid thing to do, Bill. I'll confirm.'

'Thanks. Call me back. Be quick about it.'

When Bill pulled up outside the police station, Michael remained hunched over in the cab. Bill left him fiddling with the seat belt and went to get help.

The desk clerk wasn't interested until Bill mentioned a dead body. Then a Sergeant asked for a description of the apparent lunatic and all hell broke loose. They thumped computers and made frantic phone calls.

Eventually, Michael was admitted to hospital where he greedily ate spaghetti bolognaise and gulped his way through a large milky coffee with three teaspoons of sugar. A senior doctor insisted that further questions could wait and gave Michael two sleeping tablets. The crisp white sheets and soft mattress felt like heavenly clouds.

THIRTY-FOUR

Even after hearing all that, Rebecca still felt there was something missing. She tried to explain. Michael's head tilted in the familiar way that came with his serious face. 'What more do you want, Rebecca?'

'I don't know. You once called it the goose bump theory. Well, it still hasn't gone away.'

'But, there isn't anything else.'

'There must be. Perhaps it isn't to do with you exactly. There must be another ... another *something*. If I knew, I would tell you.'

He noisily expelled a breath and left the room. Unnecessarily neatening the coasters on the table, Rebecca wondered again if she pushed too hard with her concerns. *Perhaps I should try to forget about the goose bumps.*

After a few moments, she followed Michael into the kitchen. He was standing with both hands on the sink, leaning over, staring at the plughole. He spun around when Rebecca spoke, 'Sorry, Michael, I didn't mean to upset you.'

'Look,' he said, 'I've told you everything.' He shrugged. 'Unless you want details of how to kill a wriggling rooster or perhaps I can tell you how to put up with an antiquated bathroom.' He turned back to the sink. 'There is nothing else.' He brushed a few breadcrumbs from the bench and stared out the window. His hands clenched the cold metal again.

Rebecca sensed resentment building. She hadn't meant he'd deliberately left something out. It was the feeling of attachment to Hanging Rock that she wished would go away. But it wouldn't.

She leaned against him. He sighed and moved away.

He returned to the lounge without a word. Rebecca felt like crying, but also wanted to yell at him at the same time. After trusting him enough to believe the unbelievable, she was emotional about his lack of reciprocal respect for her honesty.

Rebecca shivered as she thought of the terrifying moments on Romsey Road. She recalled the feeling of expectation after the TV report. *It all must mean something.*

She opened the fridge and stared at the cans of beer for a moment, then picked up a bar of chocolate, but changed her mind and went into the other room empty handed. Michael sat with a cushion clenched to his chest, his eyes closed.

'Michael, please listen. I'm not trying to be annoying – I can do much better than that.'

He opened his eyes, shook his head and gripped the cushion tighter. It was obvious he didn't appreciate her attempt at humour.

Rebecca continued, 'I really can't explain it. Please, I've listened to your story. Can't you try and understand my feelings?'

Michael shifted in the seat, but didn't speak.

'Please, Michael. Don't let's argue over this. It's not worth it.'

She watched as he fiddled with the edge of the cushion. He then leaned forward and placed it on the floor. It took him a moment or two to sit back. Rebecca picked up the cushion and stepped towards him.

Michael said, 'You're right. I've no right to judge you. It's just that so many people don't even try to understand what I went through. They've made so many dismissive remarks, and that's the more polite ones.' He ran his hands over his closed-cropped hair. 'For a while I thought you were making fun of me.' A hint of a smile made Rebecca step closer. 'Look, I find it hard to accept that you're crazy enough to believe me without questioning my sanity.'

Rebecca sat down next to him. 'Yep, crazy ... that's me.'

He smiled, pulled the cushion from her and tossed it onto the other chair.

She snuggled closer. 'I can't help the goose bumps you give me. They just won't go away.'

He turned and gripped her hand. 'I shouldn't have been so wound up in myself. I should've listened to you more. Let's see, if the goose bumps haven't been resolved then we just have to discover some theory which makes sense.'

'Good.' Rebecca shivered as he slipped his other hand behind her back.

Leaning against him, she tingled all the way down to her feet. He looked into her eyes with unspoken remorse. 'Is my apology accepted,' he whispered.

'Yep,' Rebecca whispered back, 'but you'll have to prove you mean it.'

He kissed her nose. 'Certainly, but that, of course, will mean lots more time together. Do you think you can manage that?'

'Mmm, let me think about it.'

Running his hand up Rebecca's back, he pushed aside her hair, curled his fingers gently around the nape of her neck and then kissed her passionately.

They managed to shed their clothes before reaching her bed. Missy leapt from her warm spot, meowing at being disturbed.

Rebecca looked over Michael's sleek body with pleasure. The pale skin of his chest contrasted with his tanned arms. His defined muscles quivered as she circled them with her fingertips. There were freckles on his stomach and Rebecca tickled the dark curls around his groin.

Michael's kisses pecked their way down her neck. She shivered as the cold silk of anticipation fell across her body. Pleasure as he tasted her nipples made her back arch. She slid her hands across his torso and pulled him closer.

'I reckon the practical is always better than the theory any day,' Michael said.

Michael now spent most nights with Rebecca. Discussing the reasons for the shivers that invariably prickled her back when they spoke of Hanging Rock, they curled up amongst the bedclothes, playfully arguing about why they ended up together.

'Maybe the universe thinks you look like Marion.'

'No, you said she was tall and thin. I'm only that in my dreams.'

'You're right. She is taller than you.'

'Very gallant of you not to mention the thinner bit.'

He prodded Rebecca's stomach. 'Perfect.'

She snuggled up against him, caressing his chest. His finger traced the outline of her lips. 'Maybe you look like Miranda.'

'Michael, that's ridiculous. You didn't see Miranda. Anyway, why would that matter?'

'I don't know. Maybe ... maybe ...'

Rebecca laughed and poked him in the ribs. He tickled her, but his kisses stopped her laughter.

'Breakfast, breakfast,' called Michael. 'Did someone order breakfast?'

As she lifted blankets from over her head, Rebecca saw Michael holding two mugs and several slices of hot buttered toast on a breadboard. 'Lovely,' Rebecca said, trying to focus her sleepy brain.

'Absolute heaven. Eat it while it's hot.' Michael pulled a robe over his bare abdomen and bit into the grainy bread. 'I don't think I'll ever stop enjoying toast with lots of butter.'

'Mmm, it's not good for you. Are you coming back into bed?'

'Just wait until I've finished this slice, then you'll find out what's good for you.'

Laughing at his corny line, she finished her piece of toast and lifted the blankets for him.

After a tedious day at work, Rebecca took out a file marked *my shop* from her desk drawer at home. She separated the pictures of colourful merchandise from a bundle of financial papers. Her coffee became cold while she re-read the lease documents of an ideal building.

She'd spent weeks lining up creative stockists, and the thought of shelves full of vibrant stock made her smile. She fingered a sample scarf and then picked up an embroidered teddy bear. *I just need to take that final step.*

When she heard Michael turn the key in the lock, Rebecca put down the teddy and walked towards the opening door.

'Hi, have a good day?' she asked.

'Hi, babe. Same as always. Monotonous.' He gave her a hug and kissed her nose.

She tucked her head into his shoulder. 'Yeah, I know what you mean.'

'Bad day, was it?'

Rebecca's eyes lifted. 'Not really.' She shrugged and said quietly, 'I got my file out again.'

Michael took her hand and led her to the couch. 'Your shop file?'

'Yep.' She paused. 'I'm going to do it.'

'Yeah? That's great. Good on you.'

'Will you go through the papers with me?'

'I thought your dad already did that.'

'Sure, but I'd like your opinion too.'

Michael stroked his chin, licked his lip and then stood up. 'Bec, here's an idea. What if I share the space with you? You know, be part of it. Sales are still going well at Jan's. So that's encouraging. I could expand a bit. Perhaps try and sell some of the bush paintings.' He plopped down next to her. 'What do you think?'

Rebecca's stomach was already churning at having made a decision, but now her mind was spinning with possibilities. She smiled and then frowned.

'It's okay, Bec. You can say no.' Michael felt uncomfortable. 'You probably think it's a terrible idea.'

'No, no. It'd be a perfect combination.' Her eyes lit up as she spoke, 'It'd be so much better.' She threw her arms around Michael's neck. 'I'd love it, but are you really sure?'

Michael squeezed her tightly then gently eased her away. 'Of course. I've thought about it a lot since I met your parents. Your mum even dropped a few hints.'

'Really?' Rebecca's grin widened. 'I missed that.'

'Remember how she showed me those picture frames. She raved on about getting a discount for large quantities. It was the wink that gave her away.'

'Mum can be a bit over enthusiastic sometimes. She keeps buying the samples. Dad's so practical, he's been a great help.'

'He seems to have covered everything, and I think you've done a thorough job with the research. I'd love to be involved. It'd be awesome to have my art in your shop. We'd have to go through the costs though. I'd want to pay my way.'

'We can talk about finances later. I think it's a cool idea.'

'We'll go through your file. See what else we have to consider changing.'

'How exciting. I can't wait to get started.'

Michael nodded. 'But there's a lot to do before we can actually open.'

'Oh dear, I'm not looking forward to telling Jan.' Rebecca stood up. 'You want something to eat?'

'Yeah, let's go out. I feel like celebrating.'

'Will you give notice too?'

Michael picked up the car keys. 'Probably, but I might see if I can go part-time at first. There's a good chance in the present climate.'

'What about Jan? Will you withdraw your art from her shop?'

'I'll talk to her. Might be good to leave some pieces there.'

'So you think the place in St Kilda will work?'

'It's perfect. Grab your bag. I'm suddenly starving.'

With input from her father Tim, Rebecca and Michael finalised plans. They negotiated terms for an overdraft and signed the lease for a building on a side street not far from Simpson's Gallery and public transport.

Rebecca spent weeks obtaining unique stock and Michael's days spent working full-time for the government were soon to be over.

A local manufacturer produced tea towels, place mats and carrier bags with Michael's popular animal prints splashed across them.

Missy insisted on checking out every box as the new stock arrived and filled the flat. A rainbow selection of animals sat next to majestic gum trees and fields of wheat in Michael's unused room at Rose's. Michael's talent showed on the artistic flyers they dropped into letterboxes in the surrounding suburbs.

The opening day of *Cats and Company* exceeded all expectations.

Both their parents arrived early. After introductions to Rebecca and her parents, Jack moved around the gallery, keeping out of the way. Janet made clucking noises and approved of the upmarket items. She shifted the painting of a purple giraffe to the middle of the window display, hiding the Daylesford coffee mugs. Tim was anxious there wouldn't be enough small change and announced he had more in the car. 'One can't be too prepared.' His wife Carol raised her eyebrows and went back to trying on another scarf.

The next dozen or so who turned up were family and friends, but many new customers wandered in throughout the day.

'You've gone soft,' teased Owen when Michael showed him some hand-knitting.

'You said your Nan's in hospital. These bed-socks are ideal.' Michael held them up for inspection, but Owen spotted Jess and Amy and ignored him. Michael was left holding several bed-socks as Jock appeared.

'Not my size, Micky,' he laughed. He waved a parcel in front of Michael and added, 'I think it's a bloody awesome place. Got some wind-chimes for my sister and a picture of a disgustingly bright pink dog for my niece.' He laughed again, 'Pippa will love it.'

Patrick couldn't decide between a patterned scarf and a fancy notebook for his mother. Erin convinced him to buy both. Jan graciously admired the gallery. She had enthusiastically agreed to retain Michael's animal art in her shop.

Rose made noises of delight as she strolled around the gallery. Mid-afternoon she busied herself in the tiny staff room and cut up a chocolate cake she brought from home. Surprised customers hesitated before accepting a small slice on a serviette.

Rebecca kept running into people she knew as she tried to be in several places at once. Sales were steady and a plethora of customers admired the black cat with the turquoise bow on the yellow front door.

Kylie arrived mid-afternoon with Luke and Thomas.

'Brec, play. Brec play with me.'

Bending down and giving her nephew a squeeze, she said, 'Sorry, precious, not this time.' She reached into a large glass jar and pulled out a striped lollypop. 'Would you like one of these?'

Tim came to the rescue and took his lolly-sucking grandson for a walk while Luke and Kylie looked around.

'All the hard work's paid off, Bec. The place looks fab.'

Giving her sister a quick hug, Rebecca said, 'Thanks, I'm glad you like it, but I'll have to keep going.'

'Sure, that's okay. I want to look around anyway. Don't need a fussy owner hanging over me.'

By closing time, Michael and Rebecca were exhausted. Once

everyone left, Michael ordered in pizza (Super Supreme, of course) and opened a bottle of sparkling wine to celebrate. 'Here's to the success of Cats and Company.'

Rebecca swished the bubbles around the glass and savoured the taste of the cold liquid. The glasses clinked and Michael added, 'And to us.'

Rebecca thought she heard Missy purr a little louder as she turned around and padded into a different spot on the rocking chair she'd claimed as her own. 'Don't get too comfy, Missy. We'll be going home soon.'

Michael laughed. 'You spoil that cat.'

'How can we have a gallery called Cats and Company without Missy?'

'Good job she likes company. Drink up. Let's take our lucky charm home.'

With long hours and continued advertising, they created a successful gallery that offered handcrafted gifts along with Michael's original artwork. Red elephants, green giraffes and the ever-reliable cats of all colours provided constancy in a world where the sale of art is spasmodic.

Rebecca created a special corner in the gallery for the pieces Michael called his *real* art. Appreciation from the customers of his beautiful watercolours depicting Australian landscapes gave Michael pure joy. His evocative paintings of Hanging Rock brought constant compliments. He was thrilled each time one sold. However, the large watercolour that hung behind the counter was not for sale.

Michael had captured the beauty of an evening in the country with its soft light on the tips of the grass bending gently in the breeze. Although the lemon tree appeared out of place amongst the distant gum trees, one could instinctively sense the importance it had with the woman who sat beneath its straggly branches. Many customers asked why the woman wore odd attire: men's trousers and an unfashionable shirt. When they leaned closer they invariably enquired about the minute piece of wood that was dated 1885. What they didn't see was the smudged charcoal drawing stuck on the back.

Two weeks later the phone at the gallery rang and Rebecca knew it would be Kylie.

'Hi, Bec, can you chat?'

'Sure, it's quiet at the moment. Anyway, Michael's here if someone comes in.'

'Is he working full time at the gallery now?'

'Yep. Things are going well enough. And it means I can get out of the shop occasionally.'

'Good, but I haven't heard from you for ages.'

'Sorry, Kyls, been busy.'

'Too busy even for your favourite sister?'

Both of them laughed.

'Come on, tell me the latest. What's stopped you from ringing? Is it the shop? Or is the gorgeous Michael keeping you from me?'

'Both, and you'd better get used to it; Michael has proposed.'

THIRTY-FIVE

As Rose was their link from the beginning, they couldn't wait to share their news with her. Armed with a bunch of carnations, they surprised her as she enjoyed a quiet moment in the garden after finishing her Sunday lunch.

'How pretty, thank you both. The kettle's still warm. Michael, will you make us a cuppa, please?'

Rose wasn't quick enough to catch Michael winking and she questioned the reason for Rebecca's amusement. 'Rebecca, what's so funny? I don't have pickle on my chin, do I?'

Giving her a quick hug, Rebecca said, 'No, your face is fine. It's that grandson of yours.'

'What's he up to?' She walked over to Michael. 'Stop playing around. Go and make the tea.'

Once inside, Michael switched on the kettle and after a conspiratorial glance at Rebecca, he spoke to his grandmother, 'It won't be long, Gran. Come and sit down. We have some news.'

'News?' Rose's face hardened. 'I don't need any bad news.'

'I hope you'll think it's good news, Gran.'

Rose sat down and placed her hands in her lap. Her eyes flicked between Michael and Rebecca. 'Tell me what you two have been up to. Stop keeping an old woman waiting.'

Grinning, Michael announced, 'Bec has promised to marry me.'

Rebecca waved her left hand in the air. 'I'm expecting a rather large rock very soon.'

'That's the best news. I was hoping ... yes, it is good news. Congratulations. Oh, that's lovely. Come here and give me a hug.'

Rebecca sprang out of the chair and folded Rose's small body in an embrace. 'Thanks. I'm glad you're pleased.'

Michael wrapped his arms around the two women.

When things calmed down, Rose said, 'Forget the tea, I'm going to find some wine.'

They sat outside under a jacaranda. Rose held up her glass and said, 'Now, Rebecca, I expect you to call me Gran.'

'We have to tell our parents,' Rebecca said, as they arrived back at her flat.

'I've been thinking about that. I wonder if I should've asked your father first.'

Rebecca poked his arm and giggled as she said, 'What, permission to marry me. I don't think so. But, we should tell them before Kylie blabs. She's not big on secrets.'

'And we'll have to tell my mum and dad.'

Rebecca thought of the urban myths she'd heard about sons and their mothers. 'I suppose we can't just ring both lots of parents.'

Michael shook his head. 'I don't think that would go down well.'

'You're right. I'd be in so much trouble.' She paused, then added, 'Mum will be in her element. God, she was a pain from the moment Kylie got engaged. She'll have us organised in two days.'

'We haven't even set a date.' Michael frowned.

Thinking of the need to decide on a venue, a dress and invitation lists, Rebecca said, 'Let's not.' She snuggled up against him on the couch. 'At least not right now.' She fondled his chest and gave him a quick kiss on his chin.

'Right then,' Michael said, 'just a matter of telling the folks, but at the moment I've another idea.'

Straight after work on Monday, Michael and Rebecca called around to her parents' home. Carol was shelling peas from the garden. Tim had just poured himself a beer.

Carol wiped her hands on her apron and gave Rebecca a hug. 'Nice to see you, love.' She patted Michael's arm. 'Nice to see you, Mike.' She popped a pea into her mouth and held the bowl towards them. 'Your father might offer to share his beer.' She saw her husband's eyebrows shoot up. 'Unless it's the last one.'

Tim grinned as he placed two more glasses on the kitchen bench. 'There's plenty. Nothing like a cold one to settle the brain after a hard day.'

'Totally. Thanks, ... Tim.' Michael picked up his beer, and then paused. 'Aren't you having one, Mrs Hannah?'

'It's Carol, please. No, I'll have pineapple juice this time. I had a glass of wine when my friend came for lunch. One can't discuss the state of the nation over water.' She picked up a cloth and peered through the glass of the oven. 'Would you like to stay for dinner? It's Shepherd's Pie. I'm sure there's enough for four.' She turned to Michael and added in a silky voice, 'It's Bec's favourite.'

'Mum, that's bribery.'

'Of course it is, but you'll stay, won't you?'

'Well, we weren't going to stay too long.' Rebecca looked sideways at Michael. He had an accepting grin on his face.

'Sure, sounds good. Thanks.' He took Rebecca's hand. 'But we really only came to give you some good news.'

Carol put down the cloth and remained where she was.

'I've asked Bec to marry me.'

Tim didn't move, but his face did gymnastics as his emotions surfaced.

Yelling, 'We're getting married,' Rebecca darted around the table and grabbed her mother. After they'd stopped hugging, Carol smothered Michael with a hug.

Managing to avoid his wife's exuberance, Tim kissed Rebecca and shook Michael's hand. 'Congratulations, I couldn't have found a better man for her myself.'

Carol, trying to mop up happy tears, wiped mascara down her cheeks. 'I think I will have a beer.'

Michael ran the gallery on Tuesdays, which meant Rebecca could sleep in before she rushed through her chores in time to arrive at Rose's for afternoon tea.

Rose became thoughtful as she fingered the photographs of her wedding day in her album. Rebecca peered at the black and white images. A newspaper clipping read, *"Local identity Miss Rose Morrison married Mr Lennard Wentworth at St Kilda Presbyterian Church in Barkley Street ..."*

'Local identity – that sounds rather important.'

'I thought they rather overstated it at the time.' Rose chuckled, 'You know, just to make a local girl sound good in the local paper, but I suppose I did have the habit of putting my hand up. Lenny always huffed and puffed when I put my hat on and kissed him farewell. Off to get them lot organised again love, he would say. I still miss him. Dear Lanky Lenny, as his army mates called him. He was a good man.'

Rebecca took Rose's hand and told her she looked spectacular in the newspaper article.

'You make me sound like a fireworks display,' Rose laughed.

Introduced to faded relatives and friends, all dressed in their finery, Rebecca lost count of the aunts and uncles on both sides of

Rose's family.

'Maud had the most wonderful veil. Look at all the lace – and the embroidery. She made it herself.'

'It's gorgeous.'

'And Annie here. She's the one with the large hat.'

'It's too big for such a little girl.'

'Here's Michael's great-uncle. Uncle Henry, what a card.' Rose turned another page. 'Now, that's the other one I wanted to show you. Here's Janet and Jack on their wedding day. Doesn't she look elegant? My son is so handsome.'

Rebecca agreed and then admitted she was a little nervous about meeting Michael's parents again. 'I hope they'll like me.'

'Janet and Jack? Why wouldn't they?' Rose paused and tipped the page up to have a closer look at their photo. 'Didn't you meet them at your opening?'

'Yes, but I was so busy. I didn't really get much of a chance to talk to them. Then they left early.'

'That was my fault. Too much excitement for one day, I'm afraid.'

Rebecca squeezed Rose's hand. 'That's okay, you were such a help.'

Rose smiled, pleased with the compliment. She pointed to the photograph again. 'They're friendly people, really. Yes, they'll like you. But you mustn't be put off by their reactions.'

'What do you mean?'

'Janet will probably burst out with lots of questions and Jack will stay silent. You might think him rude, but deep down he's a little shy and never wants to say the wrong thing. So much like his father in that way.'

Rebecca wriggled in the seat. 'Now you're making me feel awkward.'

'Rebecca dear, I didn't mean to do that. You'll be just fine. Michael will be there. They'll be pleased he's found someone so delightful.'

'Thanks, Gran.' Rebecca added a cheeky grin as she patted Rose on her knee.

The chicken and chips they shared for dinner sat heavily in Rebecca's nervous stomach. 'I hope your mum likes the flowers.'

'She'll love them. And stop worrying, they won't eat you.' Michael sighed, as he turned off the ignition.

'I'm just worried.'

'About what?'

'Your parents weren't happy about you living with your grandmother. They wanted you to go home, didn't they?' She checked her hair in the mirror on the sun-visor. It flicked back up with a snap, which made her jump.

'They did. I'm sure they've got used to it by now.'

'Yeah, but now they'll think *I've* taken you away. It'll be difficult for you all over again.'

'We're not exactly going to the moon anytime soon.'

'I know, but still ...'

Michael took Rebecca's hand. 'Bec, it's okay. It'll be fine. I stayed with Gran because of the media. Mum agreed it was for the best. Dad understood. They know I stay at your place now.' He let go of her hand. 'After the stress of Hanging Rock and all, they just tend to forget how old I am. It's okay, really.'

'I just hope they'll like me.'

'They're impressed with everything you do with the shop and ... they already love the *idea* of you.'

Rebecca frowned. 'Idea?'

'Absolutely.' Michael grinned and poked her in the ribs. 'They think it's about time I settled down and gave them grandkids.'

Laughing at the contradiction, she said, 'I thought you said they forget how old you are?'

'Well sometimes.' He pulled the keys out of the ignition and paused before adding, 'other times they want what every parent wants for their kids. Love, family – you know.'

Rebecca nodded. 'That's a good start.'

'Come on, let's go in and tell them.'

'You're what?' exclaimed Janet. Her hands came up and clapped her cheeks. Rebecca noticed her manicured fingernails and had a flashback to Michael's rough chipped nails. Janet hugged Michael and then held him away for a moment before hugging him again.

'Congratulations, son.' Jack shook his son's hand vigourously. 'Well done.' Then he clasped Rebecca's hand tenderly. 'I wish you both much happiness.'

Janet pecked Rebecca on the cheek. 'I'm so pleased.' She leaned in for a quick hug. 'When did this happen?' she asked.

'Just the other day.' Michael bowed theatrically as he said, 'You're now the official mother-of-the-groom-in-waiting.'

Janet smiled and pretended to curtsey. 'Lovely. Now then, you must tell me all the details. But first, come with me.' She led Rebecca into the dining room. 'Can you hold these, please?' She handed Rebecca one crystal wine goblet and took another from the shelf. 'We were given these when Jack and I became engaged. They've been used at every family celebration since.' As Janet held out the second goblet, she paused and said, 'You know, we really are grateful to you.' Rebecca didn't know what to say. 'Michael's had such a hard time.' Rebecca took the glass. 'I just want to thank you for believing him. It's really helped.' Janet chose two more goblets then turned towards the lounge room. 'Now be a dear and bring them through.' Rebecca smiled and followed.

Jack put on a CD and the relaxing sounds of a stringed orchestra filled the room. Janet produced some cheese and paté with biscuits.

After they were seated with their glasses filled with chilled chardonnay, Janet asked, 'When will the wedding be?'

'We haven't …' Rebecca started.

'Not for a while,' Michael said.

'I hope you're not thinking of having a long engagement,' said Janet, as she straightened the cuff on her blouse.

'No, but I …' Again, Rebecca hesitated.

Michael answered, 'We haven't thought that through yet. We've got to get a ring.' He looked at Rebecca and smiled. 'Then we'll probably have a small party. Celebrate in style.'

'Good idea, son. Take your time. From what the ladies say, there's a lot to think about.' His father relaxed his tall frame in the chair by the unlit fireplace.

'Thanks, Dad. You and I'll be the spectators. Bec's sure to organise us all. Not to mention Bec's mum. I could see her wedding planner brain ticking from the moment we told them.'

Noticing Janet's mouth clench as she patted her immaculate auburn hair, Rebecca spoke quickly. 'Mrs Wentworth, would you know of a good place for the engagement party? I'll need your help.'

Janet smiled. 'We'll have a think about it, won't we Jack? I'm sure we can help out with finances.'

THIRTY-SIX

The media somehow got wind of the celebration and turned it into a circus for a while. Apparently Michael was still worthy of a headline or two, but once the cameras stopped flashing they were able to enjoy themselves.

Rose was delighted with the posy of a yellow rose and maiden-hair-fern, which Michael presented to her. 'But it's your night, dear. I shouldn't be the one getting flowers.' She smelled the rose before letting Rebecca pin it to her new summer dress.

'Yes you should. You really were the one to get us together.'

'Nonsense, I only baked the cake.'

Those who heard her comment laughed and recounted other stories of Rose's generous hospitality.

Janet made sure everything went smoothly by keeping the service personnel on their toes. No guest held an empty glass for too long and the staff efficiently dispatched the finger food. Rebecca admired Janet's ability to look sophisticated, stay calm and have the staff follow instructions without dispute.

'Mum, Dad, have you had enough to eat?' Rebecca asked when she found them talking together, drinking cappuccinos.

Carol answered, 'Plenty thanks, Bec. It's all been so lovely.' Carol then flitted off to delight one of her aunts with her attention.

'For now, thanks, pet.' Bec's father took her hand and she suspected he might not let it go. He was emotional when he gave his speech in the early part of the evening. After welcoming everyone, he announced it was a shame he would have to share his favourite daughter.

Kylie booed heartedly, but whispered to Owen, 'He calls me that too.' She continued to join in the frivolity by wolf whistling loudly when Tim added that Michael was the best thing to happen to his youngest daughter.

'Hi, babe. How's the most gorgeous lady in the room going? I feel like I haven't seen you all night.' Michael gripped Rebecca's waist and pulled her against him. Tim relinquished her hand, nodded at Michael and took his empty cup to the table. After kissing Michael eagerly, Rebecca wiped the lipstick off his mouth.

'Get a room,' laughed Jock.

Patrick punched Michael on the shoulder. 'Hope this doesn't mean you've hung up your surfing gear?'

Rebecca snuggled in even closer to Michael. 'Surfing? There'll be no time to go surfing.'

Jock and Patrick made suggestive noises and Michael kissed her before laughingly recommending his mates should locate Owen. 'He's been monopolising Amy. You'd better keep him honest.'

The highlight of the evening was Michael's speech. After words of appreciation to their families and some bantering with his noisy mates, he became solemn and explained the struggle to find normality in his life after his experience at Hanging Rock. Rebecca sensed his deep affection for Marion as he told the silent group how having someone to share your life, is the most important thing a person can have. 'Marion did that then. Now Bec has helped me to stay sane.' He took her hand and kissed it.

'Then she didn't help enough,' yelled out Jock. The laughter relieved the seriousness of the moment.

'To my fiancé,' Michael said, as he raised a crystal glass.

The following weekend they found a quiet reputable restaurant in Flinders Lane in which to discuss their wedding plans. Wanting everything to be perfect, Rebecca bought a new dress and had her nails done at the beautician next door to their gallery.

They enjoyed a complimentary glass of sparkling wine on arrival and relaxed immediately.

'Isn't this great?' whispered Rebecca, as she checked out the surroundings. 'I love the atrium.'

Michael was particularly interested in the abstract paintings that hung around the room. 'I always wondered where they get their inspiration,' he said, as he peered at a large canvas of green and grey spattered oils.

'Probably by a large cheque book. Just look at that one.'

Michael chuckled, 'I'd rather look at you.'

Rebecca feigned embarrassment.

After deciding which delicious items to have, they watched the elegant activity around the room and sipped the wine.

'To the future Mr and Mrs Wentworth,' Michael said, as he clinked his glass against Rebecca's.

'That makes us sound so old,' she whispered.

'Wait till we're celebrating thirty-six years like my parents.'

'Will we ever get *that* old?'

Entrée arrived; tiny specks on a huge white plate. Two waiters, who simultaneously lifted the cloches with a flourish, presented the main course. Aided by another glass of wine, Rebecca giggled over the show of extravagance. Michael raised his eyebrows, but he too, was entertained.

The restaurant was warm. Rebecca removed her jacket and hung it over the back of the chair. She felt her small bag squash under her back. She took it out of the jacket pocket and placed it on the table.

As Rebecca rearranged the napkin in preparation for the next pocket-sized course, Michael snatched up her bag. 'Where did you get this?' His voice was agitated.

'My bag?'

'Yes, where did you get it? How long have you had it?'

'I'm surprised you've noticed it. My handbags don't usually come up on your radar.'

His eyes narrowed as he touched a rose-entangled letter. 'Where did you get it, Rebecca?'

Rebecca couldn't believe the change in his attitude. 'Michael, what's this all about?'

'Please, Bec.'

Not wishing to cause a commotion, Rebecca sighed, then said, 'Well, if you must know, I bought it in Woodend. From an antique shop. I suppose most of their stock is collectables, not really antiques. Anyway, it's an adorable shop. I'd love to go again. We could go together.'

Michael turned the bag over and stared at the intricate pattern. 'When?'

'When? Ah, now ... that's interesting. I remember, it was the day of that funny episode. February, yes February fourteenth actually. I wanted to avoid a stupid footy match.'

'Keep going.'

'Well, I bought the bag, and a brooch, called at a deli and got a drink for the trip home.'

'And ...?'

She put her hand out for the bag. 'I've told you all this before.'

He ignored her request and held on to the bag. 'I need to hear it again.'

'You sure?' she asked.

His lips tightened and his eyes became intense, but he nodded.

'Well, there was the willy-willy. I felt I should turn towards Hanging Rock, but by the time the wind stopped bashing the car I was too scared. It was weird. Then, as you know, everything returned to normal and I got home safely.'

Michael's eyes glazed over, as if he was somewhere else.

'I'm not going through any more details.' Rebecca tapped the table. 'You're not even listening properly.'

Trying to see past his vacant stare, she could feel tension tightening her throat. The back of her neck went clammy and a shiver shot across her shoulders.

Dessert had arrived some minutes earlier and was starting to melt. Michael couldn't have cared less. 'Let's get out of here, Rebecca. I've one more story to tell you.'

'Can't you tell me here?' Rebecca took a quick spoonful of the lime mousse.

'The thing is ...' he stood up and touched Rebecca's shoulder, 'I'll probably get emotional. So I'd rather not.'

Rebecca poked at the coconut icecream. 'Couldn't you just give me the first chapter while I finish this?'

Michael tucked the bag under his arm and took Rebecca's jacket from the back of the chair. 'Sorry, but I'd really like to go.'

She stood up and took her jacket from Michael. He reluctantly handed over her bag.

He smiled and put his arm around her waist, guiding her towards the door. 'I'm really sorry, Bec. We'll come back here again. I promise.'

Rebecca waited impatiently while he settled the bill. She stared at the bag in her hand. *How can it be significant?*

Michael remained tight-lipped until they sat in the car. Rebecca fiddled with her newly-acquired diamond ring. She felt uncomfortable with his solemn attitude, but Michael tapped her leg and assured her it was all good news. 'This bag, I think it's the catalyst for everything.'

'Catalyst?' Rebecca couldn't believe that. 'For what? It's just a pretty purse.'

He leaned over and kissed her cheek. 'No, it's not. Listen to me, Bec. You know most of what I went through at Hanging Rock, but I don't think I told you about Grandma Warren's connection.'

'Yes you did. She was Irma's granddaughter. *The* Irma Leopold who was at that picnic. I know about her.'

Michael agreed. 'But that's not all. There's an important element, that until today, until I saw your bag – Marion's bag, that I didn't think mattered.'

Rebecca eyes widened and her voice squeaked, 'Marion's bag! Are you serious?'

'Totally.'

Fixing his eyes intently on Rebecca, he said in a voice she could hardly hear. 'It's true.' Michael then rested his head on the steering wheel. 'That's the connection.'

Rebecca turned on the light above her head and tried to understand his reasoning. Touching him on the shoulder, she asked, 'How do you know it's Marion's bag?'

He lifted his head and turned to her. 'Grandma described it in detail. So did Marion.'

'Really! You're sure?' She picked up the bag and turned it around. 'It could be anyone's bag.' Rebecca couldn't fathom how this little bag could cause turmoil in so many lives. 'Impossible.'

'No, look at the initial. M for Marion. The pink roses. The cross-stitch. Even the intricate gold clasp. All there, just as Marion described it. It has pink satin lining, doesn't it?'

'Shit. How did Irma have it?'

'That's the final piece of the puzzle. You see, Bec, the story of Irma prompted me into making the trip to Hanging Rock. I've told you about that, but here's the bit that ties it all together.'

THIRTY-SEVEN

Grandma Wilma spent most of her last days going over memories.

Flashes of happy times spent with her grandmother, Granny Irma, brought back the story of the disappearance of the girls at the turn of the century.

'Never doubt that anything is possible.' Granny told Wilma when she was an impressionable teenager. 'Some things can't be explained. No matter from which angle you look.'

Wilma knew that some family members thought time had embellished the truth of the bizarre tale. Others thought it had no credence at all.

However, despite wondering if it was necessary, Grandma still felt obliged to tell Michael of Granny's revelation. She followed the compulsion and asked him to her bedside.

Michael entered the hospital room with some reluctance. Sadly, he could see her vitality had faded.

'Hi, Grandma, it's good to see you. You have something to tell me?'

'Yes, come closer, Mikey. I don't want to have to yell. My voice isn't what it used to be.'

Michael's knees hit the bed as he shuffled the chair over the vinyl flooring. 'Don't tell me you've been misbehaving, Grandma,' he said with a smile.

Her face wrinkled into a smile. She took his hand. He felt her rings move under his gentle grip. 'It's much more entertaining than that, Mikey.'

Grandma Wilma asked for fresh water and changed her mind about the need for more pillows. She kept hold of his hand and stroked it gently. 'I need you to listen carefully. It's about my grandmother.' She dithered over the start, but finally, her words came faintly, but clearly, talking about a time long ago.

Four students slipped away from their teachers. Miranda, Edith, Marion and Irma wandered through the bush and up a sloping track, which ran between the rocks. When they stopped on a level section, Edith complained about how far they'd come. 'We should go back,' she said, as she tugged at the neck of her blouse. 'We shouldn't be here.'

Miranda walked away and recommenced the climb. Marion followed. Their dream-like stare contrasted with Edith's frantic pleadings.

'Please, Miranda. Don't go.' She turned to Irma. 'Stop them. Marion! Miranda! Don't go any further.'

Irma pushed past Edith and hurried after Marion and Miranda.

Edith scampered after Irma. 'Irma, wait. Don't go without me.'

Edith caught up with Irma as they neared the top. Miranda and Marion's voices came from beyond a narrow crevice. Edith plopped down on a flat rock and tried to catch her breath. She sulked as she watched Miranda and Marion cavort, unable or unwilling to crawl through the cracks to join them. Irma peeped through the small gap and stood for a moment, enjoying the vision of the two girls.

Miranda danced sensuously and sang about the legends of the rock. Marion clapped out a rhythm and laughed at her friend's high spirits.

Irma began to step through the small opening just as a violent wind tossed leaves and sticks into the air. Irma saw her friends battling to stand upright against the swirling wind. Miranda and Marion's terrifying screams were impossible to ignore. Irma stepped back and gripped the rough edges of the rock. 'Marion. Miranda. Come back. Hurry!'

Edith ran. She didn't stop until she reached the school group.

Miranda's hat blew away as she fell to the ground. Marion screamed and reached for her friend. Miranda had just managed to stand up when the wind gathered a fresh breath. Then it blew with such force they were hurled against the rock wall. Marion was winded and her arm scraped against the rough surface as she fought to stay on her feet. Blood seeped from the wound.

Miranda shrieked when she hit the wall. Her legs buckled. She slumped to the ground. The wind whipped at her hair, blowing it across her face. She coughed away dust and dragged strands of hair from her mouth.

Irma's face went pale and she felt faint as she watched on. She continued to scream at them. She was too afraid to step through the small space and help.

'Miranda, grab my hand,' yelled Marion. The girls staggered to their feet.

Miranda gripped Marion's hand tightly until they reached over and grabbed the edge of a rock. Dust and leaves showered them as the peculiar wind encircled their bodies.

Marion stumbled forward, but something unseen stopped her reaching the gap. She ripped her small bag from her pocket and tossed it towards Irma. 'Take it. Tell them ...' she shrieked. 'Please, go for help. Ple ...' Her voice stopped as the unknown force hurled her against the ground again.

Irma reached through the gap and grabbed the bag. When she looked up, the other girls had disappeared. Her hands trembled as she tucked Marion's bag into her bodice.

The eerie wind whipped at Irma's dress and sucked her straw hat back into the hole. She clung to the rock for support. The next surge of wind tore at her hair. Irma screamed as the gale force wind hit her back. Her hands were wrenched from the rock. Blood dripped down her fingers. Stones tumbled from the rocks above. She screamed again and covered her head.

Despite being missing for four days, suffering intensive bruising and dehydration, both Mrs Appleyard and Sergeant Bumpher expected her to answer their questions. *No, I've no idea what happened. No, no, NO!*

Irma refused to speak further. She kept Marion's bag a secret. She was scared she would be blamed for her friends' disappearance.

In time, she led a relatively normal life, but as her days became numbered, she felt weighed down with her secret from the past. Alice, Irma's daughter, rolled her eyes at the story of exuberant teenagers and youthful misbehaviour. When Irma explained why she hadn't told anyone about Marion's bag before this, Alice was shocked.

'Mother, you withheld information from the police.'

'They didn't ask me directly,' said the petulant invalid.

'Omission is not any better than straight out lies. How could you?'

'I was only fifteen, Alice. So scared I couldn't sleep. Can you imagine what it was like to see your friends disappear that way? They were singing and dancing one moment – screaming and yelling the next. I couldn't see anything that was making them act that way. I grabbed Marion's little bag and to this day I honestly don't remember anything more. I've carried this secret all these years.'

Alice stood with her hands on her hips, 'So, why bother now?'

'For some reason I feel it's important.'

'I hardly think so.'

'One never knows.'

Alice was surprised to find that her daughter, Wilma, knew many stories about the embroidered bag - fanciful tales of romance, accounts of teenage exploits, as well as the story of Hanging Rock.

As a young girl, Wilma was intrigued with the tales of the woman whose name she inherited. She often begged for more stories from

Granny Irma, and the old woman reminisced with pleasure. Details of mysterious caves and beguiling teenagers kept Wilma entranced for hours. She curled up on the end of Granny's bed and listened as picnic baskets, straw hats and young lads with tight breeches were described in detail.

Alice told Wilma to forget the far-fetched stories and concentrate on her schoolwork. But Wilma loved its history and used the tapestry bag on special occasions. When Wilma moved to a nursing home, the bag remained in an unlabelled box with other possessions. It remained tucked away for many years before her daughter, Janet, sent all unwanted items to the Salvation Army depot. The owner of Bits & Bobs Collectables then purchased the bag. Wilma was angry for the disregard of her keepsakes and stubbornly avoided telling Janet the story of her ancestor.

The story fascinated Michael. However, the description of the embroidered bag would have gone unnoticed except Grandma became fidgety while describing it. She squeezed Michael's hand tightly and insisted he sit still and concentrate. He listened respectfully as she described the tapestry bag with the embroidered roses weaving their way through the initial. Grandma's vivid portrayal had him imagining a pretty lady opening the ornate gold clasp and dropping her lipstick into the silk lining. After Michael promised he would remember her tale, Grandma Wilma seemed content that the story was safe for one more generation.

Michael told Rebecca he tried to find out the truth of Irma's story. He looked through Rose's clippings, but they told him nothing new. He intended to research websites for old newspaper stories to uncover more.

'The visit to Hanging Rock was just somewhere to start,' he said. 'A place to get a feel for the story. It did that,' he added sarcastically.

As they lay with tangled legs, their faces within a breath of each other, Michael explained his theory, 'When Marion tossed that bag out of the void, fate started the journey which brought us together.'

'But, Michael. Marion ... and Miranda ... Why?'

'Strange, isn't it? You have to wonder. And me? Insane.'

'Do you really think you had to go through all that to meet me?'

He reached for her hand. 'Marion was convinced that time became distorted and somehow we were caught in its struggle to maintain reality. I don't under-stand her reasoning. But perhaps,' he said, as he pulled her closer, 'if you'd followed your instincts on that day, and gone down the road to Hanging Rock, we would've been caught in the timeless world together.'

She snuggled into his body. 'Together in a timeless world ... wonderful.'

'Yes, maybe stuck together, but perhaps not in the early nineteen hundreds.'

EPILOGUE

Hanging Rock sits 718 metres above sea level near the townships of Woodend and Mount Macedon, approximately 70 kilometres northwest of Melbourne.

Previously known as Mt. Diogenes, this rare volcanic edifice formed over six million years ago when stiff lava gushed from an aperture in the earth and solidified into rough columns.

Marion would have been pleased to study this ancient curiosity further.

Families picnic at the rock. Children scamper around the sky-reaching mass. Tourists enjoy the views and visit the cafe. Scientists take samples for analysis.

Miranda would be delighted that the rock was a place of which people were not afraid.

The Rock's beauty is in its haunting shapes. It troubles one with its mysterious qualities. Imagination runs riot when the sun splatters over the nooks and crannies. Whistling winds evoke alarming emotions when evening shadows descend.

Michael and Rebecca vowed never to visit the rock again.

ALSO BY Barbara Gurney

Poetry: **Footprints of a Stranger**
Published by Ginninderra Press of Port Adelaide
Poetry: **Life's Shadows**
Published by Ginninderra Press of Port Adelaide
Novel: **The Promise**
Published by Austin Macauley of London

CONTACT THE AUTHOR

www.barbaragurney.webs.com
www.facebook.com/Barbara.Gurney.47

FURTHER READING

Picnic at Hanging Rock
Joan Lindsay (1896-1984)
First Australian edition Cheshire Publishing, 1967

Burnt Norton
Thomas Stearns Eliot (1888-1965)

Mulga Bill's Bicycle
Banjo Paterson (1864-1941)

Middlemarch
George Eliot
Mary Anne Evans (1819-1880)

On Liberty
John Stuart Mill (1806-1873)

MUSIC

Ta-ra-ra Boom-de-ay
African-American traditional

Count Your Blessings
Johnson Oatman, Jr. (1856-1922)